28. THE AMA
HIS EDUC

(for younger readers)

29. NIGHT WATCH

30. THE WEE FREE MEN
(for younger readers)

31. MONSTROUS REGIMENT

32. A HAT FULL OF SKY
(for younger readers)

33. GOING POSTAL

34. THUD!

35. WINTERSMITH
(for younger readers)

36. MAKING MONEY

Other books about Discworld

THE SCIENCE OF DISCWORLD
(with Ian Stewart and Jack Cohen)

THE SCIENCE OF DISCWORLD II: THE GLOBE
(with Ian Stewart and Jack Cohen)

THE SCIENCE OF DISCWORLD III:
DARWIN'S WATCH
(with Ian Stewart and Jack Cohen)

THE NEW DISCWORLD COMPANION
(with Stephen Briggs)

NANNY OGG'S COOKBOOK
(with Stephen Briggs, Tina Hannan and Paul Kidby)

THE PRATCHETT PORTFOLIO
(with Paul Kidby)

THE DISCWORLD ALMANAK
(with Bernard Pearson)

THE UNSEEN UNIVERSITY CUT-OUT BOOK
(with Alan Batley and Bernard Pearson)

WHERE'S MY COW?
(illustrated by Melvyn Grant)

THE ART OF DISCWORLD
(with Paul Kidby)

THE WIT AND WISDOM OF DISCWORLD
(compiled by Stephen Briggs)

THE FOLKLORE OF DISCWORLD
(with Jacqueline Simpson)

Discworld maps

THE STREETS OF ANKH-MORPORK
(with Stephen Briggs)

THE DISCWORLD MAPP
(with Stephen Briggs)

A TOURIST GUIDE TO LANCRE –
A DISCWORLD MAPP
(with Stephen Briggs, illustrated by Paul Kidby)

DEATH'S DOMAIN
(with Paul Kidby)

A complete list of other books based on the Discworld series – illustrated screenplays, graphic novels, comics and plays, can be found on **www.terrypratchett.co.uk.**

Non-Discworld novels

GOOD OMENS (with Neil Gaiman)

STRATA

THE DARK SIDE OF THE SUN

THE UNADULTERATED CAT (illustrated by Gray Jolliffe)

Non-Discworld novels for younger readers

THE CARPET PEOPLE

TRUCKERS

DIGGERS

WINGS

ONLY YOU CAN SAVE MANKIND

JOHNNY AND THE DEAD

JOHNNY AND THE BOMB

NATION

Carpe Jugulum

Terry Pratchett

CORGI BOOKS

TRANSWORLD PUBLISHERS
61–63 Uxbridge Road, London W5 5SA
A Random House Group Company
www.rbooks.co.uk

CARPE JUGULUM

A CORGI BOOK: 9780552154208

Originally published in Great Britain by Doubleday,
a division of Transworld Publishers

PRINTING HISTORY
Doubleday edition published 1998
Corgi edition published 1999
Corgi edition reissued 2008

1 3 5 7 9 10 8 6 4 2

Addresses for Random House Group Ltd companies outside the UK can be found at: www.randomhouse.co.uk
The Random House Group Ltd Reg. No. 954009

The Random House Group Limited supports The Forest Stewardship Council (FSC), the leading international forest certification organisation. All our titles that are printed on Greenpeace-approved FSC-certified paper carry the FSC logo. Our paper procurement policy can be found at www.rbooks.co.uk/environment

Set in 12/14pt Minion by Falcon Oast Graphic Art Ltd.

Printed and bound in Great Britain by
CPI Cox & Wyman, Reading, Berkshire.

CARPE JUGULUM

THROUGH THE SHREDDED black clouds a fire moved like a dying star, falling back to earth—

—the earth, that is, of the Discworld—

—but unlike any star had ever done before, it sometimes managed to steer its fall, sometimes rising, sometimes twisting, but inevitably heading down.

Snow glowed briefly on the mountain slopes when it crackled overhead.

Under it, the land itself started to fall away. The fire was reflected off walls of blue ice as the light dropped into the beginnings of a canyon and thundered now through its twists and turns.

The light snapped off. Something still glided down the moonlit ribbon between the rocks.

It shot out of the canyon at the top of a cliff, where meltwater from a glacier plunged down into a distant pool.

Against all reason there was a valley here, or a network of valleys, clinging to the edge of the mountains before the long fall to the plains. A small lake gleamed in the warmer air. There were forests. There were tiny fields, like a patchwork quilt thrown across the rocks.

The wind had died. The air was warmer.

The shadow began to circle.

Far below, unheeded and unheeding, something else was entering this little handful of valleys. It was hard to see exactly what it was; furze rippled, heather rustled, as if a very large army made of very small creatures was moving with one purpose.

The shadow reached a flat rock that offered a magnificent view of the fields and wood below, and *there* the army came out from among the roots. It was made up of very small blue men, some wearing pointy blue caps but most of them with their red hair uncovered. They carried swords. None of them was more than six inches high.

They lined up and looked down into the new place and then, weapons waving, raised a battle cry. It would have been more impressive if they'd agreed on one before, but as it was it sounded as though every single small warrior had a battle cry of his very own and would fight anyone who tried to take it away from him.

'Nac mac Feegle!'

'Ach, stickit yer trakkans!'

'Gie you sich a kickin'!'

'Bigjobs!'

'Dere c'n onlie be whin t'ousand!'

'Nac mac Feegle wha hae!'

'Wha hae yersel, ya boggin!'

The little cup of valleys, glowing in the last shreds of evening sunlight, was the kingdom of Lancre. From its highest points, people said, you could see all the way to the rim of the world.

It was also said, although not by the people who lived in Lancre, that *below* the rim, where the seas thundered continuously over the edge, their home went through space on the back of four huge elephants that in turn stood on the shell of a turtle that was as big as the world.

The people of Lancre had heard of this. They thought it sounded about right. The world was obviously flat, although in Lancre itself the only truly flat places were tables and the top of some people's heads, and certainly turtles could shift a fair load. Elephants, by all accounts, were pretty strong too. There didn't seem any major gaps in the thesis, so Lancrastians left it at that.

It wasn't that they didn't take an interest in the world around them. On the contrary, they had a deep, personal and passionate involvement in it, but instead of asking, 'Why are we here?' they asked, 'Is it going to rain before the harvest?'

A philosopher might have deplored this lack of mental ambition, but only if he was *really certain* about where his next meal was coming from.

In fact Lancre's position and climate bred a hard-headed and straightforward people who often excelled in the world down below. It had supplied the plains with many of their greatest wizards and witches and, once again, the philosopher might have marvelled that such a four-square people could give the world so many successful magical practitioners, being quite unaware that only those with their feet on rock can build castles in the air.

And so the sons and daughters of Lancre went off into the world, carved out careers, climbed the various ladders of achievement, and always remembered to send money home.

Apart from noting the return addresses on the envelope, those who stayed didn't think much about the world outside.

The world outside thought about them, though.

The big flat-topped rock was deserted now, but on the moor below, the heather trembled in a v-shape heading towards the lowlands.

'Gin's a haddie!'

'Nac mac Feegle!'

There are many kinds of vampires. Indeed, it is said that there are as many kinds of vampires as there are types of disease.* And they're not just human (if vampires are human). All along the Ramtops may be found the belief that any apparently innocent tool, be it hammer or saw, will seek blood if left unused for more than three years. In Ghat they believe in vampire watermelons, although folklore is silent about *what* they believe about vampire watermelons. Possibly they suck back.

Two things have traditionally puzzled vampire researchers. One is: why do vampires have so much *power*? Vampires're so easy to kill, they point out. There are *dozens* of ways to despatch them, quite apart from the stake through the heart, which also works on normal people so if you have any stakes left over you don't have to waste them. Classically, they spent the day in some coffin somewhere, with no

*Which presumably means that some are virulent and deadly, and others just make you walk in a funny way and avoid fruit.

guard other than an elderly hunchback who doesn't look all that spry, and should succumb to quite a small mob. Yet just one can keep a whole community in a state of sullen obedience . . .

The other puzzle is: why are vampires always so stupid? As if wearing evening dress all day wasn't an undead giveaway, why do they choose to live in old castles which offer so much in the way of ways to defeat a vampire, like easily torn curtains and wall decorations that can readily be twisted into a religious symbol? Do they *really* think that spelling their name backwards fools anyone?

A coach rattled across the moorlands, many miles away from Lancre. From the way it bounced over the ruts, it was travelling light. But darkness came with it.

The horses were black, and so was the coach, except for the coat of arms on the doors. Each horse had a black plume between its ears; there was a black plume at each corner of the coach as well. Perhaps these caused the coach's strange effect of travelling shadow. It seemed to be dragging the night behind it.

On the top of the moor, where a few trees grew out of the rubble of a ruined building, it creaked to a halt.

The horses stood still, occasionally stamping a hoof or tossing their heads. The coachman sat hunched over the reins, waiting.

Four figures flew just above the clouds, in the silvery moonlight. By the sound of their conversation someone was annoyed, although the sharp unpleasant tone to the voice suggested that a better word might be 'vexed'.

'You let it get *away*!' This voice had a whine to it, the voice of a chronic complainer.

'It *was* wounded, Lacci.' *This* voice sounded conciliatory, parental, but with just a hint of a repressed desire to give the first voice a thick ear.

'I really *hate* those things. They're so . . . soppy!'

'Yes, dear. A symbol of a credulous past.'

'If *I* could burn like that I wouldn't skulk around just looking pretty. Why do they do it?'

'It must have been of use to them at one time, I suppose.'

'Then they're . . . what did you call them?'

'An evolutionary cul-de-sac, Lacci. A marooned survivor on the seas of progress.'

'Then I'm doing them a favour by killing them?'

'Yes, that is a point. Now, shall—'

'After all, chickens don't burn,' said the voice called Lacci. 'Not easily, anyway.'

'We heard you experiment. Killing them first might have been a good idea.' This was a third voice – young, male, and also somewhat weary with the female. It had 'older brother' harmonics on every syllable.

'What's the point in that?'

'Well, dear, it would have been quieter.'

'Listen to your father, dear.' And this, the fourth voice, could only be a mother's voice. It'd love the other voices whatever they did.

'You're *so* unfair!'

'We did let you drop rocks on the pixies, dear. Life can't be all fun.'

The coachman stirred as the voices descended through the clouds. And then four figures were standing a little way off. He clambered down and, with difficulty, opened the coach door as they approached.

'Most of the wretched things got away, though,' said Mother.

'Never mind, my dear,' said Father.

'I really hate them. Are they a dead end too?' said Daughter.

'Not quite dead enough as yet, despite your valiant efforts. Igor! On to Lancre.'

The coachman turned.

'Yeth, marthter.'

'Oh, for the last time, man . . . is that any way to talk?'

'It'th the only way I know, marthter,' said Igor.

'And I told you to take the plumes off the coach, you idiot.'

The coachman shifted uneasily.

'Gotta have black plumeth, marthter. It'th *tradithional*.'

'Remove them at once!' Mother commanded. 'What *will* people think?'

'Yeth, mithtreth.'

The one addressed as Igor slammed the door and lurched back around to the horse. He removed the plumes reverentially and placed them under his seat.

Inside the coach the vexed voice said, 'Is Igor an evolutionary dead end too, Father?'

'We can but hope, dear.'

'Thod,' said Igor to himself, as he picked up the reins.

The wording began:

'*You are cordially invited . . .*'

. . . and was in that posh runny writing that was hard to read but ever so official.

Nanny Ogg grinned and tucked the card back on the mantelpiece. She liked the idea of 'cordially'. It had a rich, a thick and above all an *alcoholic* sound.

She was ironing her best petticoat. That is to say, she was sitting in her chair by the fire while one of her daughters-in-law, whose name she couldn't remember just at this moment, was doing the actual work. Nanny was helping by pointing out the bits she'd missed.

It was a damn good invite, she thought. Especially the gold edging, which was as thick as syrup. Probably not real gold, but impressively glittery all the same.

'There's a bit there that could do with goin' over again, gel,' she said, topping up her beer.

'Yes, Nanny.'

Another daughter-in-law, whose name she'd certainly be able to recall after a few seconds' thought, was buffing up Nanny's red boots. A third was very carefully dabbing the lint off Nanny's best pointy hat, on its stand.

Nanny got up again and wandered over to open the back door. There was little light left in the sky now, and a few rags of cloud were scudding over the early stars. She sniffed the air. Winter hung on late up here in the mountains, but there was definitely a taste of spring on the wind.

A good time, she thought. Best time, really. Oh, she knew that the year started on Hogswatchnight, when the cold tide turned, but the *new* year started now, with green shoots boring upwards through the last of the snow. Change was in the air, she could feel it in her bones.

Of course, her friend Granny Weatherwax always said you couldn't trust bones, but Granny Weatherwax said a lot of things like that all the time.

Nanny Ogg closed the door. In the trees at the end of her garden, leafless and scratchy against the sky, something rustled its wings and chattered as a veil of dark crossed the world.

In her own cottage a few miles away the witch Agnes Nitt was in two minds about her new pointy hat. Agnes was generally in two minds about anything.

As she tucked in her hair and observed herself critically in the mirror she sang a song. She sang in harmony. Not, of course, with her reflection in the glass, because *that* kind of heroine will sooner or later end up singing a duet with Mr Blue Bird and other forest creatures and then there's nothing for it but a flamethrower.

She simply sang in harmony with herself. Unless she concentrated it was happening more and more these days. Perdita had rather a reedy voice, but she insisted on joining in.

Those who are inclined to casual cruelty say that inside a fat girl is a thin girl and a lot of chocolate. Agnes's thin girl was Perdita.

She wasn't sure how she'd acquired the invisible passenger. Her mother had told her that when she was small she'd been in the habit of blaming accidents and mysteries, such as the disappearance of a bowl of cream or the breaking of a prized jug, on 'the other little girl'.

Only now did she realize that indulging this sort of

thing wasn't a good idea when, despite yourself, you've got a bit of natural witchcraft in your blood. The imaginary friend had simply grown up and had never gone away and had turned out to be a pain.

Agnes disliked Perdita, who was vain, selfish and vicious, and Perdita hated going around inside Agnes, whom she regarded as a fat, pathetic, weak-willed blob that people would walk all over were she not so steep.

Agnes told herself she'd simply invented the name Perdita as some convenient label for all those thoughts and desires she knew she shouldn't have, as a name for that troublesome little commentator that lives on everyone's shoulder and sneers. But sometimes she thought Perdita had created Agnes for something to pummel.

Agnes tended to obey rules. Perdita didn't. Perdita thought that not obeying rules was somehow *cool.* Agnes thought that rules like 'Don't fall into this huge pit of spikes' were there for a purpose. Perdita thought, to take an example at random, that things like table manners were a stupid and repressive idea. Agnes, on the other hand, was against being hit by flying bits of other people's cabbage.

Perdita thought a witch's hat was a powerful symbol of authority. Agnes thought that a dumpy girl should not wear a tall hat, especially with black. It made her look as though someone had dropped a liquorice-flavoured ice-cream cone.

The trouble was that although Agnes was right, so was Perdita. The pointy hat carried a lot of weight in the Ramtops. People talked to the hat, not to the person wearing it. When people were in serious trouble they went to a witch.*

You had to wear black, too. *Perdita* liked black. Perdita thought black was cool. Agnes thought that black wasn't a good colour for the circumferentially challenged . . . oh, and that 'cool' was a dumb word used only by people whose brains wouldn't fill a spoon.

Magrat Garlick hadn't worn black and had probably never in her life said 'cool' except when commenting on the temperature.

Agnes stopped examining her pointiness in the mirror and looked around the cottage that had been Magrat's and was now hers, and sighed. Her gaze took in the expensive, gold-edged card on the mantelpiece.

Well, Magrat had certainly retired now, and had gone off to be Queen and if there was ever any doubt about that then there could be no doubt today. Agnes was puzzled at the way Nanny Ogg and Granny Weatherwax still talked about her, though. They were proud (more or less) that she'd married the King, and agreed that it was the right kind of life for her, but while they never actually articulated the thought it hung in the air over their heads in flashing mental colours: *Magrat had settled for second prize.*

Agnes had almost burst out laughing when she first realized this, but you wouldn't be able to argue with them. They wouldn't even see that there *could* be an argument.

Granny Weatherwax lived in a cottage with a thatch so old there was quite a sprightly young tree growing

*Sometimes, of course, to say, 'Please stop doing it.'

in it, and got up and went to bed alone, and washed in the rain barrel. And Nanny Ogg was the most *local* person Agnes had ever met. She'd gone off to foreign parts, yes, but she always carried Lancre with her, like a sort of invisible hat. But they took it for granted that they were top of every tree, and the rest of the world was there for them to tinker with.

Perdita thought that being a queen was just about the best thing you could be.

Agnes thought the best thing you could be was far away from Lancre, and good second best would be to be alone in your own head.

She adjusted the hat as best she could and left the cottage.

Witches never locked their doors. They never needed to.

As she stepped out into the moonlight, two magpies landed on the thatch.

The current activities of the witch Granny Weatherwax would have puzzled a hidden observer.

She peered at the flagstones just inside her back door and lifted the old rag rug in front of it with her toe.

Then she walked to the front door, which was never used, and did the same thing there. She also examined the cracks around the edges of the doors.

She went outside. There had been a sharp frost during the night, a spiteful little trick by the dying winter, and the drifts of leaves that hung on in the shadows were still crisp. In the harsh air she poked around in the flowerpots and bushes by the front door.

Then she went back inside.

She had a clock. Lancrastians liked clocks, although they didn't bother much about actual *time* in any length much shorter than an hour. If you needed to boil an egg, you sang fifteen verses of 'Where Has All The Custard Gone?' under your breath. But the tick was a comfort on long evenings.

Finally she sat down in her rocking chair and glared at the doorway.

Owls were hooting in the forest when someone came running up the path and hammered on the door.

Anyone who hadn't heard about Granny's iron self-control, which you could bend a horseshoe round, might just have thought they heard her give a tiny sigh of relief.

'Well, it's about time—' she began.

The excitement up at the castle was just a distant hum down in the mews. The hawks and falcons sat hunched on their perches, lost in some inner world of stoop and updraught. There was the occasional clink of a chain or flutter of a wing.

Hodgesaargh the falconer was getting ready in the tiny room next door when he felt the change in the air. He stepped out into a silent mews. The birds were all awake, alert, *expectant.* Even King Henry the eagle, whom Hodgesaargh would only go near at the moment when he was wearing full plate armour, was peering around.

You got something like this when there was a rat in the place, but Hodgesaargh couldn't see one. Perhaps it had gone.

For tonight's event he'd selected William the buzzard,

who could be depended upon. All Hodgesaargh's birds could be depended upon, but more often than not they could be depended upon to viciously attack him on sight. William, however, thought that she was a chicken, and she was usually safe in company.

But even William was paying a lot of attention to the world, which didn't often happen unless she'd seen some corn.

Odd, thought Hodgesaargh. And that was all.

The birds went on staring up, as though the roof simply was not there.

Granny Weatherwax lowered her gaze to a red, round and worried face.

'Here, you're not—' She pulled herself together. 'You're the Wattley boy from over in Slice, aren't you?'

'Y'g't . . .' The boy leaned against the doorjamb and fought for breath. 'You g't—'

'Just take deep breaths. You want a drink of water?'

'You g't t'—'

'Yes, yes, all right. Just *breathe* . . .'

The boy gulped air a few times.

'You got to come to Mrs Ivy and her baby missus!'

The words came out in one quick stream.

Granny grabbed her hat from its peg by the door and pulled her broomstick out of its lodging in the thatch.

'I thought old Mrs Patternoster was seeing to her,' she said, ramming her hatpins into place with the urgency of a warrior preparing for sudden battle.

'She says it's all gone wrong miss!'

Granny was already running down her garden path.

There was a small drop on the other side of the clearing, with a twenty-foot fall to a bend in the track. The broom hadn't fired by the time she reached it but she ran on, swinging a leg over the bristles as it plunged.

The magic caught halfway down and her boots dragged across the dead bracken as the broom soared up into the night.

The road wound over the mountains like a dropped ribbon. Up here there was always the sound of the wind.

The highwayman's horse was a big black stallion. It was also quite possibly the only horse with a ladder strapped behind the saddle.

This was because the highwayman's name was Casanunda, and he was a dwarf. Most people thought of dwarfs as reserved, cautious, law-abiding and very reticent on matters of the heart and other vaguely connected organs, and this was indeed true of almost all dwarfs. But genetics rolls strange dice on the green baize of life and somehow the dwarfs had produced Casanunda, who preferred fun to money and devoted to women all the passion that other dwarfs reserved for gold.

He also regarded laws as useful things and he obeyed them when it was convenient. Casanunda despised highwaymanning, but it got you out in the fresh air of the countryside, which was very good for you, especially when the nearby towns were lousy with husbands carrying a grudge and a big stick.

The trouble was that no one on the road took him seriously. He could stop the coaches all right, but people tended to say, 'What? I say, it's a lowwayman. What up? A bit short, are you? Hur, hur, hur,' and he would be forced to shoot them in the knee.

He blew on his hands to warm them, and looked up at the sound of an approaching coach.

He was about to ride out of his meagre hiding place in the thicket when he saw the *other* highwayman trot out from the wood opposite.

The coach came to a halt. Casanunda couldn't hear what transpired, but the highwayman rode around to one of the doors and leaned down to speak to the occupants . . .

. . . and a hand reached out and plucked him off his horse and into the coach.

It rocked on its springs for a while, and then the door burst open and the highwayman tumbled out and lay still on the road.

The coach moved on . . .

Casanunda waited a little while and then rode down to the body. His horse stood patiently while he untied the ladder and dismounted.

He could tell the highwayman was stone dead. Living people are expected to have some blood in them.

The coach stopped at the top of a rise a few miles further on, before the road began the long winding fall towards Lancre and the plains.

The four passengers got out and walked to the start of the drop.

The clouds were rolling in behind them but here

the air was frosty clear, and the view stretched all the way to the Rim under the moonlight. Down below, scooped out of the mountains, was the little kingdom.

'Gateway to the world,' said the Count de Magpyr.

'And entirely undefended,' said his son.

'On the contrary. Possessed of some extremely *effective* defences,' said the Count. He smiled in the night. 'At least . . . until now . . .'

'Witches should be on *our* side,' said the Countess.

'*She* will be soon, at any rate,' said the Count. 'A most . . . interesting woman. An interesting *family*. Uncle used to talk about her grandmother. The Weatherwax women have always had one foot in shadow. It's in the blood. And most of their power comes from denying it. However,' and his teeth shone as he grinned in the dark, 'she will soon find out on which side her bread is buttered.'

'Or her gingerbread is gilded,' said the Countess.

'Ah, yes. How nicely put. That's the penalty for being a Weatherwax woman, of course. When they get older they start to hear the clang of the big oven door.'

'I've heard she's pretty tough, though,' said the Count's son. 'A very sharp mind.'

'Let's kill her!' said the Count's daughter.

'Really, Lacci dear, you can't kill *everything*.'

'I don't see why not.'

'No. I rather like the idea of her being . . . useful. And she sees everything in black and white. That's always a trap for the powerful. Oh, *yes*. A mind like that is so easily . . . led. With a little help.'

There was a whirr of wings under the moonlight

and something bi-coloured landed on the Count's shoulder.

'And *this* . . .' said the Count, stroking the magpie and then letting it go. He pulled a square of white card from an inner pocket of his jacket. Its edge gleamed briefly. 'Can you believe it? Has this sort of thing ever happened before? A new world order indeed . . .'

'Do you have a handkerchief, sir?' said the Countess. 'Give it to me, please. You have a few specks . . .'

She dabbed at his chin and pushed the blood-stained handkerchief back into his pocket.

'There,' she said.

'There are other witches,' said the son, like someone turning over a mouthful that was proving rather tough to chew.

'Oh, yes. I hope we will meet them. They could be entertaining.'

They climbed back into the coach.

Back in the mountains, the man who had tried to rob the coach managed to get to his feet, which seemed for a moment to be caught in something. He rubbed his neck irritably and looked around for his horse, which he found standing behind some rocks a little way away.

When he tried to lay a hand on the bridle it passed straight through the leather and the horse's neck, like smoke. The creature reared up and galloped madly away.

It was not, the highwayman thought muzzily, going to be a good night. Well, he'd be damned if he'd lose a horse as well as some wages. Who the hell were those people? He couldn't quite remember what had happened in the carriage, but it hadn't been enjoyable.

The highwayman was of that simple class of men who, having been hit by someone bigger than them, finds someone smaller than them for the purposes of retaliation. Someone else was going to suffer tonight, he vowed. He'd get another horse, at least.

And, on cue, he heard the sound of hoofbeats on the wind. He drew his sword and stepped out into the road.

'Stand and deliver!'

The approaching horse halted obediently a few feet away. This was not going to be such a bad night after all, he thought. It really was a magnificent creature, more of a warhorse than an everyday hack. It was so pale that it shone in the light of the occasional star and, by the look of it, there was silver on its harness.

The rider was heavily wrapped up against the cold.

'Your money or your life!' said the highwayman.

I'M SORRY?

'Your money,' said the highwayman, 'or your life. Which part of this don't you understand?'

OH, I SEE. WELL, I HAVE A SMALL AMOUNT OF MONEY.

A couple of coins landed on the frosty road. The highwayman scrabbled for them but could not pick them up, a fact that only added to his annoyance.

'It's your life, then!'

The mounted figure shook its head. I THINK NOT. I REALLY DO.

It pulled a long curved stick out of a holster. The highwayman had assumed it was a lance, but now a curved blade sprang out and glittered blue along its edges.

I MUST SAY THAT YOU HAVE AN AMAZING PERSISTENCE OF VITALITY, said the horseman. It was not so much a voice, more an echo inside the head. IF NOT A PRESENCE OF MIND.

'Who *are* you?'

I'M DEATH, said Death. AND I REALLY AM NOT HERE TO TAKE YOUR MONEY. WHICH PART OF THIS DON'T YOU UNDERSTAND?

Something fluttered weakly at the window of the castle mews. There was no glass in the frame, just thin wooden slats to allow some passage of air.

And there was a scrabbling, and then a faint pecking, and then silence.

The hawks watched.

Outside the window something went *whoomph.* Beams of brilliant light jerked across the far wall and, slowly, the bars began to char.

Nanny Ogg knew that while the actual party would be in the Great Hall all the fun would be outside, in the courtyard around the big fire. Inside it'd be all quails' eggs, goose-liver jam and little sandwiches that were four to the mouthful. Outside it'd be roasted potatoes floating in vats of butter and a whole stag on a spit. Later on, there'd be a command performance by that man who put weasels down his trousers, a form of entertainment that Nanny ranked higher than grand opera.

As a witch, of course, she'd be welcome anywhere

and it was always a good idea to remind the nobs of this, in case they forgot. It was a hard choice, but she decided to stay outside and have a good dinner of venison because, like many old ladies, Nanny Ogg was a bottomless pit for free food. Then she'd go inside and fill the gaps with the fiddly dishes. Besides, they probably had that expensive fizzy wine in there and Nanny had quite a taste for it, provided it was served in a big enough mug. But you needed a good depth of beer before you loaded up on the fancy stuff.

She picked up a tankard, ambled to the front of the queue at the beer barrel, gently nudged aside the head of a man who'd decided to spend the evening lying under the tap, and drew herself a pint.

As she turned back she saw the splay-footed figure of Agnes approaching, still slightly uneasy with the idea of wearing the new pointy hat in public.

'Wotcha, girl,' said Nanny. 'Try some of the venison, it's good stuff.'

Agnes looked doubtfully at the roasting meat. Lancre people looked after the calories and let the vitamins go hang.

'Do you think I could get a salad?' she ventured.

'Hope not,' said Nanny happily.

'Lot of people here,' said Agnes.

'*Everyone* got a invite,' said Nanny. 'Magrat was very gracious about that, I thought.'

Agnes craned her head. 'Can't see Granny around anywhere, though.'

'She'll be inside, tellin' people what to do.'

'I haven't seen her around much at all lately,' said Agnes. 'She's got something on her mind, I think.'

Nanny narrowed her eyes.

'You think so?' she said, adding to herself: you're getting *good*, miss.

'It's just that ever since we heard about the birth,' Agnes waved a plump hand to indicate the general high-cholesterol celebration around them, 'she's been so . . . stretched, sort of. Twanging.'

Nanny Ogg thumbed some tobacco into her pipe and struck a match on her boot.

'You certainly notice things, don't you?' she said, puffing away. 'Notice, notice, notice. We'll have to call you Miss Notice.'

'I certainly *notice* you always fiddle around with your pipe when you're thinking thoughts you don't much like,' said Agnes. 'It's displacement activity.'

Through a cloud of sweet-smelling smoke Nanny reflected that Agnes read books. All the witches who'd lived in her cottage were bookish types. They thought you could see life through books but you couldn't, the reason being that the words got in the way.

'She has been a bit quiet, that's true,' she said. 'Best to let her get on with it.'

'I thought perhaps she was sulking about the priest who'll be doing the Naming,' said Agnes.

'Oh, old Brother Perdore's all right,' said Nanny. 'Gabbles away in some ancient lingo, keeps it short and then you just give him sixpence for his trouble, fill him up with brandy and load him on his donkey and off he goes.'

'What? Didn't you hear?' said Agnes. 'He's laid up over in Skund. Broke his wrist and both legs falling off the donkey.'

Nanny Ogg took her pipe out of her mouth.

'Why wasn't I told?' she said.

'I don't know, Nanny. Mrs Weaver told me yesterday.'

'Oo, that woman! I passed her in the street this morning! She could've said!'

Nanny poked her pipe back in her mouth as though stabbing all uncommunicative gossips. 'How can you break both your legs falling off a donkey?'

'It was going up that little path on the side of Skund Gorge. He fell sixty feet.'

'Oh? Well . . . that's a tall donkey, right enough.'

'So the King sent down to the Omnian mission in Ohulan to send us up a priest, apparently,' said Agnes.

'He did *what*?' said Nanny.

A small grey tent was inexpertly pitched in a field just outside the town. The rising wind made it flap, and tore at the poster which had been pinned on to an easel outside.

It read: GOOD NEWS! Om Welcomes You!!!

In fact no one had turned up to the small introductory service that Mightily Oats had organized that afternoon, but since he had announced one he had gone ahead with it anyway, singing a few cheerful hymns to his own accompaniment on the small portable harmonium and then preaching a very short sermon to the wind and the sky.

Now the Quite Reverend Oats looked at himself in the mirror. He was a bit uneasy about the mirror, to be honest. Mirrors had led to one of the Church's innumerable schisms, one side saying that since they encouraged vanity they were bad, and the other saying that since they reflected the goodness of Om they were holy. Oats had not quite formed his own opinion, being by nature someone who tries to see something in both sides of every question, but at least the mirrors helped him to get his complicated clerical collar on straight.

It was still very new. The Very Reverend Mekkle, who'd taken Pastoral Practice, had advised that the rules about starch were only really a guideline, but Oats hadn't wanted to put a foot wrong and his collar could have been used as a razor.

He carefully lowered his holy turtle pendant into place, noting its gleam with some satisfaction, and picked up his finely printed graduation copy of the *Book of Om.* Some of his fellow students had spent hours carefully ruffling the pages to give them that certain straight-and-narrow credibility, but Oats had refrained from this as well. Besides, he knew most of it by heart.

Feeling rather guilty, because there had been some admonitions at the college against using holy writ merely for fortune telling, he shut his eyes and let the book flop open at random.

Then he opened his eyes quickly and read the first passage they encountered.

It was somewhere in the middle of Brutha's Second Letter to the Omish, gently chiding them for not replying to the First Letter to the Omish.

'*. . . silence is an answer that begs three more*

questions. Seek and you will find, but first you should know what you seek . . .'

Oh, well. He shut the book.

What a place! What a *dump*. He'd had a short walk after the service and every path seemed to end in a cliff or a sheer drop. Never had he seen such a *vertical* country. Things had rustled at him in the bushes, and he'd got his shoes muddy. As for the people he'd met . . . well, simple ignorant country folk, salt of the earth, obviously, but they'd just stared at him carefully from a distance, as if they were waiting for something to happen to him and didn't care to be too close to him when it did.

But still, he mused, it *did* say in Brutha's Letter to the Simonites that if you wished the light to be seen you had to take it into dark places. And this was certainly a dark place.

He said a small prayer and stepped out into the muddy, windy darkness.

Granny flew high above the roaring treetops, under a half moon.

She distrusted a moon like that. A full moon could only wane, a new moon could only wax, but a half moon, balancing so precariously between light and dark . . . well, it could do anything.

Witches always lived on the edges of things. She felt the tingle in her hands. It was not just from the frosty air. There was an *edge* somewhere. Something was beginning.

On the other side of the sky the Hublights were burning around the mountains at the centre of the world, bright enough even to fight the pale light of the moon. Green and gold flames danced in the air over the central mountains. It was rare to see them at this time of the year, and Granny wondered what that might signify.

Slice was perched along the sides of a cleft in the mountains that couldn't be dignified by the name of valley. In the moonlight she saw the pale upturned face waiting in the shadows of the garden as she came in to land.

'Evening, Mr Ivy,' she said, leaping off. 'Upstairs, is she?'

'In the barn,' said Ivy flatly. 'The cow kicked her . . . hard.'

Granny's expression stayed impassive.

'We shall see,' she said, 'what may be done.'

In the barn, one look at Mrs Patternoster's face told her how little that might now be. The woman wasn't a witch, but she knew all the practical midwifery that can be picked up in an isolated village, be it from cows, goats, horses or humans.

'It's bad,' she whispered, as Granny looked at the moaning figure on the straw. 'I reckon we'll lose both of them . . . or maybe just one . . .'

There was, if you were listening for it, just the suggestion of a question in that sentence. Granny focused her mind.

'It's a boy,' she said.

Mrs Patternoster didn't bother to wonder how Granny knew, but her expression indicated that a little more weight had been added to a burden.

'I'd better go and put it to John Ivy, then,' she said.

She'd barely moved before Granny Weatherwax's hand locked on her arm.

'He's no part in this,' she said.

'But after all, he *is* the—'

'He's no part in this.'

Mrs Patternoster looked into the blue stare and knew two things. One was that Mr Ivy had no part in this, and the other was that anything that happened in this barn was never, ever, going to be mentioned again.

'I think I can bring 'em to mind,' said Granny, letting go and rolling up her sleeves. 'Pleasant couple, as I recall. He's a good husband, by all accounts.' She poured warm water from its jug into the bowl that the midwife had set up on a manger.

Mrs Patternoster nodded.

'Of course, it's difficult for a man working these steep lands alone,' Granny went on, washing her hands. Mrs Patternoster nodded again, mournfully.

'Well, I reckon you should take him into the cottage, Mrs Patternoster, and make him a cup of tea,' Granny commanded. 'You can tell him I'm doing all I can.'

This time the midwife nodded gratefully.

When she had fled, Granny laid a hand on Mrs Ivy's damp forehead.

'Well now, Florence Ivy,' she said, 'let us see what might be done. But first of all . . . no pain . . .'

As she moved her head she caught sight of the moon through the unglazed window. Between the light and the dark . . . well, sometimes that's where you had to be.

INDEED.

Granny didn't bother to turn round.

'I thought you'd be here,' she said, as she knelt down in the straw.

WHERE ELSE? said Death.

'Do you know who you're here for?'

THAT IS NOT MY CHOICE. ON THE *VERY* EDGE YOU WILL ALWAYS FIND SOME UNCERTAINTY.

Granny felt the words in her head for several seconds, like little melting cubes of ice. On the very, very edge, then, there had to be . . . judgement.

'There's too much damage here,' she said, at last. 'Too much.'

A few minutes later she felt the life stream past her. Death had the decency to leave without a word.

When Mrs Patternoster tremulously knocked on the door and pushed it open, Granny was in the cow's stall. The midwife saw her stand up, holding a piece of thorn.

'Been in the beast's leg all day,' she said. 'No wonder it was fretful. Try and make sure he doesn't kill the cow, you understand? They'll need it.'

Mrs Patternoster glanced down at the rolled-up blanket in the straw. Granny had tactfully placed it out of sight of Mrs Ivy, who was sleeping now.

'I'll tell him,' said Granny, brushing off her dress. 'As for her, well, she's strong and young and you know what to do. You keep an eye on her, and me or Nanny Ogg will drop in when we can. If she's up to it, they may need a wet nurse up at the castle, and that may be good for everyone.'

It was doubtful that anyone in Slice would defy Granny Weatherwax, but Granny saw the faintest grey shadow of disapproval in the midwife's expression.

'You still reckon I should've asked Mr Ivy?' she said.

'That's what I would have done . . .' the woman mumbled.

'You don't like him? You think he's a bad man?' said Granny, adjusting her hatpins.

'No!'

'Then what's he ever done to *me*, that I should hurt him so?'

Agnes had to run to keep up. Nanny Ogg, when roused, could move as though powered by pistons.

'But we get a lot of priests up here, Nanny!'

'Not like the Omnians!' snapped Nanny. 'We had 'em up here last year. A couple of 'em *knocked* at my *door*!'

'Well, that *is* what a door is f—'

'*And* they shoved a leaflet under it saying "Repent!"' Nanny Ogg went on. 'Repent? Me? Cheek! I can't start repenting at my time of life. I'd never get any work done. Anyway,' she added, 'I ain't sorry for most of it.'

'You're getting a bit excited, I think—'

'They set fire to people!' said Nanny.

'I think I read somewhere that they used to, yes,' said Agnes, panting with the effort of keeping up. 'But that was a long time ago, Nanny! The ones I saw in Ankh-Morpork just handed out leaflets and preached in a big tent and sang rather dreary songs—'

'Hah! The leopard does not change his shorts, my girl!'

They ran along a corridor and out from behind a screen into the hubbub of the Great Hall.

'Knee-deep in nobs,' said Nanny, craning. 'Ah, there's our Shawn . . .'

Lancre's standing army was lurking by a pillar, probably in the hope that no one would see him in his footman's powdered wig, which had been made for a much bigger footman.

The kingdom didn't have much of an executive arm of government, and most of its actual hands belonged to Nanny Ogg's youngest son. Despite the earnest efforts of King Verence, who was quite a forward-looking ruler in a nervous kind of way, the people of Lancre could not be persuaded to accept a democracy at any price and the place had not, regrettably, attracted much in the way of government. A lot of the bits it couldn't avoid were done by Shawn. He emptied the palace privies, delivered its sparse mail, guarded the walls, operated the Royal Mint, balanced the budget, helped out the gardener in his spare time and, on those occasions these days when it was felt necessary to man the borders, and Verence felt that yellow and black striped poles *did* give a country such a *professional* look, he stamped passports, or at a pinch any other pieces of paper the visitor could produce, such as the back of an envelope, with a stamp he'd carved quite nicely out of half a potato. He took it all very seriously. At times like this, he buttled when Spriggins the butler was not on duty, or if an extra hand was needed he footed as well.

'Evening, our Shawn,' said Nanny Ogg. 'I see you've got that dead lamb on your head again.'

'Aoow, *Mum*,' said Shawn, trying to adjust the wig.

'Where's this priest that's doing the Naming?' said Nanny.

'What, Mum? Dunno, Mum. I stopped shouting out the names half an hour ago and got on to serving the bits of cheese on sticks – aoow, Mum, you shouldn't take that many, Mum!'*

Nanny Ogg sucked the cocktail goodies off four sticks in one easy movement, and looked speculatively at the throng.

'I'm going to have a word with young Verence,' said Nanny.

'He *is* the King, Nanny,' said Agnes.

'That's no reason for him to go around acting like he was royalty.'

'I think it is, actually.'

'None of that cheek. You just go and find this Omnian and keep an eye on him.'

'What should I look for?' said Agnes sourly. 'A column of smoke?'

'They all wear black,' said Nanny firmly. 'Hah! Typical!'

'Well? So do we.'

'Right! But ours is . . . ours is . . .' Nanny thumped her chest, causing considerable ripples, 'ours is the *right* black, right? Now, off you go and look inconspicuous,' added Nanny, a lady wearing a

*It struck people as odd that, while Lancre people refused point-blank to have any truck with democracy, on the basis that governing was what the King ought to do and they'd be sure to tell him if he went wrong, they didn't make very good servants. Oh, they could cook and dig and wash and footle and buttle and did it very well but could never quite get the hang of the serving mentality. King Verence was quite understanding about this, and put up with Shawn ushering guests into the dining room with a cry of 'Lovely grub, get it while it's hot!'

two-foot-tall pointed black hat. She stared around at the crowd again, and nudged her son.

'Shawn, you *did* deliver an invite to Esme Weatherwax, didn't you?'

He looked horrified. 'Of *course*, Mum.'

'Shove it under her door?'

'No, Mum. You know she gave me an earbashin' when the snails got at that postcard last year. I wedged it in the hinges, good and tight.'

'There's a good boy,' said Nanny.

Lancre people didn't bother much with letterboxes. Mail was infrequent but biting gales were not. Why have a slot in the door to let in unsolicited winds? So letters were left under large stones, wedged firmly in flowerpots or slipped under the door.

There were never very many.* Lancre operated on the feudal system, which was to say, everyone feuded all the time and handed on the fight to their descendants. The chips on some shoulders had been passed down for generations. Some had antique value. A bloody good grudge, Lancre reckoned, was like a fine old wine. You looked after it carefully and left it to your children.

You never *wrote* to anyone. If you had anything to say, you said it to their face. It kept everything nice and hot.

Agnes edged into the crowd, feeling stupid. She often did. Now she knew why Magrat Garlick had

*Apart from the ones containing small postal orders attached to letters which, generally, said pretty much the same thing: Dear Mum and Dad, I am doing pretty well in Ankh-Morpork and this week I earned a whole seven dollars . . .

always worn those soppy floppy dresses and never wore the pointy hat. Wear the pointy hat and dress in black, and on Agnes there was plenty of black to go around, and everyone saw you in a certain way. You were A Witch. It had its good points. Among the *bad* ones was the fact that people turned to you when they were in trouble and never thought for a moment that you couldn't cope.

But she got a bit of respect, even from people who could remember her *before* she'd been allowed to wear the hat. They tended to make way for her, although people tended to make way in any case for Agnes when she was in full steam.

'Evening, miss . . .'

She turned and saw Hodgesaargh in full official regalia.

It was important not to smile at times like this, so Agnes kept a straight face and tried to ignore Perdita's hysterical laughter at the back of her mind.

She'd seen Hodgesaargh occasionally, around the edges of the woods or up on the moors. Usually the royal falconer was vainly fighting off his hawks, who attacked him for a pastime, and in the case of King Henry kept picking him up and dropping him again in the belief that he was a giant tortoise.

It wasn't that he was a bad falconer. A few other people in Lancre kept hawks and reckoned he was one of the best trainers in the mountains, possibly because he was so single-minded about it. It was just that he trained every feathery little killing machine so well that it became unable to resist seeing what he tasted like.

He didn't deserve it. Nor did he deserve his ceremonial costume. Usually, when not in the company of King Henry, he just wore working leathers and about three sticking plasters, but what he was wearing now had been designed hundreds of years before by someone with a lyrical view of the countryside who had never had to run through a bramble bush with a gerfalcon hanging on their ear. It had a lot of red and gold in it and would have looked much better on someone two feet taller who had the legs for red stockings. The hat was best not talked about, but if you had to, you'd talk about it in terms of something big, red and floppy. With a feather in it.

'Miss Nitt?' said Hodgesaargh.

'Sorry . . . I was looking at your hat.'

'It's good, isn't it?' said Hodgesaargh amiably. 'This is William. She's a buzzard. But she thinks she's a chicken. She can't fly. I'm having to teach her how to hunt.'

Agnes was craning her neck for any signs of overtly religious activity, but the incongruity of the slightly bedraggled creature on Hodgesaargh's wrist brought her gaze back down again.

'How?' she said.

'She walks into the burrows and kicks the rabbits to death. And I've almost cured her of crowing. Haven't I, William?'

'William?' said Agnes. 'Oh . . . yes.' To a falconer, she remembered, all hawks were 'she'.

'Have you seen any Omnians here?' she whispered, leaning down towards him.

'What kind of bird are they, miss?' said the falconer

uneasily. He always seemed to have a preoccupied air when not discussing hawks, like a man with a big dictionary who couldn't find the index.

'Oh, er . . . don't worry about it, then.' She stared at William again and said, 'How? I mean, how does a bird like *that* think he's— she's a *chicken*?'

'Can happen all too easy, miss,' said Hodgesaargh. 'Thomas Peerless over in Bad Ass pinched an egg and put it under a broody hen, miss. He didn't take the chicken away in time. So William thought if her mum was a chicken, then so was she.'

'Well, that's—'

'And that's what happens, miss. When I raise them from eggs I don't do that. I've got a special glove, miss—'

'That's absolutely fascinating, but I'd better go,' said Agnes, quickly.

'Yes, miss.'

She'd spotted the quarry, walking across the hall.

There was something unmistakable about him. It was as if he was a witch. It wasn't that his black robe ended at the knees and became a pair of legs encased in grey socks and sandals, or that his hat had a tiny crown but a brim big enough to set out your dinner on. It was because wherever he walked he was in a little empty space that seemed to move around him, just like you got around witches. No one wanted to get too close to witches.

She couldn't see his face. He was making a beeline for the buffet table.

'Excuse me, Miss Nitt?'

Shawn had appeared at her side. He stood very

stiffly, because if he made any sudden turns the over-sized wig tended to spin on his head.

'Yes, Shawn?' said Agnes.

'The Queen wants a word, miss,' said Shawn.

'With *me*?'

'Yes, miss. She's up in the Ghastly Green Drawing Room, miss.' Shawn swivelled slowly. His wig stayed facing the same way.

Agnes hesitated. It was a royal command, she supposed, even if it was only from Magrat Garlick as was, and as such it superseded anything Nanny had asked her to do. Anyway, she had spotted the priest, and it was not as though he was going to set fire to everyone over the canapes. She'd better go.

A little hatch shot open behind the doleful Igor.

'Why've we stopped *this* time?'

'Troll'th in the way, marthter.'

'A what?'

Igor rolled his eyes. 'A troll'th in the way,' he said.

The hatch shut. There was a whispered conversation inside the coach. The hatch opened.

'You mean a *troll*?'

'*Yeth*, marthter.'

'Run it down!'

The troll advanced, holding a flickering torch above its head. At some point recently someone had said 'This troll needs a uniform' and had found that the only thing in the armoury that would fit was the helmet, and then only if you attached it to his head with string.

'The old Count wouldn't have told me to run it

down,' Igor muttered, not quite under his breath. 'But, then, *he* wath a *gentleman*.'

'What was that?' a female voice snapped.

The troll reached the coach and banged its knuckles on its helmet respectfully.

'Evenin',' it said. 'Dis is a bit embarrassin'. You know a pole?'

'Pole?' said Igor suspiciously.

'It are a long wooden fing—'

'Yeth? Well? What about it?'

'I'd like you to imagine, right, dat dere's a black an' yellow striped one across dis road, right? Only 'cos we've only got der one, an' it's bein' used up on der Copperhead road tonight.'

The hatch slid open.

'Get a move on, man! Run it down!'

'I could go an' get it if you like,' said the troll, shifting nervously from one huge foot to the other. 'Only it wouldn't be here till tomorrow, right? Or you could pretend it's here right now, an' then I could pretend to lift it up, and dat'd be okay, right?'

'Do it, then,' said Igor. He ignored the grumbling behind him. The old Count had always been polite to trolls even though you couldn't bite them, and that was *real* class in a vampire.

'Only firs' I gotta stamp somethin',' said the troll. It held up half a potato and a paint-soaked rag.

'Why?'

'Shows you've bin past me,' said the troll.

'Yeth, but we will have been parthed you,' Igor pointed out. 'I mean, everyone will know we've been parthed you becauthe we *are*.'

'But it'll show you done it *officially*,' said the troll.

'What'll happen if we jutht drive on?' said Igor.

'Er . . . den I won't lift der pole,' said the troll.

Locked in a metaphysical conundrum, they both looked at the patch of road where the virtual pole barred the way.

Normally, Igor wouldn't have wasted any time. But the family had been getting on his nerves, and he reacted in the traditional way of the put-upon servant by suddenly becoming very stupid. He leaned down and addressed the coach's occupants through the hatch.

'It'th a border check, marthter,' he said. 'We got to have thomething thtamped.'

There was more whispering inside the coach, and then a large white rectangle, edged in gold, was thrust ungraciously through the hatch. Igor passed it down.

'Seems a shame,' said the troll, stamping it inexpertly and handing it back.

'What'th thith?' Igor demanded.

'Pardon?'

'Thith . . . thtupid mark!'

'Well, the potato wasn't big enough for the official seal and I don't know what a seal look like in any case but I reckon dat's a good carvin' of a duck I done there,' said the troll cheerfully. 'Now . . . are you ready? 'cos I'm liftin' der pole. Here it goes now. Look at it pointin' up in der air like dat. Dis means you can go.'

The coach rolled on a little way and stopped just before the bridge.

The troll, aware that he'd done his duty, wandered towards it and heard what he considered to be a perplexing conversation, although to Big Jim Beef most conversations involving polysyllabic words were shrouded in mystery.

'Now, I want you to all pay attention—'

'Father, we *have* done this before.'

'The point can't be hammered home far enough. *That* is the Lancre River down there. Running water. And we will cross it. It is as well to consider that your ancestors, although quite capable of undertaking journeys of hundreds of miles, nevertheless firmly believed that they couldn't cross a stream. Do I need to point out the contradiction?'

'No, Father.'

'Good. Cultural conditioning would be the death of us, if we are not careful. Drive on, Igor.'

The troll watched them go. Coldness seemed to follow them across the bridge.

Granny Weatherwax was airborne again, glad of the clean, crisp air. She was well above the trees and, to the benefit of all concerned, no one could see her face.

Isolated homesteads passed below, a few with lighted windows but most of them dark, because people would long ago have headed for the palace.

There was a story under every roof, she knew. She knew all about stories. But those down there were the stories that were never to be told, the little secret stories, enacted in little rooms . . .

They were about those times when medicines didn't help and headology was at a loss because a mind was a rage of pain in a body that had become its own enemy, when people were simply in a prison made of flesh, and at times like this she could *let them go.* There was no need for desperate stuff with a pillow, or deliberate mistakes with the medicine. You didn't push them out of the world, you just stopped the world pulling them back. You just reached in, and . . . showed them the way.

There was never anything said. Sometimes you saw in the face of the relatives the request they'd never, ever put words around, or maybe they'd say, 'Is there something you can do for him?' and this was, perhaps, the code. If you dared ask, they'd be shocked that you might have thought they meant *anything* other than, perhaps, a comfier pillow.

And any midwife, out in isolated cottages on bloody nights, would know all the other little secrets . . .

Never to be told . . .

She'd been a witch here all her life. And one of the things a witch did was stand right on the edge, where the decisions had to be made. You made them so that others didn't have to, so that others could even pretend to themselves that there *were* no decisions to be made, no little secrets, that things *just happened.* You never said what you knew. And you didn't ask for anything in return.

The castle was brightly lit, she saw. She could even make out figures around the bonfire.

Something else caught her eye, because she was going to look everywhere but at the castle now, and it jolted her out of her mood. Mist was pouring over the mountains and sliding down the far valleys under the moonlight. One strand was flowing towards the castle and pouring, very slowly, into the Lancre Gorge.

Of course you got mists in the spring, when the weather was changing, but this mist was coming from Uberwald.

The door to Magrat's room was opened by Millie Chillum, the maid, who curtseyed to Agnes, or at least to her hat, and then left her alone with the Queen, who was at her dressing table.

Agnes wasn't sure of the protocol, but tried a sort of republican curtsey. This caused considerable movement in outlying regions.

Queen Magrat of Lancre blew her nose and stuffed the hankie up the sleeve of her dressing gown.

'Oh, hello, Agnes,' she said. 'Take a seat, do. You don't have to bob up and down like that. Millie does it all the time and I get seasick. Anyway, strictly speaking, witches bow.'

'Er . . .' Agnes began. She glanced at the crib in the corner. It had more loops and lace than any piece of furniture should.

'She's asleep,' said Magrat. 'Oh, the crib? Verence ordered it all the way from Ankh-Morpork. I said the old one they'd always used was fine, but he's very, you know . . . *modern. Please* sit down.'

'You wanted me, your maj—' Agnes began, still uncertain. It was turning out to be a very complicated evening, and she wasn't sure even now how she felt about Magrat. The woman had left echoes of herself in the cottage – an old bangle lost under the bed, rather soppy notes in some of the ancient notebooks, vases full of desiccated flowers . . . You can build up a very strange view of someone via the things they leave behind the dresser.

'I just wanted a little talk,' said Magrat. 'It's a bit . . . look, I'm really very happy, but . . . well, Millie's nice but she agrees with me all the time and Nanny and Granny still treat me as if I wasn't, well, you know, Queen and everything . . . not that I *want* to be treated as Queen all the time but, well, you know, I want them to know I'm Queen but not *treat* me as one, if you see what I mean . . .'

'I *think* so,' said Agnes carefully.

Magrat waved her hands in an effort to describe the indescribable. Used handkerchiefs cascaded out of her sleeves.

'I mean . . . I get dizzy with people bobbing up and down all the time, so when they see me I like them to think, "Oh, there's Magrat, she's Queen now but I shall treat her in a perfectly normal way—"'

'But perhaps just a little bit more politely because she *is* Queen, after all,' Agnes suggested.

'Well, yes . . . exactly. Actually, Nanny's not too bad, at least she treats everyone the same all the time, but when Granny looks at me you can see her thinking, "Oh, there's Magrat. Make the tea, Magrat." One day I *swear* I'll make a very cutting remark. It's as if they think I'm doing this as a *hobby*!'

'I do know what you mean.'

'It's as if they think I'm going to get it out of my system and go back to witching again. They wouldn't say that, of course, but that's what they think. They really don't believe there's any other sort of life.'

'That's true.'

'How's the old cottage?'

'There's a lot of mice,' said Agnes.

'I know. I used to feed them. Don't tell Granny. She's here, isn't she?'

'Haven't seen her yet,' said Agnes.

'Ah, she'll be waiting for a dramatic moment,' said Magrat. 'And you know what? I've never caught her *actually* waiting for a dramatic moment, not in all the, well, things we've been involved in. I mean, if it was you or me, we'd be hanging around in the hall or something, but she just walks in and it's the right time.'

'She says you make your own right time,' said Agnes.

'Yes,' said Magrat.

'Yes,' said Agnes.

'And you say she's not here yet? It was the first card we did!' Magrat leaned closer. 'Verence got them to put extra gold leaf on it. I'm amazed it doesn't go clang when she puts it down. How are you at making the tea?'

'They always complain,' said Agnes.

'They do, don't they? Three lumps of sugar for Nanny Ogg, right?'

'It's not as if they even give me tea money,' said Agnes. She sniffed. There was a slight mustiness to the air.

'It's not worth baking biscuits, I can tell you that,' said Magrat. 'I used to spend hours doing fancy ones with crescent moons and so on. You might just as well get them from the shop.'

She sniffed too. 'That's *not* the baby,' she said. 'I'm sure Shawn Ogg's been so busy arranging things he hasn't had time to clean up the privy pit the last two weeks. The smell comes right up the garderobe in the Gong Tower when the wind gusts. I've tried hanging up fragrant herbs but they sort of dissolve.'

She looked uncertain, as if a worse prospect than lax castle sanitation had crossed her mind. 'Er . . . she must've *got* the invitation, mustn't she?'

'Shawn says he delivered it,' said Agnes. 'And she probably said,' and here her voice changed, becoming clipped and harsh, '"I can't be havin' with that at my time of life. I've never bin one to put meself forward, no one could ever say I'm one to put meself forward."'

Magrat's mouth was an O of amazement.

'That's so like her it's frightening!' she said.

'It's one of the few things I'm good at,' said Agnes, in her normal voice. 'Big hair, a wonderful personality, and an ear for sounds.' *And two minds*, Perdita added. 'She'll come anyway,' Agnes went on, ignoring the inner voice.

'But it's gone half eleven . . . Good grief, I'd better get dressed! Can you give me a hand?'

She hurried into the dressing room with Agnes tagging along behind.

'I even wrote a bit underneath asking her to be a godmother,' she said, sitting down in front of the mirror and scrabbling among the debris of make-up. 'She's always secretly wanted to be one.'

'That's something to wish on a child,' said Agnes, without thinking.

Magrat's hand stopped halfway to her face, in a little cloud of powder, and Agnes saw her horrified look in the mirror. Then the jaw tightened, and for a moment the Queen had just the same expression that Granny sometimes employed.

'Well, if it was a choice of wishing a child health, wealth and happiness, or Granny Weatherwax being on her side, I know which I'd choose,' said Magrat. 'You must have seen her in action.'

'Once or twice, yes,' Agnes conceded.

'She'll never be beaten,' said Magrat. 'You wait till you see her when she's in a tight corner. She's got that way of . . . putting part of herself somewhere safe. It's as if . . . as if she gives herself to someone else to keep hidden for a while. It's all part of that Borrowing stuff she does.'

Agnes nodded. Nanny had warned her about it but, even so, it was unnerving to turn up at Granny's cottage and find her stretched out on the floor as stiff as a stick and holding, in fingers that were almost blue, a card with the words: I ATE'NT DEAD.* It just meant that *she* was out in the world somewhere, seeing life through the eyes of a badger or a pigeon, riding as an unheeded passenger in its mind.

'And you know what?' Magrat went on. 'It's just like those magicians in Howondaland who keep their

*When there was nothing much else to occupy her time Granny Weatherwax sent her mind Borrowing, letting it piggyback inside the heads of other creatures. She was widely accepted as the most skilled exponent of the art that the Ramtops had seen for centuries, being practically able to get inside the minds of things that didn't even *have* minds. The practice meant, among other things, that Lancre people were less inclined towards the casual cruelty to animals that is a general feature of the rural idyll, on the basis that the rat you throw a brick at today might turn out to be the witch you need some toothache medicine from tomorrow.

It also meant that people calling on her unexpectedly would find her stretched out apparently cold and lifeless, heart and pulse barely beating. The sign had saved a lot of embarrassment.

heart hidden in a jar somewhere, for safety, so they can't be killed. There's something about it in a book at the cottage.'

'Wouldn't have to be a big jar,' said Agnes.

'That wasn't fair,' said Magrat. She paused. 'Well . . . not fair for most of the time. Often, anyway. Sometimes, at least. Can you help me with this bloody ruff?'

There was a gurgle from the cradle.

'What name are you giving her?' said Agnes.

'You'll have to wait,' said Magrat.

It made some sort of sense, Agnes admitted, as she followed Magrat and the maids to the hall. In Lancre you named children at midnight so that they started a day with a new name. She didn't know *why* it made sense. It just felt as though, once, someone had found that it worked. Lancrastians never threw away anything that worked. The trouble was, they seldom *changed* anything that worked, either.

She'd heard that this was depressing King Verence, who was teaching himself kinging out of books. His plans for better irrigation and agriculture were warmly applauded by the people of Lancre, who then did nothing about them. Nor did they take any notice of his scheme for sanitation, i.e. that there should *be* some, since the Lancrastian idea of posh sanitation was a non-slippery path to the privy and a mail-order catalogue with really soft pages. They'd agreed to the idea of a Royal Society for the Betterment of Mankind, but since this largely consisted of as much time as Shawn Ogg had to spare on Thursday afternoons Mankind was safe from too much Betterment for a while, although Shawn had invented draught excluders for some of the windier parts of the castle, for which the King had awarded him a small medal.

The people of Lancre wouldn't dream of living in anything other than a monarchy. They'd done so for thousands of years and knew that it worked. But they'd also found that it didn't do to pay too much attention to what the King wanted, because there was bound to be another king along in forty years or so and he'd be certain to want something different and so they'd have gone to all that trouble for nothing. In the meantime, his job as they saw it was to mostly stay in the palace, practise the waving, have enough sense to face the right way on coins and let them get on with the ploughing, sowing, growing and harvesting. It was, as they saw it, a social contract. They did what they always did, and he let them.

But sometimes, he kinged . . .

In Lancre Castle, King Verence looked at himself in the mirror and sighed.

'Mrs Ogg,' he said, adjusting his crown, 'I have, as you know, a great respect for the witches of Lancre but this is, with respect, broadly a matter of general policy which, I respectfully submit, is a matter for the King.' He adjusted the crown again, while Spriggins the butler brushed his robe. 'We must be tolerant. Really, Mrs Ogg, I haven't seen you in a state like this before—'

'They go round setting fire to people!' said Nanny, annoyed at all the respect.

'*Used to*, I believe,' said Verence.

'And it was witches they burned!'

Verence removed his crown and polished it with his sleeve in an infuriatingly reasonable manner.

'I've always understood they set fire to practically everybody,' he said, 'but that was some time ago, wasn't it?'

'Our Jason heard 'em preaching once down in Ohulan and they was saying some very nasty things about witches,' said Nanny.

'Sadly, not everyone knows witches like we do,' said Verence, with what Nanny in her overheated state thought was unnecessary diplomacy.

'And our Wayne said they tries to turn folk against other religions,' she went on. 'Since they opened up that mission of theirs even the Offlerians have upped sticks and gone. I mean, it's one thing saying you've got the best god, but sayin' it's the *only* real one is a bit of a cheek, in my opinion. I know where I can find at least two any day of the week. *And* they say everyone starts out bad and only gets good by believin' in Om, which is frankly damn nonsense. I mean, look at your little girl— What's her name going to be, now . . .?'

'Everyone will know in twenty minutes, Nanny,' said Verence smoothly.

'Hah!' Nanny's tone made it clear that Radio Ogg disapproved of this news management. 'Well, look . . . the worst she could put her little hand up to at her age is a few grubby nappies and keepin' you awake at night. That's hardly *sinful*, to my mind.'

'But you've never objected to the Gloomy Brethren, Nanny. Or to the Wonderers. And the Balancing Monks come through here all the time.'

'But none of *them* object to *me*,' said Nanny.

Verence turned. He was finding this disconcerting. He knew Nanny Ogg very well, but mainly as the person standing just behind Granny Weatherwax and smiling a lot. It was hard to deal with an angry Ogg.

'I really think you're taking this too much to heart, Mrs Ogg,' he said.

'Granny Weatherwax won't like it!' Nanny played the trump card. To her horror, it didn't seem to have the desired effect.

'Granny Weatherwax isn't King, Mrs Ogg,' said Verence. 'And the world is changing. There is a new order. Once upon a time trolls were monsters that ate people but now, thanks to the endeavours of men, and of course trolls, of goodwill and peaceful intent, we get along very well and I hope we understand each other. This is no longer a time when little kingdoms need only worry about little concerns. We're part of a big world. We have to *play* that part. For example, what about the Muntab question?'

Nanny Ogg asked the Muntab question. 'Where the hell's Muntab?' she said.

'Several thousand miles away, Mrs Ogg. But it has ambitions Hubwards, and if there's war with Borogravia we will certainly have to adopt a position.'

'This one several thousand miles away looks fine by me,' said Nanny. 'And I don't see—'

'I'm afraid you don't,' said Verence. 'Nor should you have to. But affairs in distant countries can suddenly end up close to home. If Klatch sneezes, Ankh-Morpork catches a cold. We have to pay attention. Are we always to be part of the Ankh-Morpork hegemony? Are we not in a unique position as we reach the end of the Century of the Fruitbat? The countries widdershins of the Ramtops are beginning to make themselves felt. The "werewolf economies", as the Patrician in Ankh-Morpork calls them. New powers are emerging. Old countries are blinking in the sunlight of the dawning millennium. And of course we have to maintain friendships with all blocs. And so on. Despite a turbulent past, Omnia is a friendly country . . . or, at least,' he admitted, 'I'm sure they *would* be friendly if they knew about Lancre. Being unpleasant to the priests of its state religion will serve us no good purpose. I'm sure we will not regret it.'

'Let's hope we won't,' said Nanny. She gave Verence a withering look. 'And I remember you when you were just a man in a funny hat.'

Even this didn't work. Verence merely sighed again and turned towards the door.

'I still am, Nanny,' he said. 'It's just that this one's a lot heavier. And now I must go, otherwise we shall be keeping our guests waiting. Ah, Shawn . . .'

Shawn Ogg had appeared at the door. He saluted.

'How's the army coming along, Shawn?'

'I've nearly finished the knife, sir.* Just got to do the

*It was obvious to King Verence that even if every adult were put under arms the kingdom of Lancre would still have a very small and insignificant army, and he'd therefore looked for other ways to put it on the military map. Shawn had come up with the idea of the Lancrastian Army Knife, containing a few essential tools and utensils for the soldier in the field, and research and development work had been going on for some months now. One reason for the slow progress was that the King himself was taking an active interest in the country's only defence project, and Shawn was receiving little nose-hair tweezers and the folding saw, sir. But actually I'm here as herald at the moment, sir.'

'Ah, it must be time.'

'Yes, sir.'

'A shorter fanfare this time, Shawn, I think,' said the King. 'While I personally appreciate your skill, an occasion like this calls for something a little simpler than several bars of "Pink Hedgehog Rag".'

'Yes, sir.'

'Let us go, then.'

They went out into the main passage just as Magrat's group was passing, and the King took her hand.

Nanny Ogg trailed after them. The King was right, in a way. She did feel . . . *unusual*, ill-tempered and snappish, as if she'd put on a vest that was too tight. Well, Granny would be here soon enough, and she knew how to talk to kings.

You needed a special technique for that, Nanny reasoned; for example, you couldn't say things like 'Who died and made *you* King?', because they'd *know*. 'You and whose army?' was another difficult one, although in this case Verence's army consisted of Shawn and a troll and was unlikely to be a serious threat to Shawn's own mother if he wanted to be allowed to eat his tea indoors.

notes up to three times every day with further suggestions for improvement. Generally they were on the lines of: 'A device, possibly quite small, for finding things that are lost', or 'A curiously shaped hook-like thing of many uses'. Shawn diplomatically added some of them but lost as many notes as he dared, lest he design the only pocket knife on wheels.

She pulled Agnes to one side as the procession reached the top of the big staircase and Shawn went on ahead.

'We'll get a good view from the minstrel gallery,' she hissed, dragging Agnes into the king oak structure just as the trumpet began the royal fanfare.

'That's my boy,' she added proudly, when the final flourish caused a stir.

'Yes, not many royal fanfares end with "shave and a haircut, no legs"*,' said Agnes.

'Puts people at their ease, though,' said Shawn's loyal mum.

Agnes looked down at the throng and caught sight of the priest again. He was moving through the press of guests.

'I found him, Nanny,' she said. 'He didn't make it hard, I must say. He won't try anything in a crowd, will he?'

'Which one is it?'

Agnes pointed. Nanny stared, and then turned to her.

'Sometimes I think the weight of that damn crown is turning Verence's head,' she said. 'I reckon he really doesn't know what he's lettin' into the kingdom. When Esme gets here she's going to go through this priest like cabbage soup.'

By now the guests had got themselves sorted out on either side of the red carpet that began at the bottom of the stairs. Agnes glanced up at the royal couple, waiting awkwardly, just out of sight, for the

*The *leitmotif* of the Guild of Barber-Surgeons.

appropriate moment to descend, and thought: Granny Weatherwax says you make your own right time. They're the royal family. All they need to do is walk down the stairs and it'd *be* the right time. They're doing it wrong.

Several of the Lancre guests were glancing at the big double doors, shut for this official ceremony. They'd be thrown open later, for the more public and enjoyable part, but right now they looked . . .

. . . like doors that would soon creak back and frame a figure against the firelight.

She could see the image so clearly.

The exercises Granny had reluctantly given her were working, Perdita thought.

There was a hurried conversation among the royal party and then Millie hurried back up the stairs and towards the witches.

'Mag— the Queen says, is Granny Weatherwax coming or not?' she panted.

'Of course she is,' said Nanny.

'Only, well, the King's getting a bit . . . upset. He said it *did* say RSVP on the invitation,' said Millie, trying not to meet Nanny eye to eye.

'Oh, witches *never* reservups,' said Nanny. 'They just come.'

Millie put her hand in front of her mouth and gave a nervous little cough. She glanced wretchedly towards Magrat, who was making frantic hand signals.

'Only, well, the Queen says we'd better not hold things up, so, er, would *you* be godmother, Mrs Ogg?'

The wrinkles doubled on Nanny's face as she smiled.

'Tell you what,' she said brightly. 'I'll come and sort of stand in until Granny gets here, shall I?'

Once again, Granny Weatherwax paced up and down in the spartan greyness of her kitchen. Occasionally she'd glance at the floor. There was quite a gap under the door, and sometimes things could be blown anywhere. But she'd already searched a dozen times. She must've got the cleanest floor in the country by now. Anyway, it was too late.

Even so . . . *Uberwald* . . .*

She strode up and down a few more times.

'I'll be blowed if I'll give 'em the satisfaction,' she muttered.

She sat down in her rocking chair, stood up again so quickly that the chair almost fell over, and went back to the pacing.

'I mean, I've never been the kind of person to put myself forward,' she said to the air. 'I'm not the sort to go where I'm not welcome, I'm sure.'

She went to make a cup of tea, fumbling with the kettle with shaking hands, and dropped the lid of her sugar bowl, breaking it.

A light caught her eye. The half moon was visible over the lawn.

*On the rare maps of the Ramtops that existed, it was spelled Überwald. But Lancre people had never got the hang of accents and certainly didn't agree with trying to balance two dots on another letter, where they'd only roll off and cause unnecessary punctuation.

'Anyway, it's not as if I've not got other things to do,' she said. 'Can't *all* be rushing off to parties the whole time . . . wouldn't have gone *anyway*.'

She found herself flouncing around the corners of the floor again and thought: if I'd found it, the Wattley boy would have knocked at an empty cottage. I'd have gone and enjoyed meself. And John Ivy'd be sitting alone now . . .

'Drat!'

That was the worst part about being good – it caught you coming *and* going.

She landed in the rocking chair again and pulled her shawl around her against the chill. She hadn't kept the fire in. She hadn't expected to be at home tonight.

Shadows filled the corners of the room, but she couldn't be bothered to light the lamp. The candle would have to do.

As she rocked, glaring at the wall, the shadows lengthened.

Agnes followed Nanny down into the hall. She probably wasn't meant to, but very few people will argue with a hat of authority.

Small countries were normal along this part of the Ramtops. Every glacial valley, separated from its neighbours by a route that required a scramble or, at worst, a ladder, more or less ruled itself. There seemed to Agnes to be any number of kings, even if some of them did their ruling in the evenings after they'd milked the cows. A lot of them were here, because a free meal is not to be sneezed at. There were also some senior dwarfs from Copperhead and, standing well away from them, a group of trolls. They weren't carrying weapons, so Agnes assumed they were politicians. Trolls weren't strictly subjects of King Verence, but they were there to say, in official body language, that playing football with human heads was something no one did any more, much. Hardly at all, really. Not roun' here, certainly. Dere's practic'ly a law against it.

The witches were ushered to the area in front of the thrones, and then Millie scurried away.

The Omnian priest nodded at them.

'Good, um, evening,' he said, and completely failed to set fire to anyone. He wasn't very old and had a rather ripe boil beside his nose. Inside Agnes, Perdita made a face at him.

Nanny Ogg grunted. Agnes risked a brief smile. The priest blew his nose noisily.

'You must be some of these, um, witches I've heard so much about,' he said. He had an amazing smile. It appeared on his face as if someone had operated a shutter. One moment it wasn't there, the next moment it was. And then it was gone.

'Um, yes,' said Agnes.

'Hah,' said Nanny Ogg, who could haughtily turn her back on people while looking them in the eye.

'And I am, I am, aaaa . . .' said the priest. He stopped, and pinched the bridge of his nose. 'Oh, I am sorry. The mountain air doesn't agree with me. I am the Quite Reverend Mightily Oats.'

'You are?' said Agnes. To her amazement, the man began to redden. The more she looked at him, the more she realized that he wasn't much older than she was.

'That is, Mightily-Praiseworthy-Are-Ye-Who-Exalteth-Om Oats,' he said. 'It's much shorter in Omnian, of course. Have you by any chance heard the Word of Om?'

'Which one? "Fire"?' said Nanny Ogg. 'Hah!'

The nascent religious war was abruptly cut short by the first official royal fanfare to end with a few bars from the 'Hedgehog Cakewalk'. The royal couple began to descend the stairs.

'And we'll have none of your heathen ways, thank you very much,' muttered Nanny Ogg behind the pastor. 'No sloshing water or oil or sand around or cutting any bits off and if I hears a single word I understand, well, I'm standing behind you with a pointy stick.'*

From the other side he heard, 'He's *not* some kind of horrible inquisitor, Nanny!'

'But my pointy stick's still a pointy stick, my girl!'

What's got into her? Agnes thought, watching the pastor's ears turn red. That's the way *Granny* would act. Perdita added: *Perhaps she thinks she's got to carry on like that because that old bat's not here yet.*

Agnes was quite shocked at hearing herself think that.

'You do things our way here, all right?' said Nanny.

'The, um, King did explain it all to me, um,' said the

*Lancre people considered that anything religious that wasn't said in some ancient and incomprehensible speech probably wasn't the genuine article.

pastor. 'Er, do you have anything for a headache. I'm afraid I—'

'You put the key in one hand and let her grip the crown with the other,' Nanny Ogg went on.

'Yes, um, he *did*—'

'Then you tell her what her name is and her mum's name and her dad's name, mumbling a bit over the latter if the mum ain't sure—'

'Nanny! This is *royalty*!'

'Hah, I could tell you stories, gel . . . and then, see, you give her to me and I tell her, too, and then I give her back and *you* tell the people what her name is, an' then you give her to me, and then I give her to her dad, and he takes her out through the doors and shows her to everyone, everyone throws their hats in the air and shouts "Hoorah!" and then it's all over bar the drinks and horses' doovers and findin' your own hat. Start extemporizin' on the subject of sin and it'll go hard with you.'

'What is, um, your role, madam?'

'I'm the godmother!'

'Which, um, god?' The young man was trembling slightly.

'It's from Old Lancre,' said Agnes hurriedly. 'It means something like "goodmother". It's all right . . . as witches we believe in religious toleration . . .'

'That's right,' said Nanny Ogg. 'But only for the right religions, so you watch your step!'

The royal parents had reached the thrones. Magrat took her seat and, to Agnes's amazement, gave her a sly wink.

Verence didn't wink. He stood there and coughed loudly.

'Ahem!'

'I've got a pastille somewhere,' said Nanny, her hand reaching towards her knickerleg.

'*Ahem!*' Verence's eyes darted towards his throne.

What had appeared to be a grey cushion rolled over, yawned, gave the King a brief glance, and started to wash itself.

'Oh, Greebo!' said Nanny. 'I was wonderin' where you'd got to . . .'

'Could you please remove him, Mrs Ogg?' said the King.

Agnes glanced at Magrat. The Queen had half turned away, with her elbow on the arm of the throne and her hand covering her mouth. Her shoulders were shaking.

Nanny grabbed her cat off the throne.

'A cat *can* look at a king,' she said.

'Not with that expression, I believe,' said Verence. He waved graciously at the assembled company, just as the castle's clock began to strike midnight.

'Please begin, Reverend.'

'I, um, did have a small suitable homily on the subject of, um, hope for the—' the Quite Reverend Oats began, but there was a grunt from Nanny and he suddenly seemed to jerk forward slightly. He blinked once or twice and his Adam's apple bobbed up and down. 'But alas I fear we have no time,' he concluded quickly.

Magrat leaned over and whispered something in her husband's ear. Agnes heard him say, 'Well, dear, I think we *have* to, whether she's here or not . . .'

Shawn scurried up, slightly out of breath and with

his wig on sideways. He was carrying a cushion. On the faded velvet was the big iron key of the castle.

Millie Chillum carefully handed the baby to the priest, who held it gingerly.

It seemed to the royal couple that he suddenly started to speak very hesitantly. Behind him, Nanny Ogg's was an expression of extreme interest that was nevertheless made up of one hundred per cent artificial additives. They also had the impression that the poor man was suffering from frequent attacks of cramp.

'—we are gathered here together in the sight of . . . um . . . one another . . .'

'Are you all right, Reverend?' said the King, leaning forward.

'Never better, sir, um, I assure you,' said Oats miserably, '. . . and I therefore name thee . . . that is, you . . .'

There was a deep, horrible pause.

Glassy faced, the priest handed the baby to Millie. Then he removed his hat, took a small scrap of paper from the lining, read it, moved his lips a few times as he said the words to himself, and then replaced the hat on his sweating forehead and took the baby again.

'I name you . . . Esmerelda Margaret Note Spelling of Lancre!'

The shocked silence was suddenly filled.

'*Note Spelling?*' said Magrat and Agnes together.

'*Esmerelda?*' said Nanny.

The baby opened her eyes.

And the doors swung back.

* * *

Choices. It was always choices . . .

There'd been that man down in Spackle, the one that'd killed those little kids. The people'd sent for her and she'd looked at him and seen the guilt writhing in his head like a red worm, and then she'd taken them to his farm and showed them where to dig, and he'd thrown himself down and asked *her* for mercy, because he said he'd been drunk and it'd all been done in alcohol.

Her words came back to her. She'd said, in sobriety: end it in hemp.

And they'd dragged him off and hanged him in a hempen rope and she'd gone to watch because she owed him that much, and he'd cursed, which was unfair because hanging is a clean death, or at least cleaner than the one he'd have got if the villagers had dared defy her, and she'd seen the shadow of Death come for him, and then behind Death came the smaller, brighter figures, and *then*—

In the darkness, the rocking chair creaked as it thundered back and forth.

The villagers had said justice had been done, and she'd lost patience and told them to go home, then, and pray to whatever gods they believed in that it was never done to them. The smug mask of virtue triumphant could be almost as horrible as the face of wickedness revealed.

She shuddered at a memory. Almost as horrible, but not quite.

The odd thing was, quite a lot of villagers had turned up to his funeral, and there had been mutterings from one or two people on the lines of, yes, well, but *overall* he wasn't such a bad chap . . . and anyway, maybe *she* made him say it. And she'd got the dark looks.

Supposing there was justice for all, after all? For every unheeded beggar, every harsh word, every neglected duty, every slight . . . every choice . . . Because that was the point, wasn't it? You had to choose. You might be right, you might be wrong, but you had to *choose*, knowing that the rightness or wrongness might never be clear or even that you were deciding between two sorts of wrong, that there was no *right* anywhere. And always, *always*, you did it by yourself. You were the one there, on the edge, watching and listening. Never any tears, never any apology, never any regrets . . . You saved all that up in a way that could be used when needed.

She never discussed this with Nanny Ogg or any of the other witches. That would be breaking the secret. Sometimes, late at night, when the conversation tiptoed around to that area, Nanny might just drop in some line like 'Old Scrivens went peacefully enough at the finish' and may or may not mean something by it. Nanny, as far as she could see, didn't agonize very much. To her, some things obviously had to be done, and that was that. Any of the thoughts that hung around she kept locked up tight, even from herself. Granny envied her.

Who'd come to *her* funeral when *she* died?

They didn't ask her!

Memories jostled. Other figures marched out into the shadows around the candlelight.

She'd done things and been places, and found ways

to turn anger outwards that had surprised even her. She'd faced down others far more powerful than she was, if only she'd allowed them to believe it. She'd given up so much, but she'd learned a lot . . .

It was a sign. She knew it'd come sooner or later . . . They'd realized it, and now she was no more use . . .

What had she ever earned? The reward for toil had been more toil. If you dug the best ditches they gave you a bigger shovel.

And you got these bare walls, this bare floor, this cold cottage.

The darkness in the corners grew out into the room and began to tangle in her hair.

They didn't ask her!

She'd never, ever asked for anything in return. And the trouble with not asking for anything in return was that sometimes you didn't get it.

She'd always tried to face towards the light. She'd *always* tried to face towards the light. But the harder you stared into the brightness the harsher it burned into you until, at last, the temptation picked you up and bid you turn around to see how long, rich, strong and dark, streaming away behind you, your shadow had become—

Someone mentioned her name.

There was a moment of light and noise and bewilderment.

And then she awoke and looked at the darkness flowing in, and saw things in black and white.

'So sorry . . . delays on the road, you know how it is . . .'

The newcomers hurried in and joined the crowd, who paid little attention because they were watching the unplanned entertainment around the thrones.

'Note Spelling?'

'Definitely a bit tricky,' said Nanny. 'Esmerelda, now, *that* was a good one. Gytha would have been good too, but Esmerelda, yes, you can't argue with it. But you know kids. They'll all be calling her Spelly.'

'If she's lucky,' said Agnes gloomily.

'I didn't expect anyone to *say* it!' Magrat hissed. 'I just wanted to make sure she didn't end up with "Magrat"!'

Mightily Oats was standing with his eyes cast upwards and his hands clasped together. Occasionally he made a whimpering sound.

'We can change it, can't we?' said King Verence. 'Where's the Royal Historian?'

Shawn coughed. 'It's not Wednesday evening and I'll have to go and fetch the proper hat, sire—'

'Can we change it or not, man?'

'Er . . . it has been *said*, sire. At the official time. I *think* it's her name now, but I'll need to go and look it up. Everyone heard it, sire.'

'No, you can't change it,' said Nanny, who as the Royal Historian's mum took it as read that she knew more than the Royal Historian. 'Look at old Moocow Poorchick over in Slice, for one.'

'What happened to him, then?' said the King sharply.

'His full name is James What The Hell's That Cow Doing In Here Poorchick,' said Magrat.

'That was a very strange day, I do remember that,' said Nanny.

'And if my mother had been sensible enough to *tell*

Brother Perdore *my* name instead of coming over all bashful and writing it down, life would have been a whole lot different,' said Magrat. She glanced nervously at Verence. 'Probably worse, of course.'

'So I've got to take Esmerelda out to her people and tell them one of her middle names is Note Spelling?' said Verence.

'Well, we did once have a king called My God He's Heavy the First,' said Nanny. 'And the beer's been on for the last couple of hours so, basic'ly, you'll get a cheer whatever you say.'

Besides, thought Agnes, I know for a fact there's people out there called Syphilidae Wilson and Yodel Lightley and Total Biscuit.*

Verence smiled. 'Oh well . . . let me have her . . .'

'Whifm . . .' said Mightily Oats.

'. . . and perhaps someone ought to give this man a drink.'

'I'm so terribly, terribly sorry,' whispered the priest, as the King walked between the lines of guests.

'Been on the drink already, I expect,' said Nanny.

'I never ever touch alcohol!' moaned the priest. He dabbed at his streaming eyes with a handkerchief.

'I knew there was something wrong with you as soon as I looked at you,' said Nanny. 'Where's Esme, then?'

'I don't *know*, Nanny!' said Agnes.

*This was because Lancre people had a fresh if somewhat sideways approach to names, generally just picking a sound they liked. Sometimes there was a logic to it, but only by accident. There'd be a Chlamydia Weaver toddling around today if her mother hadn't suddenly decided that Sally was easier to spell.

'She'd know about this, you mark my words. This'll be a feather in her cap, right enough, a princess named after her. She'll be crowing about it for months. I'm going to see what's going on.'

She stumped off.

Agnes grabbed the priest's arm.

'Come along, you,' she sighed.

'I really cannot, um, express how sorry—'

'It's a very strange evening all round.'

'I've, I've, I've never, um, heard of the custom before—'

'People put a lot of importance on words in these parts.'

'I'm very much afraid the King will give a bad, um, report of me to Brother Melchio . . .'

'Really.'

There are some people who could turn even the most amiable character into a bully and the priest seemed to be one of them. There was something . . . sort of *damp* about him, the kind of helpless hopelessness that made people angry rather than charitable, the total certainty that if the whole *world* was a party he'd still find the kitchen.

She seemed to be stuck with him. The VIPs were all crowded around the open doors, where loud cheering indicated that the people of Lancre thought that Note Spelling was a nice name for a future queen.

'Perhaps you should just sit there and try to get a grip,' she said. 'There's going to be dancing later on.'

'Oh, I don't dance,' said Mightily Oats. 'Dancing is a snare to entrap the weak-willed.'

'Oh. Well, I suppose there's the barbecue outside . . .'

Mightily Oats dabbed at his eyes again.

'Um, any fish?'

'I doubt it.'

'We eat only fish this month.'

'Oh.' But a deadpan voice didn't seem to work. He still wanted to talk to her.

'Because the prophet Brutha eschewed meat, um, when he was wandering in the desert, you see.'

'Each mouthful forty times?'

'Pardon?'

'Sorry, I was thinking of something else.' Against her better judgement, Agnes let curiosity enter her life. 'What meat *is* there to eat, in a desert?'

'Um, none, I think.'

'So he didn't exactly refuse to eat it, did he?' Agnes scanned the gathering crowds, but no one seemed anxious to join in this little discussion.

'Um . . . you'd have to, um, ask Brother Melchio that. I'm so sorry. I think I have a migraine coming on . . .'

You don't believe anything you're saying, do you? Agnes thought. Nervousness and a sort of low-grade terror was radiating off him. Perdita added: *What a damp little maggot!*

'I've got to go and . . . er . . . to go and . . . I've got to go and . . . help,' said Agnes, backing away. He nodded. As she left, he blew his nose again, produced a small black book from a pocket, sighed, and hurriedly opened it at a bookmark.

She picked up a tray to add some weight to the alibi, stepped towards the food table, turned to look back at the hunched figure as out of place as a lost sheep, and walked into someone as solid as a tree.

'Who is that strange person?' said a voice by her ear. Agnes heard Perdita curse her for jumping sideways, but she recovered and managed to smile awkwardly at the person who'd spoken.

He was a young man and, it dawned on her, a very attractive one. Attractive men were not in plentiful supply in Lancre, where licking your hand and smoothing your hair down before taking a girl out was considered swanky.

He's got a ponytail! squeaked Perdita. *Now* that is *cool!*

Agnes felt the blush start somewhere in the region of her knees and begin its inevitable acceleration upwards.

'Er . . . sorry?' she said.

'You can practically smell him,' said the man. He inclined his head slightly towards the sad priest. 'Looks rather like a scruffy little crow, don't you think?'

'Er . . . yes,' Agnes managed. The blush rounded the curve of her bosom, red hot and rising. A ponytail on a man was unheard of in Lancre, and the cut of his clothes also suggested that he'd spent time somewhere where fashion changed more than once a lifetime. *No one* in Lancre had ever worn a waistcoat embroidered with peacocks.

Say something to him! Perdita screamed within.

'Wstfgl?' said Agnes. Behind her, Mightily Oats had got up and was inspecting the food suspiciously.

'I beg your pardon?'

Agnes swallowed, partly because Perdita was trying to shake her by the throat.

'He does look as if he's about to flap away, doesn't he?' she said. *Oh, please, don't let me giggle . . .*

The man snapped his fingers. A waiter hurrying past with a tray of drinks turned through ninety degrees.

'Can I get you a drink, Miss Nitt?'

'Er . . . white wine?' Agnes whispered.

'No, you don't want white wine, the red is much more . . . colourful,' he said, taking a glass and handing it to her. 'What is our quarry doing now . . . Ah, applying himself to a biscuit with a very small amount of pâté on it, I see . . .'

Ask him his name! Perdita yelled. No, that'd be forward of me, Agnes thought. Perdita screamed, *You were* built *forward, you stupid lump—*

'Please let me introduce myself. I'm Vlad,' he said kindly. 'Oh, now he's . . . yes, he's about to pounce on . . . yes, a prawn vol-au-vent. Prawns up here, eh? King Verence has spared no expense, has he?'

'He had them brought up on ice all the way from Genua,' Agnes mumbled.

'They *do* very good seafood there, I believe.'

'Never been,' Agnes mumbled. Inside her head Perdita lay down and cried.

'Maybe we could visit it one day, Agnes,' said Vlad.

The blush was at Agnes's neck.

'It's *very* hot in here, don't you think?' said Vlad.

'It's the fire,' said Agnes gratefully. 'It's over there,' she added, nodding to where quite a large amount of a tree was burning in the hall's enormous fireplace and could only have been missed by a man with a bucket on his head.

'My sister and I have—' Vlad began.

'Excuse me, Miss Nitt?'

'What *is* it, Shawn?' *Drop dead, Shawn Ogg,* said Perdita.

'Mum says you're to come at once, miss. She's down in the yard. She says it's important.'

'It always is,' said Agnes. She gave Vlad a quick smile. 'Excuse me, I have to go and help an old lady.'

'I'm sure we'll meet again, Agnes,' said Vlad.

'Oh, er . . . thank you.'

She hurried out and was halfway down the steps before she remembered she hadn't told him her name.

Two steps further she thought: well, he could have asked someone.

Two steps after that Perdita said: *Why would* he *ask anyone* your *name?*

Agnes cursed the fact that she had grown up with an invisible enemy.

'Come and look at this!' hissed Nanny, grabbing her by the arm as she reached the courtyard. She was dragged out to the carriages parked near the stables. Nanny waved a finger to the door of the nearest one.

'See that?' she said.

'It looks very impressive,' said Agnes.

'See the crest?'

'Looks like . . . a couple of black and white birds. Magpies, aren't they?'

'Yeah, but look at the writin',' said Nanny Ogg, with that dark relish old ladies reserve for nastily portentous things.

'*Carpe Jugulum,*' read Agnes aloud. 'That's . . . well, *Carpe Diem* is "Seize the Day", so this means—'

'"Go for the Throat",' said Nanny. 'You know what our king has done, so we can play our part in this new changin' world order thing and get money for hedges because Klatch gets a nosebleed when Ankh-Morpork stubs its toe? He's gone an' invited some bigwigs from Uberwald, that's what he's done. Oh, *deary* deary me. Vampires and werewolves, werewolves and vampires. We'll all be murdered in one another's beds.' She walked up to the front of the coach and tapped on the wood near the driver, who was sitting hunched up in an enormous cloak. 'Where're you from, Igor?'

The shadowy figure turned.

'What maketh you think my name ith . . . Igor?'

'Lucky guess?' said Nanny.

'You think everyone from Uberwald ith called Igor, do you? I could have any one of a thouthand different nameth, woman.'

'Look, I'm Nanny Ogg and thith, excuse me, this is Agnes Nitt. And you are . . .?'

'My name ith . . . well, it'th Igor, ath a matter of facththth,' said Igor. He raised a hasty finger. 'But it might not have been!'

'It's a chilly night. Can we get you something?' said Nanny cheerfully.

'Perhaps a towel?' said Agnes.

Nanny nudged her in the ribs to be silent. 'A glass of wine, p'raps?' she said.

'I do not drink . . . wine,' said Igor haughtily.

'I've got some brandy,' said Nanny, hitching up her skirt.

'Oh, *right*. I drink *brandy* like thtink.'

Knickerleg elastic twanged in the gloom.

'So,' said Nanny, passing up the flask, 'what're you doing this far from home, Igor?'

'Why'th there a thtupid troll down there on the . . . bridge?' said Igor, taking the flask in one large hand which, Agnes noticed, was a mass of scars and stitches.

'Oh, that's Big Jim Beef. The King lets him live under there provided he looks official when we've got comp'ny comin'.'

'Beef ith an odd name for a troll.'

'He likes the sound of it,' said Nanny. 'It's like a man calling himself Rocky, I suppose. So . . . I used to know an Igor from Uberwald. Walked with a limp. One eye a bit higher than the other. Had the same manner of . . . speaking. Very good at brain juggling, too.'

'That thoundth like my Uncle Igor,' said Igor. 'He worked for the mad doctor at Blinz. Ha, an' he wath a *proper* mad doctor, too, not like the mad doctorth you get thethe dayth. And the thervantth? Even worthe. No pride thethe dayth.' He tapped the brandy flask for emphasis. 'When Uncle Igor wath thent out for a geniuth'th brain, that'th what you damn well got. There wath none of thith fumble-finger thtuff and then pinching a brain out of the "Really Inthane" jar and hopin' no one'd notithe. They alwayth do, anyway.'

Nanny took a step back. The only sensible way to hold a conversation with Igor was when you had an umbrella.

'I think I've heard of that chap,' she said. 'Didn't he stitch folk together out of dead parts?'

'No! Really?' said Agnes, shocked. 'Ow!'

'That'th right. Ith there a problem?'

'No, I call it prudent,' said Nanny, taking her foot off Agnes's toe. 'My mum was a dab hand at sewing a new sheet from bits of old ones, and people're worth more than linen. So he's your master now, is he?'

'No, my Uncle Igor thtill workth for him. Been thtruck by lightning three hundred timeth and thtill putth in a full night'th work.'

'Have a drop more of that brandy, it's very cold out here,' said Nanny. 'So who is *your* master, Igor?'

'Call them marthterth?' said Igor, with sudden venom and a light shower. 'Huh! Now the *old* Count, he *wath* a gentleman of the old thchool. *He* knew how it all workth. Proper evening dreth *at all timeth*, that'th the rule!'

'Evenin' dress, eh?' said Nanny.

'Yeth! Thith lot only wear it in the evening, can you imagine that? The retht of the time it'th all thwanning around in fanthy waithtcoatth and lacy thkirtth! Hah! D'you know what thith lot have done?'

'Do tell . . .'

'They've oiled the hingeth!' Igor took a hefty pull of Nanny's special brandy. 'Thome of thothe thqueakth took bloody *yearth* to get right. But, oh no, now it'th "Igor, clean thothe thpiderth out of the dungeon" and "Igor, order up thome proper oil lampth, all thethe flickering torcheth are tho fifteen minuteth ago"! Tho the plathe lookth old? Being a vampire'th about continuity, ithn't it? You get lotht in the mountainth and thee a light burnin' in thome carthle, you got a right to expect proper thqueakin' doorth and thome old-world courtethy, don't you?'

'Ah, right. An' a bed in the room with a balcony outside,' said Nanny.

'My point egthactly!'

'Proper billowing curtains, too?'

'Damn right!'

'Real gutterin' candles?'

'I thpend *ageth* gettin' them properly dribbly. Not that anyone careth.'

'You got to get the details right, I always say,' said Nanny. 'Well, well, well . . . so our king invited vampires, eh?'

There was a thump as Igor slumped backwards and a tinny sound as the flask landed on the cobbles. Nanny picked it up and secreted it about her person.

'Good head for his drink,' she remarked. Not many people ever *tasted* Nanny Ogg's home-made brandy; it was technically impossible. Once it encountered the warmth of the human mouth it immediately turned into fumes. You drank it via your sinuses.

'What're we going to *do*?' said Agnes.

'Do? He invited 'em. They're guests,' said Nanny. 'I bet if I asked him Verence'd tell me to mind my own business. O' course, he wouldn't put it quite like *that*,' she added, since she knew the King had no suicidal tendencies. 'He'd prob'ly use the word "respect" two or three times at least. But it'd mean the same thing in the end.'

'But *vampires* . . . what's Granny going to say?'

'Listen, my girl, they'll be gone tomorrow . . . well, today, really. We'll just keep an eye on 'em and wave 'em goodbye when they go.'

'We don't even know what they look like!'

Nanny looked at the recumbent Igor.

'On reflection, maybe I should've asked him,' she said. She brightened up. 'Still, there's one way to find them. That's something everyone knows about vampires . . .'

In fact there are many things everyone knows about vampires, without really taking into account that perhaps the vampires know them by now, too.

The castle hall was a din. There was a mob around the buffet table. Nanny and Agnes helped out.

'Can o' pee, anyone?' said Nanny, shoving a tray towards a likely-looking group.

'I beg your pardon?' said someone. 'Oh . . . canapes . . .'

He took a vol-au-vent and bit into it as he turned back to the group.

'. . . so I said to his lordship— *What the hell is this?*'

He turned to find himself under close scrutiny by the wrinkled old lady in a pointy hat.

'Sorry?' she said.

'This . . . this . . . this is just mashed garlic!'

'Don't like garlic flavour, eh?' said Nanny sternly.

'I *love* garlic, but it doesn't like *me*! This isn't just garlic flavoured, woman, it's *all* garlic!'

Nanny peered at her tray with theatrical shortsightedness.

'No, there's some . . . there's a bit of . . . you're right, perhaps we overdid it a gnat's . . . I'll just go and . . . just get some . . . I'll just go . . .'

She collided with Agnes at the entrance to the

kitchen. Two trays slid to the floor, spilling garlic vol-au-vents, garlic dip, garlic stuffed with garlic and tiny cubes of garlic on a stick, stuck into a garlic.

'Either there's a *lot* of vampires in these parts or we're doing something wrong,' said Agnes flatly.

'*I've* always said you can't have too much garlic,' said Nanny.

'Everyone else disagrees, Nanny.'

'All right, then. What else . . . ah! All vampires wear evening dress in the evenings, even this lot.'

'*Everyone* here is wearing some kind of evening dress, Nanny. Except us.'

Nanny Ogg looked down. 'This is the dress I *always* wear in the evenin'.'

'Vampires aren't supposed to show up in a mirror, are they?' said Agnes.

Nanny snapped her fingers. 'Good thinking!' she said. 'There's one in the lavvie. I'll kind of hover in there. Everyone's got to go sooner or later.'

'But what if a man comes in?'

'Oh, I won't mind,' said Nanny dismissively. 'I won't be embarrassed.'

'I think there may be objections,' said Agnes, trying to ignore the mental picture just conjured up. Nanny had a pleasant grin, but there had to be times when you didn't want it looking at you.

'We've got to do *something*. Supposing Granny were to turn up now, what would she think?' said Nanny.

'We *could* just ask,' said Agnes.

'What? "Hands up all vampires"?'

'Ladies?'

They turned. The young man who had introduced himself as Vlad was approaching.

Agnes began to blush.

'I think you were talking about vampires,' he said, taking a garlic pasty from Agnes's tray and biting into it with every sign of enjoyment. 'Could I be of assistance?'

Nanny looked him up and down.

'Do you know much about them?' she said.

'Well, I *am* one,' he said. 'So I suppose the answer is yes. Charmed to meet you, Mrs Ogg.' He bowed and reached for her hand.

'Oh no you don't!' said Nanny, snatching it away. 'I don't hold with bloodsuckers!'

'I know. But I'm sure you shall in time. Would you like to come and meet my family?'

'They can bugger off! What was the King thinking of?'

'Nanny!'

'What?'

'You don't have to shout like that. It's not very . . . polite. I don't think—'

'Vlad de Magpyr,' said Vlad, bowing.

'—is going to bite my neck!' shouted Nanny.

'Of course not,' said Vlad. 'We had some sort of bandit earlier. Mrs Ogg is, I suspect, a meal to be savoured. Any more of these garlic things? They're rather piquant.'

'You what?' said Nanny.

'You just . . . killed someone?' said Agnes.

'Of course. We *are* vampires,' said Vlad. 'Or, we prefer, vampyres. With a "y". It's more modern.

Now, do come and meet my father.'

'You actually *killed* someone?' said Agnes.

'Right! That's *it*!' snarled Nanny, marching away. 'I'm getting Shawn and he's gonna come back with a big sharp—'

Vlad coughed quietly. Nanny stopped.

'There are several other things people know about vampires,' he said. 'And one is that they have considerable control over the minds of lesser creatures. So forget all about vampires, dear ladies. That is an order. And do come and meet my family.'

Agnes blinked. She was aware that there had been . . . something. She could feel the tail of it, slipping away between her fingers.

'Seems a nice young man,' said Nanny, in a mildly stunned voice.

'I . . . he . . . yes,' said Agnes.

Something surfaced in her mind, like a message in a bottle written indistinctly in some foreign language. She tried, but she could not read it.

'I wish Granny was here,' she said at last. 'She'd know what to do.'

'What about?' said Nanny. 'She ain't good at parties.'

'I feel a bit . . . odd,' said Agnes.

'Ah, could be the drink,' said Nanny.

'I haven't had any!'

'No? Well, there's the problem right there. Come on.'

They hurried into the hall. Even though it was now well after midnight, the noise level was approaching the pain threshold. When the midnight hour lies on the glass like a big cocktail onion, there's always an extra edge to the laughter.

Vlad gave them an encouraging wave and beckoned them over to a group around King Verence.

'Ah, Agnes and Nanny,' said the King. 'Count, may I present—'

'Gytha Ogg and Agnes Nitt, I believe,' said the man the King had just been talking to. He bowed. For some reason a tiny part of Agnes was expecting a sombre-looking man with an exciting widow's-peak hairstyle and an opera cloak. She couldn't think why.

This man looked like . . . well, like a gentleman of independent means and an enquiring mind, perhaps, the kind of man who goes for long walks in the morning and spends the afternoons improving his mind in his own private library or doing small interesting experiments on parsnips and never, ever, worrying about money. There was something glossy about him, and also a sort of urgent, hungry enthusiasm, the kind you get when someone has just read a really interesting book and is determined to tell someone all about it.

'Allow me to present the Countess Magpyr,' he said. 'These are the witches I told you about, dear. I believe you've met my son? And this is my daughter, Lacrimosa.'

Agnes met the gaze of a thin girl in a white dress, with very long black hair and far too much eye make-up. There *is* such a thing as hate at first sight.

'The Count was just telling me how he is planning to move into the castle and rule the country,' said

Verence. 'And I was saying that I think we shall be honoured.'

'Well done,' said Nanny. 'But if you don't mind, I don't want to miss the weasel man . . .'

'The trouble is that people always think of vampires in terms of their diet,' said the Count, as Nanny hurried away. 'It's really rather insulting. *You* eat animal flesh and vegetables, but it hardly defines you, does it?'

Verence's face was contorted in a smile, but it looked glassy and unreal.

'But you do drink human blood?' he said.

'Of course. And sometimes we kill people, although hardly at all these days. In any case, where exactly is the harm in that? Prey and hunter, hunter and prey. The sheep was designed as dinner for the wolf, the wolf as a means of preventing overgrazing by the sheep. If you examine your teeth, sire, you'll see that they are designed for a particular kind of diet and, indeed, your whole body is constructed to take advantage of it. And so it is with us. I'm sure the nuts and cabbages do not blame you. Hunter and prey are all just part of the great cycle of life.'

'Fascinating,' said Verence. Little beads of sweat were rolling down his face.

'Of course, in Uberwald everyone understands this instinctively,' said the Countess. 'But it is rather a backward place for the children. We are so looking forward to Lancre.'

'Very glad to hear it,' said Verence.

'And so kind of you to invite us,' she went on. 'Otherwise we could not have come, of course.'

'Not *exactly*,' said the Count, beaming at his wife. 'But I have to admit that the prohibition against entering places uninvited has proved curiously . . . durable. It must be something to do with ancient territorial instincts. *But*,' he added brightly, 'I have been working on an instructional technique which I'm sure will, within a few years—'

'Oh, don't let's go through all that dull stuff *again*,' said Lacrimosa.

'Yes, I suppose it can sound a little tedious,' said the Count, smiling benevolently at his daughter. 'Has anyone any more of that wonderful garlic dip?'

The King still looked uneasy, Agnes noticed. Which was odd, because the Count and his family seemed absolutely charming and what they were saying made perfect sense. Everything was perfectly all right.

'Exactly,' said Vlad, beside her. 'Do you dance, Miss Nitt?' On the other side of the hall, the Lancre Light Symphony Orchestra (cond. S. Ogg) was striking up and out at random.

'Ur . . .' She stopped it turning into a giggle. 'Not really. Not very well . . .'

Didn't you listen to what they were saying? They're vampires!

'Shut up,' she said aloud.

'I beg your pardon?' said Vlad, looking puzzled.

'And they're . . . well, they're not a very good orchestra . . .'

Didn't you pay any attention to what they were saying at all, you useless lump?

'They're a very *bad* orchestra,' said Vlad.

'Well, the King only bought the instruments last

month and basically they're trying to learn together—'

Chop his head off! Give him a garlic enema!

'Are you all right? You really *know* there are no vampires here, don't you . . .'

He's controlling you! Perdita screamed. *They're . . . affecting people!*

'I'm a bit . . . faint from all the excitement,' Agnes mumbled. 'I think I'll go home.' Some instinct at bone-marrow level made her add, 'I'll ask Nanny to go with me.'

Vlad gave her an odd look, as if she wasn't reacting in quite the right way. Then he smiled. Agnes noticed that he had very white teeth.

'I don't think I've ever met anyone like you, Miss Nitt,' he said. 'There's something so . . . *inner* about you.'

That's me! That's me! He can't work me out! Now let's both get out of here! yelled Perdita.

'But we shall meet again.'

Agnes gave him a nod and staggered away, clutching at her head. It felt like a ball of cotton wool in which there was, inexplicably, a needle.

She passed Mightily Oats, who'd dropped his book on the floor and was sitting groaning with his head in his hands. He raised it to look at her.

'Er . . . miss, have you *anything* that might help my head?' he said. 'It really is . . . rather painful . . .'

'The Queen makes up some sort of headache pills out of willow bark,' Agnes panted, and hurried on.

Nanny Ogg was standing morosely with a pint in her hand, a hitherto unheard-of combination.

'The weasel juggler didn't turn up,' she said. 'Well,

I'm going to put out the hard word on him. He's had it in showbusiness in these parts.'

'Could you . . . help me home, Nanny?'

'So what if he got bitten on the essentials, that's all part of— Are you all right?'

'I feel really awful, Nanny.'

'Let's go, then. All the good beer's gone and I'm not stoppin' anyway if there's nothin' to laugh at.'

The wind was whistling across the sky when they walked back to Agnes's cottage. In fact there seemed more whistle than wind. The leafless trees creaked as they passed, the weak moonlight filling the eaves of the woods with dangerous shadows. Clouds were piling in, and there was more rain on the way.

Agnes noticed Nanny pick up something as they left the town behind them.

It was a stick. She'd never known a witch carry a stick at night before.

'Why have you got that, Nanny?'

'What? Oh? Dunno, really. It's a rattly old night, ain't it . . . ?'

'But you're never frightened of *anything* in Lan—'

Several things pushed through the bushes and clattered on to the road ahead. For a moment Agnes thought they were horses, until the moonlight caught them. Then they were gone, into the shadows on the other side of the road. She heard galloping among the trees.

'Haven't seen any of those for a *long* time,' said Nanny.

'I've never seen centaurs *at all* except in pictures,' said Agnes.

'Must've come down out of Uberwald,' said Nanny. 'Nice to see them about again.'

Agnes hurriedly lit the candles when she got into the cottage, and wished there were bolts on the door.

'Just sit down,' said Nanny. 'I'll get a cup of water, I know my way around here.'

'It's all right, I—'

Agnes's left arm twitched. To her horror it swung at the elbow and waved its hand up and down in front of her face, as if guided by a mind of its own.

'Feeling a bit warm, are you?' said Nanny.

'I'll get the water!' panted Agnes.

She rushed into the kitchen, gripping her left wrist with her right hand. It shook itself free, grabbed a knife from the draining board and stabbed it into the wall, dragging it so that it formed crude letters in the crumbling plaster:

VMPIR

It dropped the knife, grabbed at the hair on the back of Agnes's head and thrust her face within inches of the letters.

'You all right in there?' Nanny called from the next room.

'Er, yes, but I think I'm trying to tell me something—'

A movement made her turn. A small blue man wearing a blue cap was staring at her from the shelves over the washcopper. He stuck out his tongue, made a very small obscene gesture and disappeared behind a bag of washing crystals.

'Nanny?'

'Yes, luv?'

'Are there such things as blue mice?'

'Not while you're sober, dear.'

'I think . . . I'm owed a drink, then. Is there any brandy left?'

Nanny came in, uncorking the flask.

'I topped it up at the party. Of course, it's only shop-bought stuff, you couldn't—'

Agnes's left hand snatched it and poured it down her throat. Then she coughed so hard that some of it went up her nose.

'Hang on, hang on, it's not *that* weak,' said Nanny.

Agnes plonked the flask down on the kitchen table.

'Right,' she said, and her voice sounded quite different to Nanny. 'My name is Perdita and I'm taking over this body right *now*.'

Hodgesaargh noticed the smell of burnt wood as he ambled back to the mews but put it down to the bonfire in the courtyard. He'd left the party early. No one had wanted to talk about hawks.

The smell was *very* strong when he looked in on the birds and saw the little flame in the middle of the floor. He stared at it for a second, then picked up a water bucket and threw it.

The flame continued to flicker gently on a bare stone that was awash with water.

Hodgesaargh looked at the birds. They were watching it with interest; normally they'd be frantic in the presence of fire.

Hodgesaargh was never one to panic. He watched it for a while, and then took a piece of wood and gently touched it to the flame. The fire leapt on to the wood and went on burning.

The wood didn't even char.

He found another twig and brushed it against the flame, which slid easily from one to the other. There was one flame. It was clear there wasn't going to be two.

Half the bars in the window had been burned away, and there was some scorched wood at the end of the mews, where the old nestboxes had been. Above it, a few stars shone through rags of mist over a charred hole in the roof.

Something had burned here, Hodgesaargh saw. Fiercely, by the look of it. But also in a curiously local way, as if all the heat had been somehow contained . . .

He reached towards the flame dancing on the end of the stick. It was warm, but . . . not as hot as it should be.

Now it was on his finger. It tingled. As he waved it around, the head of every bird turned to watch it.

By its light, he poked around in the charred remains of the nestboxes. In the ashes were bits of broken eggshell.

Hodgesaargh picked them up and carried them into the crowded little room at the end of the mews which served as workshop and bedroom. He balanced the flame on a saucer. In here, where it was quieter, he could hear it making a slight sizzling noise.

In the dim glow he looked along the one crowded bookshelf over his bed and pulled down a huge ragged volume on the cover of which someone had written, centuries ago, the word 'Burds'.

The book was a huge ledger. The spine had been cut and widened inexpertly several times so that more pages could be pasted in.

The falconers of Lancre knew a lot about birds. The kingdom was on a main migratory route between the Hub and the Rim. The hawks had brought down many strange species over the centuries and the falconers had, very painstakingly, taken notes. The pages were thick with drawings and closely spaced writing, the entries copied and recopied and updated over the years. The occasional feather carefully glued to a page had added to the thickness of the thing.

No one had ever bothered with an index, but some past falconer had considerately arranged many of the entries into alphabetical order.

Hodgesaargh glanced again at the flame burning steadily in its saucer, and then, handling the crackling pages with care, turned to 'F'.

After some browsing, he eventually found what he was looking for under 'P'.

Back in the mews, in the deepest shadow, something cowered.

There were three shelves of books in Agnes's cottage. By witch standards, that was a giant library.

Two very small blue figures lay on top of the books, watching the scene with interest.

Nanny Ogg backed away, waving the poker.

'It's *all right*,' said Agnes. 'It's me again, Agnes Nitt, but . . . She's here but . . . I'm sort of holding on. Yes!

Yes! All right! All right, just shut up, will y— Look, it's *my* body, you're just a figment of my imagina— Okay! Okay! Perhaps it's not quite so clear c— Let me just talk to Nanny, will you?'

'Which one are you now?' said Nanny Ogg.

'I'm still Agnes, of course.' She rolled her eyes up. 'All *right*! I'm Agnes currently being advised by Perdita, who is also me. In a way. *And I'm not too fat, thank you so very much!*'

'How many of you are there in there?' said Nanny.

'What do you mean, "room for ten"?' shouted Agnes. 'Shut up! Listen, Perdita says there were vampires at the party. The Magpyr family, she says. She can't understand how we acted. They were putting a kind of . . . 'fluence over everyone. Including me, which is why she was able to break thr— Yes, all right, I'm telling it, thank you!'

'Why not her, then?' said Nanny.

'Because she's got a mind of her own! Nanny, can you remember anything they actually *said*?'

'Now you come to mention it, no. But they seemed nice enough people.'

'And you remember talking to Igor?'

'Who's Igor?'

The tiny blue figures watched, fascinated, for the next half-hour.

Nanny sat back at the end of it and stared at the ceiling for a while.

'Why should we believe her?' she said eventually.

'Because she's *me*.'

'They do say that inside every fat girl is a thin girl and—' Nanny began.

'Yes,' said Agnes bitterly. 'I've heard it. Yes. She's the thin girl. I'm the lot of chocolate.'

Nanny leaned towards Agnes's ear and raised her voice. 'How're you gettin' on in there? Everything all right, is it? Treatin' you all right, is she?'

'Haha, Nanny. Very funny.'

'They were saying all this stuff about drinkin' blood and killin' people and everyone was just noddin' and sayin', "Well, well, how very fascinatin' "?'

'Yes!'

'And eatin' garlic?'

'Yes!'

'That can't be right, can it?'

'I don't know, perhaps we used the wrong sort of garlic!'

Nanny rubbed her chin, torn between the vampiric revelation and prurient curiosity about Perdita.

'How does Perdita work, then?' she said.

Agnes sighed. 'Look, you know the part of you that wants to do all the things you don't dare do, and thinks the thoughts you don't dare think?'

Nanny's face stayed blank. Agnes floundered. 'Like . . . maybe . . . rip off all your clothes and run naked in the rain?' she hazarded.

'Oh, *yes*. Right,' said Nanny.

'Well . . . I suppose Perdita is that part of me.'

'Really? *I've* always been that part of me,' said Nanny. 'The important thing is to remember where you left your clothes.'

Agnes remembered too late that Nanny Ogg was in many ways a very *uncomplicated* personality.

'Mind you, I think I know what you mean,' Nanny went on in a more thoughtful voice. 'There's times when I've wanted to do things and stopped meself . . .' She shook her head. 'But . . . vampires . . . Verence wouldn't be so stupid as to send an invitation to vampires, would he?' She paused for thought. 'Yes, he would. Prob'ly think of it as offering the hand of friendship.'

She stood up. 'Right, they won't have left yet. Let's get straight to the jelly. You get *extra* garlic and a few stakes, I'll round up Shawn and Jason and the lads.'

'It won't work, Nanny. Perdita saw what they can do. The moment you get near them you'll forget all about it. They do something to your mind, Nanny.'

Nanny hesitated. 'Can't say I know *that* much about vampires,' she said.

'Perdita thinks they can tell what you're thinking, too.'

'Then this is Esme's type of stuff,' said Nanny. 'Messing with minds and so on. It's meat and drink to her.'

'Nanny, they were talking about *staying*! We have to *do* something!'

'Well, where is she?' Nanny almost wailed. 'Esme ought to be sortin' this out!'

'Maybe they've got to her first?'

'You don't think so, do you?' said Nanny, now looking quite panicky. 'I can't think about a vampire getting his teeth into Esme.'

'Don't worry, dog doesn't eat dog.' It was Perdita who blurted it out, but it was Agnes who got the blow.

It wasn't a ladylike slap of disapproval. Nanny Ogg had reared some strapping sons; the Ogg forearm was a power in its own right.

When Agnes looked up from the hearthrug Nanny was rubbing some life back into her hand. She gave Agnes a solemn look.

'We'll say no more about that, shall we?' she commanded. 'I ain't gen'rally given to physicality of that nature but it saves a lot of arguing. Now, we're goin' back to the castle. We're going to sort this out right *now*.'

Hodgesaargh shut the book and looked at the flame. It was true, then. There'd even been a picture of one just like it in the book, painstakingly drawn by another royal falconer two hundred years before. He wrote that he'd found the thing up on the high meadows, one spring. It'd burned for three years and then he'd lost it somewhere.

If you looked at it closely, you could even see the detail. It was not *exactly* a flame. It was more like a bright feather . . .

Well, Lancre *was* on one of the main migration routes, for birds of all sorts. It was only a matter of time.

So . . . the new hatchling was around. They needed time to grow, it said in the book. Odd that it should lay an egg here, because it said in the book that it always hatched in the burning deserts of Klatch.

He went and looked at the birds in the mews. They were still very alert.

Yes, it all made sense. It had flown in here, among the comfort of other birds, and laid its egg, just like it said it did in the book, and then it had burned itself up to hatch the new bird.

If Hodgesaargh had a fault, it lay in his rather utilitarian view of the bird world. There were birds that you hunted, and there were birds you hunted *with.* Oh, there were other sorts, tweeting away in the bushes, but they didn't really count. It occurred to him that if ever there was a bird you could hunt with, it'd be the phoenix.

Oh, *yes.* It'd be weak, and young, and it wouldn't have gone far.

Hmm . . . birds tended to think the same way, after all.

It would have helped if there was one picture in the book. In fact, there were several, all carefully drawn by ancient falconers who claimed it was a firebird they'd seen.

Apart from the fact that they all had wings and a beak, no two were remotely alike. One looked very much like a heron. Another looked like a goose. One, and he scratched his head about this, appeared to be a sparrow. Bit of a puzzle, he decided, and left it at that and selected a drawing that looked at least slightly foreign.

He glanced at the bird gloves hanging on their hooks. He was good at rearing young birds. He could get them eating out of his hand. Later on, of course, they just ate his hand.

Yes. Catch it young and train it to the wrist. It'd *have* to be a champion hunting bird.

Hodgesaargh couldn't imagine a phoenix as *quarry.* For one thing, how could you cook it?

. . . and in the darkest corner of the mews, something hopped on to a perch . . .

Once again Agnes had to run to keep up as Nanny Ogg strode into the courtyard, elbows pumping furiously. The old lady marched up to a group of men standing around one of the barrels and grabbed two of them, spilling their drinks. Had it not been Nanny Ogg, this would have been a challenge equal to throwing down a glove or, in slightly less exalted circles, smashing a bottle on the edge of a bar.

But the men looked sheepish and one or two of the others in the circle even scuffled their feet and made an attempt to hide their pints behind their backs.

'Jason? Darren? You come along of me,' Nanny commanded. 'We're after vampires, right? Any sharp stakes around here?'

'No, Mum,' said Jason, Lancre's only blacksmith. Then he raised his hand. 'But ten minutes ago the cook come out and said, did anyone want all these nibbly things that someone had mucked up with garlic and I et 'em, Mum.'

Nanny sniffed and then took a step back, fanning her hand in front of her face. 'Yeah, that should do it all right,' she said. 'If I give you the signal, you're to burp hugely, understand?'

'I don't think it'll work, Nanny,' said Agnes, as boldly as she dared.

'I don't see why, it's nearly knocking *me* down.'

'I *told* you, you won't get close enough, even if it'll work at all. Perdita could feel it. It's like being drunk.'

'I'll be ready for 'em this time,' said Nanny. 'I've learned a thing or two from Esme.'

'Yes, but she's—' Agnes was going to say 'better at them than you', but changed it to 'not here . . .'

'That's as may be, but I'd rather face 'em now than explain to Esme that I didn't. Come on.'

Agnes followed the Oggs, but very uneasily. She wasn't sure how far she trusted Perdita.

A few guests had departed, but the castle had laid on a pretty good feast and Ramtop people at any social level were never ones to pass up a laden table.

Nanny glanced at the crowd and grabbed Shawn, who was passing with a tray.

'Where's the vampires?'

'What, Mum?'

'That Count . . . Magpie . . .'

'Magpyr,' said Agnes.

'Him,' said Nanny.

'He's not a . . . he's gone up to . . . the solar, Mum. They all have— What's that smell of garlic, Mum?'

'It's your brother. All right, let's keep going.'

The solar was right at the top of the keep. It was old, cold and draughty. Verence had put glass in the huge windows, at his queen's insistence, which just meant that now the huge room attracted the more cunning, insidious kind of draught. But it was the royal room – not as public as the great hall, but the place where the King received visitors when he was being *formally* informal.

The Nanny Ogg expeditionary force corkscrewed

up the spiral staircase. She advanced across the good yet threadbare carpet to the group seated around the fire.

She took a deep breath.

'Ah, Mrs Ogg,' said Verence, desperately. 'Do join us.'

Agnes looked sideways at Nanny, and saw her face contort into a strange smile.

The Count was sitting in the big chair by the fire, with Vlad standing behind him. They both looked very handsome, she thought. Compared to them Verence, in his clothes that never seemed to fit right and permanently harassed expression, looked out of place.

'The Count was just explaining how Lancre will become a duchy of his lands in Uberwald,' said Verence. 'But we'll still be referred to as a kingdom, which I think is very reasonable of him, don't you agree?'

'Very handsome suggestion,' said Nanny.

'There will be taxes, of course,' said the Count. 'Not onerous. We don't want blood – figuratively speaking!' He beamed at the joke.

'Seems reasonable to me,' said Nanny.

'It *is*, isn't it?' said the Count. 'I knew it would work out so well. And I am so pleased, Verence, to see your essential modern attitude. People have quite the wrong idea about vampires, you see. Are we fiendish killers?' He beamed at them. 'Well, yes, of course we are. But only when necessary. Frankly, we could hardly hope to rule a country if we went around killing everyone *all* the time, could we? There'd be none left to rule, for one thing!' There was polite laughter, loudest of all from the Count.

It made perfect sense to Agnes. The Count was clearly a fair-minded man. Anyone who didn't think so *deserved* to die.

'And we are only human,' said the Countess. 'Well . . . in fact, not *only* human. But if you prick us do we not bleed? Which always seems such a waste.'

They've got you again, said a voice in her mind.

Vlad's head jerked up. Agnes felt him staring at her.

'We are, above all, up to date,' said the Count. 'And we do like what you've done to this castle, I must say.'

'Oh, those torches back home!' said the Countess, rolling her eyes. 'And some of the things in the dungeons, well, when I saw them I nearly died of shame. So . . . *fifteen centuries* ago. If one is a vampire then one is,' she gave a deprecating little laugh, 'a vampire. Coffins, yes, of course, but there's no point in skulking around as if you're ashamed of what you are, is there? We all have . . . needs.'

You're all standing around like rabbits in front of a fox! Perdita raged in the caverns of Agnes's brain.

'Oh!' said the Countess, clapping her hands together. 'I see you have a pianoforte!'

It stood under a shroud in a corner of the room where it had stood for four months now. Verence had ordered it because he'd heard they were very modern, but the only person in the kingdom who'd come close to mastering it was Nanny Ogg who would, as she put it, come up occasionally for a tinkle on the ivories.* Then it had been covered over on the orders of Magrat and the palace rumour was that Verence had got an earbashing for buying what was effectively a murdered elephant.

'Lacrimosa would *so* like to play for you,' the Countess commanded.

'Oh, *Mother*,' said Lacrimosa.

'I'm sure we should love it,' said Verence. Agnes wouldn't have noticed the sweat running down his face if Perdita hadn't pointed it out: *He's trying to fight it*, she said. *Aren't you glad you've got me?*

There was some bustling while a wad of sheet music was pulled out of the piano stool and the young lady sat down to play. She glared at Agnes before beginning. There was some sort of chemistry there, although it was the sort that results in the entire building being evacuated.

It's a racket, said the Perdita within, after the first few bars. *Everyone's looking as though it's wonderful but it's a din!*

Agnes concentrated. The music was beautiful but if she really paid attention, with Perdita nudging her, it wasn't really there at all. It sounded like someone playing scales, badly and angrily.

*King Verence was very keen that someone should compose a national anthem for Lancre, possibly referring to its very nice trees, and had offered a small reward. Nanny Ogg reasoned that it would be easy money because national anthems only ever have one verse or, rather, all have the same second verse, which goes 'nur . . . hnur . . . mur . . . nur nur, hnur . . . nur . . . nur, hnur' at some length until everyone remembers the last line of the first verse and sings it as loudly as they can.

I can say that at any time, she thought. Any time I want, I can just wake up.

Everyone else applauded politely. Agnes tried to, but found that her left hand was suddenly on strike. Perdita was getting stronger in her left arm.

Vlad was beside her so quickly that she wasn't even aware that he'd moved.

'You are a . . . fascinating woman, Miss Nitt,' he said. 'Such lovely hair, may I say? But who is Perdita?'

'No one, really,' Agnes mumbled. She fought against the urge to bunch her left hand into a fist. Perdita was screaming at her again.

Vlad stroked a strand of her hair. It was, she knew, good hair. It wasn't simply big hair, it was enormous hair, as if she was trying to counterbalance her body. It was glossy, it never split, and was extremely well behaved except for a tendency to eat combs.

'Eat combs?' said Vlad, coiling the hair around his finger.

'Yes, it—'

He can see what you're thinking.

Vlad looked puzzled again, like someone trying to make out some faint noise.

'You . . . can resist, can't you?' he said. 'I was watching you when Lacci was playing the piano and losing. Do you have any vampire blood in you?'

'What? No!'

'It could be arranged, haha.' He grinned. It was the sort of grin that Agnes supposed was called infectious but, then, so was measles. It filled her immediate future. Something was pouring over her like a pink fluffy cloud saying: it's all right, everything is fine, this is exactly right . . .

'Look at Mrs Ogg there,' said Vlad. 'Grinning like a pumpkin, ain't she? And she is apparently one of the more powerful witches in the mountains. It's almost distressing, don't you think?'

Tell him you know he can read minds, Perdita commanded.

And again, the puzzled, quizzical look.

'You can—' Agnes began.

'No, not exactly. Just people,' said Vlad. 'One learns, one learns. One picks things up.' He flung himself down on a sofa, one leg over the arm, and stared thoughtfully at her.

'Things will be changing, Agnes Nitt,' he said. 'My father is right. Why lurk in dark castles? Why be ashamed? We're vampires. Or, rather, vampyres. Father's a bit keen on the new spelling. He says it indicates a clean break with a stupid and superstitious past. In any case, it's not our fault. We were *born* vampires.'

'I thought you became—'

'—vampires by being bitten? Dear me, no. Oh, we can *turn* people into vampires, it's an easy technique, but what would be the point? When you eat . . . now what is it you eat? Oh yes, chocolate . . . you don't want to turn it into another Agnes Nitt, do you? Less chocolate to go around.' He sighed. 'Oh dear, superstition, superstition everywhere we turn. Isn't it true that we've been here at least ten minutes and your neck is quite free of anything except a small amount of soap you didn't wash off?'

Agnes's hand flew to her throat.

'We notice these things,' said Vlad. 'And now we're here to notice them. Oh, Father is powerful in his way, and quite an advanced thinker, but I don't think even he is aware of the *possibilities.* I can't tell you how *good* it is to be out of that place, Miss Nitt. The werewolves . . . oh dear, the werewolves . . . Marvellous people, it goes without saying, and of course the Baron has a certain rough style, but really . . . give them a good deer hunt, a warm spot in front of the fire and a nice big bone and the rest of the world can go hang. We have done our best, we really have. No one has done more than Father to bring our part of the country into the Century of the Fruitbat—'

'It's nearly over—' Agnes began.

'Perhaps that's why he's so keen,' said Vlad. 'The place is just full of . . . well, remnants. I mean . . . centaurs? Really! They've got no business surviving. They're out of place. And frankly all the lower races are just as bad. The trolls are stupid, the dwarfs are devious, the pixies are evil and the gnomes stick in your teeth. Time they were gone. Driven out. We have great hopes of Lancre.' He looked around disdainfully. 'After some redecoration.'

Agnes looked back at Nanny and her sons. They were listening quite contentedly to the worst music since Shawn Ogg's bagpipes had been dropped down the stairs.

'And . . . you're taking our country?' she said. 'Just like that?'

Vlad gave her another smile, stood up, and walked towards her. 'Oh, yes. Bloodlessly. Well . . . metaphorically. You really *are* quite remarkable, Miss Nitt.

The Uberwald girls are so sheep-like. But you ... you're concealing something from me. Everything I feel tells me you're quite under my power – and yet you're not.' He chuckled. 'This is delightful ...'

Agnes felt her mind unravelling. The pink fog was blowing through her head ...

... and looming out of it, deadly and mostly concealed, was the iceberg of Perdita.

As Agnes withdrew into the pinkness she felt the tingle spread down her arms and legs. It was not pleasant. It was like sensing someone standing right behind you and then feeling them take one step forward.

Agnes would have pushed him away. That is, Agnes would have dithered and tried to talk her way out of things, but if push had come to shove then she'd have pushed hard. But Perdita struck, and when her hand was halfway around she turned it palm out and curled her fingers to bring her nails into play ...

He caught her wrist, his hand moving in a blur.

'Well *done*,' he said, laughing.

His other hand shot out and caught her other arm as it swung.

'I like a woman with spirit!'

However, he had run out of hands, and Perdita still had a knee in reserve. Vlad's eyes crossed and he made that small sound best recorded as 'ghni ...'

'Magnificent!' he croaked as he folded up.

Perdita pulled herself away and ran over to Nanny Ogg, grabbing the woman's arm.

'Nanny, we are *leaving*!'

'Are we, dear?' said Nanny calmly, not making a move.

'And Jason and Darren too!'

Perdita didn't read as much as Agnes. She thought books were *bor-ing*. But now she really needed to know: what *did* you use against vampires?

Holy symbols! Agnes prompted from within.

Perdita looked around desperately. Nothing in the room looked particularly holy. Religion, apart from its use as a sort of cosmic registrar, had never caught on in Lancre.

'Daylight is always good, my dear,' said the Countess, who must have caught the edge of her thought. 'Your uncle always had big windows and easily twitched aside curtains, didn't he, Count?'

'Yes indeed,' said the Count.

'And when it came to running water, he always kept the moat flowing perfectly, didn't he?'

'Fed from a mountain stream, I think,' said the Count.

'And, for a vampire, he always seemed to have so many ornamental items around the castle that could be bent or broken into the shape of some religious symbol, as I recall.'

'He certainly did. A vampire of the old school.'

'Yes.' The Countess gave her husband a smile. 'The stupid school.' She turned to Perdita and looked her up and down. 'So I think you will find we are here to stay, my dear. Although you do seem to have made an impression on my son. Come here, girl. Let me have a good look at you.'

Even cushioned inside her own head Agnes felt the weight of the vampire's will hit Perdita like an iron bar, pushing her down. Like the other end of a seesaw, Agnes rose.

'Where's Magrat? What have you done with *her*?' she said.

'Putting the baby to bed, I believe,' said the Countess, raising her eyebrows. 'A lovely child.'

'Granny Weatherwax is going to hear about this, and you'll wish you'd never been born . . . or unborn or reborn or whatever you are!'

'We look forward to meeting her,' said the Count calmly. 'But here we are, and I don't seem to see this famous lady with us. Perhaps you should go and fetch her? You could take your friends. And when you see her, Miss Nitt, you can tell her that there is no reason why witches and vampires should fight.'

Nanny Ogg stirred. Jason shifted in his seat. Agnes pulled them upright and towards the stairs.

'We'll be back!' she shouted.

The Count nodded.

'Good,' he said. 'We are famous for our hospitality.'

It was still dark when Hodgesaargh set out. If you were hunting a phoenix, he reasoned, the dark was probably the best time. Light showed up better in the darkness.

He'd packed a portable wire cage after considering the charred bars of the window, and he'd also spent some time on the glove.

It was basically a puppet, made of yellow cloth with some purple and blue rags tacked on. It was not, he conceded, *very* much like the drawing of the phoenix, but in his experience birds weren't choosy observers.

Newly hatched birds were prepared to accept practically *anything* as their parent. Anyone who'd hatched eggs under a broody hen knew that ducklings could be made to think they were chicks, and poor William the buzzard was a case in point.

The fact that a young phoenix never saw its parent and therefore didn't know what it was supposed to look like might be a drawback in getting its trust, but this was unknown territory and Hodgesaargh was prepared to try anything. Like bait, for example. He'd packed meat and grain, although the drawing certainly suggested a hawk-like bird, but in case it needed to eat inflammable materials as well he also put in a bag of mothballs and a pint of fish oil. Nets were out of the question, and bird lime was not to be thought of. Hodgesaargh had his pride. Anyway, they probably wouldn't work.

Since *anything* might be worth trying, he'd also adapted a duck lure, trying to achieve a sound described by a long-dead falconer as 'like unto the cry of a buzzard yet of a lower pitch'. He wasn't too happy about the result but, on the other hand, maybe a young phoenix didn't know what a phoenix was meant to sound like, either. It might work, and if he didn't try it he'd always be wondering.

He set out.

Soon a cry like a duck in a power dive was heard among the damp, dark hills.

The pre-dawn light was grey on the horizon and a shower of sleet had made the leaves sparkle when Granny Weatherwax left her cottage. There had been so much to do.

What she'd chosen to take with her was slung in a

sack tied across her back with string. She'd left the broomstick in the corner by the fire.

She wedged the door open with a stone and then, without once looking back, strode off through the woods.

Down in the villages, the cocks crowed in response to a sunrise hidden somewhere beyond the clouds.

An hour later, a broomstick settled gently on the lawn. Nanny Ogg alighted and hurried to the back door.

Her foot kicked something holding it open. She glared at the stone as if it was something dangerous, and then edged round it and into the gloom of the cottage.

She came out a few minutes later, looking worried.

Her next move was towards the water butt. She broke the film of ice with her hand and pulled out a piece, looked at it for a moment and then tossed it away.

People often got the wrong idea about Nanny Ogg, and she took care to see that they did. One thing they often got wrong was the idea that she never thought further than the bottom of the glass.

Up in a nearby tree a magpie chattered at her. She threw a stone at it.

Agnes arrived half an hour later. She preferred to go on foot whenever possible. She suspected that she overhung too much.

Nanny Ogg was sitting on a chair just inside the door, smoking her pipe. She took it out of her mouth and nodded.

'She's gorn,' she said.

'Gone? Just when we need her?' said Agnes. 'What do you mean?'

'She ain't here,' Nanny expanded.

'Perhaps she's just out?' said Agnes.

'Gorn,' said Nanny. 'These past two hours, if I'm any judge.'

'How do you know that?'

Once – probably even yesterday – Nanny would have alluded vaguely to magical powers. It was a measure of her concern that, today, she got right to the jelly.

'First thing she does in the mornings, rain or shine, is wash her face in the water butt,' she said. 'Someone broke the ice two hours ago. You can see where it's frozed over again.'

'Oh, is that all?' said Agnes. 'Well, perhaps she's got business—'

'You come and see,' said Nanny, standing up.

The kitchen was spotless. Every flat surface had been scrubbed. The fireplace had been swept and a new fire laid.

Most of the cottage's smaller contents had been laid out on the table. There were three cups, three plates, three knives, a cleaver, three forks, three spoons, two ladles, a pair of scissors and three candlesticks. A wooden box was packed with needles and thread and pins . . .

If it was possible for anything to be polished, it had been. Someone had even managed to buff up a shine on the old pewter candlesticks.

Agnes felt the little knot of tension grow inside her. Witches didn't own much. The *cottage* owned things. They were not yours to take away.

This looked like an inventory.

Behind her, Nanny Ogg was opening and shutting drawers in the ancient dresser.

'She's left it all neat,' Nanny said. 'She's even chipped all the rust off the kettle. The larder's all bare except for some hobnailed cheese and suicide biscuits. It's the same in the bedroom. Her "I ATE'NT DEAD" card is hanging behind the door. And the guzunda's so clean you could eat your tea out of it, if the fancy took you that way. And she's taken the box out of the dresser.'

'What box?'

'Oh, she keeps stuff in it,' said Nanny. 'Memororabililia.'

'Mem—?'

'You know . . . keepsakes and whatnot. Stuff that's hers—'

'What's this?' said Agnes, holding up a green glass ball.

'Oh, Magrat passed that on to her,' said Nanny, lifting up a corner of the rug and peering under it. 'It's a float our Wayne brought back from the seaside once. It's a buoy for the fishing nets.'

'I didn't know buoys had glass balls,' said Agnes.

She groaned inwardly, and felt the blush unfold. But Nanny hadn't noticed. It was then she realized how *really* serious this was. Nanny would normally leap on such a gift like a cat on a feather. Nanny could find an innuendo in 'Good morning.' She could certainly find one in 'innuendo'. And 'buoys with glass balls' should have lasted her all week. She'd be accosting total strangers and saying, 'You'll never guess what Agnes Nitt said . . .'

She ventured 'I *said*—'

'Dunno much about fishing, really,' said Nanny. She straightened up, biting her thumbnail thoughtfully. 'Something's wrong with all this,' she said. 'The box . . . she wasn't going to leave anything behind . . .'

'Granny wouldn't *go*, would she?' said Agnes nervously. 'I mean, not actually *leave*. She's *always* here.'

'Like I told you last night, she's been herself lately,' said Nanny vaguely. She sat down in the rocking chair.

'You mean she's not been herself, don't you?' said Agnes.

'I knows exactly what I means, girl. When she's herself she snaps at people and sulks and makes herself depressed. Ain't you ever heard of taking people out of themselves? Now shut up, 'cos I'm thinkin'.'

Agnes looked down at the green ball in her hands. A glass fishing float, five hundred miles from the sea. An ornament, like a shell. Not a crystal ball. You could use it like a crystal ball but it wasn't a crystal ball . . . and she knew why that was important.

Granny was a very traditional witch. Witches hadn't always been popular. There might even be times – there *had* been times, long ago – when it was a good idea *not* to advertise what you were, and *that* was why all these things on the table didn't betray their owner at all. There was no need for that any more, there hadn't been in Lancre for hundreds of years, but some habits get passed down in the blood.

In fact things now worked the other way. Being a witch was an honourable trade in the mountains, but only the young ones invested in real crystal balls and coloured knives and dribbly candles. The old ones . . . they stuck with simple kitchen cutlery, fishing floats, bits of wood, whose very ordinariness subtly advertised their status. Any fool could be a witch with a runic knife, but it took skill to be one with an apple-corer.

A sound she hadn't been hearing stopped abruptly, and the silence echoed.

Nanny glanced up.

'Clock's stopped,' she said.

'It's not even telling the right time,' said Agnes, turning to look at it.

'Oh, she just kept it for the tick,' said Nanny.

Agnes put down the glass ball.

'I'm going to look around some more,' she said.

She'd learned to look around when she visited someone's home, because in one way it was a piece of clothing and had grown to fit their shape. It might show not just what they'd been doing, but what they'd been thinking. You might be visiting someone who expected you to know everything about everything, and in those circumstances you took every advantage you could get.

Someone had told her that a witch's cottage was her second face. Come to think of it, it had been Granny.

It should be easy to read this place. Granny's thoughts had the strength of hammer blows and they'd pounded her personality into the walls. If her cottage had been any more organic it would have had a pulse.

Agnes wandered through to the dank little scullery. The copper washpot had been scoured. A fork and a couple of shining spoons lay beside it, along with the washboard and scrubbing brush. The slop bucket gleamed, although the fragments of a broken cup in the bottom said that the recent intensive housework hadn't been without its casualties.

She pushed open the door into the old goat shed. Granny was not keeping goats at the moment, but her home-made beekeeping equipment was neatly laid out on a bench. She'd never needed much. If you needed smoke and a veil to deal with your bees, what was the point of being a witch?

Bees . . .

A moment later she was out in the garden, her ear pressed against a beehive.

There were no bees flying this early in the day, but the sound inside was a roar.

'They'll know,' said a voice behind her. Agnes stood up so quickly she bumped her head on the hive roof.

'But they won't say,' Nanny added. 'She'd have told 'em. Well done for thinkin' about 'em, though.'

Something chattered at them from a nearby branch. It was a magpie.

'Good morning, Mister Magpie,' said Agnes automatically.

'Bugger off, you bastard,' said Nanny, and reached down for a stick to throw. The bird swooped off to the other side of the clearing.

'That's bad luck,' said Agnes.

'It will be if I get a chance to aim,' said Nanny. 'Can't stand those maggoty-pies.'

'"One for sorrow,"' said Agnes, watching the bird hop along a branch.

'I always take the view there's prob'ly going to be another one along in a minute,' said Nanny, dropping a stick.

' "Two for joy"?' said Agnes.

'It's "two for mirth".'

'Same thing, I suppose.'

'Dunno about that,' said Nanny. 'I was joyful when our Jason was born, but I can't say I was *laughin'* at the time. Come on, let's have another look.'

Two more magpies landed on the cottage's antique thatch.

'That's "three for a girl—"' said Agnes nervously.

'"Three for a funeral" is what I learned,' said Nanny. 'But there's lots of magpie rhymes. Look, you take her broomstick and have a look over towards the mountains, and I'll—'

'Wait,' said Agnes.

Perdita was screaming at her to pay attention. She listened.

Threes . . .

Three spoons. Three knives. Three cups.

The broken cup thrown away.

She stood still, afraid that if she moved or breathed something awful would happen.

The clock had stopped . . .

'Nanny?'

Nanny Ogg was wise enough to recognize that something was happening and didn't waste time on daft questions.

'Yes?' she said.

'Go in and tell me what time the clock stopped at, will you?'

Nanny nodded and trotted off.

The tension in Agnes's head stretched out thin and made a noise like a plucked string. She was amazed that the whine from it couldn't be heard all round the garden. If she moved, if she tried to force things, it'd snap.

Nanny returned.

'Three o'clock?' said Agnes, before she opened her mouth.

'Just after.'

'*How much after?*'

'Two or three minutes . . .'

'Two *or* three?'

'Three, then.'

The three magpies landed together on another tree and chased one another through the branches, chattering loudly.

'Three minutes after three,' said Agnes, and felt the tension ease and the words form. 'Threes, Nanny. She was thinking in threes. There was *another* candlestick out in the goat shed, and some cutlery too. But she only put out threes.'

'Some things were in ones and twos,' said Nanny, but her voice was edged with doubt.

'Then she'd only got one or two of them,' said Agnes. 'There were more spoons and things out in the scullery that she'd missed. I mean that for some reason she wasn't putting out *more* than three.'

'I know for a fact she's got *four* cups,' said Nanny.

'Three,' said Agnes. 'She must've broken one. The bits are in the slop bucket.'

Nanny Ogg stared at her. 'She's not clumsy, as

a rule,' she mumbled. She looked to Agnes as though she was trying to avoid some huge and horrible thought.

A gust shook the trees. A few drops of rain spattered across the garden.

'Let's get inside,' Agnes suggested.

Nanny shook her head. 'It's chillier in there than out here,' she said. Something skimmed across the leaves and landed on the lawn. It was a fourth magpie. ' "Four for a birth," ' she added, apparently to herself. 'That'd be it, sure enough. I hoped she wouldn't realize, but you can't get anything past Esme. I'll tan young Shawn's hide for him when I get home! He swore he'd delivered that invite!'

'Perhaps she took it away with her?'

'No! If she'd got it she'd have been there last night, you can bet on it!' snapped Nanny.

'*What* wouldn't she realize?' said Agnes.

'Magrat's daughter!'

'What? Well, I should think she *would* realize! You can't hide a baby! Everyone in the kingdom knows about it.'

'I mean Magrat's *got a daughter*! She's a *mother*!' said Nanny.

'Well, yes! That's how it works! So?'

They were shouting at one another, and they both realized it at the same time.

It was raining harder now. Drips were flying off Agnes's hat every time she moved her head.

Nanny recovered a little. 'All right, I s'pose between us we've got enough sense to get in out of the rain.'

'And at least we can light the fire,' said Agnes as they

stepped into the chill of the kitchen. 'She's left it all laid—'

'No!'

'There's no need to *shout* again!'

'Look, *don't* light the fire, right?' said Nanny. 'Don't touch anything more than you have to!'

'I could easily get more kindling in, and—'

'Be told! That fire wasn't laid for *you* to light! And leave that door alone!'

Agnes stopped in the act of pushing away the stone.

'Be sensible, Nanny, the rain and leaves are blowing in!'

'Let 'em!'

Nanny flopped into the rocking chair, pulled up her skirt and fumbled in the depths of a lengthy knicker-leg until she came up with the spirit flask. She took a long pull. Her hands were shaking.

'I can't start being a hag at my time of life,' she muttered. 'None of my bras'll fit.'

'Nanny?'

'Yes?'

'What the hell are you going on about? Daughter? Not lighting fires? Hags?'

Nanny replaced the flask and felt around in the other leg, coming up eventually with her pipe and tobacco pouch.

'Not sure if I ought to tell you,' she said.

Now Granny Weatherwax was well beyond the local woods and high in the forests, following a track used by the charcoal burners and the occasional dwarf.

Already Lancre was dying away. She could feel it

ebbing from her mind. Down below, when things were quiet, she was always aware of the buzz of minds around her. Human and animal, they all stirred up together in some great mental stew. But here there were mainly the slow thoughts of the trees, which were frankly boring after the first few hours and could be safely ignored. Snow, still quite thick in the hollows and on the shadow sides of trees, was dissolving in a drizzle of rain.

She stepped into a clearing and a small herd of deer on the far edge raised their heads to watch her. Out of habit she stopped and gently let herself unravel, until from the deer's point of view there was hardly anyone there.

When she began to walk forward again a deer stepped out of some bushes and stopped and turned to face her.

She'd seen this happen before. Hunters talked about it sometimes. You could track a herd all day, creeping silently among the trees in search of that one clean shot, and, just as you were aiming, a deer would step out right in front of you, turn and watch – and wait. Those were the times when a hunter found out how good he was . . .

Granny snapped her fingers. The deer shook itself and galloped off.

She climbed higher, following the stony bed of a stream. Despite its swiftness, there was a border of ice along its banks. Where it dropped over a series of small waterfalls she turned and looked back down into the bowl of Lancre.

It was full of clouds.

A few hundred feet below she saw a black and white magpie skim across the forest roof.

Granny turned and scrambled quickly up the dripping, icy rocks and on to the fringes of the moorland beyond.

Up here there was more sky. Silence clamped down. Far overhead an eagle wheeled.

It seemed to be the only other life. No one ever came up here. The furze and heather stretched away for a mile between the mountains, unbroken by any path. It was matted, thorny stuff that would tear unprotected flesh to ribbons.

She sat down on a rock and stared at the unbroken expanse for a while. Then she reached into her sack and took out a thick pair of socks.

And set off, onwards and upwards.

Nanny Ogg scratched her nose. She very seldom looked embarrassed, but there was just a hint of embarrassment about her now. It was even worse than Nanny Ogg upset.

'I ain't sure if this is the right time,' she said.

'Look, Nanny,' said Agnes, 'we *need* her. If there's something I ought to know, then *tell* me.'

'It's this business with . . . you know . . . three witches,' she said. 'The maiden, the mother and . . .'

'—the other one,' said Agnes. 'Oh yes, I know *that*. But that's just a bit of superstition, isn't it? Witches don't have to come in threes.'

'Oh, no. Course not,' said Nanny. 'You can have any number up to about, oh, four or five.'

'What happens if there's more, then? Something awful?'

'Bloody great row, usually,' said Nanny. 'Over nothin' much. And then they all goes off and sulks. Witches don't like being compressed up, much. But three . . . sort of . . . works well. I don't have to draw you a picture, do I?'

'And now Magrat's a *mother*—' said Agnes.

'Ah, well, that's where it all goes a bit runny,' said Nanny. 'This maiden and mother thing . . . it's not as simple as you'd think, see? Now you,' she prodded Agnes with her pipe, 'are a maiden. You *are*, aren't you?'

'Nanny! That's not the sort of thing people discuss!'

'Well, I knows you are, 'cos I'd soon hear if you wasn't,' said Nanny, the kind of person who discussed that kind of thing all the time. 'But that ain't really important, because it ain't down to *technicalities*, see? Now me, I don't reckon I was ever a maiden *ment'ly*. Oh, you don't need to go all red like that. What about your Aunt May over in Creel Springs? Four kids and she's still bashful around men. You got your blush from her. Tell her a saucy joke and if you're quick you can cook dinner for six on her head. When you've been around for a while, miss, you'll see that some people's body and head don't always work together.'

'And what's Granny Weatherwax, then?' said Agnes, and added, a little nastily because the reference to the blush had gone home, '*Ment'ly*.'

'Damned if I've ever worked that out,' said Nanny. 'But I reckon she sees there's a new three here. That *bloody* invitation must've been the last straw. So she's gone.' She poked at her pipe. 'Can't say I fancy being a crone. I ain't the right shape and anyway I don't know what sound they make.'

Agnes had a sudden and very clear and horrible mental image of the broken cup.

'But Granny isn't a . . . wasn't a . . . I mean, she didn't *look* like a—' she began.

'There's no point in lookin' at a dog an' sayin' that's not a dog 'cos a dog don't look like that,' said Nanny simply.

Agnes fell silent. Nanny was right, of course. Nanny was someone's mum. It was written all over her. If you cut her in half, the word 'Ma' would be all the way through. Some girls were just naturally . . . mothers. *And some,* Perdita added, *were cut out to be professional maidens.* As for the third, Agnes went on, ignoring her own interruption, perhaps it wasn't so odd that people generally called Nanny out for the births and Granny for the deaths.

'She thinks we don't need her any more?'

'I reckon so.'

'What is she going to do, then?'

'Dunno. But if you had three, and now there's four . . . well, something's got to go, hasn't it?'

'What about the vampires? The two of us can't cope with them!'

'She's been telling us there's three of us,' said Nanny.

'What? Magrat? But she's—' Agnes stopped herself. 'She's no Nanny Ogg,' she said.

'Well, I sure as hell ain't an Esme Weatherwax, if it comes to that,' said Nanny. 'The ment'l stuff is meat and drink to her. Getting inside other heads, puttin' her mind somewhere else . . . that's her for-tay, right enough. She'd wipe the smile off that Count's face for him. From the inside, if I know Esme.'

They sat and stared glumly at the cold fireplace.

'Maybe we weren't always very nice to her,' said Agnes. She kept thinking of the broken cup. She was sure Granny Weatherwax hadn't done that accidentally. She may have *thought* she'd done it accidentally, but maybe everyone had a Perdita inside. She'd walked around this gloomy cottage, which was as much in tune with her thoughts by now as a dog is with its master, and she'd had *three* on her mind. Three, three, three . . .

'Esme doesn't thrive on nice,' said Nanny Ogg. 'Take her an apple pie and she'll complain about the pastry.'

'But people don't often thank her. And she *does* do a lot.'

'She's not set up for thanks, neither. Ment'ly. To tell you the honest truth, there's always been a bit of the dark in the Weatherwaxes, and that's where the trouble is. Look at old Alison Weatherwax.'

'Who was she?'

'Her own granny. Went to the bad, they say, just packed up one day and headed for Uberwald. And as for Esme's sister . . .' Nanny stopped, and restarted. 'Anyway, that's why she's always standin' behind herself and criticizin' what she's doing. Sometimes I reckon she's terrified she'll go bad without noticin'.'

'Granny? But she's as moral as—'

'Oh, yes, she is. But that's because she's got Granny Weatherwax glarin' over her shoulder the whole time.'

Agnes took another look around the spartan room.

Now the rain was leaking steadily through the ceiling. She fancied she could hear the walls settling into the clay. She fancied she could hear them thinking.

'Did she know Magrat was going to call the baby Esme?' she said.

'Probably. It's amazin' what she picks up.'

'Maybe not tactful, when you think about it,' said Agnes.

'What do you mean? *I'd* have been honoured, if it was me.'

'Perhaps Granny thought the name was being passed on. Inherited.'

'Oh. Yes,' said Nanny. 'Yes, I can just imagine Esme workin' it up to that, when she's in one of her gloomy moods.'

'My granny used to say if you're too sharp you'll cut yourself,' said Agnes.

They sat in grey silence for a while, and then Nanny Ogg said: 'My own granny has an old country sayin' she always trotted out at times like this . . .'

'Which was . . .?'

'"Bugger off, you little devil, or I'll chop off your nose and give it to the cat." Of course, that's not so very helpful at a time like this, I'll admit.'

There was a tinkle behind them.

Nanny turned her head and looked down at the table.

'There's a spoon gone . . .'

There was another jangle, this time by the door.

A magpie paused in its attempt to pick the stolen spoon off the doorstep, cocked its head and glared at them with a beady eye. It just managed to get airborne before Nanny's hat, spinning like a plate, bounced off the doorjamb.

'The devils'll pinch anything that damn well shines—' she began.

The Count de Magpyr looked out of the window at the glow that marked the rising sun.

'There you are, you see?' he said, turning back to his family. 'Morning, and here we are.'

'You've made it overcast,' said Lacrimosa sullenly. 'It's hardly *sunny*.'

'One step at a time, dear, one step at a time,' said the Count cheerfully. 'I just wished to make the point. Today, yes, it is overcast. But we can build on it. We can acclimatize. And one day . . . the beach . . .'

'You really are very clever, dear,' said the Countess.

'Thank you, my love,' said the Count, nodding his private agreement. 'How are you doing with that cork, Vlad?'

'Is this such a good idea, Father?' said Vlad, struggling with a bottle and a corkscrew. 'I thought we did not drink . . . wine.'

'I believe it's time we started.'

'Yuck,' said Lacrimosa. 'I'm not touching that, it's squeezed from *vegetables*!'

'Fruit, I think you'll find,' said the Count calmly. He took the bottle from his son and removed the cork. 'A fine claret, I understand. You'll try some, my dear?'

His wife smiled nervously, supporting her husband but slightly against her better judgement.

'Do we, er, are we, eh, supposed to warm it up?' she said.

'Room temperature is suggested.'

'That's *sickening*,' said Lacrimosa. 'I don't know how you can bear it!'

'Try it for your father, dear,' said the Countess. 'Quickly, before it congeals.'

'No, my dear. Wine stays runny.'

'Really? How very convenient.'

'Vlad?' said the Count, pouring a glass. The son watched nervously.

'Perhaps it would help if you think of it as grape blood,' said his father, as Vlad took the wine. 'And you, Lacci?'

She folded her arms resolutely. 'Huh!'

'I thought you'd like this sort of thing, dear,' said the Countess. 'It's the sort of thing your crowd does, isn't it?'

'I don't know what you're talking about!' said the girl.

'Oh, staying up until gone noon and wearing brightly coloured clothes, and giving yourselves funny names,' said the Countess.

'Like *Gertrude*,' sneered Vlad. 'And *Pam*. They think it's *cool*.'

Lacrimosa turned on him furiously, nails out. He caught her wrist, grinning.

'That's none of your business!'

'Lady Strigoiul said her daughter has taken to calling herself Wendy,' said the Countess. 'I can't imagine why she'd want to, when Hieroglyphica is such a *nice* name for a girl. And if I was her mother I'd see to it that she at least wore a bit of eyeliner—'

'Yes, but *no one* drinks *wine*,' said Lacrimosa. 'Only

real weirdos who file their teeth blunt drink wine—'

'Maladora Krvoijac does,' said Vlad. 'Or "Freda", I should say—'

'No she doesn't!'

'What? She wears a silver corkscrew on a chain round her neck and sometimes there's even a cork on it!'

'That's just a fashion item! Oh, I know she *says* she's partial to a drop of port, but really it's just blood in the glass. Henry actually brought a bottle to a party and she fainted at the smell!'

'Henry?' said the Countess.

Lacrimosa looked down sulkily. 'Graven Gierachi,' she said.

'The one who grows his hair short and pretends he's an accountant,' said Vlad.

'I just hope someone's told his father, then,' said the Countess.

'Be *quiet*,' said the Count. 'This is all just cultural conditioning, you understand? Please! I've worked hard for this! All we want is a piece of the day. Is that too much to ask? And wine is just wine. There's nothing mystical about it. Now, take up your glasses. You too, Lacci. Please? For Daddy?'

'And when you tell "Cyril" and "Tim" they'll be *so* impressed,' said Vlad to Lacrimosa.

'Shut up!' she hissed. 'Father, it'll make me sick!'

'No, your body will adapt,' said the Count. 'I've tried it myself. A little watery, perhaps, somewhat sour, but quite palatable. Please?'

'Oh, well . . .'

'Good,' said the Count. 'Now, raise the glasses—'

'*Le sang nouveau est arrivé*,' said Vlad.

'*Carpe diem*,' said the Count.

'By the throat,' said the Countess.

'People won't believe me when I tell them,' said Lacrimosa.

They swallowed.

'There,' said Count Magpyr. 'That wasn't too bad, was it?'

'A bit chilly,' said Vlad.

'I'll have a wine warmer installed,' said the Count. 'I'm not an unreasonable vampire. But within a year, children, I think I can have us quite cured of phenophobia and even capable of a little light salad—'

Lacrimosa turned her back theatrically and made throwing-up noises into a vase.

'—and then, Lacci, you'll be free. No more lonely days. No more—'

Vlad was half expecting it, and kept an entirely blank expression as his father whipped a card from his pocket and held it up.

'That is the double snake symbol of the Djelibeybian water cult,' he said calmly.

'You see?' said the Count excitedly. 'You barely flinched! Sacrephobia *can* be beaten! I've always said so! The way may have been hard at times—'

'I *hated* the way you used to leap out in corridors and flick holy water on us,' said Lacrimosa.

'It wasn't holy at all,' said her father. 'It was strongly

diluted. Mildly devout at worst. But it made you strong, didn't it?'

'I caught colds a lot, I know that.'

The Count's hand whipped out of his pocket.

Lacrimosa gave a sigh of theatrical weariness. 'The All-Seeing Face of the Ionians,' she said wearily.

The Count very nearly danced a jig.

'You see? It has worked! You didn't even wince! And apparently as holy symbols go it's pretty strong. Isn't it all worth it?'

'There'll have to be something *really* good to make up for those garlic pillows you used to make us sleep on.'

Her father took her by the shoulder and turned her towards the window.

'Will it be enough to know that the world is your oyster?'

Her forehead wrinkled in perplexity. 'Why should I want it to be some nasty little sea creature?' she said.

'Because they get eaten alive,' said the Count. 'Unfortunately I doubt if we can find a slice of lemon five hundred miles long, but the metaphor will suffice.'

She brightened up, grudgingly. 'We-ell . . .' she said.

'Good. I like to see my little girl smile,' said the Count. 'Now . . . who shall we have for breakfast?'

'The baby.'

'No, I think not.' The Count pulled a bellpull beside the fireplace. 'That would be undiplomatic. We're not *quite* there yet.'

'Well, that apology for a queen looks pretty

bloodless. Vlad should have hung on to his fat girl,' said Lacrimosa.

'Don't you start,' Vlad warned. 'Agnes is a . . . very interesting girl. I feel there is a lot in her.'

'A lot *of* her,' said Lacrimosa. 'Are you saving her for later?'

'Now, now,' said the Count. 'Your own dear mother wasn't a vampire when I met her—'

'Yes, yes, you've told us a million times,' said Lacrimosa, rolling her eyes with the impatience of someone who'd been a teenager for eighty years. 'The balcony, the nightdress, you in your cloak, she screamed—'

'Things were simpler then,' said the Count. 'And also very, very stupid.' He sighed. 'Where the hell's Igor?'

'Ahem. I've been meaning to talk to you about him, dear,' said the Countess. 'I think he'll have to go.'

'That's right!' snapped Lacrimosa. 'Honestly, even my friends laugh at him!'

'I find his more-gothic-than-thou attitude *extremely* irritating,' said the Countess. 'That *stupid* accent . . . and do you know what I found him doing in the old dungeons last week?'

'I'm sure I couldn't guess,' said the Count.

'He had a box of spiders and a whip! He was *forcing* them to make webs all over the place.'

'I wondered why there were always so many, I must admit,' said the Count.

'I agree, Father,' said Vlad. 'He's all right for Uberwald, but you'd hardly want something like him opening the door in polite society, would you?'

'And he smells,' said the Countess.

'Of course, parts of him *have* been in the family for centuries,' said the Count. 'But I must admit he's getting beyond a joke.' He yanked the bellpull again.

'Yeth, marthter?' said Igor, behind him.

The Count spun round. 'I *told* you not to do that!'

'Not to do what, marthter?'

'Turn up behind me like that!'

'It'th the only way I know how to turn up, marthter.'

'Go and fetch King Verence, will you? He's joining us for a light meal.'

'Yeth, marthter.'

They watched the servant limp off. The Count shook his head.

'He'll never retire,' said Vlad. 'He'll never take a hint.'

'And it's so old-fashioned having a servant called Igor,' said the Countess. 'He really is too much.'

'Look, it's simple,' said Lacrimosa. 'Just take him down to the cellars, slam him in the Iron Maiden, stretch him on the rack over a fire for a day or two, and then slice him thinly from the feet upwards, so he can watch. You'll be doing him a kindness, really.'

'I suppose it's the best way,' said the Count sadly.

'I remember when you told me to put my cat out of its misery,' said Lacrimosa.

'I really meant you to stop what you were doing to it,' said the Count. 'But . . . yes, you are right, he'll have to go—'

Igor ushered in King Verence, who stood there with the mildly bemused expression of someone in the presence of the Count.

'Ah, your majesty,' said the Countess, advancing. 'Do join us in a light meal.'

Agnes's hair snagged in the twigs. She managed to get one boot on a branch while holding on for dear life to the branch above, but that left her other foot standing on the broomstick, which was beginning to drift sideways and causing her to do what even ballerinas can't do without some training.

'Can you see it yet?' Nanny cried, from far too far below.

'I think this is an old nest as well— Oh, no . . .'

'What's happened?'

'I think my drawers have split . . .'

'I always go for roomy, myself,' said Nanny.

Agnes got the other leg on to the branch, which creaked.

Lump, said Perdita. *I could have climbed this like a gazelle!*

'Gazelles don't climb!' said Agnes.

'What's that?' said the voice from below.

'Oh, nothing . . .'

Agnes inched her way along, and suddenly her vision was full of black and white wings. A magpie landed on a twig a foot from her face and screamed at her. Five others swooped in from the other trees and joined in the chorus.

She didn't like birds, in any case. They were fine when they were flying, and their songs were nice, but close to they were mad little balls of needles with the intelligence of a housefly.

She tried to swat the nearest one, and it fluttered on

to a higher branch while she struggled to get her balance back. When the branch stopped rocking she moved further along, gingerly, trying to ignore the enraged birds, and looked at the nest.

It was hard to tell if it was the remains of an old one or the start of a new one, but it did contain a piece of tinsel, a shard of broken glass and, gleaming even under this sullen sky, something white . . . with a gleaming edge.

'"Five for silver . . . *six for gold* . . ."' she said, half to herself.

'It's "five for heaven, six for hell",' Nanny called up.

'I can just reach it, anyway . . .'

The bough broke. There were plenty of others below it, but they merely served as points of interest on the way down. The last one flipped Agnes into a holly bush.

Nanny took the invitation from her outflung hand. Rain had made the ink run, but the word 'Weatherwax' was still very readable. She scratched at the gold edging with her thumb.

'Too *much* gold,' she said. 'Well, that explains the invite. I *told* you them birds will steal anything that glitters.'

'I'm not hurt at all,' said Agnes pointedly. 'The holly quite cushioned my fall.'

'I'll wring their necks,' said Nanny. The magpies in the trees around the cottage screamed at her.

'I think I may have dislocated my hat, however,' said Agnes, pulling herself to her feet. But it was useless angling for sympathy in a puddle, so she gave up. 'All right, we've found the invitation. It was all a terrible mistake. No one's fault. Now let's find Granny.'

'Not if she don't want to be found,' said Nanny, rubbing the edge of the card thoughtfully.

'You can do Borrowing. Even if she left early, some creatures will have seen her—'

'I don't Borrow, as a rule,' said Nanny firmly. 'I ain't got Esme's self-discipline. I gets . . . involved. I was a rabbit for three whole days until our Jason went and fetched Esme and she brought me back. Much longer and there wouldn't have been a me to *come* back.'

'Rabbits sound dull.'

'They have their ups and downs.'

'All right, then, have a look in the buoy's glass ball,' said Agnes. 'You're good at that, Magrat told me.' Across the clearing a crumbling brick fell out of the cottage's chimney.

'Not here, then,' said Nanny, with some reluctance. 'It's giving me the willies— Oh no, as if we didn't have enough . . . What's *he* doing here?'

Mightily Oats was advancing through the wood. He walked awkwardly, as city people do when traversing real, rutted, leaf-mouldy, twig-strewn soil, and had the concerned look of someone who was expecting to be attacked at any moment by owls or beetles.

In his strange black and white clothing he looked like a human magpie himself.

The magpies screamed from the trees.

'"Seven for a secret never to be told,"' said Agnes.

'"Seven's a devil, his own sel',"' said Nanny darkly. 'You've got your rhyme, I've got mine.'

When Oats saw the witches he brightened up very slightly and blew his nose at them.

'What a waste of skin,' muttered Nanny.

'Ah, Mrs Ogg . . . and Miss Nitt,' said Oats, inching around some mud. 'Er . . . I trust I find you well?'

'Up till now,' said Nanny.

'I had, er, hoped to see Mrs Weatherwax.'

For a moment the only sound was the chattering of the ravens.

'*Hoped?*' said Agnes.

'*Mrs* Weatherwax?' said Nanny.

'Er, yes. It is part of my . . . I'm supposed to . . . one of the things we . . . Well, I heard she might be ill, and visiting the elderly and infirm is part, er, of our pastoral duties . . . Of course I realize that *technically* I have no pastoral duties, but still, while I'm here . . .'

Nanny's face was a picture, possibly one painted by an artist with a very strange sense of humour.

'I'm really sorry she ain't here,' she said, and Agnes knew she was being altogether honest and absolutely nasty.

'Oh dear. I was, er, going to give her some . . . I was going . . . er . . . Is she well, then?'

'I'm sure she'd be all the better for a visit from you,' said Nanny, and once again there was a strange, curvy sort of truth to this. 'It'd be the sort of thing she'd talk about for days. You can come back any time you want.'

Oats looked helpless. 'Then I suppose I'd better, er, be getting back to my, er, tent,' he said. 'May I accompany you ladies down to the town? There are, er, some dangerous things in the woods . . .'

'We got broomsticks,' said Nanny firmly. The priest looked crestfallen, and Agnes made a decision.

'A broomstick,' she said. 'I'll walk you— I mean, you can walk *me* back. If you like.'

The priest looked relieved. Nanny sniffed. There was a certain Weatherwax quality to the sniff.

'Back at my place, then. An' no dilly-dallyin',' she said.

'I don't dilly-dally,' said Agnes.

'Just see you don't start,' said Nanny, and went to find her broomstick.

Agnes and the priest walked in embarrassed silence for a while. At last Agnes said, 'How's the headache?'

'Oh, much better, thank you. It went away. But her majesty was kind enough to give me some pills anyway.'

'That's nice,' said Agnes. *She ought to have given him a needle! Look at the size of that boil!* said Perdita, one of nature's born squeezers. *Why doesn't he do something about it?*

'Er . . . you don't like me very much, do you?' said Oats.

'I've hardly met you.' She was becoming aware of an embarrassing draughtiness in the nether regions.

'A lot of people don't like me as soon as they've met me,' said Oats.

'I suppose that saves time,' said Agnes, and cursed. Perdita had got through on that one, but Oats didn't seem to have noticed. He sighed.

'I'm afraid I have a bit of a difficulty with people,' he went on. 'I fear I'm just not cut out for pastoral work.'

Don't get involved with this twerp, said Perdita. But Agnes said, 'You mean sheep and so on?'

'It all seemed a lot clearer at college,' said Oats, who like many people seldom paid much attention to what others said when he was unrolling his miseries, 'but here, when I tell people some of the more *accessible* stories from the *Book of Om* they say things like, "That's not right, mushrooms wouldn't grow in the desert," or, "That's a stupid way to run a vineyard." Everyone here is so very . . . literal.'

Oats coughed. There seemed to be something preying on his mind. 'Unfortunately, the *Old Book of Om* is rather unyielding on the subject of witches,' he said.

'Really.'

'Although having studied the passage in question in the original Second Omnian IV text, I have advanced the rather daring theory that the actual word in question translates more accurately as "cockroaches".'

'Yes?'

'Especially since it goes on to say that they can be killed by fire or in "traps of treacle". It also says later on that they bring lascivious dreams.'

'Don't look at me,' said Agnes. 'All you're getting is a walk home.'

To her amazement, and Perdita's crowing delight, he blushed as red as she ever did.

'Er, er, the word in question in that passage might just as easily be read in context as "boiled lobsters",' he said hurriedly.

'Nanny Ogg says Omnians used to burn witches,' said Agnes.

'We used to burn practically everybody,' said Oats gloomily. 'Although some witches did get pushed into big barrels of treacle, I believe.'

He had a boring voice, too. He did appear, she had to admit, to be a boring person. It was almost too perfect a presentation, as if he was trying to *make* himself seem boring. But one thing had piqued Agnes's curiosity.

'Why did you come to visit Granny Weatherwax?'

'Well, everyone speaks very . . . highly of her,' said Oats, suddenly picking his words like a man pulling plums from a boiling pot. 'And they said she hadn't turned up last night, which was very strange. And I thought it must be hard for an old lady living by herself. And . . .'

'Yes?'

'Well, I understand she's quite old and it's never too late to consider the state of your immortal soul,' said Oats. 'Which she must have, of course.'

Agnes gave him a sideways look. 'She's never mentioned it,' she said.

'You probably think I'm foolish.'

'I just think you are an amazingly lucky man, Mr Oats.'

On the other hand . . . here was someone who'd been *told* about Granny Weatherwax, and had *still* walked through these woods that scared him stiff to see her, *even though* she was possibly a cockroach or a boiled lobster. No one in Lancre ever came to see Granny unless they wanted something. Oh, sometimes they came with little presents (because one day they'd want something again), but they generally made sure she was out first. There was more to Mr Oats than met the eye. There had to be.

A couple of centaurs burst out of the bushes ahead

of them and cantered away down the path. Oats grabbed a tree.

'They were running around when I came up!' he said. 'Are they *usual*?'

'I've never seen them before,' said Agnes. 'I think they're from Uberwald.'

'And the horrible little blue goblins? One of them made a *very* unpleasant gesture at me!'

'Don't know about them at all.'

'And the vampires? I mean, I knew that things were *different* here, but really—'

'Vampires?!' shouted Agnes. 'You saw the vampires? Last night?'

'Well, I mean, *yes*, I studied them at length at the seminary, but I never thought I'd see them standing around talking about drinking blood and things, really, I'm surprised the King allows it—'

'And they didn't . . . affect your mind?'

'I did have that terrible migraine. Does that count? I thought it was the prawns.'

A cry rang through the woods. It seemed to have many components, but mostly it sounded as though a turkey was being throttled at the other end of a tin tube.

'*And what the heck was that?*' shouted Oats.

Agnes looked around, bewildered. She'd grown up in the Lancre woods. Oh, you got strange things sometimes, passing through, but generally they contained nothing more dangerous than other people. Now, in this tarnished light, even the trees were starting to look suspicious.

'Let's at least get down to Bad Ass,' she said, tugging at Oats's hand.

'You what?'

Agnes sighed. 'It's the nearest village.'

'*Bad Ass?*'

'Look, there was a donkey, and it stopped in the middle of the river, and it wouldn't go backwards or forwards,' said Agnes, as patiently as possible. Lancre people got used to explaining this. 'Bad Ass. See? Yes, I know that "Disobedient Donkey" might have been more . . . *acceptable*, but—'

The horrible cry echoed around the woods again. Agnes thought of all the things that were rumoured to be in the mountains, and dragged Oats after her like a badly hitched cart.

Then the sound was right in front of them and, at a turn in the lane, a head emerged from a bush.

Agnes had seen pictures of an ostrich.

So . . . start with one of them, but make the head and neck in violent yellow, and give the head a huge ruff of red and purple feathers and two big round eyes, the pupils of which jiggled drunkenly as the head moved back and forth . . .

'Is that some sort of local chicken?' warbled Oats.

'I doubt it,' said Agnes. One of the long feathers had a tartan pattern.

The cry started again, but was strangled halfway through when Agnes stepped forward, grabbed the thing's neck and pulled.

A figure rose from the undergrowth, dragged up by his arm.

'Hodgesaargh?'

He quacked at her.

'Take that thing out of your mouth,' said Agnes. 'You sound like Mr Punch.'

He removed the whistle. 'Sorry, Miss Nitt.'

'Hodgesaargh, why – and I realize I might not like the answer – why are you hiding in the woods with your arm dressed up like Hetty the Hen and making horrible noises through a tube?'

'Trying to lure the phoenix, miss.'

'The phoenix? That's a mythical bird, Hodgesaargh.'

'That's right, miss. There's one in Lancre, miss. It's very young, miss. So I thought I might be able to attract it.'

She looked at the brightly coloured glove. Oh, yes – if you raised chicks, you had to let them know what kind of bird they were, so you used a sort of glove-puppet. But . . .

'Hodgesaargh?'

'Yes, miss?'

'I'm not an expert, of course, but I seem to recall that according to the commonly accepted legend of the phoenix it would never *see* its parent. You can only have one phoenix at a time. It's automatically an orphan. You see?'

'Um, may I add something?' said Oats. 'Miss Nitt is right, I have to say. The phoenix builds a nest and bursts into flame and the new bird arises from the ashes. I've read that. Anyway, it's an allegory.'

Hodgesaargh looked at the puppet phoenix on his arm and then looked bashfully at his feet.

'Sorry about that, miss.'

'So, you see, a phoenix can never see another phoenix,' said Agnes.

'Wouldn't know about that, miss,' said Hodgesaargh, still staring at his boots.

An idea struck Agnes. Hodgesaargh was always out of doors. 'Hodgesaargh?'

'Yes, miss?'

'Have you been out in the woods all morning?'

'Oh, yes, miss.'

'Have you seen Granny Weatherwax?'

'Yes, miss.'

'You have?'

'Yes, miss.'

'Where?'

'Up in the woods over towards the border, miss. At first light, miss.'

'Why didn't you tell me?'

'Er . . . did you want to know, miss?'

'Oh. Yes, sorry . . . What were you doing up there?'

Hodgesaargh blew a couple of quacks on his phoenix lure by way of explanation. Agnes grabbed the priest again.

'Come on, let's get to the road and find Nanny—'

Hodgesaargh was left with his glove puppet and his lure and his knapsack and a deeply awkward feeling. He'd been brought up to respect witches, and Miss Nitt was a witch. The man with her *hadn't* been a witch, but his manner fitted him into that class of people Hodgesaargh mentally pigeonholed as 'my betters', although in truth this was quite a large category. He wasn't about to disagree with his betters. Hodgesaargh was a one-man feudal system.

On the other hand, he thought, as he packed up

and prepared to move on, books that were all about the world tended to be written by people who knew all about books rather than all about the world. All that stuff about birds hatching from ashes must have been written by someone who didn't know anything about birds. As for there only ever being one phoenix, well, that'd obviously been written down by a man who ought to get out in the fresh air more and meet some ladies. Birds came from eggs. Oh, the phoenix was one of those creatures that had learned to use magic, had built it right into its very existence, but magic was tricky stuff and nothing used any more of it than it needed to. So there'd be an egg, definitely. And eggs needed warmth, didn't they?

Hodgesaargh had been thinking about this a lot during the morning, as he tramped through damp bushes making the acquaintance of several disappointed ducks. He'd never bothered much about history, except the history of falconry, but he did know that there were once places – and in some cases still were – with a very high level of background magic, which made them rather exciting and not a good place to raise your young.

Maybe the phoenix, whatever it really looked like, was simply a bird who'd worked out a way of making incubation work very, *very* fast.

Hodgesaargh had actually got quite a long way, and if he'd had a bit more time he'd have worked out the next step, too.

It was well after noon before Granny Weatherwax came off the moor, and a watcher might have wondered why it took such a long time to cross a little patch of moorland.

They'd have wondered even more about the little stream. It had cut a rock-studded groove in the peat that a healthy woman could have leapt across, but someone had placed a broad stone across it for a bridge.

She looked at it for a while and then reached into her sack. She took out a long piece of black material and blindfolded herself. Then she walked out across the stone, taking tiny steps with her arms flung out wide for balance. Halfway across she fell on to her hands and knees and stayed there, panting, for several minutes. Then she crawled forward again, by inches.

A few feet below, the peaty stream rattled happily over the stones.

The sky glinted. It was a sky with blue patches and bits of cloud, but it had a strange look, as though a picture painted on glass had been fractured and then the shards reassembled wrongly. A drifting cloud disappeared against some invisible line and began to emerge in another part of the sky altogether.

Things were not what they seemed. But then, as Granny always said, they never were.

Agnes practically had to pull Oats into Nanny Ogg's house, which was in fact so far away from the concept of a witch's cottage that it, as it were, approached it from the other side. It tended towards jolly clashing colours rather than black, and smelled of polish. There were no skulls or strange candles, apart from the pink novelty one that Nanny had once bought in

Ankh-Morpork and only brought out to show to guests with the right sense of humour. There *were* lots of tables, mainly in order to display the vast number of drawings and iconographs of the huge Ogg clan. At first sight these looked randomly placed, until you worked out the code. In reality, pictures were advanced or retarded around the room as various family members temporarily fell in or out of favour, and anyone ending up on the small wobbly table near the cat's bowl had some serious spadework to do. What made it worse was that you could fall down the pecking order not because you'd done something bad, but because everyone else had done something *better*. This was why what space wasn't taken up with family pictures was occupied by ornaments, because no Ogg who travelled more than ten miles from Ankh-Morpork would dream of returning without a present. The Oggs loved Nanny Ogg and, well, there were even worse places than the wobbly table. A distant cousin had once ended up in the hall.

Most of the ornaments were cheapjack stuff bought from fairs, but Nanny Ogg never minded, provided they were colourful and shiny. So there were a lot of cross-eyed dogs, pink shepherdesses and mugs with badly spelled slogans like 'To the Wordl's Best Mum' and 'We Luove Our Nanny'. A huge gilded china beer stein that played 'Ich Bin Ein Rattarsedschwein' from *The Student Horse* was locked in a glass-fronted cabinet as a treasure too great for common display, and had earned Shirl Ogg's picture a permanent place on the dresser.

Nanny Ogg had already cleared a space on the table

for the green ball. She looked up sharply when Agnes entered.

'You were a long time. Been dallyin'?' she said, in an armour-piercing voice.

'Nanny, *Granny* would have said that,' said Agnes reproachfully.

Nanny shivered. 'You're right, gel,' she said. 'Let's find her quickly, eh? I'm too cheerful to be a crone.'

'There's odd creatures everywhere!' said Agnes. 'There's *loads* of centaurs! We had to dive into the ditch!'

'Ah, I did notice you'd got grass and leaves on your dress,' said Nanny. 'But I was too polite to mention it.'

'Where're they all coming from?'

'Down out of the mountains, I suppose. Why did you bring Soapy Sam back with you?'

'Because he's covered in mud, Nanny,' said Agnes sharply, 'and I said he could have a wash down here.'

'Er . . . is this really a witch's cottage?' said Oats, staring at the assembled ranks of Oggery.

'Oh dear,' said Nanny.

'Pastor Melchio said they are sinks of depravity and sexual excess.' The young man took a nervous step backwards, knocking against a small table and causing a blue clockwork ballerina to begin a jerky pirouette to the tune of 'Three Blind Mice'.

'Well, we've got a sink all right,' said Nanny. 'What's your best offer?'

'I suppose we should be grateful that was a Nanny Ogg comment,' said Agnes. 'Don't wind him up, Nanny. It's been a busy morning.'

'Er, which way's the pump?' said Oats. Agnes pointed. He hurried out, gratefully.

'Wetter than a thunderstorm sandwich,' said Nanny, shaking her head.

'Granny was seen up above the long lake,' said Agnes, sitting down at the table.

Nanny looked up sharply. 'On that bit of moor?' she said.

'Yes.'

'That's bad. That's gnarly country up there.'

'Gnarly?'

'All scrunched up.'

'What? I've been up there. It's just heather and gorse and there's a few old caves at the end of the valley.'

'Oh, really? Looked up at the clouds, did you? Oh well, let's have a go . . .'

When Oats came back, scrubbed and shining, they were arguing. They looked rather embarrassed when they saw him.

'I *said* it'd need three of us,' said Nanny, pushing the glass ball aside. 'Especially if she's up there. Gnarly ground plays merry hell with scrying. We just ain't got the power.'

'I don't want to go back to the castle!'

'Magrat's good at this sort of thing.'

'She's got a little baby to look after, Nanny!'

'Yeah, in a castle full of vampires. Think about that. No knowing when they'll get hungry again. Better for 'em both to be out of it.'

'But—'

'You get her out now. I'd come myself, but you said I just sit there grinnin'.'

Agnes suddenly pointed a finger at Oats. 'You!'

'Me?' he quavered.

'You said you could see they were vampires, didn't you?'

'I did?'

'*You did.*'

'That's right, I did. Er . . . and?'

'You didn't find your mind becoming all pink and happy?'

'I don't think my mind has *ever* been pink and happy,' said Oats.

'So why didn't they get through to you?'

Oats smiled uneasily and fished in his jacket.

'I am protected by the hand of Om,' he said.

Nanny inspected the pendant. It showed a figure trussed across the back of a turtle.

'You say?' she said. 'That's a good wheeze, then.'

'Just as Om reached out his hand to save the prophet Brutha from the torture, so will he spread his wings over me in my time of trial,' said Oats, but he sounded as though he was trying to reassure himself rather than Nanny. He went on: 'I've got a pamphlet if you would like to know more,' and this time the tone was much more positive, as if the existence of Om was a little uncertain whereas the existence of pamphlets was obvious to any open-minded, rational-thinking person.

'*Don't*,' said Nanny. She let the medallion go. 'Well, Brother Perdore never needed any magic jewellery for fighting off people, that's all I can say.'

'No, he just used to breathe alcohol all over them,' said Agnes. 'Well, you're coming with me, Mr Oats.

I'm not facing Prince Slime again alone! And you can shut up!'

'Er, I didn't say anything—'

'I didn't mean you, I meant— Look, you said you've studied vampires, didn't you? What's good for vampires?'

Oats thought for a moment. 'Er . . . a nice dry coffin, er, plenty of fresh blood, er, overcast skies . . .' His voice trailed off when he saw her expression. 'Ah . . . well, it depends exactly where they're from, I remember. Uberwald is a very big place. Er, cutting off the head and staking them in the heart is generally efficacious.'

'But that works on everyone,' said Nanny.

'Er . . . in Splintz they die if you put a coin in their mouth and cut their head off . . .'

'Not like ordinary people, then,' said Nanny, taking out a notebook.

'Er . . . in Klotz they die if you stick a lemon in their mouth—'

'Sounds more like it.'

'—after you cut their head off. I believe that in Glitz you have to fill their mouth with salt, hammer a carrot into both ears, and then cut off their head.'

'I can see it must've been fun finding that out.'

'And in the valley of the Ah they believe it's best to cut off the head and boil it in vinegar.'

'You're going to need someone to carry all this stuff, Agnes,' said Nanny Ogg.

'But in Kashncari they say you should cut off their toes and drive a nail through their neck.'

'And cut their head off?'

'Apparently you don't have to.'

'Toes is *easy*,' said Nanny. 'Old Windrow over in Bad Ass cut off two of his with a spade and he weren't even trying.'

'And then, of course, you can defeat them by stealing their left sock,' said Oats.

'Sorry?' said Agnes. 'I think I misheard you there.'

'Um, they're pathologically meticulous, you see. Some of the gypsy tribes in Borogravia say that if you steal their sock and hide it somewhere they'll spend the rest of eternity looking for it. They can't abide things to be out of place or missing.'

'I wouldn't have put this down as a very widespread belief,' said Nanny.

'Oh, they say in some villages that you can even slow them down by throwing poppyseed at them,' said Oats. 'Then they'll have a terrible urge to count every seed. Vampires are very anal-retentive, you see?'

'I shouldn't like meeting one that was the opposite,' said Nanny.

'Yes, well, I don't think we're going to have time to ask the Count for his precise address,' said Agnes quickly. 'We're going to go in, fetch Magrat and get back here, all right? Why are you such a vampire expert, Oats?'

'I told you, I studied this sort of thing at college. We have to know the enemy if we're to combat evil forces . . . vampires, demons, wit—' He stopped.

'Do go on,' said Nanny Ogg, as sweet as arsenic.

'But with witches I'm just supposed to show them the error of their ways.' Oats coughed nervously.

'That's something to look forward to, then,' said Nanny. 'What with me not havin' my fireproof corsets on. Off you go, then . . . all three of you.'

'There's three of us?' said Oats.

Agnes felt her left arm tremble. Against every effort of will her wrist bent, her palm curled up and she felt two fingers straining to unfold. Only Nanny Ogg noticed.

'Like having your own chaperon all the time, ain't it?' she said.

'What was she talking about?' said Oats, as they headed for the castle.

'Her mind's wandering,' said Agnes, loudly.

There were covered ox-carts rumbling up the street to the castle. Agnes and Oats stood to one side and watched them.

The drivers didn't seem interested in the bystanders. They wore drab, ill-fitting clothing, but an unusual touch was the scarf each one had wrapped around his neck so tightly that it might have been a bandage.

'Either there's a plague of sore throats in Uberwald or there will be nasty little puncture wounds under those, I'll bet,' said Agnes.

'Er . . . I do know a bit about the way they're supposed to control people,' said Oats.

'Yes?'

'It sounds silly, but it was in an old book.'

'Well?'

'They find single-minded people easier to control.'

'Single-minded?' said Agnes suspiciously. More carts rolled past.

'It doesn't sound right, I know. You'd think strong-minded people would be harder to affect. I suppose a big target is easier to hit. In some of the villages, apparently, vampire hunters get roaring drunk first. Protection, you see? You can't punch fog.'

So we're fog? said Perdita. *So's he, by the look of him . . .*

Agnes shrugged. There was a certain bucolic look to the faces of the cart drivers. Of course, you got that in Lancre too, but in Lancre it was overlaid by a mixture of guile, common sense and stubborn rock-headedness. Here the eyes behind the faces had a switched-off look.

Like cattle, said Perdita.

'Yes,' said Agnes.

'Pardon?' said Oats.

'Just thinking aloud . . .'

And she thought of the way one man could so easily control a herd of cows, any one of which could have left him as a small damp depression in the ground had it wanted to. Somehow, they never got around to thinking about it.

Supposing they *are* better than us, she thought. Supposing that, compared to them, we're just—

You're too close to the castle! snapped Perdita. *You're thinking cow thoughts.*

Then Agnes realized that there was a squad of men marching behind the carts. They didn't look at all like the carts' drivers.

And these, said Perdita, *are the cattle prods.*

They had uniforms, of a sort, with the black and white crest of the Magpyrs, but they weren't a body of men that looked smart in a uniform. They looked very much like men who killed other people for money, and not even for a lot of money. They looked, in short, like men who'd cheerfully eat a puppy sandwich. Several of them leered at Agnes when they went past, but it was only a generic leer that was simply leered on the basis that she had a dress on.

More wagons came up behind them.

'Nanny Ogg says you must take time by the fore-skin,' Agnes said, and darted forward as the last wagon rumbled past.

'She does?'

'I'm afraid so. You get used to it.'

She caught the back of the cart and pulled herself up, beckoning him hastily to follow.

'Are you trying to impress me?' he said as she hauled him on board.

'Not *you*,' she said. And realized, at this point, that what she was sitting on was a coffin.

There were two of them in the back of the cart, packed around with straw.

'Are they moving the furniture in?' said Oats.

'Er . . . I think . . . it might . . . be occupied,' said Agnes.

She almost shrieked when he removed the lid. The coffin was empty.

'You idiot! Supposing there was someone in there!'

'Vampires are weak during the day. *Everyone* knows that,' said Oats reproachfully.

'I can . . . feel them here . . . somewhere,' said Agnes. The rattling of the cart changed as it rumbled on to the cobblestones of the courtyard.

'Get off the other one and I'll have a look.'

'But supposing—'

He pushed her off and raised the lid before she could protest further. 'No, no vampire in here, either,' he said.

'Supposing one'd just reached out and grabbed you by the throat!'

'Om is my shield,' said Oats.

'Really? That's nice.'

'You may chortle—'

'I didn't chortle.'

'You can if you want to. But I'm sure we are doing the right thing. Did not Sonaton defeat the Beast of Batrigore in its very cave?'

'I don't know.'

'He did. And didn't the prophet Urdure vanquish the Dragon of Sluth on the Plain of Gidral after three days' fighting?'

'I don't know that we've got that much time—'

'And wasn't it true that the Sons of Exequial beat the hosts of Myrilom?'

'Yes?'

'You've *heard* of that?'

'No. Listen, we've stopped. I don't particularly want us to be found, do you? Not right now. And not by those guards. They didn't look like nice men at all.'

They exchanged a meaningful glance over the coffins, concerning a certain inevitability about the immediate future.

'They'll notice they're heavier, won't they?' said Oats.

'Those people driving the carts didn't look as though they notice anything very much.'

Agnes stared at the coffin beside her. There was some dirt in the bottom, but it was otherwise quite clean and had a pillow at the head end. There were also some side pockets in the lining.

'It's the easiest way in,' she said. 'You get into this one, I'll get into that one. And, look . . . those people you just told me about . . . Were they real historical characters?'

'Certainly. They—'

'Well, don't try to imitate them yet, all right? Otherwise you'll be a historical character too.'

She shut the lid, and *still* felt there was a vampire around.

Her hand touched the side pocket. There was something soft yet spiky there. Her fingers explored it in fascinated horror and discovered it to be a ball of wool with a couple of long knitting needles stuck through it, suggesting either a very domesticated form of voodoo or that someone was knitting a sock.

Who knitted socks in a coffin? On the other hand, perhaps even vampires couldn't sleep sometimes, and tossed and turned all day.

She braced herself as the coffin was picked up and tried to occupy her mind by working out where it was being taken. She heard the sound of footsteps on the cobbles, and then the ring of the flagstones on the main steps, echoing in the great hall, a sudden dip—

That meant the cellars. Logical, really, but not good.

You're doing this to impress me, said Perdita. *You're doing it to try to be extrovert and dynamic.*

Shut up, Agnes thought.

A voice outside said, 'Put them down there and puth off.'

That was the one who called himself Igor. Agnes wished she'd thought of a weapon.

'Get rid of me, would they?' the voice went on, against a background of disappearing footsteps. 'Thith ith all going to end in tearth. It'th all very well for them, but who hath to go and thweep up the dutht, eh? That'th what I'd like to know. Who'th it hath to pull their headth out of the pickle jarth? Who'th it hath to find them under the ithe? I mutht've pulled out more thtaketh than I've had wriggly dinnerth . . .'

Light flooded in as the coffin lid was removed.

Igor stared at Agnes. Agnes stared at Igor.

Igor unfroze first. He smiled – he had a geometrically interesting smile, because of the row of stitches right across it – and said, 'Dear me, thomeone'th been lithening to too many thtorieth. Got any garlic?'

'Masses,' Agnes lied.

'Won't work. Any holy water?'

'Gallons.'

'It—'

A coffin lid smacked down on Igor's head, making an oddly metallic sound. He reached up slowly to rub the spot, and then turned around. This time the lid smacked into his face.

'Oh . . . thit,' he said, and folded up. Oats appeared,

face aglow with adrenaline and righteousness.

'I smote him mightily!'

'Good, good, let's get out of here! Help me up!'

'My wrath descended upon him like—'

'It was a heavy lid and he's not that young,' said Agnes. 'Look, I used to play down here, I know how to get to the back stairs—'

'He's not a vampire? He looks like one. First time I've ever seen a patchwork man . . .'

'He's a servant. Now, please come—' Agnes paused. 'Can *you* make holy water?'

'What, here?'

'I mean bless it, or dedicate it to Om, or . . . boil the hell out of it, perhaps,' said Agnes.

'There is a small ceremony I can—' He stopped. 'That's right! Vampires can be stopped by holy water!'

'Good. We'll go via the kitchens, then.'

The huge kitchens were almost empty. They never bustled these days, since the royal couple were not the sort who demanded three meat courses with every meal, and at the moment there was only Mrs Scorbic the cook in there, calmly rolling out pastry.

'Afternoon, Mrs Scorbic,' said Agnes, deciding the best course was to march past and rely on the authority of the pointy hat. 'We've just dropped in for some water, don't worry, I know where the pump is, but if you've got a couple of empty bottles that would be helpful.'

'That's right, dear,' said Mrs Scorbic.

Agnes stopped and turned.

Mrs Scorbic was famously acerbic, especially on the subject of soya, nut cutlets, vegetarian meals and any vegetable that couldn't be boiled until it was yellow. Even the King hesitated to set foot in her kitchen but, whereas he only got an angry silence, lesser mortals got the full force of her generalized wrath. Mrs Scorbic was permanently angry, in the same way that mountains are permanently large.

Today she was wearing a white dress, a white apron, a big white mob cap and a white bandage around her throat. She also looked, for want of any better word, happy.

Agnes urgently waved Oats towards the pump. 'Find something to fill up,' she hissed, and then said brightly, 'How are you feeling, Mrs Scorbic?'

'All the better for you asking, miss.'

'I expect you're busy with all these visitors?'

'Yes, miss.'

Agnes coughed. 'And, er, what did you give them for breakfast?'

The cook's huge pink brow wrinkled. 'Can't remember, miss.'

'Well done.'

Oats nudged her. 'I've filled up a couple of empty bottles and I said the Purification Rite of Om over them.'

'And that will work?'

'You must have faith.'

The cook was watching them amiably.

'Thank you, Mrs Scorbic,' said Agnes. 'Please get on with . . . whatever you were doing.'

'Yes, miss.' The cook turned back to her rolling pin.

Plenty of meals on her, said Perdita. *Cook and larder all in one.*

'That was tasteless!' said Agnes.

'What was?' said the priest.

'Oh . . . just a thought I had. Let's go up the back stairs.'

They were bare stone, communicating with the public bits of the keep via a door at every level. On the other side of those doors it was still bare stone, but a better class of masonry altogether and with tapestries and carpets. Agnes pushed open a door.

A couple of the Uberwald people were ambling along the corridor beyond, carrying something covered in a cloth. They didn't spare the newcomers a glance as Agnes led the way to the royal apartments.

Magrat was standing on a chair when they came in. She looked down at them while little painted wooden stars and animals tangled themselves around her upraised arm.

'Wretched things,' she said. 'You'd think it would be easy, wouldn't you? Hello, Agnes. Could you hold the chair?'

'What are you doing?' said Agnes. She looked carefully. There was no bandage round Magrat's neck.

'Trying to hook this mobile on to the chandelier,' said Magrat. 'Uh . . . that's done it. But it tangles up all the time! Verence says it's very good for young children to see lots of bright colours and shapes. It speeds development, he says. But I can't find Millie anywhere.'

There's a castle full of vampires, and she's decorating the playroom, said Perdita. *What's wrong with this woodcut?*

Somehow, Agnes couldn't bring herself to blurt out

a warning. Apart from anything else, the chair looked wobbly.

'Little Esme's only two weeks old,' said Agnes. 'Isn't that a bit young for education?'

'Never too early to start, he says. What can I do for you?'

'We need you to come with us. Right now.'

'Why?' said Magrat, and to Agnes's relief she stepped down from the chair.

'Why? Magrat, there's *vampires* in the castle! The Magpyr family are *vampires*!'

'Don't be silly, they're very pleasant people. I was talking to the Countess only this morning—'

'What about?' Agnes demanded. 'I bet you can't remember!'

'I *am* Queen, Agnes,' said Magrat reproachfully.

'Sorry, but they affect people's minds—'

'Yours?'

'Um, no, not mine. I have— I'm— It seems I'm immune,' Agnes lied.

'And his?' said Magrat sharply.

'I am protected by my faith in Om,' said Oats.

Magrat raised her eyebrows at Agnes. 'Is he?'

Agnes shrugged. 'Apparently.'

Magrat leaned closer. 'He's not drunk, is he? He's holding two beer bottles.'

'They're full of holy water,' Agnes whispered.

'Verence said Omnianism seemed a very sensible and stable religion,' hissed Magrat.

They both looked at Oats, mentally trying the words on him for size.

'Are we leaving?' he said.

'Of course not!' snapped Magrat, straightening up. 'This is silly, Agnes. I'm a married woman, I'm Queen, I've got a little baby. And you come in here telling me we've got vampires! I've got guests here and—'

'The guests are *vampires*, your majesty,' said Agnes. 'The King invited them!'

'Verence says we have to learn to deal with all sorts of people—'

'We think Granny Weatherwax is in very bad trouble,' said Agnes.

Magrat stopped. 'How bad?' she said.

'Nanny Ogg is very worried. Quite snappish. She says it needs three of us to find Granny.'

'Well, I—'

'And Granny's taken the box, whatever that means,' said Agnes.

'The one she keeps in the dresser?'

'Yes. Nanny wouldn't tell me much about what was in it.'

Magrat opened up her hands like an angler measuring a medium-sized fish.

'The polished wooden box? About this size?'

'I don't know, I've never seen it. Nanny seemed to think it was important. She didn't say what was in it,' Agnes repeated, just in case Magrat hadn't got the hint.

Magrat clasped her hands together and looked down, biting her knuckles. When she looked up her face was set with purpose. She pointed at Oats.

'*You* find a bag or something and empty into it all the stuff in the top drawer over there, and take the potty, and the little truck, oh, and the stuffed animals, and the bag of nappies, and the bag for *used* nappies, and the bath, and the bag with the towels, and the box of toys, and the wind-up things, and the musical box, and the bag with the little suits, oh, and the woolly hat, and *you*, Agnes, find something we can make into a sling. You came up the back stairs? We'll go down the same way.'

'What do we need a sling for?'

Magrat leaned over the crib and picked up the baby, wrapped in a blanket.

'I'm not going to leave her here, am I?' she said.

There was a clatter from the direction of Mightily Oats. He already had both arms full, and a large stuffed rabbit in his teeth.

'Do we need all of that?' said Agnes.

'You never know,' said Magrat.

'Even the box of toys?'

'Verence thinks she might be an early developer,' said Magrat.

'She's a couple of weeks old!'

'Yes, but stimulus at an early age is vital to the development of the growing brain,' said Magrat, laying baby Esme on the table and shuffling her into a romper suit. 'Also, we have to get on top of her hand–eye co-ordination as soon as possible. It's no good just letting things slide. Oh, yes . . . If you can bring the little slide, too. And the yellow rubber duck. And the sponge in the shape of a teddy bear. And the teddy bear in the shape of a sponge.'

There was another crash from the mound around Oats.

'Why's the box so important?' said Agnes.

'Not *important* as such,' said Magrat. She looked over her shoulder. 'Oh, and put in that rag doll, will you? I'm sure she's focusing on it. Oh, blast . . . the red bag has got the medicines in it, thank you . . . What was it you asked me?'

'Granny's box,' Agnes hinted.

'Oh, it's . . . just important to her.'

'It's magical?'

'What? Oh, no. Not as far as I know. But everything in it belongs to her, you see. Not to the cottage,' said Magrat, picking up her daughter. 'Who's a good girl, then? You are!' She looked around. 'Have we forgotten anything?'

Oats spat out the rabbit. 'Possibly the ceiling,' he said.

'Then let's go.'

Magpies flocked around the castle tower. Most magpie rhymes peter out at around ten or twelve, but here were hundreds of birds, enough to satisfy any possible prediction. There are many rhymes about magpies, but none of them is very reliable because they are not the ones the magpies know themselves.

The Count sat in the darkness below, listening to their minds. Images flashed behind his eyes. This was the way to run a country, he reflected. Human minds were so hard to read, unless they were so close that you could *see* the words just hovering below actual vocalization. But the birds could get everywhere, see every worker in the fields and hunter in the forest. They were good listeners, too. Much better than bats or rats. Once again, tradition was overturned.

No sign of Granny, though. Some trick, perhaps. It didn't matter. Eventually she'd find *him*. She wouldn't hide for long. It wasn't in her nature. Weatherwaxes would always stand and fight, even when they knew they would be beaten. So predictable.

Several of the birds had seen a busy little figure trudging across the kingdom, leading a donkey laden with falconry gear. The Count had taken a look at Hodgesaargh, found a mind crammed end to end with hawks, and dismissed him. He and his silly birds would have to go eventually, of course, because he made the magpies nervous. He made a note to mention this to the guards.

'Ooaauooow!'

. . . but there was probably no combination of vowels that could do justice to the cry Nanny Ogg made on seeing a young baby. It included sounds known only to cats.

'Isn't she a little precious?' Nanny crooned. 'I've probably got a sweetie somewhere—'

'She's not on solids,' said Magrat.

'Still keeping you up at nights?'

'And days. But she's slept well today, thank goodness. Nanny, give her to Mr Oats and let's sort this out right away.'

The young priest took the baby nervously, holding it, as some men do, as if it would break or at least explode.

'There, there, there,' he said, vaguely.

'Now . . . what's this about Granny?' said Magrat.

They told her, interrupting one another at important points.

'The gnarly ground over towards the top of the forest?' said Magrat, when they were nearly finished.

'That's right,' said Nanny.

'What *is* gnarly ground?' said Agnes.

'There's a lot of magic in these mountains, right?' said Nanny. 'And everyone knows mountains get made when lumps of land bang together, right? Well, when the magic gets trapped you . . . sort of . . . get a bit of land where the space is . . . sort of . . . scrunched up, right? It'd be quite big if it could but it's like a bit of gnarly wood in an ol' tree. Or a used hanky . . . all folded up small but still big in a different way.'

'But I've been up there and it's just a bit of moorland!'

'You've got to know the right direction,' said Nanny. 'Damn hard to scry into a place like that. It goes all wobbly. It's like tryin' to look at something close up *and* a long way away at the same time. It makes your crystal ball water.'

She pulled the green ball towards her.

'Now, you two push an' I'll steer—'

'Er, are you going to do some magic?' said Oats, behind them.

'What's the problem?' said Nanny.

'I mean, does it involve, er . . .' he coloured up, 'er . . . removing your garments and dancing around and summoning lewd and salacious creatures? Only I'm afraid I couldn't be a party to that. The *Book of Om* forbids consorting with false enchanters and deceitful soothsayers, you see.'

'I wouldn't consort with false enchanters neither,' said Nanny. 'Their beards fall off.'

'We're real,' said Magrat.

'And we certainly don't summon lewd and salacious creatures,' said Agnes.

'Unless we want to,' said Nanny Ogg, almost under her breath.

'Well . . . all right, then,' said Oats.

As they unwound the power, Agnes heard Perdita think, *I don't like Magrat. She's not like she used to be.* Well, of course she's not. *But she's taking charge, she's not cringing slightly like she used to, she's not WET.* That's because she's a mother, Agnes thought. Mothers are only slightly damp.

She was not, herself, hugely in favour of motherhood in general. Obviously it was necessary, but it wasn't exactly *difficult*. Even cats managed it. But women acted as if they'd been given a medal that entitled them to boss people around. It was as if, just because they'd got the label which said 'mother', everyone else got a tiny part of the label that said 'child' . . .

She gave a mental shrug, and concentrated on the craft in hand.

Light grew and faded inside the green globe. Agnes had only scryed a few times before, but she didn't remember the light pulsing like this. Every time it dissolved into an image the light flickered and bounced to somewhere else . . . a patch of heather . . . a tree . . . boiling clouds . . .

And then Granny Weatherwax came and went. The image appeared and was gone in an instant, and the glow that rolled in with a finality told Agnes that this was all, folks.

'She was lying down,' said Magrat. 'It was all fuzzy.'

'Then she's in one of the caves. She said once she goes up there to be alone with her thoughts,' said Nanny. 'And did you catch that little twitch? She's trying to keep us out.'

'The caves up there are just scoops in the rock,' said Agnes.

'Yes . . . and no,' said Nanny. 'Did I see her holding a card in her hands?'

'The "I ate'nt dead" card?' said Magrat.

'No, she'd left that in the cottage.'

'Just when we really need her, she goes away into a cave?'

'Does she know we need her? Did she know about the vampires?' said Agnes.

'Can't we go and ask her?' said Magrat.

'We can't fly all the way,' said Nanny, scratching her chin. 'Can't fly prop'ly over gnarly ground. The broomsticks act funny.'

'Then we'll walk the rest,' said Magrat. 'It's hours to sunset.'

'You're not coming, are you?' said Agnes, aghast.

'Yes, of course.'

'But what about the baby?'

'She seems to like it in the sling and it keeps her warm and it's not as if there's monsters up there,' said Magrat. 'Anyway, *I* think it's possible to combine motherhood and a career.'

'I thought you'd given up witchcraft,' said Agnes.

'Yes . . . well . . . yes. Let's make sure Granny's all

right and get this sorted out, and then obviously I'll have other things to do . . .'

'But it could be dangerous!' said Agnes. 'Don't you think so, Nanny?'

Nanny Ogg turned her chair and looked at the baby.

'Cootchie-cootchie?' she said.

The small head looked around and Esme opened her blue eyes.

Nanny Ogg stared thoughtfully.

'Take her with us,' she said at last. 'I used to take our Jason everywhere when he was tiny. They like being with their mum.'

She gave the baby another long hard look.

'Yes,' she went on, 'I think that'd be a damn good idea.'

'Er . . . I feel perhaps there is little that I'd be able to do,' Oats said.

'Oh, it'd be too dangerous to take *you*,' said Nanny dismissively.

'But of course my prayers will go with you.'

'That's nice.' Nanny sniffed.

Drizzling rain soaked Hodgesaargh as he trudged back to the castle. The damp had got into the lure, and the noise it made now could only attract some strange, lost creature, skulking in ancient estuaries. Or possibly a sheep with a very sore throat.

And then he heard the chattering of magpies.

He tied the donkey to a sapling and stepped out into a clearing. The birds were screaming in the trees around him, but erupted away at the sight of King Henry on her perch on the donkey.

Crouched against a mossy rock was . . .

. . . a small magpie. It was bedraggled and *wrong*, as if put together by someone who had seen one but didn't know how it was supposed to work. It struggled when it saw him, there was a fluffing of feathers and, now, a smaller version of King Henry was trying to unfold its tattered wings.

He backed away. On her perch, the hooded eagle had its head turned to the strange bird . . .

. . . which was now a pigeon. A thrush. A wren . . .

A sudden intimation of doom made Hodgesaargh cover his eyes, but he saw the flash through the skin of his fingers, felt the *thump* of the flame, and smelled the scorched hairs on the back of his hand.

A few tufts of grass smouldered on the edge of a circle of scorched earth. Inside it a few pathetic bones glowed red hot and then crumbled into fine ash.

Away in the forest, the magpies screamed.

Count Magpyr stirred in the darkness of his room and opened his eyes. The pupils widened to take in more light.

'I think she has gone to ground,' he said.

'That was remarkably quick,' said the Countess. 'I thought you said she was quite powerful.'

'Oh, indeed. But human. And she's getting older. With age comes doubt. It's so simple. All alone in that barren cottage, no company but the candlelight . . . it's so simple to open up all the little cracks and let her mind turn in on itself. It's like watching a forest fire when the wind changes and suddenly it's roaring down on all the houses you thought were built so strongly.'

'So graphically put.'

'Thank you.'

'You were so successful in Escrow, I know . . .'

'A model for the future. Vampires and humans in harmony at last. There is no *need* for this animosity, just as I have always said.'

The Countess walked over to the window and gingerly pulled aside the curtain. Despite the overcast sky, grey light filtered in.

'There's no requirement to be so cautious about this, either,' said her husband, coming up behind her and jerking the curtain aside. The Countess shuddered and turned her face away.

'You see? Still harmless. Every day, in every way, we get better and better,' said Count Magpyr cheerfully. 'Self help. Positive thinking. Training. Familiarity. Garlic? A pleasant seasoning. Lemons? Merely an acquired taste. Why, yesterday I mislaid a sock and I simply don't care. I have lots of socks. Extra socks can be arranged!' His smile faded when he saw his wife's expression.

'The word "but" is on the tip of your tongue,' he said flatly.

'I was just going to say that there were no witches in Escrow.'

'And the place is all the better for it!'

'Of course, but—'

'There you go again, my dear. There is no room for "but" in our vocabulary. Verence was right, oddly enough. There's a new world coming, and there won't be any room in it for those ghastly little gnomes or witches or centaurs and especially not for the fire-birds! Away with them! Let us progress! They are unfitted for survival!'

'You only wounded that phoenix, though.'

'My point exactly. It allowed itself to be hurt, and therefore extinction looms. No, my dear, if we won't fade with the old world we must make shift in the new. Witches? I'm afraid witches are all in the past now.'

The broomsticks in the present landed just above the treeline, on the edge of the moor. As Agnes had said, it was barely big enough to deserve the term. She could even hear the little mountain brook at the far end.

'I can't see anything *gnarly*-looking,' said Agnes. She knew it was a stupid thing to say, but the presence of Magrat was getting on her nerves.

Nanny looked up at the sky. The other two followed her gaze.

'You've got to get your eye in, but you'll see it if you watch,' she said. 'You can only see it if you stands on the moor.'

Agnes squinted at the overcast.

'Oh . . . I think I can,' said Magrat.

I bet she doesn't, said Perdita, *I can't*.

And then Agnes did. It was tricky to spot, like a join between two sheets of glass, and it seemed to move away whenever she was certain she could see it, but there was an . . . *inconsistency*, flickering in and out on the edge of vision.

Nanny licked a finger and held it up to the wind. Then she pointed.

'This way. An' shut your eyes.'

'There's no path,' said Magrat.

'That's right. You hold on to my hand, Agnes will hold on to yours. I've been this way a few times. It ain't hard.'

'It's like a children's story,' said Agnes.

'Yes, we're down to the bone now, all right,' said Nanny. 'And . . . off we go . . .'

Agnes felt the heather brush her feet as she stepped forward. She opened her eyes.

Moorland stretched away on every side, even behind them. The air was darker, the clouds heavier, the wind sharper. The mountains looked a long way away. There was a distant thunder of water.

'Where are we now?' said Magrat.

'Still here,' said Nanny. 'I remember my dad saying sometimes a deer or somethin' would run into gnarly ground if it was bein' hunted.'

'It'd have to be pretty desperate,' said Agnes. The heather was darker here, and scratched so much it was almost thorny. 'Everything's so . . . nasty-looking.'

'Attitude plays a part,' said Nanny. She tapped something with her foot.

It was . . . well, it had been a standing stone, Agnes thought, but now it was a lying stone. Lichen grew thickly all over it.

'The marker. Hard to get out again if you don't know about it,' said Nanny. 'Let's head for the mountains. Esme all wrapped up, Magrat? Little Esme, I mean.'

'She's asleep.'

'Yeah,' said Nanny, in what Agnes thought was an odd tone of voice. 'Just as well, really. Let's go. Oh, I thought we might need these . . .'

She fumbled in the bottomless storeroom of her knickerleg and produced a couple of pairs of socks so thick that they could have stood up by themselves.

'Lancre wool,' she said. 'Our Jason knits 'em of an evenin' and you know what strong fingers he's got. You could kick your way through a wall.'

The heather ripped fruitlessly at the wire-like wool as the women hurried over the moor. There was still a sun here, or at least a bright spot in the overcast, but darkness seemed to come up from beneath the ground.

Agnes . . . said Perdita's voice, in the privacy of her shared brain.

What? thought Agnes.

Nanny's worried about something to do with the baby and Granny. Have you noticed?

Agnes thought: I know Nanny keeps looking at little Esme as if she's trying to make up her mind about something, if that's what you mean.

Well, I think it's to do with Borrowing . . .

She thinks Granny's using the baby to keep an eye on us?

I don't know. But something's happening . . .

The roar ahead grew louder.

'There's a little stream, isn't there?' said Agnes.

'That's right,' said Nanny. 'Just here.'

The moor fell away. They stared into the abyss, which

didn't stare back. It was huge. White water was just visible far below. Cold, damp air blew past their faces.

'That *can't* be right,' said Magrat. 'That's wider and deeper than Lancre Gorge!'

Agnes looked down into the mist. *It's a couple of feet deep*, Perdita told her. *I can see every pebble.*

'Perdita thinks it's a . . . well, an optical illusion,' Agnes said aloud.

'She could be right,' said Nanny. 'Gnarly ground, see? Bigger on the inside.'

Magrat picked up a rock and tossed it in. It bounced off the wall a few times, tumbling end over end, and then nothing was left but a stony echo. The river was too far down even to see the splash.

'It's very realistic, isn't it?' she said weakly.

'We could use the bridge,' said Nanny, pointing.

They regarded the bridge. It had a certain negative quality. That is to say, while it was possible at the limits of probability that if they tried to cross the chasm by walking out over thin air this might just work – because of sudden updraughts, or air molecules suddenly all having a crazy idea at the same time – trying to do the same thing via the bridge would clearly be laughable.

There was no mortar in it. The pillars had been piled up out of rocks laid like a drystone wall, and then a series of big flat stones dropped across the top. The result would have been called primitive even by people who were too primitive to have a word yet for 'primitive'. It creaked ominously in the wind. They could hear stone grind against stone.

'That's not right,' said Magrat. 'It wouldn't stand up to a gale.'

'It wouldn't stand up to a dead calm,' said Agnes. 'I don't think it's really real.'

'Ah, I can see where that'd make crossing it a bit tricky, then,' said Nanny.

It's just a slab laid over a ditch, Perdita insisted. *I could cartwheel over it.* Agnes blinked.

'Oh, I *understand*,' she said. 'This is some sort of test, is it? It is, isn't it? We're worried, so fear makes it a deep gorge. Perdita's always confident, so she hardly notices it . . .'

'*I'd* like to notice it's there,' said Magrat. 'It's a *bridge*.'

'We're wasting time,' said Agnes. She strode out over the slabs of stone and stopped halfway.

'Rocks a bit, but it's not too bad,' she called back. 'You just have to—'

The slab shifted under her, and tipped her off.

She flung out her hands and caught the edge of the stone by sheer luck. But, strong though her fingers were, a lot of Agnes was penduluming underneath.

She looked down. She didn't want to, but it was a direction occupying a lot of the world.

The water's about a foot below you, it really is, said Perdita. *All you have to do is drop, and you'd be good at that . . .*

Agnes looked down again. The drop was so long that probably no one would hear the splash. It didn't just look deep, it *felt* deep. Clammy air rose around her. She could feel the sucking emptiness under her feet.

'Magrat threw a stone down there!' she hissed.

Yes, and I saw it fall a few inches.

'Now, I'm lyin' flat and Magrat's holdin' on to my legs,' said Nanny Ogg conversationally, right above her. 'I'm going to grab your wrists and, you know, I reckon if you swings a little sideways you ought to get your foot on one of the stone pillars and you'll be right as ninepence.'

'You don't have to talk to me as if I'm some kind of frightened idiot!' snapped Agnes.

'Just tryin' to be pleasant.'

'I can't move my hands!'

'Yes, you can. See, I've got your arm now.'

'I can't move my hands!'

'Don't rush, we've got all day,' said Nanny. 'Whenever you're ready.'

Agnes hung for a while. She couldn't even *sense* her hands now. That presumably meant that she wouldn't feel it when her grip slipped.

The stones groaned.

'Er . . . Nanny?'

'Yep?'

'Can you talk to me a bit more as if I'm some kind of frightened idiot?'

'Okay.'

'Er . . . why do they say "right as ninepence"? As opposed to, say, tenpence?'

'Interestin'. Maybe it's—'

'And can you speak up? Perdita's shouting at me that if I drop eighteen inches I'll be standing in the stream!'

'Do you think she's right?'

'Not about the eighteen inches!'

The bridge creaked.

'People seldom are,' said Nanny. 'Are you getting anywhere, dear? Only I can't lift you up, you see. And my arms are going numb, too.'

'I can't reach the pillar!'

'Then let go,' said Magrat, from somewhere behind Nanny.

'Magrat!' snapped Nanny.

'Well, perhaps it *is* only a little stream to Perdita. Gnarly ground can be two things at the same time, can't it? So if that's how she sees it . . . well, can't you let her get on with it? Let *her* sort it out. Can't you let her take over?'

'She only does that when I'm really under stress! Shut up!'

'I only—'

'Not you, her! Oh, *no*—'

Her left hand, white and almost numb, pulled itself off the stone and out of Nanny's grip.

'Don't let her do this to us!' Agnes shrieked. 'I'll fall hundreds of feet on to sharp rocks!'

'Yes, but since you're going to do that anyway, anything's worth a try, isn't it?' said Nanny. 'I should shut your eyes, if I was you—'

The right hand came loose.

Agnes shut her eyes. She fell.

Perdita opened her eyes. She was standing in the stream.

'Damn!' And Agnes would never say 'damn', which was why Perdita did so at every suitable occasion.

She reached up to the slab just above her, got a grip, and hauled herself up. Then, catching sight of Nanny Ogg's expression, she jerked her hands around into a new position and kicked her legs up.

That stupid Agnes never realizes how strong she is, Perdita thought. There's all these muscles she's afraid of using . . .

She pushed gently until her toes pointed at the sky and she was doing a handstand on the edge. The effect, she felt, was spoilt by her skirt falling over her eyes.

'You've still got that tear in yer knickers,' said Nanny sharply.

Perdita flicked herself on to her feet.

Magrat had her eyes tight shut. 'She didn't do a handstand on the *edge*, did she?'

'She did,' said Nanny. 'Now then, A— Perdita, stop that showing off, we've wasted too much time. Let Agnes have the body back, you know it's hers really.'

Perdita did a cartwheel. 'This body's wasted on her,' she said. 'And you should see the stuff she eats! Do you know she's still got two shelves full of soft toys? And dolls? And she wonders why she can't get along with boys!'

'Nothing like being stared at by a teddybear to put a young man off his stroke,' said Nanny Ogg. 'Remember old Mrs Sleeves, Magrat? Used to need two of us when she had one of her nasty turns.'

'What's that got to do with toys?' said Perdita suspiciously.

'And what's it— Oh, yes,' said Magrat.

'Now, I recall that old bellringer down in Ohulan,' said Nanny, leading the way. 'He had no fewer than *seven* personalities in his head. Three of 'em were women and four of 'em were men. Poor old chap. He said he was always the odd one out. He said they let him get on with all the work and the breathin' and eatin' and they had all the fun. Remember? He said it was hellish when he had a drink and they all started fightin' for a tastebud. Sometimes he couldn't hear himself think in his own head, he said— *Now! Now! Now!*'

Agnes opened her eyes. Her jaw hurt.

Nanny Ogg was peering at her closely, while rubbing some feeling back into her wrist. From a couple of inches away her face looked like a friendly pile of elderly laundry.

'Yes, that's Agnes,' she said, standing back. 'Her face goes sharper when it's the other one. See? I told you she'd be the one that came back. She's got more practice.'

Magrat let go of her arms. Agnes rubbed her chin.

'That *hurt*,' she said reproachfully.

'Just a bit of tough love,' said Nanny. 'Can't have that Perdita running around at a time like this.'

'You just sort of *grabbed* the bridge and came right back up,' said Magrat.

'I felt her stand on the ground!' said Agnes.

'And that too, then,' said Nanny. 'Come on. Not far now. Sometimes. And let's just take it easy, shall we? Some of us might have further to fall than others.'

They edged forward, despite an increasingly insistent voice in Agnes's head that kept telling her she was being a stupid coward and *of course* she wouldn't be hurt. She tried to ignore it.

The caves that Agnes remembered hadn't been much more than rock overhangs. *These* were caverns.

The difference is basically one of rugged and poetic grandeur. These had a lot of both.

'Gnarly ground's a bit like icebergs,' said Nanny, leading them up a little gully to one of the largest.

'Nine-tenths of it is under water?' said Agnes. Her chin still hurt.

'There's more to it than meets the eye, I mean.'

'There's someone there!' said Magrat.

'Oh, that's the witch,' said Nanny. 'She's not a problem.'

Light from the entrance fell on a hunched figure, sitting among pools of water. Closer to, it looked like a statue, and perhaps not quite as human as the eye at first suggested. Water glistened on it; drops formed on the end of the long hooked nose and fell into a pool with the occasional *plink*.

'I come up here with a young wizard once, when I was a girl,' said Nanny. 'He liked nothing so much as bashing at rocks with his little hammer . . . well, almost nothing,' she added, with a smile towards the past and then a happy sigh. 'He said the witch was just a lot of ol' stuff from the rocks, left there by the water drippin'. But my granny said it was a witch that sat up here to think about some big spell, and she turned to stone. Person'ly, I keep an open mind.'

'It's a long way to bring someone,' said Agnes.

'Oh, there was a lot of us kids at home and it was rainin' a lot and you need a lot of privacy for really good geology,' said Nanny vaguely. 'I think his hammer's still around here somewhere. He quite forgot about it after a while. Mind how you tread, the rocks is very slippery. How's young Esme doing, Magrat?'

'Oh, gurgling away. I'll have to feed her soon.'

'We've got to look after her,' said Nanny.

'Well, yes. Of course.'

Nanny clapped her hands together and pulled them apart gently. The glow between them wasn't the showy light that wizards made, but a grainy graveyard glimmer. It was just enough to ensure that no one fell down a hole.

'Probably some dwarfs in a place like this,' said Magrat, as they picked their way along a tunnel.

'Shouldn't think so. They don't like places that don't stay the same. No one comes up here now but animals and Granny when she wants to be alone with her thoughts.'

'And you when you were banging rocks,' said Magrat.

'Hah! But it was different then. There was flowers on the moor and the bridge was just stepping stones. That's 'cos I was in love.'

'You mean it really does change because of the way you feel?' said Agnes.

'You spotted it. It's amazing how high and rocky the bridge can be if you're in a bad mood, I know that.'

'I wonder how high it was for Granny, then?'

'Probably clouds could go underneath, girl.'

Nanny stopped where the path forked, and then pointed.

'I reckon she's gone this way. Hold on—'

She thrust out an arm. Stone groaned, and a slab of roof thudded down, throwing up spray and pebbles.

'So we'll just have to climb over this bit, then,'

Nanny went on, in the same matter-of-fact tone of voice.

'Something's trying to push us out,' said Agnes.

'But it won't,' said Nanny. 'And I don't think it'll harm us.'

'That was a big slab!' said Agnes.

'Yeah. But it missed us, didn't it?'

There was an underground river further on, sheer white water blurred with speed. It poured around and almost over a dam of driftwood, topped by an inviting long log.

'Look, this isn't safe for the baby!' said Agnes. 'Do you both see that? You're her mother, Magrat!'

'Yes, I know, I was there,' said Magrat, with infuriating calm. 'But this doesn't *feel* unsafe. Granny's here somewhere.'

'That's right,' said Nanny. 'Really close now, I think.'

'Yes, but she can't control rivers and rocks—' Agnes began.

'Here? Dunno. Very . . . *responsive* place, this.'

They inched their way across the log, passing the baby from one to the other.

Agnes leaned against the stone wall. 'How much *further*?'

'Well, *technic'ly* a few inches,' said Nanny. 'That's helpful to know, isn't it?'

'Is it just me,' said Magrat, 'or is it getting warmer?'

'Now *that*,' said Agnes, pointing ahead, 'I don't believe.'

At the end of a slope a crevasse had opened in the rock. Red light spilled out. As they stared at it, a ball of flame rolled up and burst across the ceiling.

'Oh deary deary me,' said Nanny, who had taken a turn to carry the baby. 'An' it's not even as if there's any volcanoes anywhere near here. What *can* she be thinking?' She headed purposefully towards the fire.

'Careful!' Agnes shouted. 'Perdita says it's real!'

'What's that got to do with the price of fish?' said Nanny, and stepped into the fire.

The flames snapped out.

The other two stood in the chilly, damp gloom.

Magrat shuddered. 'Nanny, you are carrying the *baby*.'

'The harm you come to here is what you brings with you,' said Nanny. 'And it's Granny's thoughts that are shaping this place. But she wouldn't raise a hand to a child. Couldn't do it. Hasn't got it in her.'

'This place is reacting to what she's thinking?' said Agnes.

'I reckon so,' said Nanny, setting off again.

'I'd hate to be inside her head!'

'You nearly are,' said Nanny. 'Come on. We've passed the fire. I don't think there'll be anything else.'

They found her in a cavern. It had sand on the floor, smooth and unmarked by anything except one set of footprints. Her hat had been placed neatly beside her. Her head rested on a rolled-up sack. She held a card in stiff hands.

It read:

GOE AWAY.

'That's not very helpful,' said Magrat, and sat down with the baby across her lap. 'After all this, too.'

'Can't we wake her up?' said Agnes.

'That's dangerous,' said Nanny Ogg. 'Trying to

call her back when she ain't ready to come? Tricky.'

'Well, can we at least take her out of here?'

'She won't bend round corners but, hah, maybe we could use her as a bridge,' said Nanny. 'No, she came here for a reason . . .'

She pulled the sack out from under Granny's head, which did not move, and opened it.

'Wrinkly apple, bottle of water and a cheese sandwich you could bend horseshoes round,' she said. 'And her old box.'

She set it down on the floor between them.

'What *is* in there?' said Agnes.

'Oh, keepsakes. Memorororabililia, like I said. That sort of thing,' said Nanny. 'She always says it's full of things she's got no further use for.' She drummed her fingers on the box as if accompanying a thought on the piano, and then picked it up.

'Should you do that?' said Agnes.

'No,' said Nanny. She lifted out a bundle of papers tied with ribbon and put them on one side.

They all saw the light shining up from underneath. Nanny reached in and took out a small glass medicine bottle, tightly corked, and held it up. A little glow inside was quite bright in the gloom of the cave.

'Seen this bottle before,' said Nanny. 'She's got all kinds of odds and ends in here. Never noticed it glowing, though.'

Agnes took the bottle. Inside there was what looked like a piece of fern, or . . . no, it was a feather, quite black except for the very tip, which was as yellow and bright as a candle flame.

'Do you know what it is?'

'No. She's always pickin' up stuff. She's had the bottle a long time, 'cos I've seen it in there—'

'I faw her fick it uff—' Magrat removed a safetypin from her mouth. 'I saw her pick that thing up years ago,' she tried again. 'It was around this time of year, too. We were walking back through the woods and there was a shooting star and this sort of light fell off it and we went to look and there it was. It looked like a flame but she was able to pick it up.'

'Sounds like a firebird feather,' said Nanny. 'There used to be old stories about them. They pass through here. But if you touch their feathers you'd better be damn sure of yourself, because the old stories say they burn in the presence of evil—'

'Firebird? You mean a phoenix?' said Agnes. 'Hodgesaargh was going on about one.'

'Haven't seen one go over for years,' said Nanny. 'Sometimes you'd see two or three at a time when I was a girl, just lights flying high up in the sky.'

'No, no, the phoenix . . . there's only *one* of it, that's the whole point,' said Agnes.

'One of anything's no bloody use,' said Nanny.

Granny Weatherwax smacked her lips, like someone emerging from a very deep sleep. Her eyelids flickered.

'Ah, I knew opening her box'd work,' said Nanny happily.

Granny Weatherwax's eyes opened. She stared straight up for a moment, and then swivelled them towards Nanny Ogg.

'W't'r,' she mumbled. Agnes hastily passed her the

water bottle. She touched Granny's fingers, and they were as chilly as stone.

The old witch took a gulp.

'Oh. It's you three,' she whispered. 'Why did you come here?'

'You told us to,' said Agnes.

'No, I didn't!' Granny snapped. 'Wrote you a note, did I?'

'No, but the stuff—' Agnes stopped. 'Well, we thought you wanted us to.'

'Three witches?' said Granny. 'Well, no reason why not. The maiden, the mother and the—'

'Go carefully,' Nanny Ogg warned.

'—the other one,' said Granny. 'That's up to you, I'm sure. It's not something about which I would venture any sort of opinion. So I expect you've got some dancin' to be doing, and good day to you. I'll have my pillow back, thank you very much.'

'You know there's vampires in Lancre?' Nanny demanded.

'Yes. *They* got invited.'

'You know they're taking over?'

'Yes!'

'So why did you run away up here?' said Agnes.

The temperature of a deep cave should remain constant, but suddenly this one was a lot colder.

'I can go where I like,' said Granny.

'Yes, but you ought—' Agnes began. She wished she could bite the word back, but it was too late.

'Oh, *ought*, is it? Where does it say *ought*? I don't remember it saying *ought* anywhere. Anyone going to tell me where it says *ought*? There's lots of things that *ought*, I dare say. But they *ain't*.'

'You know a magpie stole your invite?' said Nanny. 'Shawn delivered it okay, but them thieving devils had it away and into a nest.'

She flourished the crumpled, smudged yet gold-laden invitation.

In the moment of silence Agnes fancied she could hear the stalactites grow.

'Yes, of course I did,' said Granny. 'Worked that out first thing.' But the moment had been just slightly too long, and just slightly too quiet.

'And you know Verence got an Omnian priest in to do the Naming of young Esme?'

Again . . . fractionally too long, infinitesimally too silent.

'You know I put my mind to business,' said Granny. She glanced at the baby sitting on Magrat's lap.

'Why's she got a pointy head?' she said.

'It's the little hood Nanny knitted for her,' said Magrat. 'It's meant to look like that. Would you like to hold her?'

'She looks comfortable where she is,' said Granny diffidently.

She didn't know the baby's name! Perdita whispered. *I told you! Nanny thinks Granny's been in the baby's mind, I can tell by the way she's been looking at her, but if she had she'd know the name and she doesn't, I swear. She wouldn't do anything that might hurt a child . . .*

Granny shook herself. 'Anyway, if there's a problem, well, you've got your three witches. It doesn't say anywhere that one of them *ought*,' she nodded at Agnes, 'to be Granny Weatherwax. You sort it out. I've been witching in these parts for altogether too long and it's time to . . . move on . . . do something else . . .'

'You're going to hide up here?' said Magrat.

'I'm not going to keep on repeating myself, my girl. People aren't going to tell me what I ought to do no more. I know what's ought and what's not. Your husband invited vampires into the country, did he? That's *modern* for you. Well, everyone else knows that a vampire don't have no power over you 'less you invite it in, and if it's a king as does the inviting, then they've got their teeth into the whole country. And I'm an ol' woman living in the woods and I've got to make it all better? When there's three of you? I've had a lifetime of *ought* from can to can't and now it's over, and I'll thank you for gettin' out of my cave. And that's an end of it.'

Nanny glanced at the other two and shrugged.

'Come on, then,' she said. 'If we get a wiggle on we can be back at the broomsticks before dark.'

'Is that *all*?' said Magrat.

'Things come to an end,' said Granny. 'I'm going to rest up here and then I'm on my way. Plenty of places to go.'

Now get her to tell you the truth, said Perdita. Agnes bit down. *Ought* had been bad enough.

'So we'll be getting along,' said Nanny. 'Come on.'

'But—'

'But me no buts,' said Nanny. 'As Granny would have said.'

'That's right!' said Granny, lying back.

As they filed back into the caves Agnes heard Perdita start counting.

Magrat patted her pockets. Nanny patted her knickerlegs.

Magrat said, 'Oh, I must have le—'

'Blow, I left my pipe back there,' said Nanny, so quickly that the sentence overtook the one in front.

Five seconds, said Perdita. 'I didn't see you take it out,' said Agnes.

Nanny gave her a piercing look. 'Really? Then I'd better go and leave it there, hadn't I? Was there something you'd left too, Magrat? Never mind, I'll be sure to look for it, whatever it was going to be.'

'Well!' said Magrat, as Nanny darted back.

'Granny was certainly not telling the truth,' said Agnes.

'Of course she wasn't, she never does,' said Magrat. 'She expects you to work it out for yourself.'

'But she's right about us being three witches.'

'Yes, but I never intended to come back to it, I've got other things to do. Oh, perhaps when Esme's older I thought, maybe, a bit of part-time aromatherapy or something, but not serious full-time witching. This power-of-three business is . . . well, it's very old-fashioned . . .'

And what have we got now? Perdita chimed in. *The knowing but technically inexperienced young woman, the harassed young mother and the silver-haired golden ager . . . doesn't exactly sound mythic, does it? But Magrat just bundled up her little baby as soon as she heard Granny was in trouble and she didn't even stop to worry about her husband . . .*

'Wait a moment . . . listen,' said Agnes.

'What for?'

'Just listen . . . the sound echoes in these caves . . .'

Nanny Ogg sat down on the sand and wriggled slightly to settle in firmly. She took out her pipe.

'So,' she said to the recumbent figure, 'apart from all that, how are you feeling?'

There was no reply.

'Saw Mrs Patternoster this morning,' Nanny went on chattily. 'Her from over in Slice. Just passed the time of day. Mrs Ivy is bearing up well, she says.'

She blew out a cloud of smoke.

'I put her right about a few things,' she said.

There was still silence from the shadowy figure.

'The Naming went off all right. The priest's as wet as a snow omelette, though.'

'I can't beat 'em, Gytha,' said Granny. 'I can't beat 'em, and that's a fact.'

One of Nanny Ogg's hidden talents was knowing when to say nothing. It left a hole in the conversation that the other person felt obliged to fill.

'They've got minds like steel. I can't touch 'em. I've been tryin' everything. Every trick I've got! They've been searching for me but they can't focus right when I'm in here. The best one nearly got to me at the cottage. My *cottage*!'

Nanny Ogg understood the horror. A witch's cottage was her fortress.

'I've never felt anything like it, Gytha. He's had hundreds of years to get good. You noticed the magpies? He's using 'em as eyes. And he's clever, too. He's not going to fall to a garlic sandwich, that one. I can pick up that much. These vampires has *learned.* That's what they've never done before. I can't find a way into 'em *anywhere.* They're more powerful, stronger, they think quick . . . I tell you, going mind to mind with him's like spittin' at a thunderstorm.'

'So what're you going to do?'

'Nothing! There's nothing I can do! Can't you understand what I've been tellin' you? Don't you know I've been lying here all day tryin' to think of something? They know all about magic, Borrowing's second nature to them, they're fast, they think we're like cattle that can talk . . . I never expected anything like this, Gytha. I've thought about it round and round and there's not a thing I can see to do.'

'There's always a way,' said Nanny.

'I can't see it,' said Granny. 'This is it, Gytha. I might as well lie here until the water drips on me and I go into stone like the ol' witch at the door.'

'You'll find a way,' said Nanny. 'Weatherwaxes don't let 'emselves get beaten. It's something in the blood, like I've always said.'

'I am beaten, Gytha. Even before I start. Maybe someone else has a way, but I haven't. I'm up against a mind that's better'n mine. I just about keep it away from me but I can't get in. I can't fight *back.*'

The chilly feeling crept over Nanny Ogg that Granny Weatherwax meant it.

'I never thought I'd hear you say that,' she muttered.

'Off you go. No sense in keepin' the baby out in the cold.'

'And what are *you* going to do?'

'Maybe I shall move on. Maybe I'll just stop here.'

'Can't stop here for ever, Esme.'

'Ask her that is by the door.'

That seemed to be all there was going to be. Nanny walked out, found the others looking slightly too innocent in the next cave, and led the way to the open air.

'Found your pipe, then,' said Magrat.

'Yes, thank you.'

'What's she going to do?' said Agnes.

'You tell me,' said Nanny. 'I knows you was listenin'. You wouldn't be witches if you wasn't listenin' somehow.'

'Well, what can we do that she can't? If *she's* beaten, then so are we, aren't we?'

'What did Granny mean, "from can to can't"?' said Magrat.

'Oh, from the first moment in the morning when you can see to the last moment in the evenin' when you can't,' said Nanny.

'She's really feeling low, isn't she?'

Nanny paused by the stone witch. Her pipe had gone out. She struck a match on the hooked nose.

'There's three of us,' she said. 'The right number. So we'll start by having a proper coven meetin' . . .'

'Aren't you *worried*?' said Agnes. 'She's . . . giving up . . .'

'Then it's up to us to carry on, isn't it?' said Nanny.

Nanny had placed the cauldron in the middle of the floor for the look of the thing, although an indoor coven meeting didn't feel right, and one without Granny Weatherwax felt worse.

Perdita said it made them look like soppy girls playing at it. The only fire in the room was in the huge black iron range, the very latest model, recently installed for Nanny by her loving sons. On it, the kettle began to boil.

'I'll make the tea, shall I?' said Magrat, getting up.

'No, you sit down. It's Agnes's job to make the tea,' said Nanny. 'You're the mother, so it's your job to pour.'

'What's your job, Nanny?' said Agnes.

'I drinks it,' said Nanny promptly. 'Right. We've got to find out more while they're still actin' friendly. Agnes, you go back to the castle with Magrat and the baby. She needs extra help anyway.'

'What good will that do?'

'You told me yourself,' said Nanny. 'Vampires don't affect you. As soon as they try to see Agnes's mind it sinks down and up pops Perdita like a seesaw. Just when they're looking at Perdita, here comes Agnes again. Young Vlad's definitely got his eye on you, ain't he?'

'Certainly not!'

'Yeah, right,' said Nanny. 'Men always like women that've got a bit of mystery to 'em. They like a challenge, see? And while he's got his eye on you keeping your eye on Magrat, you've got your other eye on him, understand? Everyone's got a weakness. Maybe we'll not see the back of these vampires by going over to the curtains and saying, "My, isn't it stuffy in here?" but there's got to be some other way.'

'And if there isn't?'

'Marry him,' said Nanny firmly. Magrat gasped. The teapot rattled in her hand.

'That's horrible!' she said.

'I'd rather kill myself,' said Agnes. *In the morning*, said Perdita.

'Dun't have to be a long marriage,' said Nanny. 'Put a pointy stake in your garter and our lad'll be getting cold even before they've finished cutting up the wedding cake.'

'Nanny!'

'Or maybe you could just sort of . . . make him change his ways a bit,' Nanny went on. 'It's amazing what a wife can do if she knows her own mind, or minds in your case, course. Look at King Verence the First, for one. He used to toss all his meat bones over his shoulder until he was married and the Queen made him leave them on the side of the plate. I'd only bin married to the first Mr Ogg for a month before he was getting out of the bath if he needed to pee. You can refine a husband. Maybe you could point him in the direction of blutwurst and black puddings and underdone steak.'

'You really *haven't* got any scruples, have you, Nanny?' said Agnes.

'No,' said Nanny simply. 'This is Lancre we're talkin' about. If we was men, we'd be talking about layin' down our lives for the country. As women, we can talk about laying down.'

'I just don't want to hear this,' said Magrat.

'I ain't asking her to do what I wouldn't do,' said Nanny.

'Really? Then why—'

'Because no one wants me to do it,' said Nanny. 'But if I was fifty years younger I reckon I could have Sonny Jim bitin' turnips by midsummer.'

'You mean just because she's a woman she should use sexual wiles on him?' said Magrat. 'This is so . . . so . . . well, it's so Nanny Ogg, that's all I can say.'

'She should use any wile she can lay her hands on,' said Nanny. 'I don't care what Granny said, there's always a way. Like the hero in Tsort or wherever it was, who was completely invincible except for his heel and someone stuck a spear in it and killed him . . .'

'What are you expecting her to do, prod him all over?'

'I never understood that story, anyway,' said Nanny. 'I mean, if *I* knew I'd got a heel that would kill me if someone stuck a spear in it, I'd go into battle wearing very heavy boots—'

'You don't know what he's like,' said Agnes, ignoring the diversion. 'He looks at me as if he's undressing me with his eyes.'

'Eyes is allowed,' said Nanny.

'And he's *laughing* at me all the time! As if he knows I don't like him and that adds to the fun!'

'Now you get into that castle!' Nanny growled. 'For Lancre! For the King! For everyone in the country! And if he gets too much, let Perdita take over, 'cos I reckon there's some things she's better at!'

In the shocked silence there was a faint clinking noise from Nanny's sideboard.

Magrat coughed. 'J-just like the old days,' she said. 'Arguing all the time.'

Nanny stood up and unhooked a cast-iron saucepan from the beam over the kitchen range.

'You can't treat people like this,' said Agnes sullenly.

'I can,' said Nanny, tiptoeing in the direction of the sideboard. 'I'm the other one now, see?'

Ornaments flew and shattered as she brought the saucepan down hard, bottom upwards.

'Got you, you little blue devil!' she shouted. 'Don't think I didn't see you!'

The saucepan rose. Nanny leaned her weight on the handle but it still moved slowly along the dresser, rocking slightly from side to side, until it reached the edge.

Something red and blue dropped on to the floor and started moving towards the closed door.

At the same time Greebo shot past Agnes, accelerating. And then, just as he was about to spring, he changed his mind. All four feet extended their claws at the same time and bit into the floorboards. He rolled, sprang on to his feet, and started to wash himself.

The red and blue blur hit the door and picked itself up, becoming a blue man, six inches tall, with red hair. He carried a sword about the same size as himself.

'Ach, hins tak yer scaggie, yer dank yowl callyake!' he screamed.

'Oh, it's *you*,' said Nanny, relaxing. 'Do you want a drink?'

The sword was lowered slightly, but with a definite hint that it could be raised again at a moment's notice.

''tazit?'

Nanny reached down to the crate by her chair and sorted through the bottles.

'Scumble? My best. Vintage,' she said.

The wee man's tiny eyes lit up. 'Las' *Tuesda*?'

'Right. Agnes, open that sewing box and pass me a thimble, will you? Come away here, man,' said Nanny, uncorking the bottle well away from the fire and filling up the thimble. 'Ladies, this here's . . . let's see them tattoos . . . yeah, this here's one of the Nac mac Feegle. The little bastards comes down and raids my still about once a year. I reckon I recognize the pattern.'

'Yings, yow graley yin! Suz ae rikt dheu,' said the blue man, taking the thimble.

'What *is* he?' said Magrat.

'They're gnomes,' said Nanny.

The man lowered the thimble. 'Pictsies!'

'Pixies, if you insist,' said Nanny. 'They live up on the high moors over towards Uberwald—'

'Ach! Bae, yon snae rikt speel, y'ol behennit! Feggers! Yon ken sweal boggin bludsuckers owl dhu tae—'

Nanny nodded while she listened. Halfway through the little man's rant she topped up his thimble.

'Ah, right,' she said, when he seemed to have finished. 'Well, he says the Nac mac Feegle have been forced out by the vampires, see? They've been driving out all the . . .' her lips moved as she tried out various translations '. . . old people . . .'

'That's very cruel!' said Magrat.

'No . . . I mean . . . old races. The people that live in

... the corners. You know, the ones you don't see around a lot . . . centaurs, bogeys, gnomes—'

'Pictsies!'

'Yeah, right . . . driving 'em out of the country.'

'Why should they do that?'

'Probably not fashionable any more,' said Nanny.

Agnes looked hard at the pixie. On a scale of ethereal from one to ten he looked as if he was on some other scale, probably one buried in deep ocean sludge. The blueness of his skin, she could see now, was made up of tattoos and paint. His red hair stuck out at all angles. His sole concession to the temperature was a leather loincloth. He saw her looking at him.

'Yist, awa' fra' yeeks, ye stawking gowt that'ya! Bigjobs!'

'Er, sorry,' said Agnes.

'Good language, ain't it?' said Nanny. 'A hint o' heather and midden. But when you've got the Nac mac Feegle on your side you're doing okay.'

The pixie waved the empty thimble at Nanny.

'Ghail o' bludy "lemonade", callyake!'

'Ah, no foolin' you, *you* want the *real* stuff,' said Nanny. She pulled back a chair cushion, and produced a black glass bottle with its cork held on by wire.

'You're not giving him *that*, are you?' said Magrat. 'That's your medicinal whisky!'

'And you always tell people it's strictly for external use only,' said Agnes.

'Ah, the Nac mac Feegle are a hard-headed race,' said Nanny, handing it down to the tiny man. To Agnes's amazement, he grasped a bottle bigger than himself with insolent ease. 'There you go, man. Share it with your mates, 'cos I know they're around here somewhere.'

There was a clink from the dresser. The witches looked up. Hundreds of pixies had simply appeared among the ornaments. Most of them wore pointed hats that curved so that the point was practically pointing down, and they all carried swords.

'Amazin' how they can just fade into the foreground like that,' said Nanny. 'That's what's kept 'em so safe all these years. That and killin' most people who saw 'em, of course.'

Greebo, very quietly, went and sat under her chair.

'So . . . you gentlemen have been turned out by the vampires, have ye?' said Nanny, as the bottle bobbed through the throng. A roar went up.

'Blaznet!'

'Ach, yon weezit fash' deveel!'

'Arnoch, a hard tickut!'

'Bigjobs!'

'I daresay you can stop in Lancre,' said Nanny, above the din.

'Just a moment, Nanny—' Magrat began.

Nanny waved a hand at her hurriedly. 'There's that island up on the lake,' she went on, raising her voice. 'It's where the herons nest. Just the place, eh? Lots of fish, lots of hunting up the valley.'

The blue pixies went into a huddle. Then one of them looked up.

'Priznae? Yowl's nae brennit, moy ghail!'

'Oh, you'd be left to yourself,' said Nanny. 'But no stealing cattle, eh?'

'*These* steal *cattle*?' said Agnes. 'Full-size cattle? How many of them does it take?'

'Four.'

'Four?'

'One under each foot. Seen 'em do it. You see a cow in a field, mindin' its own business, next minute the grass is rustlin', some little bugger shouts, "Hup, hup, hup," and the poor beast goes past voom! without its legs movin",' said Nanny. 'They're stronger'n cockroaches. You step on a pixie, you'd better be wearing good thick soles.'

'Nanny, you can't give them the island! It doesn't belong to you!' said Magrat.

'It doesn't belong to anyone,' said Nanny.

'It belongs to the King!'

'Ah. Well, what's his is yours, so give 'em the island and Verence can sign a bit o' paper later on. It's worth it,' Nanny added. 'A rent of not stealing our cows is well worth it. Otherwise you'll see cows zippin' around very fast. Backwards, sometimes.'

'Without their legs moving?' said Agnes.

'Right!'

'Well—' Magrat began.

'And they'll be useful,' Nanny added, lowering her voice. 'Fighting's what they like best.'

'Whist, yon fellaight fra' aquesbore!'

'Drinkin's what they like best,' Nanny corrected herself.

'Nae, hoon a scullen!'

'Drinkin' *and* fightin's what they like best,' said Nanny.

'An' snaflin' coobeastie.'

'And stealing cows,' said Nanny. 'Drinkin', fightin' and stealin' cows is what they like best. Listen, Magrat, I'd rather have 'em in here pissin' out than outside pissin' in. There's more of them and they'll make your ankles all wet.'

'But what can they *do*?' said Magrat.

'Well . . . Greebo's frightened of 'em,' said Nanny.

Greebo was two worried eyes, one yellow, one pearly white, in the shadows. The witches were impressed. Greebo had once brought down an elk. There was practically nothing that he wouldn't attack, including architecture.

'I'd have thought they'd have no trouble with vampires, then,' said Agnes.

'Ach, c'na flitty-flitty! Ye think we're flowers o' the forest fairies?' sneered a blue man.

'They can't fly,' said Nanny.

'It's quite a nice island, even so . . .' Magrat mumbled.

'Gel, your husband was messin' around with politics, which is why we're in this trouble, and to get you've got to give. Now he's ill and you're Queen so you can do as you like, right? There's no one who can tell you what to do, isn't that so?'

'Yes, I suppos—'

'So damn well give 'em the island and then they've got somethin' here to fight for. Otherwise they'll just push on through anyway *and* nick all our livestock on the way. Dress that up in fancy talk, and you've got politics.'

'Nanny?' said Agnes.

'Yup?'

'Don't get angry, but you don't think Granny's doing this on purpose, do you? Keeping back, I mean, so that we have to form a three and work together?'

'Why'd she do that?'

'So we develop insights and pull together and learn valuable lessons,' said Magrat.

Nanny paused with her pipe halfway to her lips. 'No,' she said, 'I don't reckon Granny'd be thinking like that, because that's soppy garbage. Here, you blokes . . . here's the key to the drinks cupboard in the scullery. Bugger off and have fun, don't touch the stuff in the green bottles because it's— Oh, I expect you'll be all right.'

There was a blue blur, and the room was cleared.

'We got things Granny ain't got,' said Nanny.

'Yes?' said Agnes.

'Magrat's got a baby. I've got no scruples. And we've both got you.'

'What good will I be?'

'Well, for one thing . . . you're in two minds about everything—'

There was a tinkle of glass from the scullery, and a scream of '*Ach, ya skivens! Yez lukin' at a faceful o' heid!*'

'*Crives! Sezu? Helweit! Summun hol' me cote! Gude! Now, summun hol' his arms!*'

'*Stitch this, f'ra ma brinnit goggel!*' Some more glass broke.

'We'll all go back into the castle,' said Nanny. 'On our terms. Face this count down. And we'll take garlic and lemons and all the other stuff. And some of Mr

Oats's holy water. You can't tell me all that stuff together won't work.'

'And they'll let us in, will they?' said Agnes.

'They'll have a lot to think about,' said Nanny. 'What with a mob at the gates. We can nip in round the back.'

'What mob?' said Magrat.

'We'll organize one,' said Nanny.

'You don't *organize* a mob, Nanny,' said Agnes. 'A mob is something that happens spontaneously.'

Nanny Ogg's eyes gleamed.

'There's seventy-nine Oggs in these parts,' she said. 'Spontaneous it is, then.'

Her gaze fell for a moment on the forest of familial pictures, and then she removed a boot and hammered on the wall beside her. After a few seconds they heard a door bang and footsteps pass in front of the window.

Jason Ogg, blacksmith and head male of the Ogg clan, poked his head around the front door.

'Yes, Mum?'

'There's going to be a spontaneous mob stormin' the castle in, oh, half an hour,' said Nanny. 'Put the word out.'

'Yes, Mum.'

'Tell everyone I said it ain't compuls'ry for them to be there, of course,' Nanny added. Jason glanced at the hierarchy of Oggs. Nanny didn't have to add anything more to that sentence. Everyone knew the cat's box sometimes needed lining.

'Yes, Mum. I'll tell 'em you said they didn't have to come if they don't want to.'

'Good boy.'

'Is it flaming torches or, you know, scythes and stuff?'

'That's always tricky,' said Nanny. 'But I'd say both.'

'Battering ram, Mum?'

'Er . . . no, I don't think so.'

'Good! It is my door, after all,' said Magrat.

'Anythin' special for people to yell, Mum?'

'Oh, general yellin', I think.'

'Anything to throw?'

'Just rocks on this occasion,' said Nanny.

'Not large ones!' said Magrat. 'Some of the stonework around the main gate is quite fragile.'

'Okay, nothin' harder than sandstone, understand? And tell our Kev to roll out a barrel of my Number Three beer,' said Nanny. 'Better pour a bottle of brandy in it to keep out the chill. It can really strike right through your coat when you're hanging around outside a castle chantin' and wavin'. And get our Nev to run up to Poorchick's and say Mrs Ogg presents her compliments and we want half a dozen big cheeses and ten dozen eggs, and tell Mrs Carter will she be so good as to let us have a big jar of those pickled onions she does so well. It's a shame that we've not time to roast something, but I suppose you have to put up with that sort of inconvenience when you're being spontaneous.' Nanny Ogg winked at Agnes.

'Yes, Mum.'

'Nanny?' said Magrat, when Jason had hurried away.

'Yes, dear?'

'A couple of months ago, when Verence suggested

that tax on liquor exports, there was a big crowd protesting in the courtyard and he said, "Oh, well, if that's the will of the people . . ."'

'Well, it was the will of the people,' said Nanny.

'Oh. Right. Good.'

'Only sometimes they temp'ry forget what their will is,' said Nanny. 'Now, you can leave young Esme next door with Jason's wife . . .'

'I'm keeping her with me,' said Magrat. 'She's happy enough on my back.'

'You can't do that!' said Agnes.

'Don't you dare argue with me, Agnes Nitt,' said Magrat, drawing herself up. 'And not a word out of you, Nanny.'

'Wouldn't dream of it,' said Nanny. 'The Nac mac Feegle always take their babies into battle, too. Mind you, for use as a weapon if it comes to it.'

Magrat relaxed a little. 'She said her first word this morning,' she said, looking proud.

'What, at fourteen days?' said Nanny doubtfully.

'Yes. It was "blup".'

'Blup?'

'Yes. It was . . . more of a bubble than a word, I suppose.'

'Let's get the stuff together,' said Nanny, standing up. 'We're a coven, ladies. We're a trio. I miss Granny as much as you do, but we've got to deal with things as she would.' She took a few deep breaths. 'I can't be having with this.'

'It sounds better the way she says it,' said Agnes.

'I know.'

* * *

Hodgesaargh ate his meal in the servants' dining room off the kitchen, and ate alone. There were new people around, but Hodgesaargh generally didn't pay much attention to non-falconers. There were always other people in the castle, and they had jobs to do, and if pressed Hodgesaargh would vaguely acknowledge the fact that if he left his laundry in a sack by the kitchen door every week it'd be washed and dried two days later. There were his meals. The game he left on the cold slab in the long pantry got dealt with. And so on.

He was returning to the mews when one of the shadows pulled him into the darkness, with a hand clamped over his mouth.

'Mph?'

'It's me. Mrs Ogg,' said Nanny. 'You all right, Hodgesaargh?'

'Mph,' and by this Hodgesaargh contrived to indicate that he was fine except for someone's thumb blocking his breathing.

'Where are the vampires?'

'Mph?'

Nanny released her grip.

'Vampires?' the falconer panted. 'They the ones that walk around slowly?'

'No, that's the . . . food,' said Nanny. 'Any swish-looking buggers about as well? Any soldiers?'

There was a soft thud from somewhere in the shadows, and someone said, 'Blast, I've dropped the nappy bag. Did you see where it rolled?'

'Er, there's some new ladies and gentlemen,' said Hodgesaargh. 'They're hanging around the kitchens. There's some men in chainmail, too.'

'Damn!' said Nanny.

'There's the little door off the main hall,' said Magrat. 'But that's always locked on the inside.'

Agnes swallowed. 'All right. I'll go in and unlock it, then.'

Nanny tapped her on the shoulder. 'You'll be all right?'

'Well, they can't control me . . .'

'They can grab you, though.'

Vlad won't want you hurt, said Perdita. *You saw the way he looked at us . . .*

'I . . . think I'll be all right,' said Agnes.

'You know your own minds best, I'm sure,' said Nanny. 'Got the holy water?'

'Let's hope it works better than the garlic,' said Agnes.

'Good luck.' Nanny cocked her head. 'Sounds like the mob is spontaneously arriving at the gate. Go!'

Agnes ran off into the rain, around the castle to the doors of the kitchen. They were wide open. She made it to the corridor beyond the kitchens when a hand grabbed her shoulder, and then in a blur of speed two young men were standing in front of her.

They were dressed something like the young opera-goers she'd seen in Ankh-Morpork, except that their fancy waistcoats would have been considered far too fast by the staider members of the community, and they wore their hair long like a poet who hopes that romantically flowing locks will make up for a wretched inability to find a rhyme for 'daffodil'.

'Why are you in such a hurry, girl?' one said.

Agnes sagged. 'Look,' she said, 'I'm very busy. Can

we speed this up? Can we dispense with all the leers and "I like a girl with spirit" stuff? Can we get right to the bit where I twist out of your grip and kick you in the—'

One of them struck her hard across the face.

'No,' he said.

'I'll tell Vlad of you!' Perdita screamed in Agnes's voice.

The other vampire hesitated.

'Hah! Yes, he *knows* me!' said Agnes and Perdita together. 'Hah!'

One of the vampires looked her up and down.

'What, *you*?' he said.

'Yes, her,' said a voice.

Vlad strolled towards them, thumbs hooked into the pockets of his waistcoat.

'Demone? Crimson? To me, please?'

The two went and stood meekly in front of him. There was a blur, and then his thumbs were back in his waistcoat and the two vampires were in mid-crumple and sinking to the floor.

'This is the kind of thing we *don't* do to our guests,' said Vlad, stepping over Demone's twitching body and holding out his hands to Agnes. 'Did they hurt you? Say the word and I'll turn them over to Lacrimosa. She's just discovered you have a torture chamber here. And to think we thought Lancre was backward!'

'Oh, that old thing,' said Agnes weakly. Crimson was making bubbling noises. *I didn't even see his hands move*, said Perdita. 'Er . . . it's been there for centuries . . .'

'Oh, really? She did say there weren't enough straps and buckles. Still, she is . . . inventive. Just say the word.'

Say the word, Perdita prompted. *That'd be two less of them.*

'Er . . . no,' said Agnes. *Ah . . . moral cowardice from the fat girl.* 'Er . . . who are they?'

'Oh, we brought some of the clan in on the carts. They can make themselves useful, Father said.'

'Oh? They're relatives?' *Granny Weatherwax would've said yes,* Perdita whispered.

Vlad coughed gently. 'By blood,' he said. 'Yes. In a way. But . . . subservient. Do come this way.'

He gently took her arm and led her back up the passage, treading heavily on Crimson's twitching hand as he did so.

'You mean vampirism is like . . . pyramid selling?' said Agnes. She was alone with Vlad. Admittedly this had the edge over being alone with the other two, but somehow at a time like this it seemed vital to hear the sound of her own voice, if only to remind herself that she was alive.

'I'm sorry?' said Vlad. 'Who sells pyramids?'

'No, I mean . . . you bite five necks, and in two months' time you get a lake of blood of your very own?'

He smiled, but a little cautiously. 'I can see we will have a lot to learn,' he said. 'I understood every word in that sentence, but not the sentence itself. I'm sure there is a lot you could teach me. And, indeed, I could teach you . . .'

'No,' said Agnes, flatly.

'But when we— Oh, what is that *moron* doing now?'

A cloud of dust was advancing from the direction of the kitchens. In the middle of it, holding a bucket and a shovel, was Igor.

'Igor!'

'Yeth, marthter?'

'You're putting down dust again, aren't you?'

'Yeth, marthter.'

'And why are you putting down dust, Igor?' said Vlad icily.

'You've *got* to have dutht, marthter. It'th *tradi—*'

'Igor, Mother *told* you. We don't *want* dust. We don't *want* huge candlesticks. We don't *want* eyeholes cut in all the pictures, and we certainly don't want your wretched box of damn spiders and your *stupid* little whip!'

In the ringing, red-hot silence Igor looked down at his feet.

'... thpiderth webth ith what people ecthpect, marthter ...' he mumbled.

'We don't want them!'

'... the old Count *liked* my thpiderth ...' said Igor, his voice like some little insect that would nevertheless not be squashed.

'It's *ridiculous*, Igor.'

'... he uthed to thay, "Good webth today, Igor ..."'

'Look, just ... just *go away*, will you? See if you can't sort out that dreadful smell from the garderobe. Mother says it makes her eyes water. And stand up straight and walk properly!' Vlad called after him. 'No one's impressed by the limp!'

Agnes saw Igor's retreating back pause for a moment, and she expected him to say something. But then he continued his wobbly walk.

'He's such a big baby,' said Vlad, shaking his head. 'I'm sorry you had to see that.'

'Yes, I think I'm sorry too,' said Agnes.

'He's going to be replaced. Father's only been keeping him on out of sentiment. I'm afraid he came with the old castle, along with the creaking roof and the strange smell halfway up the main stairs which, I have to say, is not as bad as the one we've noticed here. Oh dear . . . look at this, will you? We turn our back for five minutes . . .'

There was a huge and very dribbly candle burning in a tall black candlestick.

'King Verence had all those oil lamps put in, a lovely modern light, and Igor's been going around replacing them with candles again! We don't even know where he gets them from. Lacci thinks he saves his earwax . . .'

They were in the long room beside the great hall now. Vlad lifted the candlestick up so that the flame's glow lit the wall.

'Ah, they've put the pictures up. You ought to get to know the family . . .'

The light fell on a portrait of a tall, thin, grey-haired man in evening dress and a red-lined cloak. He looked quite distinguished in a distant, aloof sort of way. There was the glimmer of a lengthened canine on his lower lip.

'My great-uncle,' said Vlad. 'The last . . . incumbent.'

'What's the sash and star he's wearing?' said Agnes. She could hear the sounds of the mob, far off but growing louder.

'The Order of Gvot. He built our family home. Don'tgonearthe Castle, we call it. I don't know whether you've heard of it?'

'It's a strange name.'

'Oh, he used to laugh about it. The local coachmen used to warn visitors, you see. "Don't go near the castle," they'd say. "Even if it means spending a night up a tree, never go up there to the castle," they'd tell people. "Whatever you do, don't set foot in that castle." He said it was marvellous publicity. Sometimes he had every bedroom full by 9 p.m. and people would be hammering on the door to get in. Travellers would go miles out of their way to see what all the fuss was about. We won't see his like again, with any luck. He did rather play to the crowd, I'm afraid. Rose from the grave so often that he had a coffin with a revolving lid. Ah . . . Aunt Carmilla . . .'

Agnes stared at a very severe woman in a figure-hugging black dress and deep-plum lipstick.

'She was said to bathe in the blood of up to two hundred virgins at a time,' Vlad said. 'I don't believe that. Use more than eighty virgins and even quite a large bath will overflow, Lacrimosa tells me.'

'These little details are important,' said Agnes, buoyed up by the excitement of terror. 'And, of course, it is so hard to find the soap.'

'Killed by a mob, I'm afraid.'

'People can be so ungrateful.'

'And *this* . . .' the light passed along the hall '. . . is my grandfather . . .'

A bald head. Dark-rimmed, staring eyes. Two teeth like needles, two ears like batwings, fingernails that hadn't been trimmed for years . . .

'But half the picture's just bare canvas,' said Agnes.

'The family story is that old Magyrato got hungry,' said Vlad. 'A very direct approach to things, my grandfather. See the reddish-brown stains just here? Very much in the old style. And here . . . well, some distant ancestor, that's all I know.'

This picture was mostly dark varnish. There was a suggestion of a beak on a hunched figure.

Vlad turned away, quickly. 'We've come a long way, of course,' he said. 'Evolution, Father says.'

'They look very . . . powerful,' said Agnes.

'Oh, yes. So very powerful, and yet so very, very dumb,' said Vlad. 'My father thinks stupidity is somehow built into vampirism, as if the desire for fresh blood is linked to being as thick as a plank. Father is a very unusual vampire. He and Mother raised us . . . differently.'

'Differently,' said Agnes.

'Vampires aren't very family orientated. Father says that's natural. Humans are raising their successors, you see, but we live for a very long time so a vampire is raising *competitors*. There's not a lot of family feeling, you could say.'

'Really.' In the depths of her pocket Agnes's fingers closed around the bottle of holy water.

'But Father said self-help was the only way out. Break the cycle of stupidity, he said. Little traces of garlic were put into our food to get us used to it. He tried early exposure to various religious symbols – oh dear, we must have had the oddest nursery wallpaper in the world, never mind the jolly frieze of Gertie the Dancing Garlic – and I have to say that their efficacy isn't that good in any case. He even made us go out and play during the day. That which does not kill us, he'd say, makes us strong—'

Agnes's arm whirled. The holy water spiralled out of the bottle and hit Vlad full in the chest.

He threw his arms wide and screamed as water cascaded down and poured into his shoes.

She'd never expected it to be this easy.

He raised his head and winked at her.

'*Look* at this waistcoat! Will you *look* at this waistcoat? Do you know what water does to silk? You just never get it out! No matter what you do, there's always a mark.' He looked at her frozen expression and sighed.

'I suppose we'd better get some things off our chest, hadn't we?' he said. He looked up at the wall and took down a very large and spiky axe. He thrust it at her.

'Take this and cut my head off, will you?' he said. 'Look, I'll loosen my cravat. Don't want blood on it, do we? There. See?'

'Are you trying to tell me that you were brought up with this, too?' she said hotly. 'What was it, a little light hatchet practice after breakfast? Cut your head off a little bit every day and the real thing won't hurt?'

Vlad rolled his eyes. '*Everyone* knows that cutting off a vampire's head is internationally acceptable,' he said. 'I'm sure Nanny Ogg would be swinging right now. Come along, there's a lot of muscle in those rather thick arms, I'm—'

She swung.

He reached around from behind her and whisked the axe out of her arms.

'—sure,' he finished. 'We are also very, very fast.'

He tested the blade with his thumb. 'Blunt, I notice. My dear Miss Nitt, it may just be more trouble than it's worth to try to get rid of us, do you see? Now, old Magyrato there would not have made the kind of offer we are making to Lancre. Dear me, no. Are we ravaging across the country? No? Forcing our way into bedrooms? Certainly not. What's a little blood, for the good of the community? Of course Verence will have to be demoted a little but, let's face it, the man is rather more of a clerk than a king. And . . . our friends may find us grateful. What is the *point* of resisting?'

'Are vampires ever grateful?'

'We can learn.'

'You're just saying that in exchange for not actually being evil you'll simply be bad, is that it?'

'What we are saying, my dear, is that our time has come,' said a voice behind them.

They both turned.

The Count had stepped into the gallery. He was wearing a smoking jacket. There was an armed man strolling on either side of him.

'Oh dear, Vlad . . . Playing with your food? Good evening, Miss Nitt. We appear to have a mob at the gates, Vlad.'

'Really? That's exciting. I've never seen a *real* mob.'

'I wish your first could have been a better one,' said the Count, and sniffed. 'There's no *passion* in it. Still, it'd be too tiresome to let it go on all through dinner. I shall tell them to go away.'

The doors of the hall swung open without apparent aid.

'Shall we go and watch?' said Vlad.

'Er, I think I'll go and powder my, I'll just go and . . . I'll just be a minute,' said Agnes, backing away.

She darted down the little corridor that led to the small door, and drew the bolts.

'About time,' said Nanny, hurrying in. 'It's really clammy out here.'

'They've gone to look at the mob. But there's other vampires here, not just the guards! The rest must've come in on the carts! They're like . . . not quite servants but they take orders.'

'How many are there?' said Magrat.

'I haven't found out! Vlad is trying to get to know me better!'

'Good plan,' said Nanny. 'See if he talks in his sleep.'

'Nanny!'

'Let's see his lordship in action, shall we?' said Nanny. 'We can nip into the old guardroom alongside the door and look through the squint.'

'I want to get Verence!' said Magrat.

'He's not going anywhere,' said Nanny, striding into the little room by the door. 'And I don't reckon they're planning to kill him. Anyway, he's got some protection now.'

'I think these really *are* new vampires,' said Agnes. 'They really *aren't* like the old sort.'

'Then we face 'em here and now,' said Nanny. 'That's what Esme would do, sure enough.'

'But are *we* strong enough?' said Agnes. *Granny wouldn't have asked*, said Perdita.

'There's three of us, isn't there?' said Nanny. She produced a flask and uncorked it. 'And a bit of help. Anyone else want some?'

'That's *brandy*, Nanny!' said Magrat. 'Do you want to face the vampires *drunk*?'

'Sounds a whole lot better than facin' them sober,' said Nanny, taking a gulp and shuddering. 'Only sensible bit of advice Agnes got from Mister Oats, I reckon. Vampire hunters need to be a little bit tipsy, he said. Well, I always listen to good advice . . .'

Even inside Mightily Oats's tent the candle streamed in the wind. He sat gingerly on his camp bed, because sudden movements made it fold up with nail-blackening viciousness, and leafed through his notebooks in a state of growing panic.

He hadn't come here to be a vampire expert. 'Revenants and Ungodly Creatures' had been a one-hour lecture from deaf Deacon Thrope every fortnight, for Om's sake! It hadn't even counted towards the final examination score! They'd spent twenty times that on Comparative Theology, and right now he wished, he really *wished*, that they'd found time to tell him, for example, exactly where the heart was and how much force you needed to drive a stake through it.

Ah . . . here they were, a few pages of scribble, saved only because the notes for his essay on

Thrum's *Lives of the Prophets* were on the other side.

'*. . . The blood is the life . . . vampires are subservient to the one who turned them into a vampire . . . allyl disulphide, active ingredient in garlic . . . porphyria, lack of? Learned reaction? . . . native soil v. important . . . as many as possible will drink of a victim so that he is the slave of all . . . "clustersuck" . . . blood as an unholy sacrament . . . Vampire controls: bats, rats, creatures of the night, weather . . . contrary to legend, most victims merely become passive, NOT vampires . . . intended vampire suffers terrible torments & craving for blood . . . socks . . . Garlic, holy icons . . . sunlight – deadly? . . . kill vampire, release all victims . . . physical strength & . . .*'

Why hadn't anyone told them this was *important*? He'd covered half the page with a drawing of Deacon Thrope, which was practically a still life.

Oats dropped the book into his pocket and grasped his medallion hopefully. After four years of theological college he wasn't at all certain of what he believed, and this was partly because the Church had schismed so often that occasionally the entire curriculum would alter in the space of one afternoon. But also—

They had been warned about it. Don't expect it, they'd said. It doesn't happen to anyone except the prophets. Om doesn't work like that. Om works from inside.

—but he'd hoped that, just once, Om would make himself known in some obvious and unequivocal way that couldn't be mistaken for wind or a guilty conscience. Just once he'd like the clouds to part for the space of ten seconds and a voice to cry out, 'YES, MIGHTILY-PRAISEWORTHY-ARE-YE-WHO-EXALTETH-OM OATS! IT'S ALL COMPLETELY TRUE! INCIDENTALLY, THAT WAS A VERY THOUGHTFUL PAPER YOU WROTE ON THE CRISIS OF RELIGION IN A PLURALISTIC SOCIETY!'

It wasn't that he'd lacked faith. But faith wasn't enough. He'd wanted knowledge.

Right now he'd settle for a reliable manual of vampire disposal.

He stood up. Behind him, unheeded, the terrible camp bed sprang shut.

He'd found knowledge, and knowledge hadn't helped.

Had not Jotto caused the Leviathan of Terror to throw itself on to the land and the seas to turn red with blood? Had not Orda, strong in his faith, caused a sudden famine thoughout the land of Smale?

They certainly had. He believed it utterly. But a part of him also couldn't forget reading about the tiny little creatures that caused the rare red tides off the coast of Urt and the effect this apparently had on local sea life, and about the odd wind cycle that sometimes kept rainclouds away from Smale for years at a time.

This had been . . . worrying.

It was because he was so very good at old languages that he'd been allowed to study in the new libraries that were springing up around the Citadel, and this had been fresh ground for worry, because the seeker after truth had found truths instead. The Third Journey of the Prophet Cena, for example, seemed remarkably like a retranslation of the Testament of Sand in the *Laotan Book of the Whole.* On one shelf alone he found forty-three remarkably similar accounts of a great flood, and in every single one of them a man very much like Bishop Horn had saved the elect of mankind by building a magical boat. Details varied, of course. Sometimes the boat was made of wood, sometimes of banana leaves. Sometimes the news of the emerging dry land was brought by a swan, sometimes by an iguana. *Of course* these stories in the chronicles of other religions were mere folktales and myth, while the voyage detailed in the Book of Cena was holy truth. But nevertheless . . .

Oats had gone on to be fully ordained, but he'd progressed from Slightly Reverend to Quite Reverend a troubled young man. He'd wanted to discuss his findings with someone, but there were so many schisms going on that no one would stand still long enough to listen. The hammering of clerics as they nailed their own versions of the truth of Om on the temple doors was deafening, and for a brief while he'd even contemplated buying a roll of paper and a hammer of his own and putting his name on the waiting list for the doors, but he'd overruled himself.

Because he was, he knew, in two minds about everything.

At one point he'd considered asking to be exorcized but had drawn back from this because the Church traditionally used fairly terminal methods for this and in any case serious men who seldom smiled would not be amused to hear that the invasive spirit he wanted exorcized was his own.

He called the voices the Good Oats and the Bad Oats. The trouble was, each of them agreed with the terminology but applied it in different ways.

Even when he was small there'd been a part of him that thought the temple was a silly boring place, and tried to make him laugh when he was supposed to be listening to sermons. It had grown up with him. It was the Oats that read avidly and always remembered those passages which cast doubt on the literal truth of the *Book of Om* – and nudged him and said, if *this* isn't true, what *can* you believe?

And the other half of him would say: there must be other kinds of truth.

And he'd reply: other kinds than the kind that is actually *true*, you mean?

And he'd say: define *actually*!

And he'd shout: well, *actually* Omnians would have tortured you to death, not long ago, for even *thinking* like this. Remember that? Remember how many died for using the brain which, you seem to think, their god *gave* them? What kind of truth excuses all that pain?

He'd never quite worked out how to put the answer into words. And then the headaches would start, and the sleepless nights. The Church schismed all the time these days, and this was surely the ultimate one, starting a war inside one's head.

To think he'd been sent here for his health, because Brother Melchio had got worried about his shaky hands and the way he talked to himself!

He did not gird his loins, because he wasn't certain how you did that and had never dared ask, but he adjusted his hat and stepped out into the wild night under the thick, uncommunicative clouds.

The castle gates swung open and Count Magpyr stepped out, flanked by his soldiers.

This was not according to the proper narrative tradition. Although the people of Lancre were technically new to all this, down at genetic level they knew that when the mob is at the gate the mobee should be screaming defiance in a burning laboratory or engaged in a cliffhanger struggle with some hero on the battlements.

He shouldn't be lighting a cigar.

They fell silent, scythes and pitchforks hovering in mid-shake. The only sound was the crackling of the torches.

The Count blew a smoke ring.

'Good evening,' he said, as it drifted away. 'You must be the mob.'

Someone at the back of the crowd, who hadn't been keeping up to date, threw a stone. Count Magpyr caught it without looking.

'The pitchforks are good,' he said. 'I like the pitchforks. As pitchforks they certainly pass muster. And the torches, well, that goes without saying. But the scythes . . . no, no, I'm afraid not. They simply will not do. *Not* a good mob weapon, I have to tell you. Take it from me. A simple sickle is much better. Start waving scythes around and someone could lose an ear. Do try to learn.'

He ambled over to a very large man who was holding a pitchfork.

'And what is your name, young man?'

'Er . . . Jason Ogg, sir.'

'The blacksmith?'

'Yessir?'

'Wife and family doing well?'

'Yessir.'

'Well done. Got everything you need?'

'Er . . . yessir.'

'Good man. Carry on. If you could keep the noise down over dinner I would be grateful, but of course I appreciate you have a vital traditional role to play. I'll have the servants bring out some mugs of hot toddy shortly.' He knocked the ash off his cigar. 'Oh, and may I introduce you to Sergeant Kraput, known to his friends as "Bent Bill", I believe, and this gentleman here picking his teeth with his knife is Corporal Svitz, who I understand has no friends at all. I suppose it is faintly possible that he will make some here. They and their men, who I suppose *could* be called soldiers in a sort of informal, easy-come easy-go, cut-and-thrust sort of way' – here Corporal Svitz leered and flicked a gobbet of anonymous rations from a yellowing molar – 'will be going on duty in, oh, about an hour. Purely for reasons of security, you understand.'

'An' then we'll gut yer like a clam and stuff yer with straw,' said Corporal Svitz.

'Ah. This is technical military language of which I know little,' said the Count. 'I do so hope there is no unpleasantness.'

'I don't,' said Sergeant Kraput.

'What scamps they are,' said the Count. 'Good evening to you all. Come, gentlemen.'

He stepped back into the courtyard. The gates, their wood so heavy and toughened with age that it was like iron, swung shut.

On the other side of it was silence, followed by the puzzled mumbling of players who have had their ball confiscated.

The Count nodded at Vlad and flung out his hands theatrically.

'Ta-da! And that is how we do it—'

'And d'you think you'd do it twice?' said a voice from the steps.

The vampires looked up at the three witches.

'Ah, Mrs Ogg,' said the Count, waving the soldiers away impatiently. 'And your majesty. And Agnes . . . Now . . . was it three for a girl? Or three for a funeral?'

The stone cracked under Nanny's feet as Magpyr walked forward.

'Do you think I'm stupid, dear ladies?' he said. 'Did you really think I'd let you run around if there was the least chance that you could harm us?'

Lightning crackled across the sky.

'I can control the weather,' said the Count. 'And lesser creatures which, let me tell you, includes humans. And yet you plot away and think you can have some kind of . . . of *duel*? What a lovely image. However . . .'

The witches were lifted off their feet. Hot air curled around them. A rising wind outside made the torches of the mob stream flames like flags.

'What happened to us harnessing the power of all three of us together?' hissed Magrat.

'That rather depended on him standing still!' said Nanny.

'Stop this at once!' Magrat shouted. 'And how dare you smoke in my castle! That can have a very serious effect on people around you!'

'Is anyone going to say, "You'll never get away with it"?' said the Count, ignoring her. He walked up the steps. They bobbed helplessly along ahead of him, like so many balloons. The hall doors slammed shut after him.

'Oh, *someone* must,' he said.

'*You won't get away with this!*'

The Count beamed. 'And I didn't even see your lips move—'

'*Depart from here and return to the grave whence thou camest, unrighteous revenant!*'

'Where the hell did *he* come from?' said Nanny, as Mightily Oats dropped to the ground in front of the vampires.

He was creeping along the minstrel gallery, said Perdita to Agnes. *Sometimes you just don't pay attention.*

The priest's coat was covered with dust and his collar was torn, but his eyes blazed with holy zeal.

He thrust something in front of the vampire's face. Agnes saw him glance down hurriedly at a small book in his other hand.

'Er . . . "Get thee hence, thou worm of Rheum, and vex not—"'

'Excuse me?' said the Count.

'"—trouble not more the—"'

'Could I just make a point?'

'"—thou spirit that troubles thee, thou" . . . What?'

The Count took the notebook out of Oats's suddenly unresisting hand.

'This is from Ossory's *Malleus Maleficarum*,' he said. 'Why do you look so surprised? I helped *write* it, you silly little man!'

'But . . . you . . . but that was hundreds of years ago!' Oats managed.

'So? *And* I contributed to *Auriga Clavorum Maleficarum*, *Torquus Simiae Maleficarum* . . . the whole damn *Arca Instrumentorum*, in fact. None of those stupid fictions work on vampires, didn't you even know that?' The Count almost growled. 'Oh, I remember your prophets. They were mad bearded old men with the sanitary habits of a stoat but, by all that's crazed, they had *passion*! *They* didn't have holy little minds full of worry and fretfulness. They spoke the idiot words as though they believed them, with specks of holy foam bubbling away in the corners of their mouths. Now *they* were *real* priests, bellies full of fire and bile! *You* are a joke.'

He tossed the notebook aside and took the pendant. 'And this is the holy turtle of Om, which I believe should make me cringe back in fear. My, my. Not even a very good replica. Cheaply made.'

Oats found a reserve of strength. He managed to say, 'And how would you know, foul fiend?'

'No, no, that's for demons,' sighed the Count.

He handed the turtle back to Oats.

'A commendable effort, none the less,' he said. 'If I ever want a nice cup of tea and a bun and possibly also a cheery sing-song, I will be sure to patronize your mission. But, at the moment, you are in my way.'

He hit the priest so hard that he slid under the long table.

'So much for piety,' he said. 'All that remains is for Granny Weatherwax to turn up. It should be any minute now. After all, did you think she'd trust you to get it *right*?'

The sound of the huge iron doorknocker reverberated through the hall.

The Count nodded happily. 'And that will be her,' he said. 'Of course it will. Timing is everything.'

The wind roared in when the doors were opened, swirling twigs and rain and Granny Weatherwax, blown like a leaf. She was soaked and covered in mud, her dress torn in several places.

Agnes realized that she'd never actually seen Granny Weatherwax wet before, even after the worst storm, but now she was drenched. Water poured off her and left a trail on the floor.

'Mistress Weatherwax! So good of you to come,' said the Count. 'Such a long walk on a dark night. Do sit by the fire for a while and rest.'

'I'll not rest here,' said Granny.

'At least have a drink or something to eat, then.'

'I'll not eat nor drink here.'

'Then what *will* you do?'

'You know well why I've come.'

She looks small, said Perdita. *And tired, too.*

'Ah, yes. The set-piece battle. The great gamble. The Weatherwax trademark. And . . . let me see . . . your shopping list today will be . . . "If I win I will expect you to free everyone and go back to Uberwald," am I right?'

'No. I will expect you to die,' said Granny.

To her horror, Agnes saw that the old woman was swaying slightly.

The Count smiled. 'Excellent! But . . . I know how you think, Mistress Weatherwax. You always have more than one plan. You're standing there, clearly one step away from collapse, and yet . . . I'm not entirely certain that I believe what I'm seeing.'

'I couldn't give a damn what you're certain of,' said Granny. 'But you daren't let me walk out of here, I do know that. 'Cos you can't be sure of where I'll go, or what I'll do. I could be watching you from any pair of eyes. I might be behind any door. I have a few favours I might call in. I could come from any direction, at any time. An' I'm good at malice.'

'So? If I was so impolite, I could kill you right now. A simple arrow would suffice. Corporal Svitz?'

The mercenary gave a wave that was as good as he'd ever get to a salute, and raised his crossbow.

'Are you *sure*?' said Granny. 'Is your ape sure he'd have time for a second shot? That I'd still be here?'

'You're not a shape-changer, Mistress Weatherwax. And by the look of it you're in no position to run.'

'She's talking about moving her self into someone else's head,' said Vlad.

The witches looked at one another.

'Sorry, Esme,' said Nanny Ogg, at last. 'I couldn't stop meself thinking. I don't think I drunk quite enough.'

'Oh, yes,' said the Count. 'The famous Borrowing trick.'

'But you don't know where, you don't know how far,' said Granny wearily. 'You don't even know what kind of head. You don't know if it has to be a head. All you know about me is what you can get out of other people's minds, and *they* don't know all about me. Not by a long way.'

'And so your self is put elsewhere,' said the Count. 'Primitive. I've met them, you know, on my travels. Strange old men in beads and feathers who could put their inner self into a fish, an insect . . . even a tree. And as if it mattered. Wood burns. I'm sorry, Mistress Weatherwax. As King Verence is so fond of saying, there's a new world order. We are it. You are history—'

He flinched. The three witches dropped to the ground.

'Well *done*,' he said. 'A shot across my bows. I felt that. I actually *felt* it. No one in Uberwald has ever managed to get through.'

'I can do better'n that,' said Granny.

'I don't think you can,' said the Count. 'Because if you could you would have done so. No mercy for the vampire, eh? The cry of the mob throughout the ages!'

He strolled towards her. 'Do you really think we're like some inbred elves or gormless humans and can be cowed by a firm manner and a bit of trickery? We're out of the casket now, Mistress Weatherwax. I have tried to be understanding towards you, because really we do have a lot in common, but now—'

Granny's body jerked back like a paper doll caught by a gust of wind.

The Count was halfway towards her, hands in the

pockets of his jacket. He broke his step momentarily.

'Oh dear, I hardly felt that one,' he said. '*Was* that your best?'

Granny staggered, but raised a hand. A heavy chair by the wall was picked up and tumbled across the room.

'For a human that was quite good,' said the Count. 'But I don't think you can keep *on* sending it away.'

Granny flinched and raised her other hand. A huge chandelier began to swing.

'Oh dear,' said the Count. 'Still not good enough. Not *nearly* good enough.'

Granny backed away.

'But I will promise you this,' said the Count. 'I won't kill you. On the contrary—'

Invisible hands picked her up and slammed her against the wall.

Agnes went to step forward, but Magrat squeezed her arm.

'Don't think of it as losing, Granny Weatherwax,' said the Count. 'You *will* live for ever. I would call that a bargain, wouldn't you?'

Granny managed a sniff of disapproval.

'*I*'d call that unambitious,' she said. Her face screwed up in pain.

'Goodbye,' said the Count.

The witches felt the mental blow. The hall wavered.

But there was something else, in a realm outside normal space. Something bright and silvery, slipping like a fish . . .

'She's gone,' whispered Nanny. 'She sent her self somewhere . . .'

'Where? Where?' hissed Magrat.

'Don't think about it!' said Nanny.

Magrat's expression froze.

'Oh, *no* . . .' she began.

'Don't think it! Don't think it!' said Nanny urgently. 'Pink elephants! Pink elephants!'

'She wouldn't—'

'Lalalala! Ee-ie-ee-ie-oh!' shouted Nanny, dragging Magrat towards the kitchen door. 'Come on, let's go! Agnes, it's up to you two!'

The door slammed behind them. Agnes heard the bolts slide home. It was a thick door and they were big bolts; the builders of Lancre Castle hadn't understood the concept of planks less than three inches thick or locks that couldn't withstand a battering ram.

The situation would, to an outsider, have seemed very selfish. But, logically, three witches in danger had been reduced to one witch in danger. Three witches would have spent too much time worrying about one another and what they were going to do. One witch was her own boss.

Agnes knew all this, and it still seemed selfish.

The Count was walking towards Granny. Out of the corner of her eye Agnes could see Vlad and his sister approaching her. There was a solid door behind her. Perdita wasn't coming up with any ideas.

So she screamed.

That was a talent. Being in two minds wasn't a talent, it was merely an affliction. But Agnes's vocal range could melt earwax at the top of the scale.

She started high and saw that she'd judged right. Just after the point where bats and woodworm fell out of the rafters, and dogs barked down in the town, Vlad clapped his hands over his ears.

Agnes gulped for breath.

'Another step and I'll do it louder!' she shouted.

The Count picked up Granny Weatherwax as though she were a doll.

'I'm sure you will,' he said. 'And sooner or later you *will* run out of breath. Vlad, she followed you home, you may keep her, but she's your responsibility. You have to feed her and clean out her cage.'

The younger vampire approached cautiously.

'Look, you're really not being sensible,' he hissed.

'Good!'

And then he was beside her. But Perdita had been expecting this even if Agnes hadn't, and as he arrived her elbow was already well into its thrust and caught him in the stomach before he could stop it.

She strode forward as he doubled up, noting that inability to learn was a vampire trait that was hard to shake off.

The Count laid Granny Weatherwax on the table.

'Igor!' he shouted. 'Where are you, you stupid—'

'Yeth, marthter?'

The Count spun round.

'Why do you *always* turn up behind me like that!'

'The old Count alwayth . . . ecthpected it of me, marthter. It'th a profethional thing.'

'Well, stop it.'

'Yeth, marthter.'

'And the ridiculous voice, too. Go and ring the dinner gong.'

'Yeth, marrrtthhter.'

'And I've told you before about that walk!' the Count shouted, as Igor limped across the hall. 'It's not even amusing!'

Igor walked past Agnes, lisping nastily under his breath.

Vlad caught up with Agnes as she strode towards the table, and she was slightly glad because she didn't know what she'd do when she got there.

'You must go,' he panted. 'I wouldn't have let him hurt you, of course, but Father can get . . . testy.'

'Not without Granny.'

A faint voice in her head said: Leave . . . me . . .

That wasn't me, Perdita volunteered. *I think that was her.*

Agnes stared at the prone body. Granny Weatherwax looked a lot smaller when she was unconscious.

'Would you like to stay to dinner?' said the Count.

'You're going to . . . after all this talk, you're going to . . . suck her blood?'

'We *are* vampires, Miss Nitt. It's a vampire thing. A little . . . sacrament, shall we say.'

'How can you? She's an old lady!'

He spun round and was suddenly standing too close to her.

'The idea of a younger aperitif is attractive, believe me,' he said. 'But Vlad would sulk. Anyway, blood develops . . . character, just like your old wines. She won't be killed. Not as such. At her time of life I should welcome a little immortality.'

'But she hates vampires!'

'This may present her with a problem when she

comes round, since she will be a rather subservient one. Oh dear . . .' The Count reached down and picked up Oats from under the table by one arm. 'What a bloodless performance. I remember Omnians when they were full of certainty and fire and led by men who were courageous and unforgiving, albeit quite unbelievably insane. How they would despair of all this milk and water stuff. Take him away with you, please.'

'Shall I see you again tomorrow?' said Vlad, proving to Agnes that males of every species could possess a stupidity gene.

'You won't be able to turn her into a vampire!' she said, ignoring him.

'She won't be able to help it,' said the Count. 'It's in the blood, if we choose to put it there.'

'She'll resist.'

'That would be worth seeing.'

The Count dropped Oats on to the floor again.

'Now go away, Miss Nitt. Take your soggy priest. Tomorrow, well, you can have your old witch back. But she'll be ours. There's a hierarchy. Everyone knows that . . . who knows anything about vampires.'

Behind him Oats was being sick.

Agnes thought of the hollow-eyed people now working in the castle. No one deserved that.

She grabbed the priest by the back of his jacket and held him like a bag.

'*Goodbye*, Miss Nitt,' said the Count.

She hauled the limp Oats to the main doors. Now it was raining hard outside, great heavy unmerciful rain slanting out of the sky like steel rods. She kept close to the wall for the slight shelter that this gave and propped him up under the gush from a gargoyle.

He shuddered. 'Oh, that poor old woman,' he moaned, slumping forward so that a flattened star of rain poured off his head.

'Yes,' said Agnes. The other two had run off. They'd shared a thought – and Perdita had too. They'd all felt the shock as Granny set her mind free and . . . well, the baby was even *called* Esme, wasn't she? But . . . she couldn't have imagined Granny's voice in her head. She had to be somewhere close . . .

'I really made a terrible mess of it, didn't I?' said Oats.

'Yes,' said Agnes vaguely. No, lending her *self* to the baby did have a sort of *rightness* to it, a folklore touch, a romantic ring, and that's why Nanny and Magrat would probably believe it and that was why Granny wouldn't do it. Granny had no romance in her soul, Agnes thought. But she *did* have a very good idea of how to manipulate the romance in other people.

So . . . where else was she? *Something* had happened. She'd put the essence of herself somewhere for safety, and no matter what she'd told the Count she couldn't have put it very far away. It had to be in something alive, but if it was in a human the owner wouldn't even know it—

'If only I'd used the right exorcism,' Oats mumbled.

'Wouldn't have worked,' said Agnes sharply. 'I don't think they're very religious vampires.'

'It's probably only once in his life that a priest gets a chance like this . . .'

'You were just the wrong person,' said Agnes. 'If a pamphlet had been the right thing to scare them away, then you'd have been the very best man for the job.'

She stared down at Oats. So did Perdita.

'Brother Melchio is going to get very abrupt about this,' he said, pulling himself to his feet. 'Oh, look at me, all covered in mud. Er . . . why *are* you looking at me like that?'

'Oh . . . just an odd thought. The vampires still don't affect your head?'

'What do you mean?'

'They don't affect your mind? They don't know what you're thinking?'

'Hah! Most of the time even *I* don't know what I'm thinking,' said Oats miserably.

'Really?' said Agnes. *Really?* said Perdita.

'He was right,' mumbled Oats, not listening. 'I've let everyone down, haven't I? I should have stayed in the college and taken that translating post.'

There wasn't even any thunder and lightning with the rain. It was just hard and steady and grim.

'But I'm . . . ready to have another go,' said Oats.

'You are? Why?'

'Did not Kazrin return three times into the valley of Mahag, and wrest the cup of Hiread from the soldiers of the Oolites while they slept?'

'Did he?'

'Yes. I'm . . . I'm sure of it. And did not Om say to the Prophet Brutha, "I will be with you in dark places"?'

'I imagine he did.'

'Yes, he did. He must have done.'

'And,' said Agnes, 'on that basis you'd go back in?'

'Yes.'

'Why?'

'Because if I didn't, what use am I? What use am I anyway?'

'I don't think we'd survive a second time,' said Agnes. 'They let us go this time because it was the cruel thing to do. Dang! *I've* got to decide what to do now, and it shouldn't be *me*. I'm the maiden, for goodness' sake!' She saw his expression and added, for reasons she'd find hard to explain at the moment, 'A technical term for the junior member of a trio of witches. I shouldn't have to *decide* things. Yes, I know it's better than making the tea!'

'Er ... I didn't say anything about making the tea—'

'No, sorry, that was someone else. What is it she wants me to *do*?'

Especially since now you think you know where she's hiding, said Perdita.

There was a creak, and they heard the hall doors open. Light spilled out, shadows danced in the mist raised by the driving rain, there was a splash and the doors shut again. As they closed, there was the sound of laughter.

Agnes hurried to the bottom of the steps, with the priest squelching along beside her.

There was already a wide and muddy puddle at this end of the courtyard. Granny Weatherwax lay in it, her dress torn, her hair uncoiling from its rock-hard bun.

There was blood on her neck.

'They didn't even lock her in a cell or something,'

said Agnes, steaming with rage. 'They just threw her like . . . like a meat bone!'

'I suppose they think she *is* locked up now, the poor soul,' said Oats. 'Let's get her under cover, at least . . .'

'Oh . . . yes . . . of course.'

Agnes took hold of Granny's legs, and was amazed that someone so thin could be so heavy.

'Perhaps there'd be someone in the village?' said Oats, staggering under his end of the load.

'Not a good idea,' said Agnes.

'Oh, but surely—'

'What would you say to them? "This is Granny, can we leave her here, oh, and when she wakes up she'll be a vampire"?'

'Ah.'

'It's not as though people are that happy to see her anyway, unless they're ill . . .'

Agnes peered around through the rain.

'Come on, let's go round to the stables and the mews, there's sheds and things . . .'

King Verence opened his eyes. Water was pouring down the window of his bedroom. There was no light but that which crept in under the door, and he could just make out the shapes of his two guards, nodding in their seats.

A windowpane tinkled. One of the Uberwaldians went and opened the window, looked out into the wild night, found nothing of interest and shuffled back to his seat.

Everything felt very . . . pleasant. It seemed to Verence that he was lying in a nice warm bath, which was very relaxing and comfortable. The cares of the world belonged to someone else. He bobbed like happy flotsam on the warm sea of life.

He could hear very faint voices, apparently coming from somewhere below his pillow.

'Rikt, gi' tae yon helan bigjobs?'

'Ach, fashit keel!'

'Hyup?'

'Nach oona whiel ta' tethra . . . yin, tan, TETRA!'

'Hyup! Hyup!'

Something rustled on the floor. The chair of one man jerked up into the air and bobbed at speed to the window.

'Hyup!' The chair and its occupant crashed through the glass.

The other guard managed to get to his feet, but something was growing in the air in front of him. To Verence, an alumnus of the Fools' Guild, it looked very much like a very tall human pyramid made up of very small acrobats.

'Hup! Hup!'

'Hyup!'

'Hup!'

It grew level with the guard's face. The single figure at the top yelled: 'What ya lookin' a', chymie? Ha' a wee tastie!' and launched itself directly at a point between the man's eyes. There was a little cracking noise, and the man keeled over backwards.

'Hup! Hup!'

'Hyup!'

The living pyramid dissolved to floor level. Verence heard tiny pattering feet and suddenly there was a small, heavily tattooed man in a blue pointy hat standing on his chin.

'Seyou, kingie! Awa' echt ta' branoch, eh?'

'Well done,' Verence murmured. 'How long have you been a hallucination? *Jolly* good.'

'Ken ye na' saggie, ye spargit?'

'That's the way,' said Verence dreamily.

'Auchtahelweit!'

'Hyup! Hyup!'

Verence felt himself lifted off the bed. Hundreds of little hands passed him from one to the other and he was glided through the window and out into the void.

It was a sheer wall and, he told himself dreamily, he had no business drifting down it so slowly, to cries of 'Ta ya! Ta me! Hyup!' Tiny hands caught his collar, his nightshirt, his bedsocks . . .

'Good show,' he murmured, as he slid gently to the ground and then, six inches above ground level, was carried off into the night.

There was a light burning in the rain. Agnes hammered on the door, and the wet wood gave way to the slightly better vision of Hodgesaargh the falconer.

'We've got to come in!' she said.

'Yes, Miss Nitt.'

He stood back obediently as they carried Granny into the little room.

'She been hurt, miss?'

'You *do* know there's vampires in the castle?' said Agnes.

'Yes, miss?' said Hodgesaargh. His voice suggested that he'd just been told a fact and he was waiting with polite interest to be told whether this was a good fact or a bad fact.

'They bit Granny Weatherwax. We need to let her lie down somewhere.'

'There's my bed, miss.'

It was small and narrow, designed for people who went to bed because they were tired.

'She might bleed on it a bit,' said Agnes.

'Oh, I bleed on it all the time,' said Hodgesaargh cheerfully. 'And on the floor. I've got any amount of bandages and ointment, if that will be any help.'

'Well, it won't do any harm,' said Agnes. 'Er . . . Hodgesaargh, you *do* know vampires suck people's blood, do you?'

'Yes, miss? They'll have to queue up behind the birds for mine, then.'

'It doesn't worry you?'

'Mrs Ogg made me a huge tub of ointment, miss.'

That seemed to be that. Provided they didn't touch his birds, Hodgesaargh didn't much mind who ran the castle. For hundreds of years the falconers had simply got on with the important things, like falconry, which needed a lot of training, and left the kinging to amateurs.

'She's soaking wet,' said Oats. 'At least let's wrap her up in a blanket or something.'

'And you'll need some rope,' said Agnes.

'Rope?'

'She'll wake up.'

'You mean . . . we ought to tie her up?'

'If a vampire wants to turn you into a vampire, what happens?'

Oats's hands clasped his turtle pendant for comfort as he tried to remember. 'I . . . think they put something in the blood,' he said. 'I think if they want to turn you into a vampire you get turned. That's all there is to it. I don't think you can fight it when it's in the blood. You can't say you don't want to join. I don't think it's a power you can resist.'

'She's good at resisting,' said Agnes.

'That good?' said Oats.

One of the Uberwald people shuffled along the corridor. It stopped when it heard a sound, looked around, saw nothing that had apparently made a noise, and plodded on again.

Nanny Ogg stepped out of the shadows, and then beckoned Magrat to follow her.

'Sorry, Nanny, it's very hard to keep a baby quiet—'

'Shh! There's quite a bit of noise coming from the kitchens. What could vampires want to cook?'

'It's those people they've brought with them,' hissed Magrat. 'They've been moving in new furniture. They've got to be fed, I suppose.'

'Yeah, like cattle. I reckon our best bet is to walk out bold as brass,' said Nanny. 'These folk don't look like they're big on original thinkin'. Ready?' She absent-mindedly took a swig from the bottle she was carrying. 'You just follow me.'

'But look, what about Verence? I can't just leave him. He's my husband!'

'What will they do to him that you could prevent if

you was here?' said Nanny. 'Keep the baby safe, that's the important thing. It always has been. Anyway . . . I told you, he's got protection. I saw to that.'

'What, magic?'

'Much better'n that. Now, you just follow me and act snooty. You must've learned that, bein' a queen. Never let 'em even think you haven't got a right to be where you are.'

She strode out into the kitchen. The shabbily dressed people there gave her a dull-eyed look, like dogs waiting to see if a whipping was in prospect. On the huge stove, in place of Mrs Scorbic's usual array of scoured-clean pots, was a large, blackened cauldron. The contents were a basic grey. Nanny wouldn't have stirred it for a thousand dollars.

'Just passing through,' she said sharply. 'Get on with whatever you were doing.'

The heads all turned to watch them. But towards the back of the kitchen a figure unfolded from the old armchair where Mrs Scorbic sometimes held court and ambled towards them.

'Oh, blast, it's one of the bloody hangers-on,' said Nanny. 'He's between us and the door . . .'

'Ladies!' said the vampire, bowing. 'May I be of assistance?'

'We were just leaving,' said Magrat haughtily.

'Possibly not,' said the vampire.

''scuse me, young man,' said Nanny, in her soft old biddy voice, 'but where are you from?'

'Uberwald, madam.'

Nanny nodded and referred to a piece of paper she'd pulled out of her pocket. 'That's nice. What part?'

'Klotz.'

'Really? That's nice. 'scuse me.' She turned her back and there was a brief twanging of elastic before she turned round again, all smiles.

'I just likes to take an interest in people,' she said. 'Klotz, eh? What's the name of that river there? The Um? The Eh?'

'The Ah,' said the vampire.

Nanny's hand shot forward and wedged something yellow between the vampire's teeth. He grabbed her but, as she was dragged forward, she hit him on the top of the head.

He fell to his knees, clutching at his mouth and trying to scream through the lemon he'd just bitten into.

'Seems an odd superstition, but there you are,' said Nanny, as he started to foam around the lips.

'You have to cut their heads off, too,' said Magrat.

'Really? Well, I saw a cleaver back there—'

'Shall we just go?' Magrat suggested. 'Before someone else comes, perhaps?'

'All right. He's not a high-up vampire, anyway,' said Nanny dismissively. 'He's not even wearing a very interestin' waistcoat.'

The night was silver with rain. Heads down, the witches dashed through the murk.

'I've got to change the baby!'

'For a raincoat'd be favourite,' muttered Nanny. 'Now?'

'It's a bit urgent . . .'

'All right, then, in here . . .'

They ducked into the stables. Nanny peered back into the night and shut the door quietly.

'It's very dark,' whispered Magrat.

'I could always change babies by feel when I was young.'

'I'd prefer not to have to. Hey . . . there's a light . . .'

The weak glow of a candle was just visible at the far end of the loose boxes.

Igor was brushing the horses until they shone. His muttering kept time with the strokes of the brush. Something seemed to be on his mind.

'Thilly voithe, eh? Thilly walk? What the hell doth he know? Jumped-up whipper-thnapper! Igor thtop thith, Igor thtop that . . . all thethe kidth thwanning around, trying to puth *me* around . . . there'th a *covenant* in thethe thingth. The *old* marthter knew that! A thervant ith not a thlave . . .'

He glanced around. A piece of straw drifted to the ground.

He began brushing again. 'Huh! Fetch thith, fetch that . . . never a morthel of rethpect, oh no . . .'

Igor stopped and pulled another piece of straw off his sleeve.

'. . . and another thing . . .'

There was a creak, a rush of air, the horse reared in its stall and Igor was borne to the ground, his head feeling as though it was caught in a vice.

'Now, if I brings my knees together,' said a cheerful female voice above him, 'it's very probable I could make your brains come right down your nose. But I know that ain't going to happen, because I'm sure we're all friends here. Say yes.'

''th.'

'That's the best we're going to get, I expect.'

Nanny Ogg got up and flicked straw off her dress.

'I've been in cleaner haylofts,' she said. 'Up you get, Mr Igor. And if you're thinking of anything clever, my colleague over there is holdin' a pitchfork and she ain't much good at aiming so who knows *what* part of you she might hit?'

'Ith that a baby thee'th carrying?'

'We're very modern,' said Nanny. 'We've got hedge money and everything. And now we'll have your coach, Igor.'

'Will we?' said Magrat. 'Where're we going?'

'It's a wicked night. I don't want to keep the babby out, and I don't know where we'd be safe near here. Maybe we can get down on to the plains before morning.'

'I *won't* leave Lancre!'

'Save the child,' said Nanny. 'Make sure there's going to be a future. Besides . . .' She mouthed something at Magrat which Igor did not catch.

'We can't be sure of that,' said Magrat.

'You know the way Granny thinks,' said Nanny. 'She'll want us to keep the baby safe,' she added loudly. 'So hitch up the horses, Mr Igor.'

'Yeth, mithtreth,' said Igor meekly.

'Are you kicking my bucket, Igor?'*

'No, it'th a pleathure to be commanded in a clear, firm authoritative voithe, mithtreth,' said Igor, lurching over to the bridles. 'None of thith "Would you

*In a society that had progressed beyond the privy and the earth closet she would have said 'pulling my chain'.

mind . . ." rubbith. An Igor liketh to know where he thtandth.'

'Slightly lopsidedly?' said Magrat.

'The *old* marthter uthed to whip me every day!' said Igor proudly.

'You *liked* that?' said Magrat.

'Of courthe not! But it'th *proper*! He wath a *gentleman*, whothe bootth I wath not fit to lick clean . . .'

'But you did, though?' said Nanny.

Igor nodded. 'Every morning. Uthed to get a lovely thine, too.'

'Well, help us out and I'll see you're flogged with a scented bootlace,' said Nanny.

'Thankth all the thame, but I'm leaving anyway,' said Igor, tightening a strap. 'I'm thick up to here with thith lot. They thouldn't be doing thith! They're a dithgrathe to the thpethieth!'

Nanny wiped her face. 'I like a man who speaks his mind,' she said, 'and is always prepared to lend a towel – did I say towel? I mean hand.'

'Are you going to *trust* him?' said Magrat.

'I'm a good judge of character, me,' said Nanny. 'And you can always rely on a man with stitches *all round* his head.'

'Waley, waley, waley!'

'Ta' can onlie be one t'ousan!'

'Bigjobs!'

A fox peered cautiously around a tree.

Through the rain-swept woods a man was moving at speed, while apparently lying down. He wore a nightcap, the bobble of which bounced on the ground.

By the time the fox realized what was going on it was too late. A small blue figure leapt out from under the rushing man and landed on its nose, smacking it between the eyes with his head.

'Seeyu? Grich' ta' bones outa t'is yan!'

The Nac mac Feegle leapt down as the fox collapsed, grabbed its tail with one hand and ran after the others, punching the air triumphantly.

'Obhoy! We 'gan eat t'nicht!'

They'd pulled the bed out into the middle of the room. Now Agnes and Oats sat on either side of it, listening to the distant sounds of Hodgesaargh feeding the birds. There was the rattle of tins and the occasional yelp as he tried to remove a bird from his nose.

'Sorry?' said Agnes.

'Pardon?'

'I thought you whispered something,' said Agnes.

'I was, er, saying a short prayer,' said Oats.

'Will that help?' said Agnes.

'Er . . . it helps me. The Prophet Brutha said that Om helps those who help one another.'

'And does he?'

'To be honest, there are a number of opinions of what was meant.'

'How many?'

'About one hundred and sixty, since the Schism of 10.30 a.m., February 23. That was when the Re-United Free Chelonianists (Hubwards Convocation) schismed from the Re-United Free Chelonianists (Rimwards Convocation). It was rather serious.'

'Blood spilled?' said Agnes. She wasn't really interested, but it took her mind off whatever might be waking up in a minute.

'No, but there were fisticuffs and a deacon had ink spilled on him.'

'I can see that was pretty bad.'

'There was some serious pulling of beards as well.'

'Gosh.' *Sects maniacs*, said Perdita.

'You're making fun of me,' said Oats solemnly.

'Well, it does sound a little . . . trivial. You're always arguing?'

'The Prophet Brutha said, "Let there be ten thousand voices,"' said the priest. 'Sometimes I think he meant that it was better to argue amongst ourselves than go out putting unbelievers to fire and the sword. It's all very complicated.' He sighed. 'There are a hundred pathways to Om. Unfortunately I sometimes think someone left a rake lying across a lot of them. The vampire was right. We've lost the fire . . .'

'But you used to burn people with it.'

'I know . . . I know . . .'

Agnes saw a movement out of the corner of her eye.

Steam was rising from under the blanket they'd pulled over Granny Weatherwax.

As Agnes looked down Granny's eyes sprang open and swivelled from side to side.

Her mouth moved once or twice.

'And how are you, Miss Weatherwax?' said Mightily Oats, in a cheerful voice.

'She was bitten by a vampire! What sort of question is that?' Agnes hissed.

'One that's better than "*What* are you?"' Oats whispered.

Granny's hand twitched. She opened her mouth again, arched her body against the rope and then slumped back against the pillow.

Agnes touched her forehead, and drew her hand back sharply.

'She's burning up! Hodgesaargh! Bring some water!'

'Coming, miss!'

'Oh, no . . .' whispered Oats. He pointed to the ropes. They were unknotting themselves, stealthily moving across one another like snakes.

Granny half rolled, half fell out of the bed, landing on her hands and knees. Agnes went to pick her up and received a blow from an elbow that sent her across the room.

The old witch dragged the door open and crawled out into the rain. She paused, panting, as the drops hit her. Agnes swore that some of them sizzled.

Granny's hands slipped. She landed in the mud and struggled to push herself upright.

Blue-green light spilled out from the mews's open door. Agnes looked back inside. Hodgesaargh was staring at a jamjar, in which a point of white light was surrounded by a pale blue flame that stretched well beyond the jar, and curled and pulsed.

'What's *that*?'

'My phoenix feather, miss! It's burning the air!'

Outside, Oats had pulled Granny upright and

had got his shoulder under one of her arms.

'She said something,' he said. '"I am", I think . . .'

'She might be a *vampire*!'

'She just said it again. Didn't you hear?'

Agnes moved closer, and Granny's limp hand was suddenly gripping her shoulder. She could feel the heat of it through her sodden dress and made out the word in the hiss of the rain.

'Iron?' said Oats. 'Did she say iron?'

'There's the castle forge next door,' said Agnes. 'Let's get her in there.'

The forge was dark and cold, its fire only lit when there was work to be done. They pulled Granny inside and she slipped out of their grip and landed on hands and knees on the flagstones.

'But iron's no good against vampires, is it?' said Agnes. 'I've never heard of people using iron—'

Granny made a noise somewhere between a snort and a growl. She pulled herself across the floor, leaving a trail of mud, until she reached the anvil.

It was simply a great long lump of iron to accommodate the half-skilled metal-bashing occasionally needed to keep the castle running. Still kneeling, Granny grabbed at it with both hands and laid her forehead against it.

'Granny, what can—' Agnes began.

'Go where the others . . . are,' Granny Weatherwax croaked. 'It'll need three . . . witches if this goes . . . wrong . . . you'll have to face . . . something terrible . . .'

'What terrible thing?'

'*Me*. Do it *now*.'

Agnes backed away. On the black iron, by Granny's fingers, little flecks of rust were spitting and jumping.

'I'd better go! Keep an eye on her!'

'But what if—'

Granny flung her head back, her eyes screwed shut. '*Get away!*' she screamed.

Agnes went white.

'You heard what she said!' she shouted, and ran out into the rain.

Granny's head slumped forward against the iron again. Around her fingers red sparks danced on the metal.

'Mister priest,' she said in a hoarse whisper. 'Somewhere in this place is an axe. Fetch it here!'

Oats looked around desperately. There *was* an axe, a small double-headed one, lying by a grindstone.

'Er, I've found one,' he ventured.

Granny's head jerked back. Her teeth were gritted, but she managed to say, 'Sharpen it!'

Oats glanced at the grindstone and licked his lips nervously.

'Sharpen it right now, I said!'

He pulled off his jacket, rolled up his sleeves, took up the axe and put a foot on the wheel's treadle.

Sparks leapt off the blade as the wheel spun.

'Then find some wood an' . . . cut a point on it. And find . . . a hammer . . .'

The hammer was easy. There was a rack of tools by the wheel. A few seconds' desperate rummaging in the debris by the wall produced a fence post.

'Madam, what are you wanting me to—'

'Something . . . will get up . . . presently,' Granny

panted. 'Make sure . . . you know well . . . what it is . . .'

'But you're not expecting me to behead—'

'I'm commandin' you, religious man! What do you really . . . believe? What did you . . . think it was all about? Singing songs? Sooner or later . . . it's all down to . . . the blood . . .'

Her head lolled against the anvil.

Oats looked at her hands again. Around them the iron was black, but just a little way from her fingers there was a faint glow to the metal, and the rust still sizzled. He touched the anvil gingerly, then pulled his hand away and sucked at his fingers.

'Mistress Weatherwax a bit poorly, is she?' said Hodgesaargh, coming in.

'I think you could certainly say that, yes.'

'Oh dear. Want some tea?'

'What?'

'It's a nasty night. If we're stopping up I'll put the kettle on.'

'Do you realize, man, that she might get up from there a bloodthirsty vampire?'

'Oh.' The falconer looked down at the still figure and the smoking anvil. 'Good idea to face her with a cup of tea inside you, then,' he said.

'Do you *understand* what's going on here?'

Hodgesaargh took another slow look at the scene. 'No,' he said.

'In that case—'

''s not my job to understand this sort of thing,' said the falconer. 'I wasn't trained. Probably takes a lot of training, understanding this. That's your job. And her job. Can you understand what's going on when a bird's been trained and'll make a kill and still come back to the wrist?'

'Well, no—'

'There you are, then. So that's all right. Cup of tea, was it?'

Oats gave up. 'Yes, please. Thank you.'

Hodgesaargh bustled off.

The priest sat down. If the truth were known, he *wasn't* sure he understood what was happening. The old woman had been burning up and in pain, and now . . . the iron was getting hot, as if the pain and the heat had been moved away. Could anyone do that? Well, of course, the prophets could, he told himself conscientiously, but that was because Om had given them the power. But by all accounts the old woman didn't believe in anything.

She was very still now.

The others had talked about her as though she was some great magician, but the figure he'd seen in the hall had been just a tired, worn-out old woman. He'd seen people down in the hospice in Aby Dyal, stiff and withdrawn until the pain was too great and all they had left was a prayer and then . . . not even that. That seemed to be where she was now.

She was *really* still. Oats had only seen stillness like that when movement was no longer an option.

Up the airy mountain and down the rushy glen ran the Nac mac Feegle, who seemed to have no concept of stealth. Progress was a little slower now, because some of the party broke away occasionally to have a fight amongst themselves or an impromptu hunt, and in addition to the King of Lancre there was now, bobbing through the heather, the fox, a stunned stag, a wild boar, and a weasel who'd been suspected of looking at a Nac mac Feegle in a funny way.

Verence saw, muzzily, that they were heading for a bank at the edge of a field, long deserted and over-grown, topped with some ancient thorn trees.

The pixies stopped with a jolt when the King's head was a few inches away from a large rabbit hole.

'Danna fittit!'

'G'shovitt, s'yust!'

Verence's head was banged hopefully against the wet soil once or twice.

'Hakkis lugs awa'!'

'Bigjobs!'

One of the pixies shook his head. 'Canna' do't, ken? Els' y'ole carlin'll hae oor guts fae garters . . .'

Unusually, the Nac mac Feegle fell silent for a moment. Then one of them said, 'Na one's got tha' much guts, right eno'.'

'An' b'side, she'll gi'us uskabarch muckell. We oathit. Y' canna' cross a hag.'

'Al' at it noo, then . . .'

Verence was dropped on the ground. There was a brief sound of digging, and mud showered over him. Then he was picked up again and carried through a much enlarged hole, his nose brushing tree roots in the ceiling. Behind him there was the sound of a tunnel being rapidly filled in.

Then there was just a bank where rabbits obviously lived, topped with thorn trees. Unseen in the wild night, the occasional wisp of smoke drifted among the trunks.

Agnes leaned against the castle wall, which was streaming with water, and fought for breath. Granny hadn't just *told* her to go away. The command had hit her brain like a bucket of ice. Even Perdita had felt it. There was no question of not obeying.

Where would Nanny have gone? Agnes felt a pressing desire to be near her. Nanny Ogg radiated a perpetual field of It'll-be-all-rightness. If they'd got out through the kitchens she could be *anywhere* . . .

She heard the coach rattle out through the arch that led to the stables. It was just a looming shape, shrouded in spray from the rain, as it bounced across the cobbles of the courtyard. A figure by the driver, holding a sack over its head against the wind and rain, might have been Nanny. It hardly mattered. No one would have seen Agnes running through the puddles and waving.

She trooped back to the arch as the coach disappeared down the hill. Well, they had been trying to get away, hadn't they? And stealing a vampire's coach had a certain Nanny Ogg style . . .

Someone gripped both her arms from behind. Instinctively she tried to thrust back with her elbows. It was like trying to move against rock.

'Why, Miss Agnes Nitt,' said Vlad coldly. 'A pleasant stroll to take in a little rain?'

'They've got away from you!' she snapped.

'You think so? Father could send that coach right into the gorge in a moment if he wanted to,' said the vampire. 'But he won't. We much prefer the personal touch.'

'The in-your-neck approach,' said Agnes.

'Hah, yes. But he really is trying to be reasonable. So I can't persuade you to become one of us, Agnes?'

'What, someone who lives by taking life from other people?'

'We don't usually go as far as that any more,' said Vlad, dragging her forward. 'And when we do . . . well, we make sure that we only kill people who deserve to die.'

'Oh, well, that's all right, then, isn't it?' said Agnes. 'I'm sure I'd trust a vampire's judgement.'

'My sister can be a bit too . . . rigorous at times, I admit.'

'I've seen the people you brought with you! They practically moo!'

'Oh, *them*. The domestics. Well? It's not much different from the lives they would have had in any case. Better, in fact. They are well fed, sheltered—'

'—milked.'

'And is that bad?'

Agnes tried to twist out of his grip. Just here there was no castle wall. There hadn't been any need. Lancre Gorge was all the wall anyone could need, and Vlad was walking her right to the sheer drop.

'What a *stupid* thing to say!' she said.

'Is it? I understand you've travelled, Agnes,' said Vlad, as she struggled. 'So you'll know that so many people lead *little* lives, always under the whip of some king or ruler or master who won't hesitate to sacrifice them in battle or turn them out when they can't work any more.'

But they can run away, Perdita prompted.

'But they can run away!'

'Really? On foot? With a family? And no money? Mostly they never even try. Most people put up with most things, Agnes.'

'That's the most unpleasant, cynical—'

Accurate, Perdita said.

'—accur— No!'

Vlad raised his eyebrows. 'You have such a strange mind, Agnes. Of course, *you* are not one of the . . . cattle. I expect that no witch is. You people tend to know your own mind.' He gave her a toothy grin, and on a vampire this was not pleasant. 'I wish I did. Come along.'

There was no resisting the pull, unless she wanted to be dragged along the ground.

'Father's very impressed with you witches,' he said, over his shoulder. 'He says we should make you *all* vampires. He says you're halfway there anyway. But I'd much rather you came to see how marvellous it could be.'

'You would, would you? I'd like to be constantly craving blood?'

'You constantly crave chocolate, don't you?'

'How dare you!'

'Blood tends to be low in carbohydrates. Your body will adapt. The pounds will just drop away . . .'

'That's sickening!'

'You'll have complete control over yourself . . .'

'I'm not listening!'

'All it takes is a little prick—'

'It's not going to be yours, mister!'

'Hah! Wonderful!' said Vlad and, dragging Agnes behind him, he leapt into the Lancre Gorge.

Granny Weatherwax opened her eyes. At least, she had to assume they were open. She'd felt the lids move.

Darkness lay in front of her. It was velvet black, starless, a hole in space. But there was light behind her. She was standing with her back to the light, she could sense it, see it on her hands. It was streaming past, outlining the darkness that was the long rich deep shadow of her on the . . .

. . . black sand. It crunched under her boots as she shifted her weight.

This was a test. Everything was a test. Everything was a competition. Life put them in front of you every day. You watched yourself all the time. You had to make choices. You never got told which ones were right. Oh, some of the priests said you got given marks *afterwards*, but what was the point of that?

She wished her mind was working faster. She couldn't think properly. Her head felt full of fog.

This . . . wasn't a real place. No, that wasn't the *right* way of thinking about it. It wasn't a *usual* place. It might be more real than Lancre. Across it her shadow stretched, waiting . . .

She glanced up at the tall, silent figure beside her.

GOOD EVENING.

'Oh . . . you again.'

ANOTHER CHOICE, ESMERELDA WEATHERWAX.

'Light and dark? It's never as simple as that, you know, even for you.'

Death sighed. NOT EVEN FOR ME.

Granny tried to line up her thoughts.

Which light and *which* dark? She hadn't been prepared for this. This didn't feel right. This wasn't the fight she had expected. *Whose* light? Whose mind was this?

Silly question. She was always her.

Never lose your grip on that . . .

So . . . light behind her, darkness in front . . .

She'd always said witches stood between the light and the dark.

'Am I dyin'?'

YES.

'Will I die?'

YES.

Granny thought this over.

'But from your point of view, everyone is dying and everyone will die, right?'

YES.

'So you aren't actually bein' a lot of help, strictly speakin'.'

I'M SORRY, I THOUGHT YOU WANTED THE TRUTH. PERHAPS YOU WERE EXPECTING JELLY AND ICE CREAM?

'Hah . . .'

There was no movement in the air, no sound but her own breathing. Just the brilliant white light on one side, and the heavy darkness on the other . . . waiting.

Granny had listened to people who'd nearly died but had come back, possibly because of a deft thump in the right place or the dislodging of some wayward mouthful that'd gone down the wrong way. Sometimes they talked about seeing a light—

That's where she ought to go, a thought told her. But . . . was the light the way in, or the way out?

Death snapped his fingers.

An image appeared on the sand in front of them. She saw herself, kneeling in front of the anvil. She admired the dramatic effect. She'd always had a streak of theatrics, although she'd never admit it, and she appreciated in a disembodied way the strength with which she had thrust her pain into the iron. Someone had slightly spoiled the effect by putting a kettle on one end.

Death reached down and took a handful of sand. He held it up, and let it slip between his fingers.

CHOOSE, he said. YOU ARE GOOD AT CHOOSING, I BELIEVE.

'Is there any advice you could be givin' me?' said Granny.

CHOOSE RIGHT.

Granny turned to face the sheer white brilliance, and closed her eyes.

And stepped backwards.

The light dwindled to a tiny distant point and vanished.

The blackness was suddenly all around, closing in like quicksand. There seemed to be no way, no direction. When she moved she did not sense movement.

There was no sound but the faint trickle of sand inside her head.

And then, voices from her shadow.

'... *Because of you, some died who may have lived...*'

The words lashed at her, leaving livid lines across her mind.

'Some lived who surely would have died,' she said.

The dark pulled at her sleeves.

'... *you killed...*'

'No. I showed the way.'

'... *hah! That's just words...*'

'Words is important,' Granny whispered into the night.

'... *you took the right to judge others...*'

'I took the duty. I'll own up to it.'

'... *I know every evil thought you've ever had...*'

'I know.'

'... *the ones you'd never dare tell anyone...*'

'I know.'

'... *all the little secrets, never to be told...*'

'I know.'

'... *how often you longed to embrace the dark...*'

'Yes.'

'... *such strength you could have...*'

'Yes.'

'... *embrace the dark...*'

'No.'

'... *give in to me...*'

'No.'

'... *Lilith Weatherwax did. Alison Weatherwax did...*'

'That's never been proved!'

'... *give in to me...*'

'No. I know you. I've always known you. The Count just let you out to torment me, but I've always known you were there. I've fought you every day of my life and you'll get no victory now.'

She opened her eyes and stared into the blackness.

'I knows who you are now, Esmerelda Weatherwax,' she said. 'You don't scare me no more.'

The last of the light vanished.

Granny Weatherwax hung in the dark for a time she couldn't measure. It was as if the absolute emptiness had sucked all the time and direction into it. There wasn't anywhere to go, because there wasn't any *anywhere.*

After a length of time without any measure, she began to hear another sound, the faintest of whispers on the borders of hearing. She pushed towards it.

Words were rising through the blackness like little wriggling golden fish.

She fought her way towards them, now that there was a direction.

The slivers of light turned into sounds.

'*—and asketh you in your infinite compassion to see your way clear to possibly intervening here . . .*'

Not normally the kind of words she'd associate with light. Perhaps it was the way they were said. But they had a strange echo to them, a *second* voice, woven in amongst the first voice, glued to every syllable . . .

'*. . . what compassion? How many people prayed at the stake? How foolish I look, kneeling like this . . .*'

Ah . . . one mind, split in half. There were more Agneses in the world than Agnes dreamed of, Granny told herself. All the girl had done was give a thing a name, and once you gave a thing a name you gave it a life . . .

There was something *else* near by, a glimmer a few photons across, which winked out as she looked for it again. She turned her attention away for a moment, then jerked it back. Again, the tiny spark blinked out.

Something was hiding.

The sand stopped rushing. Time was up.

Now to find out what she was.

Granny Weatherwax opened her eyes, and there was light.

The coach swished to a halt on the mountain road. Water poured around its wheels.

Nanny got out and paddled over to Igor, who was standing where the road wasn't.

Water was foaming where it should have been.

'Can we get acroth?' said Igor.

'Probably, but it'll be worse down below, where there's really bad run-off,' said Nanny. 'The plains have been cut off all winter before now . . .'

She looked at the other way. The road wound further into the mountains, awash but apparently sound.

'Where's the nearest village that way?' she said. 'One with a good stone building in it. Slake, isn't it? There's a coaching inn up there.'

'That'th right. Thlake.'

'Well, we ain't going anywhere on foot in this weather,' said Nanny. 'Slake it's got to be, then.'

She got back into the coach and felt it turn round.

'Is there a problem?' said Magrat. 'Why are we going uphill?'

'Road's washed out,' said Nanny.

'We're heading *into* Uberwald?'

'Yes.'

'But there's werewolves and vampires and—'

'Yes, but not *everywhere*. We should be safe on the main road. Anyway, there's not much of a choice.'

'I suppose you're right,' said Magrat reluctantly.

'And it could be worse,' said Nanny.

'How?'

'Well . . . there could be snakes in here with us.'

Agnes saw the rocks rush past, looked down and saw the foam of the swollen river.

The world spun around her when Vlad stopped in mid-air. Water washed over her toes.

'Let there be . . . lightness,' he said. 'You'd like to be as light as the air, wouldn't you, Agnes?'

'We – we've got broomsticks . . .' Agnes panted. Her life had just flashed past her eyes *and wasn't it dull?* Perdita added.

'Useless cumbersome stupid things,' he said. 'And they can't do *this*—'

The walls of the gorge went past in a blur. The castle dropped away. Clouds drenched her. Then they unrolled as a silver-white fleece, under the silent cold light of the moon.

Vlad wasn't beside her. Agnes slowed in her rise, flung out her arms to grip what wasn't there, and began to fall back—

He appeared, laughing, and grabbed her around the waist.

'—can they?' he said.

Agnes couldn't speak. Her life passing in front of her eyes one way had met it passing in front of her eyes going in the opposite direction, and words would fail her now until she could decide when *now* was.

'And you haven't seen anything yet,' said Vlad. Wisps of cloud coiled behind them as he raced forward.

The clouds vanished under them. They might have been as thin as smoke but their presence, their imitation of *groundness*, had been a comfort. Now they were a departing edge, and far below were the moonlit plains.

'Ghjgh,' gurgled Agnes, too tense and terrified even to scream. *Wheee!* crowed Perdita, inside.

'See that?' said Vlad, pointing. 'See the light all around the Rim?'

Agnes stared, because anything now was better than looking down.

The sun was under the Disc. Around the dark Rim, though, it found its way up through the endless waterfall, creating a glowing band between the night-time ocean and the stars. It was, indeed, beautiful, but Agnes felt that beauty was even more likely to be in the eye of the beholder if the feet of the beholder were on something solid. At ten thousand feet up, the eye of the beholder tends to water.

Perdita thought it was beautiful. Agnes wondered if, should Agnes end up as a circle of pink splash marks on the rocks, Perdita would still be there.

'Everything you want,' whispered Vlad. 'For ever.'

'I want to get down,' said Agnes.

He let go.

There was this about Agnes's shape. It was a good one for falling. She turned automatically belly down, hair streaming behind her, and floated in the rushing wind.

Oddly enough, the terror had gone. That had been fear of a situation out of her control. Now, arms outspread, skirts whipping her legs, eyes streaming in the freezing air, she could at least see what the future held even if it was not big enough to hold very much.

Perhaps she could hit a snowbank, or deep water—

It might have been worth a try, said Perdita. *He doesn't seem entirely bad.*

'Shut up.'

It'd just be nice if you could stop looking as though you were wearing saddlebags under your skirt . . .

'Shut up.'

And it'd be nice if you didn't hit the rocks like a balloon full of water . . .

'Shut up. Anyway, I can see a lake. I think I can sort of angle across towards it.'

At this speed it will be like hitting the ground.

'How do *you* know that? I don't know that. So how do *you* know?'

Everyone knows that.

Vlad appeared alongside Agnes, lounging on the air as though it were a sofa.

'Enjoying it?' he said.

'It's fine so far,' said Agnes, not looking at him.

She felt him touch her wrist. There was no real sense of pressure, but the fall stopped. She felt as light as the air again.

'Why are you *doing* this?' she said. 'If you're going to bite me, then get it over with!'

'Oh, but I couldn't be having with that!'

'You did it to Granny!' said Agnes.

'Yes, but when it's against someone's will . . . well, they end up so . . . compliant. Little more than thinking food. But someone who embraces the night of their own volition . . . ah, that's another thing entirely, my dear Agnes. And you're *far* too interesting to be a slave.'

'Tell me,' said Agnes, as a mountaintop floated by, 'have you had many girlfriends?'

He shrugged. 'One or two. Village girls. Housemaids.'

'And what happened to them, may I ask?'

'Don't look at me like that. We still find employment for them in the castle.'

Agnes loathed him. Perdita merely hated him, which is the opposite pole to love and just as attractive.

. . . but Nanny said if the worst came to the worst . . . and then he'll trust you . . . and they've already got Granny . . .

'If I'm a vampire,' she said, 'I won't know good from evil.'

'That's a bit childish, isn't it? They're only ways of looking at the same thing. You don't always have to do what the rest of the world wants you to do.'

'Are you *still* toying with her?'

Lacrimosa was walking towards them on the air. Agnes saw the other vampires behind her.

'Bite her or let her go,' the girl went on. 'Good grief, she's so *blobby*. Come on, Father wants you. They're heading for our castle. Isn't that just too stupid?'

'This is my affair, Lacci,' said Vlad.

'Every boy should have a hobby, but . . . *really*,' said Lacrimosa, rolling her black-rimmed eyes.

Vlad grinned at Agnes.

'Come with us,' he said.

Granny did say you need to be with the others, Perdita pointed out.

'Yes, but how will I find them when we're there?' said Agnes aloud.

'Oh, we'll find them,' said Vlad.

'I meant—'

'*Do* come. We don't intend to hurt your friends—'

'Much,' said Lacrimosa.

'Or . . . we could leave you here,' said Vlad, smiling.

Agnes looked around. They had touched down on the mountain peak, above the clouds. She felt warm and light, which was wrong. Even on a broomstick she'd never felt like this, she'd always been aware of gravity sucking her down, but with the vampire holding her arm every part of her felt that it could float for ever.

Besides, if she didn't go with them it was going to be either a very long or an extremely short journey down to the ground.

Besides, she *would* find the other two, and you couldn't do that when you were dying in some crevasse somewhere.

Besides, even if he did have small fangs and a terrible taste in waistcoats, Vlad actually seemed *attracted* to her. It wasn't even as if she had a very interesting neck.

She made up both minds.

'If you attached a piece of string to her I suppose we could tow her like some sort of balloon,' said Lacrimosa.

Besides, there was always the chance that, at some point, she might find herself in a room with Lacrimosa. When that happened, she wouldn't need garlic, or a stake, or an axe. Just a little talk about people who were too unpleasant, too malicious, too *thin*. Just five minutes alone.

And perhaps a pin, said Perdita.

Under the rabbit hole, down below the bank, was a wide, low-roofed chamber. Tree roots wound among the stones in the wall.

There were plenty of such things around Lancre. The kingdom had been there many years, ever since the ice withdrew. Tribes had pillaged, tilled, built and died. The clay walls and reed thatch of the living houses had long since rotted and been lost but, down under the moundy banks, the abodes of the dead survived. No one knew now who'd been buried there. Occasionally the spoil heap outside a badger sett would reveal a piece of bone or a scrap of corroded armour. The Lancrastians didn't go digging themselves, reckoning in their uncomplicated country way that it was bad luck to have your head torn off by a vengeful underground spirit.

One or two of the old barrows had been exposed over the years, their huge stones attracting their own folklore. If you left your unshod horse at one of them overnight and placed a sixpence on the stone, in the morning the sixpence would be gone and you'd never see your horse again, either . . .

Down on the earth floor under the bank a fire was burning darkly, filling the barrow with smoke which exited through various hidden crannies. There was a pear-shaped rock beside it.

Verence tried to sit up, but his body didn't want to obey.

'Dinna scanna' whista,' said the rock.

It unfolded its legs. It was, he realized, a woman, or at least a female, blue like the other pixies but at least a foot high and so fat that it was almost spherical. It looked exactly like the little figurines back in the days of ice and mammoths, when what men *really* looked for in a woman was quantity. For the sake of modesty, or merely to mark the equator, it wore what Verence could only think of as a tutu. The whole effect reminded him of a spinning top he'd had when he was a child.

'The Kelda says,' said a cracked voice by his ear, 'that ye . . . must get . . . ready.'

Verence turned his head the other way and tried to focus on a small wizened pixie right in front of his nose. Its skin was faded. It had a long white beard. It walked with two sticks.

'Ready? For what?'

'Good.' The old pixie banged its sticks on the ground. 'Craik'n shaden ach, Feegle!'

The blue men rushed at Verence from the shadows. Hundreds of hands grabbed him. Their bodies formed a human pyramid, pulling him upright against the wall. Some clung to the tree roots that looped across the ceiling, tugging on his nightshirt to keep him vertical.

A crowd of others ran across the floor with a full-sized crossbow and propped it on a stone close to him.

'Er . . . I say . . .' Verence murmured.

The Kelda waddled into the shadows and returned with her pudgy fists clenched. She went to the fire and held them over the flames.

'Yin!' said the old pixie.

'I say, that's aimed right at my—'

'Yin!' shouted the Nac mac Feegle.

'. . . ton!'

'Ton!'

'Um, it's, er, right . . .'

'Tetra!'

The Kelda dropped something on the fire. A white flame roared up, etching the room in black and white. Verence blinked.

When he managed to see again there was a crossbow bolt sticking in the wall just by his ear.

The Kelda growled some order, while white light still danced around the walls. The bearded pixie rattled his sticks again.

'Now ye must walk awa'. Noo!'

The Feegle let Verence go. He took a few tottering steps and collapsed on the floor, but the pixies weren't watching him.

He looked up.

His shadow twisted on the wall where it had been pinned. It writhed for a moment, trying to clutch at the arrow with insubstantial hands, and then faded.

Verence raised his hand. There seemed to be a shadow there, too, but at least this one looked as if it was the regular kind.

The old pixie hobbled over to him.

'All fine now,' he said.

'You shot my shadow?' said Verence.

'Aye, ye *could* call it a shade,' said the pixie. 'It's the 'fluence they put on ye. But ye'll be up and aboot in no time.'

'A boot?'

'Aboot the place,' said the pixie evenly. 'All hail, your kingy. I'm Big Aggie's Man. Ye'd call me the prime minister, I'm hazardin'. Will ye no' have a huge dram and a burned bannock while yer waitin'?'

Verence rubbed his face. He did feel better already. The fog was drifting away.

'How can I ever repay you?' he said.

The pixie's eyes gleamed happily.

'Oh, there's a wee bitty thing the carlin' Ogg said you could be givin' us, hardly important at all,' he said.

'Anything,' said Verence.

A couple of pixies came up staggering under a rolled-up parchment, which was unfolded in front of Verence. The old pixie was suddenly holding a quill pen.

'It's called a signature,' he said, as Verence stared at

the tiny handwriting. 'An' make sure ye initial all the sub-clauses and codicils. We of the Nac mac Feegle are a simple folk,' he added, 'but we write verra complicated documents.'

Mightily Oats blinked at Granny over the top of his praying hands. She saw his gaze slide sideways to the axe, and then back to her.

'You wouldn't reach it in time,' said Granny, without moving. 'Should've got hold of it already if you were goin' to use it. Prayer's all very well. I can see where it can help you get your mind right. But an axe is an axe no matter what you believes.'

Oats relaxed a little. He'd expected a leap for the throat.

'If Hodgesaargh's made any tea, I'm parched,' said Granny. She leaned against the anvil, panting. Out of the corner of her eye she saw his hand move slowly.

'I'll get— I'll ask— I'll—'

'Man with his head screwed on properly, that falconer. A biscuit wouldn't come amiss.'

Oats's hand reached the axe handle.

'Still not quick enough,' said Granny. 'Keep hold of it, though. Axe first, pray later. You look like a priest. What's your god?'

'Er . . . Om.'

'That a he god or a she god?'

'A he. Yes. A he. Definitely a he.' It was one thing the Church hadn't schismed over, strangely. 'Er . . . you don't mind, do you?'

'Why should I mind?'

'Well . . . your colleagues keep telling me the Omnians used to burn witches . . .'

'They never did,' said Granny.

'I'm afraid I have to admit that the records show—'

'They never burned witches,' said Granny. 'Probably they burned some old ladies who spoke up or couldn't run away. I wouldn't look for witches bein' burned,' she added, shifting position. 'I might look for witches doin' the burning, though. We ain't *all* nice.'

Oats remembered the Count talking about contributing to the *Arca Instrumentorum* . . .

Those books were ancient! *But so were vampires, weren't they?* And they were practically canonical! The freezing knife of doubt wedged itself deeper in his brain. Who knew who really wrote *anything*? What could you *trust*? Where was the *holy* writ? Where was the *truth*?

Granny pulled herself to her feet and tottered over to the bench, where Hodgesaargh had left his jar of flame. She examined it carefully.

Oats tightened his grip on the axe. It was, he had to admit, slightly more comforting than prayer at that moment. Perhaps you could start with the small truths. Like: he had an axe in his hand.

'I wa— want to be certain,' he said. 'Are you . . . are you a vampire?'

Granny Weatherwax appeared not to hear the question.

'Where's Hodgesaargh with that tea?' she said.

The falconer came in with a tray.

'Nice to see you up and about, Mistress Weatherwax.'

'Not before time.'

The tea slopped as she took the proffered cup. Her hand was shaking.

'Hodgesaargh?'

'Yes, mistress?'

'So you've got a firebird here, have you?'

'No, mistress.'

'I saw you out huntin' it.'

'And I found it, miss. But it had been killed. There was nothing but burnt ground, miss.'

'You'd better tell me all about it.'

'Is this the right time?' said Oats.

'Yes,' said Granny Weatherwax.

Oats sat and listened. Hodgesaargh was an original storyteller and quite good in a very specific way. If he'd had to recount the saga of the Tsortean War, for example, it would have been in terms of the birds observed, every cormorant noted, every pelican listed, every battlefield raven taxonomically placed, no tern unturned. Some men in armour would have been involved at some stage, but only because the ravens were perching on them.

'The phoenix doesn't lay eggs,' said Oats, at one point. This was a point a few points after the point where he asked the falconer if he'd been drinking.

'She's a bird,' said Hodgesaargh. 'That's what birds do. I've never seen a bird that doesn't lay eggs. I collected the eggshell.'

He scuttled off into the mews. Oats smiled nervously at Granny Weatherwax.

'Probably a bit of chicken shell,' he said. 'I've read

about the phoenix. It's a mythical creature, a symbol, it—'

'Can't say for sure,' said Granny. 'I've never seen one that close to.'

The falconer returned, clutching a small box. It was full of tufts of fleece, in the middle of which was a pile of shell fragments. Oats picked up a couple. They were a silvery grey and very light.

'I found them in the ashes.'

'No one's ever claimed to have found phoenix eggshell before,' said Oats accusingly.

'Didn't know that, sir,' said Hodgesaargh innocently. 'Otherwise I wouldn't have looked.'

'Did anyone else ever look, I wonder?' said Granny. She poked at the fragments. 'Ah . . .' she said.

'I thought p'raps the phoenixes used to live somewhere very dangerous—' Hodgesaargh began.

'Everywhere's like that when you're newborn,' said Granny. 'I can see you've been thinking, Hodgesaargh.'

'Thank you, Mistress Weatherwax.'

'Shame you didn't think further,' Granny went on.

'Mistress?'

'There's the bits of more than one egg here.'

'Mistress?'

'Hodgesaargh,' said Granny patiently, 'this phoenix laid more than one egg.'

'What? But it can't! According to mythology—' Oats said.

'Oh, *mythology*,' said Granny. 'Mythology's just the folktales of people who won 'cos they had bigger swords. They're *just* the people to spot the finer points of ornithology, are they? Anyway, one of anything ain't going to last for very long, is it? Firebirds have got enemies, same as everything else. Give me a hand up, Mister Oats. How many birds in the mews, Hodgesaargh?'

The falconer looked at his fingers for a moment.

'Fifty.'

'Counted 'em lately?'

They stood and watched while he walked from post to post. Then they stood and watched while he walked back and counted them again. Then he spent some time looking at his fingers.

'Fifty-one?' said Granny helpfully.

'I don't understand it, mistress.'

'You'd better count them by types, then.'

This produced a count of nineteen lappet-faced worriers where there should have been eighteen.

'Perhaps one flew in because it saw the others,' said Oats. 'Like pigeons.'

'It doesn't work like that, sir,' said the falconer.

'One of 'em won't be tethered,' said Granny. 'Trust me.'

They found it at the back, slightly smaller than the other worriers, hanging meekly from its perch.

Fewer birds could sit more meekly than the Lancre wowhawk, or lappet-faced worrier, a carnivore permanently on the lookout for the vegetarian option. It spent most of its time asleep in any case, but when forced to find food it tended to sit on a branch out of the wind somewhere and wait for something to die. When in the mews the worriers would initially perch like other birds and then, talons clamped around the pole, doze off peacefully upside down. Hodgesaargh bred them because they were found only in Lancre and he liked the plumage, but all reputable falconers agreed that for hunting purposes the only way you could reliably bring down prey with a wowhawk was by using it in a slingshot.

Granny reached out towards it.

'I'll fetch you a glove,' said Hodgesaargh, but she waved him away.

The bird hopped on to her wrist.

Granny gasped, and little threads of green and blue burned like marsh gas along her arm for a moment.

'Are you all right?' said Oats.

'Never been better. I'll need this bird, Hodgesaargh.'

'It's dark, mistress.'

'That won't matter. But it'll need to be hooded.'

'Oh, I never hood wowhawks, mistress. They're never any trouble.'

'This bird . . . *this* bird,' said Granny, 'is a bird I reckon no one's ever seen before. Hood it.'

Hodgesaargh hesitated. He recalled the circle of scorched earth and, before it, something looking for a shape in which it could survive . . .

'It *is* a wowhawk, isn't it, mistress?'

'And what makes you ask that?' said Granny slowly. 'After all, you're the falconer in these parts.'

'Because I found . . . in the woods . . . I saw . . .'

'What did you see, Hodgesaargh?'

Hodgesaargh gave up in the face of her stare. To think that he'd tried to *capture* a phoenix! At least the worst the other birds could do would be to draw blood. Supposing he'd been *holding* it . . . He was overcome by a very definite *burning* desire to get this bird out of here.

Strangely, though, the other birds weren't disturbed at all. Every hooded head was turned towards the little bird on Granny Weatherwax's wrist. Every blind, hooded head.

Hodgesaargh picked up another hood. As he fastened it over the bird's head he thought, for a moment, that there was a flash of gold from underneath.

He put that down as not his business. He'd survived quite happily in the castle for many years by knowing where his business was, and he was suddenly very clear that it wasn't here, thank goodness.

Granny took a few deep breaths.

'Right,' she said. 'Now we'll go up to the castle.'

'What for? Why?' said Oats.

'Good grief, man, why d'you think?'

'The vampires are gone,' said the priest. 'While you were . . . getting better. Mr Hodges . . . aargh found out. They've just left the soldiers and the, er, servants. There was a lot of noise and the coach went, too. There's guards all over the place.'

'How did the coach get out, then?'

'Well, it was the vampires' coach and their servant was driving it, but Jason Ogg said he saw Mrs Ogg, too.'

Granny steadied herself against the wall.

'Where did they go?'

'I thought you could read their minds or something,' said Oats.

'Young man, right now I don't think I can read my *own* mind.'

'Look, Granny Weatherwax, it's obvious to me you're still weak from loss of blood—'

'Don't you dare tell me what I am,' said Granny. 'Don't you *dare*. Now, where would Gytha Ogg've taken them?'

'I think—'

'Uberwald,' said Granny. 'That'll be it.'

'What? How can you know that?'

'Because nowhere in the village'd be safe, she wouldn't go up to the gnarly ground on a night like this and with a baby to carry as well, and heading down on to the plains'd be downright daft 'cos there's no cover and I wouldn't be surprised if the road is washed out by now.'

'But that'll be right into danger!'

'More dangerous than here?' said Granny. 'They *know* about vampires in Uberwald. They're used to 'em. There's safe places. Pretty strong inns all along the coach road, for a start. Nanny's practical. She'll think of that, I'm betting.' She winced, and added, 'But they'll end up in the vampires' castle.'

'Oh, surely not!'

'I can feel it in my blood,' said Granny. 'That's the trouble with Gytha Ogg. Far *too* practical.' She paused. 'You mentioned guards?'

'They've locked themselves in the keep, mistress,' said a voice in the doorway. It was Shawn Ogg, with the rest of the mob behind him. He advanced awkwardly, one hand held in front of him.

'That's a blessing, then,' said Granny.

'But we can't get in, mistress,' said Shawn.

'So? Can they get out?'

'Well . . . no, not really. But the armoury's in there. All our weapons! *And* they're boozing!'

'What's that you're holding?'

Shawn looked down. 'It's the Lancrastian Army Knife,' he said. 'Er . . . I left my sword in the armoury, too.'

'Has it got a tool for extracting soldiers from castles?'

'Er . . . no.'

Granny peered closer. 'What's the curly thing?' she said.

'Oh, that's the Adjustable Device for Winning Ontological Arguments,' said Shawn. 'The King asked for it.'

'Works, does it?'

'Er . . . if you twiddle it properly.'

'And this?'

'That's the Tool for Extracting the Essential Truth from a Given Statement,' said Shawn.

'Verence asked for that one too, did he?'

'Yes, Granny.'

'Useful to a soldier, is it?' said Oats. He glanced at Granny. She'd changed as soon as the others had entered. Before, she'd been bowed and tired. Now she was standing tall and haughty, supported by a scaffolding of pride.

'Oh, yes, sir, 'cos of when the other side are yelling, "We're gonna cut yer tonk— yer *tongue* off,"' Shawn blushed and corrected himself, 'and things like that . . .'

'Yes?'

'Well, you can tell if they're going to be right,' said Shawn.

'I need a horse,' said Granny.

'There's old Poorchick's plough horse—' Shawn began.

'Too slow.'

'I . . . er . . . I've got a mule,' said Oats. 'The King was kind enough to let me put it in the stables.'

'Neither one thing nor t'other, eh?' said Granny. 'It suits you. That'll do for me, then. Fetch it up here and I'll be off to get the girls back.'

'What? I thought you wanted it to take you up to your cottage! Into Uberwald? Alone? I couldn't let you do that!'

'I ain't asking you to *let* me do anything. Now off you go and fetch it, otherwise Om will be angry, I expect.'

'But you can hardly stand up!'

'Certainly I can! Off you go.'

Oats turned to the assembled Lancrastians for support.

'You wouldn't let a poor old lady go off to confront monsters on a wild night like this, would you?'

They watched him owlishly for a while just in case something interestingly nasty was going to happen to him.

Then someone near the back said, 'So why should we care what happens to monsters?'

And Shawn Ogg said, 'That's Granny Weatherwax, that is.'

'But she's an old lady!' Oats insisted.

The crowd took a few steps back. Oats was clearly a dangerous man to be around.

'Would *you* go out alone on a night like this?' he said.

The voice at the back said, 'Depends if I knew where Granny Weatherwax was.'

'Don't think I didn't hear that, Bestiality Carter,' said Granny, but there was just a hint of satisfaction in her voice. 'Now, are we fetchin' your mule, Mr Oats?'

'Are you *sure* you can walk?'

'Of course I can!'

Oats gave up. Granny smirked triumphantly at the crowd and strode through them and towards the stables, with him trotting after her.

When he hurried around the corner he almost collided with her, standing as stiff as a rod.

'Is there anyone watchin' me?' she said.

'What? No, I don't think so. Apart from me, of course.'

'You don't count,' said Granny.

She sagged, and almost collapsed. He caught her, and she pummelled him on the arm. The wowhawk flapped its wings desperately.

'Let go! I just lost my footin', that's all!'

'Yes, yes, of course. You just lost your footing,' he said soothingly.

'And don't try to humour me, either.'

'Yes, yes, all *right*.'

'It's just that it don't do to let things slide, if you must know.'

'Like your foot did just then . . .'

'Exactly.'

'So perhaps I'll take your arm, because it's very muddy.'

He could just make out her face. It was a picture, but not one you'd hang over the fireplace. Some sort of inner debate was raging.

'Well, if you think *you're* going to fall over . . .' she said.

'That's right, that's right,' said Oats gratefully. 'I nearly hurt my ankle back there as it is.'

'I've always said young people today don't have the stamina,' said Granny, as if testing out an idea.

'That's right, we don't have the stamina.'

'And your eyesight is prob'ly not as good as mine owin' to too much readin',' said Granny.

'Blind as a bat, that's right.'

'All right.'

And so, at cross purposes and lurching occasionally, they reached the stables.

The mule shook its head at Granny Weatherwax when they arrived at its loose box. It knew trouble when it saw her.

'It's a bit cantankerous,' said Oats.

'Is it?' said Granny. 'Then we shall see what we can do.'

She walked unsteadily over to the creature and pulled one of its ears down to the level of her mouth. She whispered something. The mule blinked.

'That's sorted out, then,' she said. 'Help me up.'

'Just let me put the bridle on—'

'Young man, I might be temp'ry not at my best, but when I need a bridle on any creature they can put me to bed with a shovel. Give me a hand up, and kindly avert your face whilst so doing.'

Oats gave up and made a stirrup of his hands to help her into the saddle.

'Why don't I come with you?'

'There's only one mule. Anyway, you'd be a hindrance. I'd be worrying about you all the time.'

She slid gently off the other side of the saddle and landed in the straw. The wowhawk fluttered up and perched on a beam, and if Oats had been paying attention he'd have wondered how a hooded bird could fly so confidently.

'Drat!'

'Madam, I *do* know something about medicine! You are in *no* state to ride anything!'

'Not right now, I admit,' said Granny, her voice slightly muffled. She pulled some straw away from her face and waved a hand wildly to be helped up. 'But you just wait until I find my feet . . .'

'All right! All *right*! Supposing I ride and you hang on behind me? You can't weigh more than the harmonium, and I managed that all right.'

Granny looked owlishly at him. She seemed drunk, at that stage when hitherto unconsidered things seem a good idea, like another drink. Then she appeared to reach a decision.

'Oh . . . if you insist . . .'

Oats found a length of rope and, after some difficulties caused by Granny's determined belief that she was doing him some sort of favour, got her strapped into a pillion position.

'Just so long as you understand that I didn't ax you

to come along and I don't need your help,' said Granny.

'Ax?'

'Ask, then,' said Granny. 'Slipped into a bit of rural there.'

Oats stared ahead for a while. Then he dismounted, lifted Granny down, propped her up while she protested, disappeared into the night, came back shortly carrying the axe from the forge, used more rope to tie it to his waist, and mounted up again.

'You're learnin',' said Granny.

As they left she raised an arm. The wowhawk fluttered down and settled on her wrist.

The air in the rocking coach was acquiring a distinct personality.

Magrat sniffed. 'I'm *sure* I changed Esme not long ago . . .'

After a fruitless search of the baby they looked under the seat. Greebo was lying asleep with his legs in the air.

'Isn't that just like him?' said Nanny. 'He can't see an open door without going through it, bless 'im. And he likes to be near his mum.'

'Could we open a window?' said Magrat.

'The rain'll get in.'

'Yes, but the smell will go out.' Magrat sighed. 'You know, we've left at least one bag of toys. Verence was really very keen on those mobiles.'

'I still think it's a bit early to start the poor little mite on education,' said Nanny, as much to take

Magrat's mind off the current dangers as from a desire to strike a blow for ignorance.

'Environment is so very important,' said Magrat solemnly.

'Did I hear he told you to read improvin' books and listen to posh music while you were expecting?' said Nanny, as the coach rushed through a puddle.

'Well, the books were all right, but the piano doesn't work properly and all I could hear was Shawn practising the trumpet solo,' said Magrat.

'It's not his fault if no one wants to join in,' said Nanny. She steadied herself as the coach lurched. 'Good turn of speed on this thing.'

'I wish we hadn't forgotten the bath, too,' Magrat mused. 'And I think we left the bag with the toy farm. And we're low on nappies . . .'

'Let's have a look at her,' Nanny said.

Baby Esme was passed across the swaying coach.

'Yes, let's have a look at you . . .' said Nanny.

The small blue eyes focused on Nanny Ogg. The pink face on the small lolling head gave her a speculative look, working out whether she'd do as a drink or a toilet.

'That's good, at this age,' said Nanny. 'Focusing like that. Unusual in a babby.'

'If she *is* at this age,' said Magrat darkly.

'Hush, now. If Granny's in there she's not interfering. She never interferes. Anyway, it wouldn't be her *mind* in there, that's not how she works it.'

'What is it, then?'

'You've seen her do it. What do *you* think?'

'I'd say . . . all the things that make her *her*,' Magrat ventured.

'That's about right. She wraps 'em all up and puts 'em somewhere safe.'

'You know how she can even be silent in her own special way.'

'Oh, yes. No one can be quiet like Esme. You can hardly hear yourself think for the silence.'

They bounced in their seats as the coach sprang in and out of a pothole.

'Nanny?'

'Yes, love?'

'Verence *will* be all right, won't he?'

'Yep. I'd trust them little devils with anything except a barrel of stingo or a cow. Even Granny says the Kelda's damn good—'

'The Kelda?'

'Sort of a wise lady. I think the current one's called Big Aggie. You don't see much of their women. Some say there's only ever one at a time, and she's the Kelda an' has a hundred kids at a go.'

'That sounds . . . very . . .' Magrat began.

'Nah, I reckons they're a bit like the dwarfs and there's hardly any difference except under the loin-cloth,' said Nanny.

'I expect Granny knows,' said Magrat.

'And she ain't sayin',' said Nanny. 'She says it's their business.'

'And . . . he'll be all right with them?'

'Oh, yes.'

'He's very . . . kind, you know.' Magrat's sentence hung in the air.

'That's nice.'

'And a good king, as well.'

Nanny nodded.

'It's just that I wish people took him . . . more seriously,' Magrat went on.

'It's a shame,' said Nanny.

'He does work very hard. And he worries about everything. But people just seem to ignore him.'

Nanny wondered how to approach it.

'He could try having the crown taken in a bit,' she ventured, as the coach bounced over another rut. 'There's plenty of dwarfs up at Copperhead'd be glad to make it smaller for him.'

'It *is* the traditional crown, Nanny.'

'Yes, but if it wasn't for his ears it'd be a collar on the poor man,' said Nanny. 'He could try bellowing a bit more, too.'

'Oh, he couldn't do that, he *hates* shouting!'

'That's a shame. People like to see a bit of bellowing in a king. The odd belch is always popular, too. Even a bit of carousing'd help, if he could manage it. You know, quaffing and such.'

'I think he thinks that isn't what people want. He's very conscious of the needs of today's citizen.'

'Ah, well, I can see where there's a problem, then,' said Nanny. 'People need something today but they generally need something else tomorrow. Just tell him to concentrate on bellowing and carousing.'

'And belching?'

'That's optional.'

'And . . .'

'Yes, dear?'

'He'll be all right, will he?'

'Oh, yes. Nothing's going to happen to him. It's like that chess stuff, see? Let the Queen do the fightin', 'cos if you lose the King you've lost everything.'

'And us?'

'Oh, *we're* always all right. You remember that. We happen to other people.'

A lot of people were happening to King Verence. He lay in a sort of warm, empty daze, and every time he opened his eyes it was to see scores of the Feegle watching him in the firelight. He overheard snatches of conversation or, more correctly, argument.

'... he's oor kingie noo?'

'Aye, sortaley.'

'That pish of a hobyah?'

'Hushagob! D'man's sicken, can y'no vard?'

'Aye, mucken! Born sicky, imhoe!'

Verence felt a small yet powerful kick on his foot.

'See you, kingie? A'ye a lang stick o'midlin or wha', bigjobs?'

'Yes, well done,' he mumbled.

The interrogating Feegle spat near his ear.

'Ach, I wouldna' gi'ye skeppens for him—'

There was a sudden silence, a real rarity in any space containing at least one Feegle. Verence swivelled his eyes sideways.

Big Aggie had emerged from the smoke.

Now that he could see her clearly, the dumpy creature looked like a squat version of Nanny Ogg. And there was something about the eyes. Verence was technically an absolute ruler and would continue to be so provided he didn't make the mistake of repeatedly asking Lancrastians to do anything they didn't want to do. He was aware that the commander-in-chief of his armed forces was more inclined to take orders from his mum than his king.

Whereas Big Aggie didn't even have to *say* anything. Everyone just watched her, and then went and got things done.

Big Aggie's man appeared at her side.

'Ye'll be wantin' to save yer ladie and yer bairn, Big Aggie's thinkin'," he said.

Verence nodded. He didn't feel strong enough to do anything else.

'But ye'll still be verra crassick from loss o' blud, Big Aggie reckons. The heelins put something in their bite that makes ye biddable.'

Verence agreed absolutely. Anything anyone said was all right by him.

Another pixie appeared through the smoke, carrying an earthenware bowl. White suds slopped over the top.

'Ye canna be kinging lyin' down,' said Big Aggie's man. 'So she's made up some brose for ye . . .'

The pixie lowered the bowl, which looked as though it was full of cream, although dark lines spiralled on its surface. Its bearer stood back reverentially.

'What's in it?' Verence croaked.

'Milk,' said Big Aggie's man promptly. 'And some o' Big Aggie's brewin'. An' herbs.'

Verence grasped the last word thankfully. He shared with his wife the curious but unshakeable conviction that anything with herbs in it was safe and wholesome and nourishing.

'So you'll be having a huge dram,' said the old pixie. 'And then we'll be finding you a sword.'

'I've never used a sword,' said Verence, trying to pull himself into a sitting position. 'I— I believe violence is the last resort . . .'

'Ach, weel, so long as ye've brung yer bucket and spade,' said Big Aggie's man. 'Now you just drink up, kingie. Ye'll soon see things differently.'

The vampires glided easily over the moonlit clouds. There was no weather up here and, to Agnes's surprise, no chill either.

'I thought you turned into bats!' she shouted to Vlad.

'Oh, we could if we wanted to,' he laughed. 'But that's a bit too melodramatic for Father. He says we should not conform to crass stereotypes.'

A girl glided alongside them. She looked rather like Lacrimosa; that is, she looked like someone who admired the way Lacrimosa looked and so had tried to look like her. *I bet she's not a natural brunette,* said Perdita. *And if I used that much mascara I'd at least try not to look like Harry the Happy Panda.*

'This is Morbidia,' said Vlad. 'Although she's been calling herself Tracy lately, to be cool. Mor— Tracy, this is Agnes.'

'What a good name!' said Morbidia. 'How clever of you to come up with it! Vlad, everyone wants to stop off at Escrow. Can we?'

'It's my real—' Agnes began, but her words were carried away on the wind.

'I thought we were going to the castle,' said Vlad.

'Yes, but some of us haven't fed for days and that old woman was hardly even a snack and the Count won't allow us to feed in Lancre yet and he says it'll be all right and it's not much out of our way.'

'Oh. Well, if Father says . . .'

Morbidia swooped away.

'We haven't been to Escrow for weeks,' said Vlad. 'It's a pleasant little town.'

'You're going to *feed* there?' said Agnes.

'It's not what you think.'

'You don't *know* what I think.'

'I can guess, though.' He smiled at her. 'I wonder if Father said yes because he wants you to see? It's so easy to be frightened of what you don't know. And then, perhaps, you could be a sort of ambassador. You could tell Lancre what life under the Magpyrs is really like.'

'People being dragged out of their beds, blood on the walls, that sort of thing?'

'There you go again, Agnes. It's most unfair. Once people find out you're a vampire they act as if you're some kind of monster.'

They curved gently through the night air.

'Father's rather proud of his work in Escrow,' said Vlad. 'I think you'll be impressed. And then perhaps I could dare hope—'

'No.'

'I'm really being rather understanding about this, Agnes.'

'You attacked Granny Weatherwax! You *bit* her.'

'Symbolically. To welcome her into the family.'

'Oh, really? Oh, that makes it all better, does it? And she'll be a vampire?'

'Certainly. A good one, I suspect. But that's only horrifying if you believe being a vampire is a bad thing. We don't. You'll come to see that we're right, in time,' said Vlad. 'Yes, Escrow would be good for you. For us. We shall see what can be done . . .'

Agnes stared.

He does smile nicely . . . He's a vampire! *All right, but apart from that—* Oh, *apart* from that, eh? *Nanny would tell you to make the most of it.* That might work for Nanny, but can you imagine *kissing* that? *Yes, I can.* I will admit, he does smile nicely, and he looks good in those waistcoats, but look at what he is— *Do you notice?* Notice what? *There's something different about him.* He's just trying to get round us, that's all. *No . . . there's something . . . new . . .*

'Father says Escrow is a model community,' said Vlad. 'It shows what happens if ancient enmity is put aside and humans and vampires learn to live in peace. Yes. It's not far now. Escrow is the future.'

A low ground mist drifted between the trees, curling up in little tongues as the mule's hooves disturbed it. Rain dripped off the branches. There was even a bit of sullen thunder now, not the outgoing sort that cracks the sky but the other sort, which hangs around the horizons and gossips nastily with other storms.

Mightily Oats had tried a conversation with himself a few times, but the problem with a conversation was that the other person had to join in. Occasionally he heard a snore from behind him. When he looked around, the wowhawk on her shoulder flapped its wings in his face.

Sometimes the snoring would stop with a grunt, and a hand would tap him on a shoulder and point out a direction which looked like every other direction.

It did so now.

'What's that you're singing?' Granny demanded.

'I wasn't singing very loudly.'

'What's it called?'

'It's called "Om Is In His Holy Temple".'

'Nice tune,' said Granny.

'It keeps my spirits up,' Oats admitted. A wet twig slapped his face. After all, he thought, I *may* have a vampire behind me, however good she is.

'You take comfort from it, do you?'

'I suppose so.'

'Even that bit about "smiting evil with thy sword"? That'd worry me, if I was an Omnian. Do you get just a little sort of tap for a white lie but minced up for murder? That's the sort of thing that'd keep *me* awake o' nights.'

'Well, actually . . . I shouldn't be singing it at all, to be honest. The Convocation of Ee struck it from the songbook as being incompatible with the ideals of modern Omnianism.'

'That line about crushing infidels?'

'That's the one, yes.'

'You sung it anyway, though.'

'It's the version my grandmother taught me,' said Oats.

'She was keen on crushing infidels?'

'Well, mainly I think she was in favour of crushing

Mrs Ahrim next door, but you've got the right idea, yes. She thought the world would be a better place with a bit more crushing and smiting.'

'Prob'ly true.'

'Not as much smiting and crushing as *she*'d like, though, I think,' said Oats. 'A bit judgemental, my grandmother.'

'Nothing wrong with that. Judging is human.'

'We prefer to leave it ultimately to Om,' said Oats and, out here in the dark, that statement sounded lost and all alone.

'Bein' human means judgin' all the time,' said the voice behind him. 'This and that, good and bad, making choices every day . . . that's human.'

'And are you so sure you make the right decisions?'

'No. But I do the best I can.'

'And hope for mercy, eh?'

A bony finger prodded him in the back.

'Mercy's a fine thing, but judgin' comes first. Otherwise you don't know what you're bein' merciful about. Anyway, I always heard you Omnians were *keen* on smitin' and crushin'.'

'Those were . . . different days. We use crushing arguments now.'

'And long pointed debates, I suppose?'

'Well, there *are* two sides to every question . . .'

'What do you do when one of 'em's wrong?' The reply came back like an arrow.

'I meant that we are enjoined to see things from the other person's point of view,' said Oats patiently.

'You mean that from the point of view of a torturer, torture is all right?'

'Mistress Weatherwax, you are a natural disputant.'

'No, I ain't!'

'You'd certainly enjoy yourself at the Synod, anyway. They've been known to argue for days about how many angels can dance on the head of a pin.'

He could almost feel Granny's mind working. At last she said, 'What size pin?'

'I don't know that, I'm afraid.'

'Well, if it's a ordinary household pin, then there'll be sixteen.'

'Sixteen angels?'

'That's right.'

'Why?'

'I don't know. Perhaps they like dancing.'

The mule picked its way down a bank. The mist was getting thicker here.

'You've *counted* sixteen?' said Oats eventually.

'No, but it's as good an answer as any you'll get. And that's what your holy men discuss, is it?'

'Not usually. There is a very interesting debate raging at the moment about the nature of sin, for example.'

'And what do they think? Against it, are they?'

'It's not as simple as that. It's not a black and white issue. There are so many shades of grey.'

'Nope.'

'Pardon?'

'There's no greys, only white that's got grubby. I'm surprised you don't know that. And sin, young man, is when you treat people as things. Including yourself. That's what sin is.'

'It's a lot more complicated than that—'

'No. It ain't. When people say things are a lot more complicated than that, they means they're getting worried that they won't like the truth. People as things, that's where it starts.'

'Oh, I'm sure there are worse crimes—'

'But they *starts* with thinking about people as things . . .'

Granny's voice tailed off. Oats let the mule walk on for a few minutes, and then a snort told him that Granny had awoken again.

'You strong in your faith, then?' she said, as if she couldn't leave things alone.

Oats sighed. 'I try to be.'

'But you read a lot of books, I'm thinking. Hard to have faith, ain't it, when you read too many books?'

Oats was glad she couldn't see his face. Was the old woman reading his mind through the back of his head?

'Yes,' he said.

'Still got it, though?'

'Yes.'

'Why?'

'If I didn't, I wouldn't have anything.'

He waited for a while, and then tried a counterattack.

'You're not a believer yourself, then, Mistress Weatherwax?'

There were a few moments' silence as the mule picked its way over the mossy tree roots. Oats thought he heard, behind them, the sound of a horse, but then it was lost in the sighing of the wind.

'Oh, I reckon I believes in tea, sunrises, that sort of thing,' said Granny.

'I was referring to religion.'

'I know a few gods in these parts, if that's what you mean.'

Oats sighed. 'Many people find faith a great solace,' he said. He wished he was one of them.

'Good.'

'Really? Somehow I thought you'd argue.'

'It's not my place to tell 'em what to believe, if they act decent.'

'But it's not something that you feel drawn to, perhaps, in the darker hours?'

'No. I've already got a hot water bottle.'

The wowhawk fluttered its wings. Oats stared into the damp, dark mist. Suddenly he was angry.

'And that's what you think religion is, is it?' he said, trying to keep his temper.

'I gen'rally don't think about it at all,' said the voice behind him.

It sounded fainter. He felt Granny clutch his arm to steady herself . . .

'Are you all right?' he said.

'I wish this creature would go faster . . . I ain't entirely myself.'

'We could stop for a rest.'

'No! Not far now! Oh, I've been so *stupid* . . .'

The thunder grumbled. He felt her grip lessen, and heard her hit the ground.

Oats leapt down. Granny Weatherwax was lying awkwardly on the moss, her eyes closed. He took her wrist. There was a pulse there, but it was horribly weak. She felt icy cold.

When he patted her face she opened her eyes.

'If you raise the subject of religion at this point,' she wheezed, 'I'll give you such a hidin' . . .' Her eyes shut again.

Oats sat down to get his breath back. Icy cold . . . yes, there *was* something cold about all of her, as though she always pushed heat away. Any kind of warmth.

He heard the sound of the horse again, and the faint jingle of a harness. It stopped a little way away.

'Hello?' said Oats, standing up. He strained to see the rider in the darkness, but there was just a dim shape further along the track.

'Are you following us? Hello?'

He took a few steps and made out the horse, head bowed against the rain. The rider was just a darker shadow in the night.

Suddenly awash with dread, Oats ran and slithered back to Granny's silent form. He struggled out of his drenched coat and put it over her, for whatever good that would do, and looked around desperately for anything that could make a fire. *Fire*, that was the thing. It brought life and drove away the darkness.

But the trees were tall firs, dripping wet with dank bracken underneath among the black trunks. There was nothing that would burn here.

He fished hurriedly in his pocket and found a waxed box with his last few matches in it. Even a few dry twigs or a tuft of grass would do, anything that'd dry out *another* handful of twigs . . .

Rain oozed through his shirt. The air was full of water.

Oats hunched over so that his hat kept the drips off, and pulled out the *Book of Om* for the comfort that it brought. In times of trouble, Om would surely show the way—

. . . I've already got a hot water bottle . . .

'Damn you,' he said, under his breath.

He opened the book at random, struck a match and read:

'*. . . and in that time, in the land of the Cyrinites, there was a multiplication of camels . . .*'

The match hissed out.

No help there, no clue. He tried again.

'*. . . and looked upon Gul-Arah, and the lamentation of the desert, and rode then to . . .*'

Oats remembered the vampire's mocking smile. What words could you trust? He struck the third match with shaking hands and flicked the book open again and read, in the weak dancing light:

'*. . . and Brutha said to Simony, "Where there is darkness we will make a great light . . ."*'

The match died. And there was darkness.

Granny Weatherwax groaned. At the back of his mind Oats thought he could hear the sound of hooves, slowly approaching.

Oats knelt in the mud and tried a prayer, but there was no answering voice from the sky. There never had been. He'd been told never to expect one. That wasn't how Om worked any more. Alone of all the gods, he'd been taught, Om delivered the answers straight into the depths of the head. Since the prophet Brutha, Om was the silent god. That's what they said.

If you didn't have faith, then you weren't anything. There was just the dark.

He shuddered in the gloom. Was the god silent, or was there no one to speak?

He tried praying again, more desperately this time, fragments of childish prayer, losing control of the words and even of their direction, so that they tumbled out and soared away into the universe addressed simply to The Occupier.

The rain dripped off his hat.

He knelt and waited in the wet darkness, and listened to his own mind, and remembered, and took out the *Book of Om* once more.

And made a great light.

The coach thundered through pinetrees by a lake, struck a tree root, lost a wheel and skidded to a halt on its side as the horses bolted.

Igor picked himself up, lurched to the coach and raised a door.

'Thorry about that,' he said. 'I'm afraid thith alwayth happenth when the marthter ithn't on board. Everyone all right down there?'

A hand grabbed him by the throat.

'You could have warned us!' Nanny growled. 'We were thrown all over the place! Where the hell are we? Is this Slake?'

A match flared and Igor lit a torch.

'We're near the cathle,' he said.

'Whose?'

'The Magpyrth.'

'We're near the *vampires'* castle?'

'Yeth. I think the old marthter did thomething to the road here. The wheelth alwayth come off, ath thure ath eggth ith eggth. Bringth in the vithitorth, he thed.'

'It didn't occur to you to mention it?' said Nanny, climbing out and giving Magrat a hand.

'Thorry. It'th been a buthy day . . .'

Nanny took the torch. The flames illuminated a crude sign nailed to a tree.

'"Don't go near the Castle!!"' Nanny read. 'Nice of them to put an arrow pointing the way to it, too.'

'Oh, the marthter did that,' said Igor. 'Otherwithe people wouldn't notithe it.'

Nanny peered into the gloom. 'And who's in the castle now?'

'A few thervantth.'

'Will they let us in?'

'That'th not a problem.' Igor fished in his noisome shirt and pulled out a very big key on a string.

'We're going to go *into* their *castle*?' said Magrat.

'Looks like it's the only place around,' said Nanny Ogg, heading up the track. 'The coach is wrecked. We're miles from anywhere else. Do you want to keep the baby out all night? A castle's a castle. It'll have locks. All the vampires are in Lancre. And—'

'Well?'

'It's what Esme would've done. I feels it in my blood.'

A little way off something howled. Nanny looked at Igor.

'Werewolf?' she said.

'That'th right.'

'Not a good idea to hang around, then.'

She pointed to a sign painted on a rock.

'"Don't take thiſ quickeſt route to the Caſtle,"' she read aloud. 'You've got to admire a mind like that. Definitely a student of human nature.'

'Won't there be a lot of ways in?' said Magrat as they walked past a sign that said: 'Don't go Nere the Coach Park, 20 yds. on left.'

'Igor?' said Nanny.

'Vampireth uthed to fight amongtht themthelveth,' said Igor. 'There'th only one way in.'

'Oh, all *right*, if we must,' said Magrat. 'You take the rocker, and the used nappy bag. And the teddies. And the thing that goes round and round and plays noises when she pulls the string—'

A sign near the drawbridge said, 'Laſt chance not to Go near the Caſtle', and Nanny Ogg laughed and laughed.

'The Count's not going to be very happy about you, Igor,' she said, as he unlocked the doors.

'Thod him,' he said. 'I'm going to pack up my thtuff and head for Blintth. There'th alwayth a job for an Igor up there. More lightning thtriketh per year than anywhere in the mountainth, they thay.'

Nanny Ogg wiped her eye. 'Good job we're soaked already,' she said. 'All right, let's get in. And, Igor, if you haven't been thtraight with us, sorry, straight with us, I'll have your guts for garters.'

Igor looked down bashfully. 'Oh, that'th more than a man could pothibly hope for,' he murmured.

Magrat giggled and Igor pushed open the door and hurriedly shuffled inside.

'What?' said Nanny.

'Haven't you noticed the looks he's been giving you?' said Magrat, as they followed the lurching figure.

'What, *him*?' said Nanny.

'Could be carrying a torch for you,' said Magrat.

'I thought it was just to see where he's going!' said Nanny, a little bit of panic in her voice. 'I mean, I haven't got my best drawers on or anything!'

'I think he's a bit of a romantic, actually,' said Magrat.

'Oh, I don't know, I really don't,' said Nanny. 'I mean, it's flattering and everything, but I really don't think I could be goin' out with a man with a limp.'

'Limp what?'

Nanny Ogg had always considered herself unshockable, but there's no such thing. Shocks can come from unexpected directions.

'I *am* a married woman,' said Magrat, smiling at her expression. And it felt good, just once, to place a small tintack in the path of Nanny's carefree amble through life.

'But is . . . I mean, is Verence, you know, all right in the—'

'Oh, yes. Everything's . . . fine. But now I understand what your jokes were about.'

'What, *all* of them?' said Nanny, like someone who'd found all the aces removed from their favourite pack of cards.

'Well, not the one about the priest, the old woman and the rhinoceros.'

'I should just about hope so!' said Nanny. 'I

didn't understand *that* one until I was forty!'

Igor limped back.

'There'th jutht the thervantth,' he said. 'You could thtay down in my quarterth in the old tower. There'th thick doorth.'

'Mrs Ogg would really like that,' said Magrat. 'She was saying just now what good legs you've got, weren't you, Nanny . . .'

'Do you want thome?' said Igor earnestly, leading the way up the steps. 'I've got plenty and I could do with the thpathe in the ithehouthe.'

'You what?' said Nanny, stopping dead.

'I'm your man if there'th any organ you need,' said Igor.

There was a strangled coughing noise from Magrat.

'You've got – bits of people stored on ice?' said Nanny, horrified. 'Bits of strange people? Chopped up? I'm not taking another step!'

Now Igor looked horrified.

'Not *thtrangerth*,' he said. '*Family*.'

'You chopped up your *family*?' Nanny backed away.

Igor waved his hands frantically.

'It's a tradithion!' he said. 'Every Igor leaveth hith body to the family! Why wathte good organth? Look at my Uncle Igor, he died of buffaloeth, tho there wath a perfectly good heart and thome kidneyth going begging, pluth he'd thtill got Grandad'th handth and they were damn good handth, let me tell you.' He sniffed. 'I with I'd had them, he wath a great thurgeon.'

'We-ll . . . I know every family says things like "He's got his father's eyes"—' Nanny began.

'No, my thecond couthin Igor got *them*.'

'But— but . . . who does the cutting and sewing?' said Magrat.

'I do. An Igor learnth houthehold thurgery on hith father'th knee,' said Igor. 'And then practitheth on hith grandfather'th kidneyth.'

''scuse me,' said Nanny. 'What did you say your uncle died of?'

'Buffaloeth,' said Igor, unlocking another door.

'He broke out in them?'

'A herd fell on him. A freak acthident. We don't talk about it.'

'Sorry, are you telling us you do surgery on *yourself*?' said Magrat.

'It'th not hard when you know what you're doing. Thometimeth you need a mirror, of courth, and it helpth if thomeone can put a finger on the knotth.'

'Isn't it painful?'

'Oh, no, I alwayth tell them to take it away jutht before I pull the thtring tight.'

The door creaked open. It was a long, tortured, groaning noise. In fact there was more creak than door, and it went on just a few seconds after the door had stopped.

'That sounds *dreadful*,' said Nanny.

'Thank you. It took dayth to get right. Creakth like that don't jutht happen by themthelveth.'

There was a woof from the darkness and *something* leapt at Igor, knocking him off his feet.

'Get off, you big thoppy!'

It was a dog. Or several dogs rolled, as it were, into one. There were four legs, and they were nearly all the same length although not, Magrat noted, all the same colour. There was one head, although the left ear was black and pointed while the right ear was brown and white and flopped. It was a very enthusiastic animal in the department of slobber.

'Thith ith Thcrapth,' said Igor, fighting to get to his feet in a hail of excited paws. 'He'th a thilly old thing.'

'Scraps . . . yes,' said Nanny. 'Good name. Good name.'

'He'th theventy-eight yearth old,' said Igor, leading the way down a winding staircase. 'Thome of him.'

'Very neat stitching,' said Magrat. 'He looks well on it, too. Happy as a dog with two— Oh, I see he *does* have two . . .'

'I had one thpare,' said Igor, leading the way with Scraps bounding along beside him. 'I thought, he'th tho happy with one, jutht think of the fun he could have with two . . .'

Nanny Ogg's mouth didn't even get half open—

'Don't you even *think* of saying anything, Gytha Ogg!' snapped Magrat.

'Me?' said Nanny innocently.

'Yes! And you *were*. I could *see* you! You *know* he was talking about tails, not . . . anything else.'

'Oh, I thought about *that* long ago,' said Igor. 'It'th obviouth. Thaveth wear and tear, pluth you can uthe one while you're replathing the other. I ecthperimented on mythelf.'

Their footsteps echoed on the stairs.

'Now, what are we talking about here, exactly?' said Nanny, in a quiet, I'm-only-asking-out-of-interest tone of voice.

'Heartth,' said Igor.

'Oh, two *hearts.* You've got two hearts?'

'Yeth. The other one belonged to poor Mr Thwinetth down at the thawmill, but hith wife thed it wath no uthe to him after the acthident, what with him not having a head to go with it.'

'You're a bit of a self-made man on the quiet, aren't you?' said Magrat.

'Who did your brain?' said Nanny.

'Can't do brainth yourthelf,' said Igor.

'Only . . . you've got all those stitches . . .'

'Oh, I put a metal plate in my head,' said Igor. 'And a wire down my neck all the way to my bootth. I got fed up with all thothe lightning thtriketh. Here we are.' He unlocked another groaning door. 'My little plathe.'

It was a dank vaulted room, clearly lived in by someone who didn't spend a lot of social time there. There was a fireplace with a dog basket in front of it, and a bed with a mattress and one blanket. Crude cupboards lined one wall.

'There'th a well under that cover there,' he said, 'and there'th a privy through there . . .'

'What's through *that* door?' said Nanny, pointing to one with heavy bolts across it.

'Nothing,' said Igor.

Nanny shot him a glance. But the bolts were very firmly on this side.

'This looks like a crypt,' she said. 'With a fireplace.'

'When the *old* Count wath alive he liked to get warm of an evening before going out,' said Igor. 'Golden dayth, them wath. I wouldn't give you tuppenth for thith lot. D'you know, they wanted me to get rid of Thcrapth?'

Scraps leapt up and tried to lick Nanny's face.

'I thaw Lacrimotha *kick* him onthe,' said Igor darkly. He rubbed his hands together. 'Can I get you ladieth anything to eat?'

'No,' said Nanny and Magrat together.

Scraps tried to lick Igor. He was a dog with a lot of lick to share.

'Thcrapth, play dead,' said Igor. The dog dropped and rolled over with his legs in the air.

'Thee?' said Igor. 'He rememberth!'

'Won't we be cornered down here if the Magpyrs come?' said Magrat.

'They don't come down here. It'th not *modern* enough for them,' said Igor. 'And there'th wayth out if they do.'

Magrat glanced at the bolted door. It didn't look the kind of way out anyone would want to take.

'What about weapons?' she said. 'I shouldn't think there'd be any anti-vampire stuff in a vampire's castle, would there?'

'Why, thertainly,' said Igor.

'There is?'

'Ath much ath you want. The old marthter wath very keen on that. When we had vithitorth ecthpected, he alwayth thed, "Igor, make thertain the windowth are clean and there'th lotth of lemonth and bitth of ornament that can be turned into religiouth thymbolth around the plathe." He enjoyed it when people played by the ruleth. Very fair, the old marthter.'

'Yeah, but that'd mean he'd die, wouldn't it?' said Nanny. She opened a cupboard and a stack of wrinkled lemons fell out.

Igor shrugged. 'You win thome, you lothe thome,' he said. 'The old marthter uthed to thay, "Igor, the day vampireth win all the time, that'th the day we'll be knocked back beyond return." Mind you, he got annoyed when people pinched hith thockth. He'd thay, "Thod, that wath thilk, ten dollarth a pair in Ankh-Morpork."'

'And he probably spent a lot of money on blotting paper, too,' said Nanny. Another cupboard revealed a rack of stakes, along with a mallet and a simple anatomical diagram with an X over the heart area.

'The chart wath my idea, Mithith Ogg,' said Igor proudly. 'The old marthter got fed up with people just hammering the thtaketh in any old where. He thed he didn't mind the dying, that wath quite rethtful, but he did object to looking like a colander.'

'You're a bright chap, aren't you, Igor?' said Nanny.

Igor beamed. 'I've got a good brain in my head.'

'Chose it yourself, did you? No, only joking. You can't do brains.'

'I've got a dithtant couthin at Untheen Univerthity, you know.'

'Really? What's he do there?'

'Floatth around in hith jar,' said Igor proudly. 'Thall I thow you the holy water thellar? The old marthter built up a very good collection.'

'Sorry? A *vampire* collected *holy water*?' said Magrat.

'I think I'm beginning to understand,' said Nanny. 'He was a sportsman, right?'

'Egthactly!'

'And a good sportsman always gives the valiant prey a decent chance,' said Nanny. 'Even if it means having a cellar of Chateau Nerf de Pope. Sounds an intelligent bird, your old boy. Not like this new one. He's just clever.'

'I don't follow you,' said Magrat.

'Being killed's nothing to a vampire,' said Nanny. 'They always find a way of coming back. Everyone knows that, who knows anything about vampires. If they're not *too* hard to kill and it's all a bit of an adventure for people, well, like as not they'll just stake him or chuck him in the river and go home. Then he has a nice restful decade or so, bein' dead, and comes back from the grave and away he goes again. That way he never gets totally wiped out and the lads of the village get some healthy exercise.'

'The Magpyrs will come after us,' said Magrat, clutching the baby to her. 'They'll see we're not in Lancre and they'll know we couldn't have gone down to the plains. They'll find the smashed coach, too. They'll *find* us, Nanny.'

Nanny looked at the array of jars and bottles, and the stakes neatly organized in order of size.

'It'll take them a little while,' she said. 'We've got time to get . . . prepared.'

She turned around with a bottle of blessed water in one hand, a crossbow loaded with a wooden bolt, and a bag of musty lemons in her mouth.

'Eg oo it I ay,' she said.

'Pardon?' said Magrat.

Nanny spat out the lemons.

'Now we'll try things my way,' she said. 'I'm not good at thinkin' like Granny but I'm bloody good at actin' like me. Headology's for them as can handle it. Let's kick some bat.'

The wind soughed across the moors on the edge of Lancre, and hissed through the heather.

Around some old mounds, half buried in brambles, it shook the wet branches of a single thorn tree, and shredded the curling smoke that drifted up through the roots.

There was a single scream.

Down below, the Nac mac Feegle were doing their best, but strength is not the same as weight and mass and even with pixies hanging on to every limb and Big Aggie herself sitting on Verence's chest he was still hard to control.

'I think mebbe the drink was a wee bitty too trackle?' said Big Aggie's man, looking down at Verence's bloodshot eyes and foaming mouth. 'I'm sayin', mebbe it was wrong jus' giving him fifty times more than we tak'. He's not used to it . . .'

Big Aggie shrugged.

In the far corner of the barrow half a dozen pixies backed out of the hole they'd hacked into the next chamber, dragging a sword. For bronze, it was quite well preserved – the old chieftains of Lancre reckoned to be buried with their weapons in order to fight their enemies in the next world, and since you didn't become a chieftain of ancient Lancre without sending a great many enemies to the next world, they liked to take weapons that could be relied upon to last.

Under the direction of the old pixie, they manoeuvred it within reach of Verence's flailing hand.

'Are ye scrat?' said Big Aggie's man. 'Yin! Tan! Tetra!'

The Feegle leapt away in every direction. Verence rose almost vertically, bounced off the roof, grabbed the sword, hacked madly until he'd cut a hole through to the outside world, and escaped into the night.

The pixies clustered around the walls of the barrow turned their eyes to their Kelda.

Big Aggie nodded.

'Big Aggie says ye'd best see him come to nae harm,' said the old pixie.

A thousand small but very sharp weapons waved in the smoky air.

'Hoons!'

'Kill 'em a'!'

'Nac mac Feegle!'

A few seconds later the chamber was empty.

Nanny hurried across the castle's main hall, burdened with stakes, and stopped dead.

'What the hell's that thing?' she said. 'Takes up a whole wall!'

'Oh, that wath the old Count'th pride and joy,' said Igor. 'He wathn't very modern, he alwayth thaid, but the Thentury of the Fruitbat had it'th compenthathionth. Thometimeth he'd play with it for hourth on end . . .'

It was an organ, or possibly what an organ hoped to

be when it grew up, because it dominated the huge room. A music lover to the core, Nanny couldn't help trotting over to inspect it. It was black, its pipes framed and enclosed in intricate ebony fretwork, with the stops and keyboard made of dead elephant.

'How does it work?' she said.

'Water power,' said Igor proudly. 'There'th an underground river. The marthter had thith made thpethially to hith own dethign . . .'

Nanny ran her fingers over a brass plate screwed above the keyboard.

It read: 'HLISTEN TO ZER CHILTREN OFF DER NIGHT . . . VOT VONDERFUL MHUSICK DEY MAKE. Mnftrd. by Bergholt Stuttley Johnson, Ankh-Morpork.'

'It's a Johnson,' she breathed. 'I haven't got my hands on a Johnson for ages . . .' She looked closer. 'What's this? "Scream 1"? "Thunderclap 14"? "Wolf Howl 5"? There's a whole set of stops just marked "Creaky Floors"! Can't you play *music* on this thing?'

'Oh, yeth. But the old marthter wath more interethted in . . . effectth.'

There was still a dust-covered sheet of music on the stand, which someone had been filling in carefully, with many crossings-out.

'"Return Of The Bride Of The Revenge Of The Son Of Count Magpyr"', Nanny said aloud, noting that 'From 20,000 Fathoms(?)' had been written in subsequently and then crossed out. '"Sonata for Thunderstorm, Trapdoors and Young Women in Skimpy Clothing". Bit of an artist too, then, your old master?'

'In a . . . *thpethial* way,' said Igor wistfully.

Nanny stepped back.

'Magrat's going to be safe, isn't she?' she said, picking up the stakes again.

'It'th a mob-proof door,' said Igor. 'And Thcrapth ith nine-thirtyeighth Rottweiler.'

'Which parts, as a matter of interest?'

'Two legth, one ear, lotth of tubeth and lower jaw,' said Igor promptly as they hurried off again.

'Yes, but he's got a spaniel brain,' said Nanny.

'It'th in the bone,' said Igor. 'He holdth people in hith jawth and beatth them thentheleth with hith tailth.'

'He wags people to death?'

'Thometimeth he drownth them in dribble,' said Igor.

The rooftops of Escrow loomed out of the darkness as the vampires drifted lower. A few windows were glowing with candlelight when Agnes's feet touched the ground.

Vlad dropped down beside her.

'Of course, you can't see it at its best in this weather,' he said. 'Some quite good architecture in the town square, and a very fine town hall. Father paid for the clock.'

'Really.'

'And the belltower, naturally. Local labour, of course.'

'Vampires have a lot of cash, do they?' said Agnes. The town looked quite large, and pretty much like the country towns down on the plains save for a certain amount of gingerbread carving on the eaves.

'Well, the family has always owned land,' said Vlad, ignoring the sarcasm. 'The money mounts up, you know. Over the centuries. And obviously we've not enjoyed a particularly active social life.'

'Or spent much on food,' said Agnes.

'Yes, yes, very good—'

A bell started to toll, somewhere above them.

'Now you'll see,' said Vlad. 'And you'll understand.'

Granny Weatherwax opened her eyes. There were flames roaring right in front of her.

'Oh,' she said. 'So be it, then . . .'

'Ah. Feeling better, are we?' said Oats.

Her head spun round. Then she looked down at the steam rising from her dress.

Oats ducked between the branches of two firs and threw another armful of dead wood on the flames. It hissed and spluttered.

'How long was I . . . resting?' said Granny.

'About half an hour, I'd say.' Red light and black shadows danced among the trees. The rain had turned to sleet, but it was flashing into steam overhead.

'You did well to get a fire going in this murk,' said Granny.

'I thank Om for it,' said Oats.

'Very kind of him, I'm sure. But we've got to . . . get on.' Granny tried to stand up. 'Not far now. All downhill . . .'

'The mule ran away,' said Oats.

'We've got feet, haven't we? I feel better for the . . . rest. The fire's put a . . . bit of life into me.'

'It's too dark and far too wet. Wait until morning.'

Granny pulled herself up. 'No. Find a stick or something I can lean on. Go on.'

'Well . . . there's a hazel grove just along the slope, but . . .'

'Just the thing, a good bit of hazel. Well, don't just stand there. I'm feeling better every minute. Off you go.'

He disappeared into the dripping shadows.

Granny flapped her skirts in front of the blaze to circulate some warm air, and something small and white flew up from the ashes, dancing in the fire and sleet.

She picked it up from the moss where it had landed.

It was a piece of thin paper, the charred corner of a page. She could just make out, in the red light, the words '. . . of Om . . . aid unto . . . Ossory smote . . .' The paper was attached to a burnt strip of leather binding.

She regarded it for a while, and then dropped it carefully into the flames as the sound of crackling twigs indicated Oats's return.

'Can you even find the way in all this?' he said, handing her a long hazel pole.

'Yes. You go on one side of me, and I've got this staff. Then it's just a walk in the woods, eh?'

'You don't *look* better.'

'Young man, if we're going to wait for me to look interestin' we'll be here for years.'

She raised a hand and the wowhawk flew down out of the shadows.

'Good thing you were able to get a fire going, all the same,' she said, without turning round.

'I have always found that if I put my trust in Om a way will be found,' said Oats, hurrying after her.

'I reckon Om helps those who helps themselves,' said Granny.

Through the town of Escrow the windows glowed as lamps were lit and there was the sound of doors being unbolted. Over all, the bell went on ringing out through the fog.

'Normally we congregate in the town square,' said Vlad.

'It's the middle of the night!' said Agnes.

'Yes, but it doesn't happen very often, and our covenant says never more than twice in a month,' said Vlad. 'Do you see how prosperous the place is? People are *safe* in Escrow. They've seen reason. No shutters on the windows, do you see? They don't have to bar their windows or hide in the cellar, which I have to admit is what people do in the . . . less well regulated areas of our country. They exchanged fear for security. They—' He stumbled, and steadied himself against a wall. Then he rubbed his forehead. 'Sorry. I felt a little . . . strange. What was I saying?'

'How should I know?' snapped Agnes. 'You were talking about how happy everyone is because the vampires visit, or something.'

'Oh, yes. Yes. Because of co-operation, not enmity. Because . . .' he pulled a handkerchief from his pocket and wiped his face '. . . because . . . well, you'll see . . . is it rather cold here?'

'Just clammy,' said Agnes.

'Let's get to the square,' Vlad muttered. 'I'm sure I shall feel better.'

It was just ahead. Torches had been lit. People had congregated there, most of them with blankets across their shoulders or a coat over their night clothes, standing around in aimless groups like people who'd heard the fire alarm but hadn't seen the smoke.

One or two of them caught sight of Vlad and there was a certain amount of coughing and shuffling.

Other vampires were descending through the mist. The Count landed gently and nodded to Agnes.

'Ah, Miss Nitt,' he said vaguely. 'Are we all here, Vlad?'

The bell stopped. A moment later Lacrimosa descended.

'You've *still* got her?' she said to Vlad, raising her eyebrows. 'Oh, well . . .'

'I will just have a brief chat to the mayor,' said the Count. 'He appreciates being kept informed.'

Agnes watched him walk towards a small, dumpy man who, despite getting out of bed in the middle of a wet night, seemed to have had the foresight to put on a gold chain of office.

She noticed the vampires taking up positions in a line in front of the belltower, about four or five feet apart. They joked and called out to one another, except for Lacrimosa, who was glaring directly at her.

The Count was deep in conversation with the mayor, who was staring down at his feet.

Now, across the square, the people were beginning to form lines. A couple of small children pulled away from their parents' hands and chased one another up and down the lines of people, laughing.

And the suspicion bloomed slowly in Agnes like a great black, red-edged rose.

Vlad must have felt her body stiffen, because his grip tightened on her arm.

'I know what you're thinking—' he began.

'You *don't* know what I'm thinking but I'll *tell* you what I'm thinking,' she said, trying to keep the tremble out of her voice. 'You're—'

'Listen, it could be so much worse, it *used* to be so much worse—'

The Count bustled. 'Good news,' he said. 'Three children have just turned twelve.' He smiled at Agnes. 'We have a little . . . ceremony, before the main lottery. A rite of passage, as it were. I think they look forward to it, to tell you the truth.'

He's watching you to see how you react, said Perdita. *Vlad is just stupid and Lacrimosa would weave your hair into a face flannel if she had the chance but this one will go for the throat if you so much as blink at the wrong time . . . so don't blink at the wrong time, thank you, because even figments of the imagination want to live . . .*

But Agnes felt the terror rising around her. And it was *wrong,* the wrong *kind* of terror, a numbing, cold, sick feeling that froze her where she stood. She had to do something, do anything, break its horrible grip—

It was Vlad who spoke.

'It's nothing dramatic,' he said quickly. 'A little drop

of blood . . . Father went to the school and explained all about citizenship . . .'

'How nice,' she croaked. 'Do they get a badge?' It must have been Perdita behind that; she couldn't imagine Agnes being so tasteless, even in the cause of sarcasm.

'Hah, no. But what a *good* idea,' said the Count, giving her another quick smile. 'Yes . . . perhaps a badge, or a small plaque. Something to be treasured in later life. I shall make a mental note of this. And so . . . let us begin. Ah, the mayor has assembled the dear children . . .'

There was a shout somewhere at the back of the crowd and, for a moment, Agnes caught sight of a man trying to press forward. The mayor nodded at a couple of the nearby men. They hurried back into the crowd. There was a scuffle in the shadows. She thought she heard a woman's scream, suddenly muffled. A door slammed.

As the mayor turned back, he met Agnes's stare. She looked away, not wanting to see that expression. People were good at imagining hells, and some they occupied while they were alive.

'Shall we get on?' said the Count.

'Will you let go of my arm, Vlad?' said Agnes sweetly.

They're just waiting for you to react, whispered Perdita. Oh, said Agnes inside her head, so I should just stand here and watch? Like everybody else? *I just thought I'd point it out. What's been done to them? They're like pigs queueing for Hogswatch!* I think they saw reason, said Agnes. *Oh well . . .*

just wipe that smile off Lacrimosa's face, that's all I ask . . .

They could move very fast. Even a scream wouldn't work. She might be able to get in one good wallop, and that would be it. And perhaps she'd wake up as a vampire, and not know the difference between good and evil. But that wasn't the point. The point was here and now, because here and now she *did.*

She could see every drop of moisture hanging in the air, smell the woodsmoke from damped-down fires, hear the rats in the thatch of the houses. Her senses were working overtime, to make the most of the last few seconds—

'I don't see why!' Lacrimosa's voice cut through the mist like a saw.

Agnes blinked. The girl had reached her father and was glaring at him.

'Why do *you* always start?' she demanded.

'Lacrimosa! What has got into you? I am the head of the clan!'

'Oh, really? For ever?'

The Count looked astonished. 'Well, yes. Of course!'

'So we'll always be pushed around by you, for *ever*? We'll just be your children for *ever*?'

'My dear, what *do* you think you—'

'And don't try that voice on me! That only works on the meat! So I'll be sent to my room for being disobedient *for ever*?'

'We did let you have your own rack—'

'Oh, yes! And for that I have to nod and smile and be nice with *meat*?'

'Don't you dare talk to your father like that!' screamed the Countess.

'And don't talk about Agnes like that!' snarled Vlad.

'Did I use the word Agnes? Did I refer to her in any way?' said Lacrimosa, coldly. 'I don't believe I did. I wouldn't dream of mentioning her at *all*.'

'I can't be having with this *arguing*!' shouted the Count.

'That's *it*, isn't it?' said Lacrimosa. 'We *don't* argue! We just do what you say, for *ever*.'

'We agreed—'

'No, you agreed, and no one disagreed with *you*. Vlad was right!'

'Indeed?' said the Count, turning to his son. 'Right about what, pray?'

Vlad's mouth opened and shut once or twice as he hastily assembled a coherent sentence. 'I may have mentioned that the whole Lancre business might be considered unwise—'

'Oh,' said the Countess. 'You know so much about wisdom all of a sudden and you're barely two hundred?'

'Unwise?' said the Count.

'*I'd* say stupid!' said Lacrimosa. 'Little badges? Gifts? We don't *give* anything! We're *vampires*! We *take* what we want, like *this*—'

She reached out, grabbed a man standing near her, and turned, mouth open and hair flying.

And stopped, as if she'd been frozen.

Then she buckled, one hand reaching for her throat, and glared at her father.

'What . . . did you do?' she gasped. 'My throat . . . feels . . . You *did* something!'

The Count rubbed his forehead and pinched the bridge of his nose. 'Lacci—'

'And *don't* call me that! You know how I hate that!'

There was a brief scream from one of the lesser vampires behind them. Agnes couldn't remember his name, it was probably Fenrir or Maledicta or something, but she did recall that he preferred to be known as Gerald. He sagged to his knees, clawing at his throat. None of the other vampires looked very happy, either. A couple of them were kneeling and groaning, to the bewilderment of the citizens.

'I don't . . . feel very well,' said the Countess, swaying slightly. 'I did say I didn't think wine was a good idea . . .'

The Count turned and stared at Agnes. She took a step back.

'It's you, isn't it?' he said.

'Of course it is!' moaned Lacrimosa. 'You know that old woman put her self somewhere, and she must've known Vlad was soppy on that lump!'

She's not in here, is she? said Perdita. Don't you know? Agnes thought, backing away again. *Well, I don't think she is, but is it me doing the thinking?* Look, she's hidden her self in that priest, we *know* it. *No, we don't, you just thought that'd be a smart thing for her to do because everyone would think she's hiding in the baby.*

'Why don't you just crawl back into your coffin and rot, you slimy little maggot?' Agnes said. It wasn't that good, but impromptu insults are seldom well crafted.

Lacrimosa leapt at her, but something else was

wrong. Instead of gliding through the air like velvet death she lurched like a bird with a broken wing. But fury let her rear up in front of Agnes, one claw out to scratch—

Agnes hit her as hard as she could and felt Perdita get behind the blow as well. It shouldn't have been possible for it to connect, the girl was quick enough to run around Agnes three times before it could, but it did.

The people of Escrow watched a vampire stagger back, bleeding.

The mayor raised his head.

Agnes went into a crouch, fists raised.

'I don't know where Granny Weatherwax went,' she said. 'Maybe she *is* in here with me, eh?' A flash of mad inspiration struck her and she added, in Granny's sharp tones, 'And if you strike me down again I'll bite my way up through your boots!'

'A nice try, Miss Nitt,' said the Count, striding towards her. 'But I don't *think* so—'

He stopped, clutching at the gold chain that was suddenly around his neck.

Behind him the mayor hauled on it with all his weight, forcing the vampire to the ground.

The citizens looked at one another, and all moved at once.

Vampires rose into the air, trying to gain height, kicking at clutching hands. Torches were snatched from walls. The night was suddenly full of screams.

Agnes looked up at Vlad, who was staring in horror. Lacrimosa was surrounded by a closing ring of people.

'You'd better run,' she said, 'or they'll—'

He turned and lunged, and the last thing she saw was teeth.

The track downhill was worse than the climb. Springs had erupted in every hollow, and every path was a rivulet.

As Granny and Oats lurched from mud slough to bog, Oats reflected on the story in the *Book of Om* – *the* story, really – about the prophet Brutha and his journey with Om across the burning desert, which had ended up changing Omnianism for ever. It had replaced swords with sermons, which at least caused fewer deaths except in the case of the really very long ones, and had broken the Church into a thousand pieces which had then started arguing with one another and finally turned out Oats, who argued with himself.

Oats wondered how far across the desert Brutha would have got if he'd been trying to support Granny Weatherwax. There was something unbending about her, something hard as rock. By about halfway the blessed prophet might, he felt guiltily, have yielded to the temptation to . . . well, at least say something unpleasant, or give a meaningful sigh. The old woman had got very crotchety since being warmed up. She seemed to have something on her mind.

The rain had stopped but the wind was sharp, and there were still occasional stinging bursts of hail.

'Won't be long now,' he panted.

'You don't know that,' said Granny, splashing through black, peaty mud.

'No, you're absolutely right,' said Oats. 'I was just saying that to be cheerful.'

'Hasn't worked,' said Granny.

'Mistress Weatherwax, would you like me to leave you here?' said Oats.

Granny sniffed. 'Wouldn't worry me,' she said.

'Would you *like* me to?' said Oats.

'It's not my mountain,' said Granny. 'I wouldn't be one to tell people where they should be.'

'I'll go if you want me to,' said Oats.

'I never asked you to come,' said Granny simply.

'You'd be dead if I hadn't!'

'That's no business of yours.'

'My god, Mistress Weatherwax, you try me sorely.'

'Your god, Mister Oats, tries everyone. That's what gods generally does, and *that's* why I don't truck with 'em. And they lays down rules all the time.'

'There have to be rules, Mistress Weatherwax.'

'And what's the first one that your Om requires, then?'

'That believers should worship no other god but Om,' said Oats promptly.

'Oh yes? That's gods for you. Very self-centred, as a rule.'

'I think it was to get people's attention,' said Oats. 'There are many commandments about dealing well with other people, if that's what you're getting at.'

'Really? And s'pose someone doesn't want to believe in Om and tries to live properly?'

'According to the prophet Brutha, to live properly *is* to believe in Om.'

'Oho, that's clever! He gets you coming *and* going,'

said Granny. 'It took a good thinker to come up with that. Well done. What other clever things did he say?'

'He doesn't say things to be clever,' said Oats hotly. 'But, since you ask, he said in his Letter to the Simonites that it is through other people that we truly become people.'

'Good. He got that one right.'

'And he said that we should take light into dark places.'

Granny didn't say anything.

'I thought I'd mention that,' said Oats, 'because when you were . . . you know, kneeling, back in the forge . . . you said something very similar . . .'

Granny stopped so suddenly that Oats nearly fell over.

'I did *what*?'

'You were mumbling and—'

'I was talkin' in my . . . sleep?'

'Yes, and you said something about darkness being where the light needs to be, which I remember because in the *Book of Om*—'

'You *listened*?'

'No, I wasn't listening, but I couldn't help hearing, could I? And you sounded as if you were having an argument with someone . . .'

'Can you remember everything I said?'

'I think so.'

Granny staggered on a little, and stopped in a puddle of black water that began to rise over her boots.

'Can you forget?' she said.

'Pardon?'

'You wouldn't be so unkind as to pass on to anyone else the ramblings of a poor ol' woman who was probably off her head, would you?' said Granny slowly.

Oats thought for a moment. 'What ramblings were these, Mistress Weatherwax?'

Granny seemed to sag with relief.

'Ah. Good thing you asked, really, bein' as there weren't any.'

Black bubbles arose from the bog around Granny Weatherwax as the two of them watched each other. Some sort of truce had been declared.

'I wonder, young man, if you would be so good as to pull me out?'

This took some time and involved a branch from a nearby tree and, despite Oats's best efforts, Granny's first foot came out of its boot. And once one boot has said goodbye in a peat bog, the other one is bound to follow out of fraternal solidarity.

Granny ended up on what was comparatively dry and comparatively land wearing a pair of the heaviest-looking socks Oats had ever seen. They looked as if they could shrug off a hammer blow.

'They was good boots,' said Granny, looking at the bubbles. 'Oh, well, let's get on.'

She staggered a little as she set off again, but to Oats's admiration managed to stay upright. He was beginning to form yet another opinion of the old woman, who caused a new opinion to arise about once every half-hour, and it was this: she needed someone to beat. If she didn't have someone to beat, she'd probably beat herself.

'Shame about your little book of holy words . . .' she said, when she was further down the track.

There was a long pause before Oats replied.

'I can easily get another,' he said levelly.

'Must be hard, not having your book of words.'

'It's only paper.'

'I shall ask the King to see about getting you another book of words.'

'I wouldn't trouble him.'

'Terrible thing to have to burn all them words, though.'

'The worthwhile ones don't burn.'

'You're not too stupid, for all that you wear a funny hat,' said Granny.

'I know when I'm being pushed, Mistress Weatherwax.'

'Well done.'

They walked on in silence. A shower of hail bounced off Granny's pointy hat and Oats's wide brim.

Then Granny said, 'It's no good you trying to make me believe in Om, though.'

'Om forbid that I should try, Mistress Weatherwax. I haven't even given you a pamphlet, have I?'

'No, but you're trying to make me think, "Oo, what a nice young man, his god must be something special if nice young men like him helps old ladies like me," aren't you?'

'No.'

'Really? Well, it's not working. People you can believe in, sometimes, but not gods. And I'll tell you this, Mister Oats . . .'

He sighed. 'Yes?'

She turned to face him, suddenly alive. 'It'd be as well for you if I didn't believe,' she said, prodding him with a sharp finger. 'This Om . . . anyone seen him?'

'It is said three thousand people witnessed his manifestation at the Great Temple when he made the Covenant with the prophet Brutha and saved him from death by torture on the iron turtle—'

'But I bet that *now* they're arguing about what they actually saw, eh?'

'Well, indeed, yes, there are many opinions—'

'Right. Right. That's people for you. Now if I'd seen him, really there, really alive, it'd be in me like a fever. If I thought there was some god who really did care two hoots about people, who watched 'em like a father and cared for 'em like a mother . . . well, you wouldn't catch me sayin' things like "There are two sides to every question," and "We must respect other people's beliefs." You wouldn't find *me* just being gen'rally nice in the hope that it'd all turn out right in the end, not if that flame was burning in me like an unforgivin' sword. And I did say burnin', Mister Oats, 'cos that's what it'd be. You say that you people don't burn folk and sacrifice people any more, but that's what true faith would mean, y'see? Sacrificin' your own life, one day at a time, to the flame, declarin' the truth of it, workin' for it, breathin' the soul of it. *That*'s religion. Anything else is just . . . is just bein' *nice*. And a way of keepin' in touch with the neighbours.'

She relaxed slightly, and went on in a quieter voice: 'Anyway, that's what I'd be, if I really believed. And I don't think that's fashionable right now, 'cos it seems that if you sees evil now you have to wring your hands and say, "Oh deary me, we must debate this." That's my two penn'orth, Mister Oats. You be happy to let things lie. Don't chase faith, 'cos you'll never catch it.' She added, almost as an aside, 'But, perhaps, you can live faithfully.'

Her teeth chattered as a gust of icy wind flapped her wet dress around her legs.

'You got another book of holy words on you?' she added.

'No,' said Oats, still shocked. He thought: my god, if she ever finds a religion, what would come out of these mountains and sweep across the plains? My god . . . I just said, 'My god' . . .

'A book of hymns, maybe?' said Granny.

'No.'

'A slim volume o' prayers, suitable for every occasion?'

'No, Granny Weatherwax.'

'Damn.' Granny slowly collapsed backwards, folding up like an empty dress.

He rushed forward and caught her before she landed in the mud. One thin white hand gripped his wrist so hard that he yelped. Then she relaxed, and sagged in his grasp.

Something made Oats look up.

A hooded figure sat on a white horse a little way away, outlined in the faintest blue fire.

'Go away!' he screamed. 'You be gone right now or . . . or . . .'

He lowered the body on to some tufts of grass,

grabbed a handful of mud and flung it into the gloom. He ran after it, punching wildly at a shape that was suddenly no more than shadows and curling mist.

He dashed back, picked up Granny Weatherwax, slung her over his shoulder and ran on, downhill.

The mist behind him formed a shape on a white horse.

Death shook his head.

IT WASN'T EVEN AS IF I SAID ANYTHING, he said.

Waves of black heat broke over Agnes, and then there was a pit, and a fall into hot, suffocating darkness.

She felt the *desire.* It was tugging her forward like a current.

Well, she thought dreamily, at least I'll lose some weight . . .

Yes, said Perdita, *but all the eyeliner you'll have to wear must add a few pounds . . .*

The hunger filled her now, accelerating her.

And there was light, behind her, shining past her. She felt the fall gradually slow as if she'd hit invisible feathers, and then the world spun and she was rising again, moving up faster than an eagle stoops, towards an expanding circle of cold white—

It couldn't possibly be words that she heard. There was no sound but a faint rushing noise. But it was the shadow of words, the effect they leave in the mind after they have been said, and she felt her own voice rushing in to fill the shape that had appeared there. *I . . . can't . . . be . . . having . . . with . . . this . . .*

Light exploded.

And someone was about to hammer a stake through her heart.

'Stdt?' she said, knocking the hand away. She spluttered for a moment and then spat the lemon out of her mouth. 'Hey, stop that!' she tried again, this time with all the authority she could muster. 'What the heck are you doing? Do I *look* like a vampire?'

The man with the stake and mallet hesitated, and then tapped a finger to the side of his neck.

Agnes reached to hers, and found two raised weals.

'He must have missed!' she said, pushing the stake away and sitting up. 'Who took my stocking off? Who took off my left stocking? Is that boiling vinegar I can smell? What're all these poppyseeds doing poured down my bra? If it wasn't a woman who took my stocking off there's going to be some *serious* trouble, I can tell you!'

The crowd around the table looked at one another, suddenly uncertain in the face of her rage. Agnes glanced up as something brushed her ear. Hanging over her were stars and crosses and circles and more complex designs she recognized as religious symbols. She'd never felt inclined to believe in religion, but she knew what it looked like.

'And this is just a very tasteless display,' she said.

'She doesn't *act* like a vampire,' said a man. 'She doesn't look like one. And she did fight the others.'

'We saw that one bite her!' said a woman.

'Bad aim in poor light,' said Agnes, knowing that it wasn't. There was a hunger welling up. It was not like the black urge she'd felt in the dark, but sharp and urgent all the same. She had to give in to it.

'I'd kill for a cup of tea,' she added.

That seemed to clinch it. Tea wasn't the liquid usually associated with vampires.

'And for goodness' sake let me shake some of these poppyseeds out,' she went on, adjusting her bosom. 'I feel like a wholemeal loaf.'

They moved aside as she swung her legs off the table, which now meant that she could see the vampire lying on the floor. She nearly thought of it as the *other* vampire.

It was a man wearing a long frock coat and a fancy waistcoat, both covered in mud and blood; there was a stake through his heart. Further identification, though, would have to await finding where they'd put his head.

'I see you got one, then,' she said, trying not to be sick.

'Got two,' said the man with the hammer. 'Set fire to the other one. They killed the mayor and Mr Vlack.'

'You mean the rest got away?' said Agnes.

'Yes. They're still strong but they can't fly much.'

Agnes indicated the headless vampire. 'Er . . . is that one Vlad?' she said.

'Which one was he?'

'The one that . . . bit me. Tried to bite me,' she corrected herself.

'We can check. Piotr, show her the head.'

A young man obediently went to the fireplace, pulled on a glove, lifted the lid of a big saucepan and held up a head by its hair.

'That's not Vlad,' said Agnes, swallowing. *No*, said Perdita, *Vlad was taller.*

'They'll be heading back to their castle,' said Piotr. 'On foot! You should see them trying to fly! It's like watching chickens panicking.'

'The castle . . .' said Agnes.

'They'll have to make it before cock-crow,' said Piotr, with some satisfaction. 'And they can't cut through the woods, 'cos of the werewolves.'

'What? I thought werewolves and vampires would get along fine,' said Agnes.

'Oh, maybe it looks like that,' said Piotr. 'But they're watching one another all the time to see who's going to be the first to blink.' He looked around the room. 'We don't mind the werewolves,' he went on, to general agreement. 'They leave us alone most of the time because we don't run fast enough to be interesting.'

He looked Agnes up and down.

'What was it you did to the vampires?' he said.

'Me? I didn't do— I don't know,' said Agnes.

'They couldn't even bite us properly.'

'And they were squabbling like kids when they left,' said the man with the mallet.

'You've got a pointy hat,' said Piotr. 'Did you put a spell on them?'

'I— I don't know. I really don't.' And then natural honesty met witchcraft. One aspect of witchcraft is the craftiness, and it's seldom unwise to take the credit for unexplained but fortuitous events. 'I may have done,' she added.

'Well, we're going after them,' said Piotr.

'Won't they have got well away?'

'We can cut through the woods.'

Blood tinted the rain that ran off the wound on Jason Ogg's shoulder. He dabbed at it with a cloth.

'Reckon I'll be hammerin' left-handed for a week or two,' he said, wincing.

'They got very good fields of fire,' said Shawn, who had taken refuge behind the beer barrel used so recently to wet the baby's head. 'I mean, it's a *castle.* A frontal attack simply won't work.'

He sighed, and shielded his guttering candle to keep the wind from blowing it out. They'd tried a frontal attack nevertheless, and the only reason no one had been killed was that the drink seemed to be flowing freely within the keep. As it was, one or two people would be limping for a while. Then they'd tried what Jason persisted in referring to as a backal attack, but there were arrow slots even over the kitchens. One man creeping up to the walls very slowly – a sidle attack, as Shawn had thought of it – had worked, but since all the doors were very solidly barred this had just meant that he'd stood there feeling like a fool.

He was trying to find some help in the ancient military journals of General Tacticus, whose intelligent campaigning had been so successful that he'd lent his very name to the detailed prosecution of martial endeavour, and had actually found a section headed What to Do If One Army Occupies a Well-fortified and Superior Ground and the Other Does Not, but since the first sentence read

'Endeavour to be the one inside' he'd rather lost heart.

The rest of the Lancre militia cowered behind buttresses and upturned carts, waiting for him to lead them.

There was a respectful clang as Big Jim Beef, who was acting as cover for two other part-time soldiers, saluted his commander.

'I reckon,' he ventured, 'dat if we got big fires goin' in frun' of the doors we could smoke dem out.'

'Good idea,' said Jason.

'That's the *King's* door,' Shawn protested. 'He's already been a bit sharp with me for not cleaning the privy pit this week—'

'He can send Mum the bill.'

'That's seditious talk, Jason! I could have you arr— I could arr— Mum would have something to say about you talking like that!'

'Where is the King, anyway?' said Darren Ogg. 'Sittin' back and lettin' Mum sort everything out while we get shot at?'

'You know he's got a weak chest,' said Shawn. 'He does very well considering he—'

He stopped as a sound rolled out across the countryside. It had a hoarse, primal quality, the sound of an animal who is in pain but also intends to pass it on as soon as possible. The men looked around nervously.

Verence came thundering through the gates. Shawn recognized him only by the embroidery on his nightshirt and his fluffy slippers. He held a long sword over his head in both hands and was running straight for the door of the keep, trailing a scream behind him.

The sword struck the wood. Shawn heard the whole door shudder.

'He's gone mad!' shouted Darren. 'Let's grab the poor creature before he gets shot!'

A couple of them scurried across to the struggling King, who was standing horizontally on the door in an effort to get the sword out.

'Now, see here, your maj— Aargh!'

'Ach, tak a faceful o'heid!'

Darren staggered back, clutching at his face.

Little shapes swarmed across the courtyard after the King, like some kind of plague.

'Gibbins!'

'Fackle!'

'Nac mac Feegle!'

There was another scream as Jason, trying to restrain his monarch's enthusiasm, found that while the touch of a monarch may indeed cure certain scalp conditions, the scalp of a king itself is capable of spreading someone's nose into an interesting flat shape.

Arrows thudded into the ground around them.

Shawn grabbed Big Jim. 'They're all going to get shot, drink or not!' he shouted above the din. 'You come with me!'

'What we gonna do?'

'Clean the privies!'

The troll scuttled after him as he edged his way around the keep, to where the Gong Tower loomed against the night in all its odoriferous splendour. It was the bane of Shawn's life. All the keep's garderobes discharged into it. One of his jobs was to clean it out and take the contents to the pits in the gardens where Verence's efforts at composting were gradually turning them into, well, Lancre.* But now that the castle was a lot busier than it used to be his weekly efforts with shovel and wheelbarrow weren't the peaceful and solitary interludes they had been. Of *course* he'd let the job sort of . . . pile up these last few weeks, but did they expect him to do *everything*?

He waved Big Jim towards the door at the bottom of the tower. Fortunately, trolls have not much interest in organic odours, although they can easily distinguish types of limestone by smell.

'I want you to open it when I say,' he said, tearing a strip off his shirt and wrapping it round an arrow. He searched his pockets for a match. 'And when you've opened the door,' he went on, as the cloth caught, 'I want you to run away very, very fast, right? Okay . . . open the door!'

Big Jim pulled at the handle. There was a very faint whoosh as the door swung back.

'Run!' Shawn shouted. He drew back the bowstring and fired through the doorway.

The flaming arrow vanished into the noisome darkness. There was a pause of a few heartbeats. Then the tower exploded.

It happened quite slowly. The green-blue light mushroomed up from storey to storey in an almost leisurely way, blowing out stones at every level to give the tower a nice sparkling effect. The roofing leads

*The role of the lower intestine in the efforts to build a better nation is one that is often neglected by historians.

opened up like a daisy. A faint flame speared the clouds. Then time, sound and motion came back with a *thump.*

After a few seconds the main doors burst open and the soldiers ran out. The first one was smacked between the eyes by a ballistic king.

Shawn had just started to run back to the fight when someone landed on his shoulders, bearing him to the ground.

'Well, well, one of the toy soldiers,' sneered Corporal Svitz, leaping up and drawing his sword.

As he raised it Shawn rolled over and struck upwards with the Lancrastian Peace-time Army Knife. He might have had time to select the Device for Dissecting Paradoxes, or the Appliance for Detecting Small Grains of Hope, or the Spiral Thing for Ascertaining the Reality of Being, but as it happened it was the Instrument for Ending Arguments Very Quickly that won the day.

Presently, there came a short shower of soft rain.

Well . . . certainly a shower.

Definitely soft, anyway.

Agnes hadn't seen a mob like this before. Mobs, in her limited experience, were noisy. This one was silent. Most of the town was in it, and to Agnes's surprise they'd brought along many of the children.

It didn't surprise Perdita. *They're going to kill the vampires,* she said, *and the children will watch.*

Good, thought Agnes, that's exactly right.

Perdita was horrified. *It'll give them nightmares!*

No, thought Agnes. It'll take the nightmares away.

Sometimes everyone has to know the monster is dead, and remember, so that they can tell their grandchildren.

'They tried to turn people into things,' she said aloud.

'Sorry, miss?' said Piotr.

'Oh . . . just thinking aloud.'

And where had she got that other idea? Perdita wondered, the one where she'd told the villagers to send runners out to other towns to report on the night's work. That was unusually nasty of her.

But she remembered the look of horror on the mayor's face and, later, the blank engrossed expression when he was trying to throttle the Count with his chain of office. The vampire had killed him with a blow that had almost broken him in half.

She fingered the wounds on her neck. She was pretty certain vampires didn't miss, but Vlad must have done, because she clearly *wasn't* a vampire. She didn't even like the idea of rare steak. She'd tried to see if she could fly, when she thought people weren't looking, but she was as attractive to gravity as ever. The blood-sucking . . . no, never that, even if it was the ultimate diet programme, but she'd have liked the flying.

It's changed you, said Perdita.

'How?'

'Sorry, miss?'

You're sharper . . . edgier . . . nastier.

'Maybe it's about time I was, then.'

'Sorry, miss?'

'Oh, nothing. Do you have a spare sickle?'

The vampires travelled fast but erratically, appearing not so much to fly as to be promising entries in the world long-jump championships.

'We'll burn that *ungrateful* place to the ground,' moaned the Countess, landing heavily.

'*Afterwards* we'll burn that place to the ground,' said Lacrimosa. 'This is what kindness leads to, Father. I do hope you're paying attention.'

'After you paid for that belltower, too,' said the Countess.

The Count rubbed his throat, where the links of the gold chain still showed as a red weal. He wouldn't have believed that a human could be so strong.

'Yes, that might be a good course of action,' he said. 'We would have to make sure the news got around, of course.'

'You think *this* news won't get around?' said Lacrimosa, landing beside him.

'It will be dawn soon, Lacci,' said the Count, with heavy patience. 'Because of my training, you will regard it as rather a nuisance, not a reason to crumble into a little pile of dust. Reflect on this.'

'That Weatherwax woman did this, didn't she?' said Lacrimosa, ignoring this call to count her blessings. 'She put her self somewhere and she's attacking us. She can't be in the baby. I suppose she wasn't in your fat girl, Vlad? Plenty of room in there. Are you listening, brother?'

'What?' said Vlad distantly as they turned a corner in the road and saw the castle ahead of them.

'I saw you give in and bite her. So romantic. They still dragged her off, though. They'll have to use quite a long stake to hit any useful organ.'

'She'd have put her self somewhere close,' said the Count. 'It stands to reason. It must've been someone in the hall . . .'

'One of the other witches, surely,' said the Countess.

'I wonder . . .'

'That stupid priest,' said Lacrimosa.

'That would probably appeal to her,' said the Count. 'But I suspect not.'

'Not . . . Igor?' said his daughter.

'I wouldn't give that a moment's thought,' said the Count.

'I still think it was Fat Agnes.'

'She wasn't that fat,' said Vlad sulkily.

'You'd have got tired of her in the end and we'd have ended up with her always getting in the way, just like the others,' said Lacrimosa. '*Traditionally* a keep-sake is meant to be a lock of their hair, not their entire skull—'

'She's different.'

'Just because you can't read her mind? How interesting would that be?'

'At least I did *bite* someone,' said Vlad. 'What was wrong with you?'

'Yes, you were acting very strangely, Lacci,' said the Count, as they reached the drawbridge.

'If she was hiding in *me* I'd know!' snarled Lacrimosa.

'I wonder if you would,' said the Count. 'She just

has to find a weak spot . . .'

'She's just a witch, Father. Honestly, we're acting as though she's got some sort of terrible power—'

'Perhaps it was Vlad's Agnes after all,' said the Count. He gave his son a slightly longer stare than was strictly necessary.

'We're nearly at the castle,' said the Countess, trying to rally them. 'We'll all feel better for an early day.'

'Our best coffins got taken to Lancre,' said Lacrimosa sullenly. '*Someone* was so sure of themselves.'

'Don't you adopt that tone with me, young woman!' said the Count.

'I'm two hundred years old,' said Lacrimosa. 'Pardon me, but I think I can choose any tone I like.'

'That's no way to speak to your father!'

'Really, Mother, you might at least act as if you had two brain cells of your own!'

'It is *not* your father's fault that everything's gone wrong!'

'It has *not* all gone wrong, my dear! This is just a temporary setback!'

'It won't be when the Escrow meat tell their friends! Come on, Vlad, stop moping and back me up here . . .'

'If they tell them, what can they do? Oh, there will be a little bit of protesting, but then the survivors will see reason,' said the Count. 'In the meantime, we have those witches waiting for us. With the baby.'

'And we've got to be polite to them, I suppose?'

'Oh, I don't think we need go that far,' said the Count. 'Let them live, perhaps—'

Something bounced on the bridge beside him. He reached down to pick it up and dropped it with a yelp.

'But . . . garlic shouldn't burn . . .' he began.

'*Thith ith water from the Holy Turtle Pond of Thquintth*,' said a voice above them. 'Blethed by the Bithop himthelf in the Year of the Trout.' There was a glugging noise and the sound of someone swallowing. 'That wath a good year for beatitude,' Igor went on. 'But you don't have to take *my* word for it. Duck, you thuckerth!'

The vampires dived for cover as the bottle, turning over and over, arced down from the battlements.

It shattered on the bridge, and most of the contents hit a vampire, who burst into flame as if hit by burning oil.

'Now *really*, Cryptopher, there's no call for that sort of thing,' said the Count, as the blazing figure screamed and spun around in a circle. 'It's all in your mind, you know. Positive thinking, that's the ticket—'

'He's turning black,' said the Countess. 'Aren't you going to do something?'

'Oh, very well. Vlad, just kick him off the drawbridge, will you?'

The luckless Cryptopher was pushed, squirming, into the chasm.

'You know, that should not have happened,' said the Count, looking at his blistered fingers. 'He obviously was not . . . truly one of us.' Far below, there was a splash.

The rest of the vampires scrambled for the cover of the gate arch as another bottle exploded near the

Count. A drop splashed his leg, and he glanced down at the little wisp of smoke.

'Some error appears to have crept in,' he said.

'I've never been one to put myself forward,' said the Countess, 'but I strongly suggest you find a *new* plan, dear. One which works, perhaps?'

'I have one already formed,' he said, tapping his knuckles against the huge oak gates. 'If everyone would perhaps stand aside . . .'

Up on the battlement Igor nudged Nanny Ogg, who lowered a decanter of water from the Holy Fountain of Seven-Handed Sek and followed his pointing thumb.*

Clouds were suddenly spiralling, with blue light flashing inside them.

'There'th going to be a thtorm!' he said. 'The top of my head'th tingling! Run!'

They reached the tower just as a single bolt of lightning blew the doors apart and shattered the stones where they had been standing.

'Well, *that* was easy,' said Nanny, lying full length on the floor.

'They can control the weather,' said Igor.

'Blast!' said Nanny. 'That's right. Everyone knows that, who knows anything about vampires.'

'Thorry. But they won't be able to try that on the inthide doorth. Come on!'

'What's that smell?' said Nanny, sniffing. 'Igor, your boots are on fire!'

*Igor had two thumbs on his right hand. If something was useful, he always said, you may as well add another.

'Damn! And thethe feet were nearly new thicth month ago,' said Igor, as Nanny's holy water sizzled over the smoking leather. 'It'th my wire, it pickth up thtray currentth.'

'What happened, someone was hit by a falling buffalo?' said Nanny, as they hurried down the stairs.

'It wath a tree,' said Igor reproachfully. 'Mikhail Thwenitth up at the logging camp, the poor man. Practically nothing left, but hith parentth thaid I could have hith feet to remember him by.'

'That was strangely kind of them.'

'Well, I gave him a thpare arm after the acthe acthident a few yearth ago and when old Mr Thwenitth'th liver gave out I let him have the one Mr Kochak left to me for giving Mithith Kochak a new eye.'

'People round here don't so much die as pass on,' said Nanny.

'What goeth around cometh around,' said Igor.

'And your new plan is . . .?' said Lacrimosa, stepping across the rubble.

'We'll kill everyone. Not an original plan, I admit, but tried and tested,' said the Count. This met with general approval, but his daughter looked unsatisfied.

'What, everyone? All at once?'

'Oh, you can save some for later if you must.'

The Countess clutched his arm.

'Oh, this does so remind me of our honeymoon,' she said. 'Don't you remember those wonderful nights in Grjsknvij?'

'Oh, fresh morning of the world indeed,' said the Count solemnly.

'Such romance . . . and we met such lovely people, too. Do you remember Mr and Mrs Harker?'

'Very fondly. I recall they lasted nearly all week. Now, listen all of you. Holy symbols will *not* hurt us. Holy water is just water – yes, I know, but Cryptopher just wasn't concentrating. Garlic is just another member of the allium family. Do onions hurt us? Are we frightened of shallots? No. We've just got a bit tired, that's all. Malicia, call up the rest of the clan. We will have a little holiday from reason. And afterwards, in the morning, there will be room for a new world order I can't be having with this at all . . .'

He rubbed his forehead. The Count prided himself on his mind, and tended it carefully. But right now it felt exposed, as though someone was looking over his shoulder. He wasn't certain he was thinking right. She couldn't have got into his head, could she? He'd had hundreds of years of experience. There was no way some village witch could get past his defences. It stood to reason . . .

His throat felt parched. At least he could obey the call of his nature. But this time it was an oddly disquieting one.

'Do we have any . . . tea?' he said.

'What is tea?' said the Countess.

'It . . . grow on a bush, I think,' said the Count.

'How do you bite it, then?'

'You . . . er . . . lower it into boiling water, don't you?' The Count shook his head, trying to free himself of this demonic urge.

'While it's still alive?' said Lacrimosa, brightening up.

'. . . sweet biscuits . . .' mumbled the Count.

'I think you should try to get a grip, dear,' said the Countess.

'This . . . tea,' said Lacrimosa. 'Is it . . . brown?'

'Yes,' whispered the Count.

'Because when we were in Escrow I was going to put the bite on one of them and I had this horrible mental picture of a cup full of the wretched stuff,' said his daughter.

The Count shook himself again.

'I don't know what's happening to me,' he said. 'So let's stick to what we *do* know, shall we? Obey our blood . . .'

The second casualty in the battle for the castle was Vargo, a lank young man who actually became a vampire because he thought he'd meet interesting girls, or any girls at all, and had been told he looked good in black. And then he'd found that a vampire's interests always centre, sooner or later, on the next meal, and hitherto he'd never really thought of the neck as the most interesting organ a girl could have.

Right now all he wanted to do was sleep, so as the vampires surged into the castle proper he sauntered gently away in the direction of his cellar and nice comfortable coffin. Of course he was hungry, since all he'd got in Escrow was a foot in the chest, but he had just enough sense of self-preservation to let the others get on with the hunting so that he could turn up later for the feast.

His coffin was in the centre of the dim cellar, its lid lying carelessly on the floor beside it. He'd always been messy with the bedclothes, even as a human.

Vargo climbed in, twisted and turned a few times to get comfortable on the pillow, then pulled the lid down and latched it.

As the eye of narrative drew back from the coffin on its stand, two things happened. One happened comparatively slowly, and this was Vargo's realization that he never recalled the coffin having a pillow before.

The other was Greebo deciding that he was as mad as hell and wasn't going to take it any more. He'd been shaken around in the wheely thing and then sat on by Nanny, and he was angry about that because he knew, in a dim, animal way, that scratching Nanny might be the single most stupid thing he could do in the whole world, since no one else was prepared to feed him. This hadn't helped his temper.

Then he'd encountered a dog, which had tried to lick him. He'd scratched and bitten it a few times, but this had had no effect apart from encouraging it to try to be more friendly.

He'd finally found a comfy resting place and had curled up into a ball, and *now* someone was using him as a *cushion*—

There wasn't a great deal of noise. The coffin rocked a few times, and then pivoted around.

Greebo sheathed his claws and went back to sleep.

'—burn, with a clear bright light—'

Splash, suck, splash.

'—and I in mine . . . Om be praised.'

Squelch, splash.

Oats had worked his way though most of the hymns he knew, even the old ones you shouldn't really sing any more but you nevertheless remembered because the words were so good. He sang them loudly and defiantly, to hold back the night and the doubts. They helped take his mind off the weight of Granny Weatherwax. It was amazing how she'd apparently gained in the last mile or so, especially whenever he fell over and she landed on top of him.

He'd lost one of his own boots in a mire. His hat was floating in a pool somewhere. Thorns had ripped his coat to tatters—

He slipped and fell once again as the mud shifted under his feet. Granny rolled off and landed in a clump of sedge.

If Brother Melchio could only see him now . . .

The wowhawk swooped past and landed on the branch of a dead tree a few yards away. Oats hated the thing. It appeared demonic. It flew even though it surely couldn't see through the hood. Worse, whenever he thought about it, as now, the hooded head turned to fix him with an invisible stare. He took off his other useless shoe, its shiny leather all stained and cracked, and flung it inexpertly.

'Go away, you wicked creature!'

The bird didn't stir. The shoe flew past it.

Then, as he tried to get to his feet, he smelled burning leather.

Two wisps of smoke were curling up from either side of the hood.

Oats reached to his neck for the security of the turtle, and it wasn't there. It had cost him five *obols* in the Citadel, and it was too late now to reflect that perhaps he shouldn't have hung it from a chain worth a tenth of an *obol.* It was probably lying in some pool, or buried in some muddy, squelching marsh . . .

Now the leather burned away, and the yellow glow from the holes was so bright he could barely see the outline of the bird. It turned the dank landscape into lines and shadows, put a golden edge on every tuft of grass and stricken tree – and winked out so quickly that it left Oats's eyes full of purple explosions.

When he'd recovered his breath and his balance, the bird was swooping away down the moor.

He picked up Granny Weatherwax's unconscious body and ran after it.

The track did lead downhill, at least. Mud and bracken slipped under his feet. Rivulets were running from every hole and gully. Half the time it seemed to him that he wasn't walking, merely controlling a slide, bouncing off rocks, slithering through puddles of mud and leaves.

And then there was the castle, seen through a gap in the trees, lit by a flash of lightning. Oats staggered through a clump of thorn bushes, managed to keep upright down a slope of loose boulders, and collapsed on the road with Granny Weatherwax on top of him.

She stirred.

'. . . holiday from reason . . . kill them all . . . can't be havin' with this . . .' she murmured.

The wind blew a branchful of raindrops on her face, and she opened her eyes. For a moment they seemed to Oats to have red pupils, and then the icy blue gaze focused on him.

'Are we here, then?'

'Yes.'

'What happened to your holy hat?'

'It got lost,' said Oats abruptly. Granny peered closer.

'Your magic amulet's gone too,' she said. 'The one with the turtle and the little man on it.'

'It's *not* a magic amulet, Mistress Weatherwax! Please! A magic amulet is a symbol of primitive and mechanistic superstition, whereas the Turtle of Om is . . . is . . . is . . . Well, it's not, do you understand?'

'Oh, right. Thank you for explaining,' said Granny. 'Help me up, will you?'

Oats was having some difficulty with his temper. He'd carried the old bit— biddy for miles, he was frozen to the bone, and now they were here she acted as if she'd somehow done him a favour.

'What's the magic word?' he snarled.

'Oh, I don't think a holy man like you should be having with *magic* words,' said Granny. 'But the *holy* words are: do what I tell you or get smitten. They should do the trick.'

He helped her to her feet, alive with badly digested rage, and supported her as she swayed.

There was a scream from the castle, suddenly cut off.

'Not female,' said Granny. 'I reckon the girls have started. Let's give 'em a hand, shall we?'

Her arm shook as she raised it. The wowhawk fluttered down and settled on her wrist.

'Now help get me to the gate.'

'Don't mention it, glad to be of service,' Oats mumbled. He looked at the bird, whose hood swivelled to face him.

'That's the . . . other phoenix, isn't it?' he said.

'Yes,' said Granny, watching the door. 'A phoenix. You can't have just one of anything.'

'But it looks like a little hawk.'

'It was born among hawks, so it looks like a hawk. If it was hatched in a hen roost it'd be a chicken. Stands to reason. And a hawk it'll remain, until it needs to be a phoenix. They're shy birds. You could say a phoenix is what it may *become* . . .'

'Too much eggshell . . .'

'Yes, Mister Oats. And when does the phoenix sometimes lay two eggs? When it needs to. Hodgesaargh was right. A phoenix is of the nature of birds. Bird first, myth second.'

The doors were hanging loose, their iron reinforcements twisted out of shape and their timbers smouldering, but some effort had been made to pull them shut. Over what remained of the arch, a bat carved in stone told visitors everything they needed to know about this place.

On Granny's wrist the hood of the hawk was crackling and smoking. As Oats watched, little flames erupted from the leather again.

'He knows what they did,' said Granny. 'He was *hatched* knowing. Phoenixes share their minds. And they don't tolerate evil.'

The head turned to look at Oats with its white-hot stare and, instinctively, he backed away and tried to cover his eyes.

'Use the doorknocker,' said Granny, nodding to the big iron ring hanging loosely from one splintered door.

'What? You want me to *knock* on the *door*? Of a vampire's *castle*?'

'We're not going to sneak in, are we? Anyway, you Omnians are good at knocking on doors.'

'Well, *yes*,' said Oats, 'but normally just for a shared prayer and to interest people in our pamphlets' – he let the knocker fall a few times, the boom echoing around the valley – 'not to have my throat ripped out!'

'Think of this as a particularly difficult street,' said Granny. 'Try again . . . mebbe they're hidin' behind the sofa, eh?'

'Hah!'

'You're a good man, Mister Oats?' said Granny, conversationally, as the echoes died away. 'Even without your holy book and holy amulet and holy hat?'

'Er . . . I try to be . . .' he ventured.

'Well . . . this is where you find out,' said Granny. 'To the fire we come at last, Mister Oats. This is where we *both* find out.'

Nanny raced up some stairs, a couple of vampires at her heels. The vampires were hampered because they hadn't got to grips with not being able to fly, but there was something else wrong with them as well.

'Tea!' one screamed. 'I must have . . . *tea*!'

Nanny pushed open the door to the battlements. They followed her, and tripped over Igor's leg as he stepped out of the shadows.

He raised two sharpened table legs.

'How d'you want your thtaketh, boyth?' he shouted excitedly, as he struck. 'You thould have thed you *liked* my thpiderth!'

Nanny leaned against the wall to get her breath back.

'Granny's somewhere here,' she panted. 'Don't ask me how. But those two were craving a cup of tea, and I reckon only Esme could mess up someone's head like that—'

The sounds of the doorknocker boomed around the courtyard below. At the same time the door at the other end of the battlements opened. Half a dozen vampires advanced.

'They're acting very dumb, aren't they?' said Nanny. 'Give me a couple more stakes.'

'Run out of thtaketh, Nanny.'

'Okay, then, pass me a bottle of holy water . . . Hurry up . . .'

'None left, Nanny.'

'We've got *nothing*?'

'Got'n orange, Nanny.'

'What for?'

'Run out of lemonth.'

'What good will an orange do if I hit a vampire in the mouth with it?' said Nanny, eyeing the approaching creatures.

Igor scratched his head. 'Well, I thuppothe they won't catch coldth tho eathily . . .'

The knocking reverberated around the castle again. Several vampires were creeping across the courtyard.

Nanny caught a flicker of light around the edge of

the door. Instinct took over. As the vampires began to run, she grabbed Igor and pulled him down.

The arch exploded, every stone and plank drifting away on an expanding bubble of eyeball-searing flame. It lifted the vampires off their feet and they screamed as the fire carried them up.

When the brightness had faded a little Nanny peered carefully into the courtyard.

A bird, house-sized, wings of flame wider than the castle, reared in the broken doorway.

Mightily Oats pushed himself up on to his hands and knees. Hot flames roared around him, thundering like fiercely burning gas. His skin should have been blackening already, but against all reason the fire felt no more deadly than a hot desert wind. The air smelled of camphor and spices.

He looked up. The flames wrapped Granny Weatherwax, but they looked oddly transparent, not *entirely* real. Here and there little gold and green sparks glittered on her dress, and all the time the fire whipped and tore around her.

She looked down at him. 'You're in the wings of the phoenix now, Mister Oats,' she shouted, above the noise, 'and you ain't burned!'

The bird flapping its wings on her wrist was incandescent.

'How can—'

'You're the scholar! But male birds are always ones for the big display, aren't they?'

'Males? This is a *male* phoenix?'

'Yes!'

It leapt. What flew . . . what flew, as far as Oats could see, was a great bird-shape of pale flame, with the little form of the real bird inside like the head of a comet. He added to himself: if that is indeed the real bird . . .

It swooped up into the tower. A yell, cut off quickly, indicated that a vampire hadn't been fast enough.

'It doesn't burn itself?' Oats said weakly.

'Shouldn't think so,' said Granny, stepping over the wreckage. 'Wouldn't be much point.'

'Then it must be magical fire . . .'

'They say that whether it burns you or not is up to you,' said Granny. 'I used to watch them as a kid. My granny told me about 'em. Some cold nights you see them dancin' in the sky over the Hub, burnin' green and gold . . .'

'Oh, you mean the aurora coriolis,' said Oats, trying to make his voice sound matter of fact. 'But actually that's caused by magic particles hitting the—'

'Dunno what it's *caused* by,' said Granny sharply, 'but what it *is* is the phoenix dancin'.' She reached out. 'I ought to hold your arm.'

'In case I fall over?' said Oats, still watching the burning bird.

'That's right.'

As he took her weight the phoenix above them flung back its head and screamed at the sky.

'And to think I thought it was an allegorical creature,' said the priest.

'Well? Even allegories have to live,' said Granny Weatherwax.

* * *

Vampires are not naturally co-operative creatures. It's not in their nature. Every other vampire is a rival for the next meal. In fact, the ideal situation for a vampire is a world in which every other vampire has been killed off and no one seriously believes in vampires any more. They are by nature as co-operative as sharks.

Vampyres are just the same, the only real difference being that they can't spell properly.

The remnant of the clan scurried through the keep and headed for a door that for some reason had been left ajar.

The bucket containing a cocktail of waters blessed by a Knight of Offler, a High Priest of Io and a man so generically holy that he hadn't cut his hair or washed for seventy years, landed on the first two to run through.

They did not include the Count and his family, who had moved as one into a side tower. There's no point in having underlings if you don't let them be the first to go through suspicious doors.

'How could you have been so—' Lacrimosa began, and to her shock got a slap across the face from her father.

'All we need to do is remain calm,' said the Count. 'There's no need to panic.'

'You *struck* me!'

'And most satisfying it was, too,' said the Count. 'Careful thought is what will save us. That is why we will survive.'

'It's not *working*!' said Lacrimosa. 'I'm a vampire!

I'm supposed to crave blood! And all I can think about is a cup of tea with three sugars in it, whatever the hell that is! That old woman's doing something to us, can't you see?'

'Not possible,' said the Count. 'Oh, she's sharp for a human, but I don't reckon there's any way she could get into your head or mine—'

'You're even talkin' like her!' shouted Lacrimosa.

'Be resolute, my dear,' said the Count. 'Remember – that which does not kill us can only make us stronger.'

'And that which *does* kill us leaves us *dead*!' snarled Lacrimosa. 'You saw what happened to the others! *You* got your fingers burned!'

'A moment's lapse of concentration,' said the Count. 'That old witch is *not* a threat. She's a vampire. *Subservient* to us. She'll be seeing the world differently—'

'Are you mad? Something killed Cryptopher.'

'He let himself be frightened.'

The rest of the family looked at the Count. Vlad and Lacrimosa exchanged a glance.

'I am supremely confident,' said the Count. His smile looked like a death mask, waxen and disturbingly tranquil. 'My mind is like a rock. My nerve is firm. A vampire with his wits about him, or her, of course, can never be defeated. Didn't I teach you this? What's *this* one?'

His hand flew from his pocket, holding a square of white cardboard.

'Oh, Father, this is really no time for—' Lacrimosa froze, then jerked her arm in front of her face. 'Put it away! Put it away! It's the Agatean Chlong of Destiny!'

'Exactly, which is merely three straight lines and two curved lines pleasantly arranged which—'

'—I'd never have known about if you hadn't told me, you old fool!' screamed the girl, backing away.

The Count turned to his son.

'And do *you*—' he began. Vlad sprang back, putting his hand over his eyes.

'It *hurts*!' he shouted.

'Dear me, the two of you haven't been practising—' the Count began, and turned the card around so that he could look at it.

He screwed up his eyes and turned his face away.

'What have you *done* to us?!' Lacrimosa screamed. 'You've taught us how to see hundreds of the damned holy things! They're everywhere! Every religion has a different one! *You* taught us that, you stupid bastard! Lines and crosses and circles . . . Oh, my . . .' She caught sight of the stone wall behind her astonished brother and shuddered. 'Everywhere I *look* I see something holy! You've taught us to see *patterns*!' she snarled at her father, teeth exposed.

'It'll be dawn soon,' said the Countess nervously. 'Will it hurt?'

'It won't! Of course it won't!' shouted Count Magpyr, as the others glanced up at the pale light coming through a high window. 'It's a learned psychochromatic reaction! A superstition! It's all in the mind!'

'What *else* is in our minds, Father?' said Vlad coldly.

The Count was circling, trying to keep an eye on Lacrimosa. The girl was flexing her fingers and snarling.

'I said—'

'Nothing's in our minds that we didn't put there!' the Count roared. 'I saw that old witch's mind! It's *weak*. She relies on trickery! She couldn't possibly find a way in! I wonder if there are *other* agendas here?'

He bared his teeth at Lacrimosa.

The Countess fanned herself desperately. 'Well, I think we're all getting a *little* bit overexcited,' she said. 'I think we should all settle down and have a nice cup of . . . a nice . . . of tea . . . a cup of . . .'

'We're *vampires*!' Lacrimosa shouted.

'Then let's act like them!' screamed the Count.

Agnes opened her eyes, kicked up, and the man with the hammer and stake lost all interest in vampires and in consciousness as well.

'Whsz—' Agnes removed from her mouth what was, this time, a fig. 'Can you get it into your stupid heads that I'm not a vampire? And this isn't a lemon. It's a fig. And I'd watch that bloke with the stake. He's altogether too keen on it. I reckon there's some psychology there—'

'I wouldn't have let him use it,' said Piotr, close by her ear. 'But you did act very odd and then you just collapsed. So we thought we'd better see what woke up.'

He stood up. The citizens of Escrow stood watching among the trees, their faces gaunt in the flickering torchlight.

'It's all right, she's still not one,' he said. There was some general relaxation.

You really have changed, said Perdita.

'You're not affected?' said Agnes. She felt as if she was on the end of a string with someone jerking the other end.

No. I'm the bit of you that watches, remember?

'What?' said Piotr.

'I really, really hope this wears off,' said Agnes. 'I keep tripping over my own feet! I'm walking wrong! My whole body feels wrong!'

'Er . . . can we go on to the castle?' said Piotr.

'*She*'s already there,' said Agnes. 'I don't know how, but—'

She stopped and looked at the worried faces, and for a moment she found herself thinking in the way Granny Weatherwax thought.

'Yes,' she said, more slowly. 'I reckon . . . I mean, I think we ought to get there right away. People have to kill their own vampires.'

Nanny hurried down the steps again.

'I *told* you!' she said. 'That's Esme Weatherwax down there, that is. I told you! I *knew* she was just biding her time! Hah, I'd like to see the bloodsucker who could put one over on her!'

'I wouldn't,' said Igor, fervently.

Nanny stepped over a vampire who hadn't noticed, in the shadows, a cunning combination of a tripwire, a heavy weight and a stake, and opened a door into the courtyard.

'Coo-ee, Esme!'

Granny Weatherwax pushed Oats away and stepped forward.

'Is the baby all right?' she said.

'Magrat and Es . . . *young* Esme are locked up in the crypt. It's a very strong door,' said Nanny.

'And Thcrapth ith guarding them,' said Igor. 'He'th a wonderful guard dog.'

Granny raised her eyebrows and looked Igor up and down.

'I don't think I know this . . . *these* gentlemen,' she said.

'Oh, this is Igor,' said Nanny. 'A man of many parts.'

'So it seems,' said Granny.

Nanny glared at Mightily Oats. 'What did you bring him for?' she said.

'Couldn't seem to shake him off,' said Granny.

'I always try hiding behind the sofa, myself,' said Nanny. Oats looked away.

There was a scream from somewhere on the battlements. The phoenix had spotted another vampire.

'All over now bar sweeping up the dust, then,' said Nanny. 'They didn't seem very smart—'

'The Count's still here,' said Granny flatly.

'Oh, I vote we just set fire to the place and go home,' said Nanny. 'It's not as though he'll be coming back to Lancre in a hurry—'

'There'th a crowd coming,' said Igor.

'I can't hear anything,' said Nanny.

'I've got very good earth,' said Igor.

'Ah, well, of course some of us don't get to choose,' said Nanny.

There was a clattering of footsteps across the bridge and people were suddenly swarming over the rubble.

'Isn't that Agnes?' said Nanny. Normally there'd be

no mistaking the figure advancing across the courtyard, but there was something about the walk, the way every foot thudded down as though the boots were not on speaking terms with the earth. And the arms, too, swung in a way—

'I can't be having with this!' Agnes shouted, marching up to Granny. 'I can't think straight. It's you, isn't it?'

Granny reached out and touched the wounds on her neck.

'Ah, I see,' she said. 'One of them bit you, yes?'

'Yes! And somehow *you* spoke to me!'

'Not me. That was something in your blood talkin', I reckon,' said Granny. 'Who're all these people? Why's that man trying to set fire to the wall? Don't he know stone don't burn?'

'Oh, that's Claude, he's a bit single-minded. Just let me know if he picks up a stake, will you? Look, they're from Escrow, it's a town not far away . . . The Magpyrs treated them like . . . well . . . *pets.* Farm animals! Just like they were trying to do back home!'

'We ain't leaving until we've dealt with the Count,' said Granny. 'Otherwise he'll be sneaking back—'

'Er, excuse me,' said Oats, who seemed to have been thinking about something. 'Excuse me, but did someone mention that the Queen was locked up in the crypt?'

'Safe as houses,' said Nanny. 'Huge thick door and you can bar it from the inside.'

'How safe are houses from vampires?' said Oats.

Granny's head turned sharply. 'What do you mean?'

Oats took a step backwards.

'Ah, I know what he means,' said Nanny. 'It's all right, we're not daft, she won't open up until she knows it's us—'

'I meant, how does the door stop vampires?'

'Stop them? It's a *door*.'

'So . . . they can't turn themselves into some sort of mist, then?' said Oats, frying in the joint radiation of their stares. 'Only I thought that vampires could, you see. I thought everyone knew that who knows anything about vampires . . .'

Granny turned on Igor. 'D'you know anything about this?'

Igor's mouth opened and shut a few times.

'The old Count never did anything like *that*,' he said.

'Yes,' said Nanny, 'But *he* played *fair*.'

There was a rising howl from the depths of the castle, cut off suddenly.

'That was Thcrapth!' said Igor, breaking into a run.

'Thcraapthhh?' said Agnes, wrinkling her brow. Nanny grabbed her arm and dragged her after Igor.

Granny swayed a little. Her eyes had an unfocused look.

Oats glanced at her, made up his mind, staggered rather theatrically and sprawled in the dust.

Granny blinked, shook her head and glared down at him.

'Hah! All too much for you, eh?' she said hoarsely.

Trembling fingers reached down for Oats. He took them, taking care not to pull, and stood up.

'If you could just give me a hand,' he said, as her grateful weight hit his shoulder.

'Right,' said Granny. 'Now let's find the kitchens.'

'Huh? What do we want with the kitchens?'

'After a night like this we could all do with a cup of tea,' said Granny.

Magrat leaned against the door as a second thump rattled the bolts. Beside her, Scraps started to growl. Perhaps it was something to do with his extensive surgery, but Scraps growled in half a dozen different pitches all at once.

Then there was silence, which was even more terrifying than the thumping.

A faint noise made her look down. A green smoke was pouring through the keyhole.

It was thick, and had an oily quality . . .

She darted across the room and snatched up a jar that had contained lemons so sportingly provided by the mysterious old Count that Igor thought so highly of. She wrenched off the lid and held it under the keyhole. When the smoke had filled it up she dropped a few cloves of garlic in and slammed the lid back on.

The jar rocked urgently on the floor.

Then Magrat glanced at the lid of the well. When she lifted it up she heard rushing water a long way below. Well, that was likely, wasn't it? There must be lots of underground rivers in the mountains.

She held the jar over the centre of the hole and let it go. Then she slammed the lid back down.

Young Esme gurgled in the corner. Magrat hurried over to her and shook a rattle.

'Look at the pretty bunny rabbit,' she said, and darted back again.

There was whispering on the other side of the door. Then Nanny Ogg's voice said, 'It's all right, dear, we've got them. You can open the door now. Lawks.'

Magrat rolled her eyes.

'Is that really you, Nanny?'

'That's right, dear.'

'Thank goodness. Just tell me the joke about the old woman, the priest and the rhinoceros then and I'll let you in.'

There was a pause, and some more whispering.

'I don't think we've got time for that, dear,' said the voice.

'Ha ha, nice try,' said Magrat. 'I've dropped one of you in the river! Who was it?'

After some silence the voice of the Count said, 'We *thought* the Countess could persuade you to listen to reason.'

'Not in a jar she can't,' said Magrat. 'And I've got more jars if you want to try it again!'

'We had hoped that you would be sensible about this,' said the Count. 'However . . .'

The door slammed back, pulling the bolts out of the wall.

Magrat grabbed the baby and stepped backwards, her other hand raised.

'You come near me and I'll stab you with this!' she shouted.

'It's a teddybear,' said the Count. 'I'm afraid it wouldn't work, even if you sharpened it.'

* * *

The door was so hard that the wood was like stone with a grain. Someone had once thought hard about the maximum amount of force a really determined mob would be able to apply, and had then overdesigned.

It hung open.

'But we heard her put the bars across!' wailed Nanny.

A variously coloured lump was sprawled in front of the door. Igor knelt down and picked up a limp paw.

'They've killed Thcrapth! The bathtardth!'

'They've got Magrat and the babby!' snapped Nanny.

'He wath my only friend!'

Nanny's arm shot out and, despite his bulk, Igor was lifted up by his collar.

'You're going to have one very *serious* enemy really soon, my lad, unless you help us out right *now*! Oh, for heaven's sake . . .' With her spare hand she reached into her knickerleg and produced a large crumpled handkerchief. 'Have a good blow, will you?'

There was a noise like a foghorn being trodden on.

'Now, where would they take them? The place is swarming with righteous peasants!' said Nanny, when he'd finished.

'He wath alwayth ready with hith waggy tailth and hith cold nothe—' Igor sobbed.

'*Where*, Igor?'

Igor pointed with his finger, or at least one that he currently owned, to the far door.

'That goeth to the vaultth,' he said. 'An' they can get

out through the iron gate down in the valley. You'll never catch them!'

'But it's still bolted,' said Agnes.

'Then they're thtill in the cathle, which ith thtupid—'

He was interrupted by several huge organ chords, which made the floor rumble.

'Any of the Escrow folk big musicians?' said Nanny, lowering Igor.

'How do I know?' said Agnes, as another couple of descending chords brought dust down from the ceiling. 'They wanted to hammer a stake in me and boil my head! That is *not* the time to ask them to give a little whistle!'

The organ piped its summons once more.

'Why'd they stay?' said Nanny. 'They could be dug in deep somewhere by now— Oh . . .'

'Granny wouldn't run,' said Agnes.

'No, Granny Weatherwax likes a showdown,' said Nanny, grinning artfully. 'And they're thinkin' like her. Somehow she's making them think like *her* . . .'

'*She* thinks like her, too,' said Agnes.

'Let's hope she's had more practice, then,' said Nanny. 'Come on!'

Lacrimosa pulled an organ stop marked 'Ghastly Face at Window' and was rewarded with a chord, a crash of thunder and a slightly mechanical scream.

'Thank goodness we don't take after your side of the family, Father, that's all I can say,' she said. 'Although I suppose it could be fun if we could arrange some sort of mechanical linkage to the torture chamber. That certainly wasn't a very realistic scream.'

'This is ridiculous,' said Vlad. 'We've got the child. We've got the woman. Why don't we just leave? There're plenty of other castles.'

'That would be running away,' said the Count.

'And surviving,' said Vlad, rubbing his head.

'We don't run,' said the Count. 'And— No, step back, please . . .'

This was to the mob, which was hovering uncertainly just inside the doors. Mobs become uncertain very quickly, in view of the absence of a central brain, and in this case the hesitation was caused by the sight of Magrat and the baby.

Vlad had a bruise on his forehead. A push-and-go wooden duck on wheels can cause quite a lot of damage if wielded with enough force.

'Well done,' said the Count, cradling baby Esme on one arm. Magrat writhed to escape the grip of his other hand, but it clamped her wrist like steel. 'You see? Absolute obedience. It's just as in chess. If you take the Queen, you've as good as won. It doesn't matter if a few pawns are lost.'

'That's a very nasty way to talk about Mother,' said Vlad.

'I am very attached to your mother,' said the Count. 'And she'll find a way to return, in the fullness of time. A voyage will be good for her health. Some fisherman will find the jar and next thing you know she'll be back with us, fat and healthy— Ah, the inestimable Mrs Ogg . . .'

'Don't you go smarming me!' snapped Nanny,

pushing her way through the bewildered crowd. 'I'm fed up with you smarming at me smarmily as if you were Mister Smarm! Now you just free the both of them or—'

'Ah, so quickly we get to *or*,' sighed the Count. 'But *I* will say: you will all leave the castle, and then we shall see. Perhaps we shall let the Queen go. But the little princess . . . Isn't she charming? She can remain as our guest. She'll brighten the place up—'

'She's coming back to Lancre with us, you bastard!' screamed Magrat. She twisted in the Count's grip and tried to slap him, but Agnes saw her face whiten as his hand tightened on her wrist.

'That's very bad language for a queen,' said the Count. 'And I am still very strong, even for a vampire. But you're right. We shall *all* go back to Lancre. One big happy family, living in the castle. I must say, this place is losing its attractions. Oh, don't blame yourself, Mrs Ogg. I'm sure others will do that for you—'

He stopped. A sound that had been on the edge of hearing was getting louder. It had a rhythmic, almost tinny sound.

The crowd parted. Granny Weatherwax walked forward, slowly stirring.

'No milk in this place,' she said. 'Not to be wondered at, really. I sliced a bit of lemon, but it's not the same, I always think.'

She laid the spoon in the saucer with a clink that echoed around the hall, and gave the Count a smile.

'Am I too late?' she said.

* * *

The bolts rattled back, one by one.

'. . . 'th gone too far,' Igor muttered. 'The old marthter wouldn't . . .'

The door creaked back on lovingly rusted hinges. Cool dry air puffed out of the darkness.

Igor fumbled with some matches and lit a torch.

'. . . it'th all very well wanting a nithe long retht, but thith ith a dithgrathe . . .'

He ran along the dark corridors, half rough masonry, half sheer naked rock, and reached another chamber that was completely empty apart from a large stone sarcophagus in the centre, on the side of which was carved *magpyr*.

He stuffed the torch into a bracket, removed his coat and after considerable pushing heaved the stone lid aside.

'Thorry about thith, marthter,' he grunted as it thudded to the ground.

Inside the coffin grey dust twinkled in the torchlight.

'. . . coming up here, mething everything up . . .' Igor picked up his coat and took a thick wad of material out of his pocket. He unrolled it on the edge of the stone. Now the light glinted off an array of scalpels, scissors and needles.

'. . . threatening little babieth now . . . *you* never done that . . . only adventurouth femaleth over the age of theventeen and looking good in a nightie, you alwayth thed . . .'

He selected a scalpel and, with some care, nicked the little finger of his left hand.

A drop of blood appeared, swelled and dropped on

to the dust, where it smoked.

'That one'th for Thcrapth,' said Igor with grim satisfaction.

By the time he'd reached the door white mist was already pouring over the edge of the coffin.

'I'm an old lady,' said Granny Weatherwax, looking around sternly. 'I'd like to sit down, thank you so very much.'

A bench was rushed forward. Granny sat, and eyed the Count.

'What were you saying?' she said.

'Ah, Esmerelda,' said the Count. 'At last you come to join us. The call of the blood is too strong to be disobeyed, yes?'

'I hope so,' said Granny.

'We're all going to walk out of here, Miss Weatherwax.'

'You're not leaving here,' said Granny. She stirred the tea again. The eyes of all three vampires swivelled to follow the spoon.

'You have no choice but to obey me. You know that,' said the Count.

'Oh, there's always a choice,' said Granny.

Vlad and Lacrimosa leaned down on either side of their father. There was some hurried whispering. The Count looked up.

'No, you *couldn't* have resisted it,' he said. 'Not even you!'

'I won't say it didn't cost me,' said Granny. She stirred the tea again.

There was more whispering.

'We *do* have the Queen and the baby,' said the Count. 'I believe you think highly of them.'

Granny raised the cup halfway to her lips. 'Kill 'em,' she said. 'It won't benefit you.'

'Esme!' snapped Nanny Ogg and Magrat together.

Granny put the cup back in the saucer. Agnes thought she saw Vlad sigh. She could feel the pull herself . . .

I know what she did, whispered Perdita. So do I, thought Agnes.

'He's bluffing,' Granny said.

'Oh? You'd like a vampire queen one day, would you?' said Lacrimosa.

'Had one once, in Lancre,' said Granny conversationally. 'Poor woman got bitten by one of you people. Got by on blue steak and such. Never laid a tooth on anyone, the way I heard it. Griminir the Impaler, she was.'

'The *Impaler*?'

'Oh, I just said she wasn't a bloodsucker. I didn't say she was a nice person,' said Granny. 'She didn't mind shedding blood, but she drew the line at drinking it. You don't have to, neither.'

'You know *nothing* about *true* vampires!'

'I know more'n you think, and I know about Gytha Ogg,' said Granny. Nanny Ogg blinked.

Granny Weatherwax raised the teacup again, and then lowered it. 'She likes a drink. She'll *tell* you it has to be best brandy . . .' Nanny nodded affirmation '. . . and that's certainly what she *desires*, but really she'll settle for beer just like everyone else.' Nanny Ogg shrugged as Granny went on: 'But you wouldn't settle for black puddings, would you, because what you really drink is power over people. I know you like I know myself. And one of the things I know is that you ain't going to hurt a hair of that child's head. Leastways,' and here Granny absentmindedly stirred the tea again, 'if she had any yet, you wouldn't. You can't, see.'

She picked up the cup and carefully scraped it on the edge of the saucer. Agnes saw Lacrimosa's lips part, hungrily.

'So all I'm really here for, d'you see, is to see whether you get justice or mercy,' said Granny. 'It's just a matter of choosing.'

'You really think we wouldn't harm *meat*?' said Lacrimosa, striding forward. 'Watch!'

She brought her hand down hard towards the baby, and then jerked back as if she'd been stung.

'Can't do it,' said Granny.

'I nearly broke my arm!'

'Shame,' said Granny calmly.

'You've put some . . . something magical in the child, have you?' said the Count.

'Can't imagine who'd think I'd do such a thing,' said Granny, while behind her Nanny Ogg looked down at her boots. 'So here's my offer, you see. You hand back Magrat and the baby and we'll chop your heads off.'

'And that's what you call justice, is it?' said the Count.

'No, that's what I call mercy,' said Granny. She put the cup back in the saucer.

'*For goodness' sake, woman, are you going to drink that damn tea or not?*' roared the Count.

Granny sipped it and made a face.

'Why, what *have* I been thinkin' of? I've been so busy talking it's got cold,' she said, and daintily tipped the contents of the cup on to the floor.

Lacrimosa groaned.

'It'll probably wear off soon,' Granny went on, in the same easy voice. 'But until it does, you see, you'll not harm a child, you'll not harm Magrat, you hate the thought of drinking blood, and you won't run because you'll never run from a challenge . . .'

'*What* will wear off?' said Vlad.

'Oh, they're strong, your walls of thought,' said Granny dreamily. 'I couldn't get through them.'

The Count smiled.

Granny smiled, too. 'So I didn't,' she added.

The mist rolled through the crypt, flowing along the floor, walls and ceiling. It poured up the steps and along a tunnel, the billows boiling ahead on one another as though engaged in a war.

An unwary rat, creeping across the flagstones, was too late. The mist flowed over it. There was a squeak, cut off, and when the mist had gone a few small white bones were all that remained.

Some equally small bones, but fully assembled and wearing a black hooded robe and carrying a tiny scythe, appeared out of nowhere and walked over to them. Skeletal claws tippy-tapped on the stone.

'Squeak?' said the ghost of the rat pathetically.

SQUEAK, said the Death of Rats. This was really all it needed to know.

* * *

'You wanted to know where I'd put my self,' said Granny. 'I didn't go anywhere. I just put it in something alive, and you took it. You invited me in. I'm in every muscle in your body and I'm in your head, oh yes. I was in the *blood*, Count. In the blood. I ain't been vampired. You've been Weatherwaxed. All of you. And you've always listened to your blood, haven't you?'

The Count stared at her, open-mouthed.

The spoon dropped out of her saucer and tinkled on to the floor, raising a wave in a thin white mist. It was rolling in from the walls, leaving a shrinking circle of black and white tiles in the middle of which were the vampires.

Igor pushed his way through the crowd until he was alongside Nanny.

'It'th all right,' he said, 'I couldn't let it go on, it wath dithgratheful . . .'

The mist rose in a boiling tower, there was a moment of discontinuity, a feeling of sliced time, and then a figure stood behind Vlad and Lacrimosa. He was rather taller than most men, and wearing evening dress that might have been in style once upon a time. His hair was streaked with grey and brushed back over his ears in a way that gave the impression his head had been designed for its aerodynamic efficiency.

Beautifully manicured hands gripped the shoulders of the younger vampires. Lacrimosa turned to scratch him, and cowered when he snarled like a tiger.

Then the face returned to something closer to human, and the newcomer smiled. He seemed genuinely pleased to see everyone.

'Good morning,' he said.

'Another bloody vampire?' said Nanny.

'Not any old vampire,' said Igor, hopping from one foot to the other. 'It'th the old marthter! Old Red Eyeth ith back!'

Granny stood up, ignoring the tall figure firmly holding the two suddenly docile vampires. She advanced on the Count.

'I know all about what you can and can't do,' she said, 'because you let me in. An' that means you can't do what I can't do. An' you think just like me, the difference bein' I've done it longer and I'm better'n you at it.'

'You're *meat*,' snarled the Count. 'Clever *meat*!'

'And you *invited* me in,' said Granny. 'I'm not the sort to go where I'm not welcome, I'm sure.'

In the Count's arms the baby started to cry. He stood up.

'How *sure* are you that I won't harm this child?' he said.

'I wouldn't. So you can't.'

The Count's face contorted as he wrestled with his feelings and also with Magrat, who was kicking him on the shins.

'It could have worked . . .' he said, and for the first time the certainty had been drained from his voice.

'You mean it could have worked for you!' shouted Agnes.

'We are vampires. We cannot help what we are.'

'Only animals can't help what they are,' said Granny. 'Will you give me the child now?'

'If I . . .' the Count began, and then straightened up.

'No! I don't have to bargain! I *can* fight you, just as you fought me! And if I walk out of here now, I don't think there's anyone who'll dare stop me. Look at you . . . all of you . . . and look at me. And now look at . . . him.' He nodded at the figure holding Vlad and Lacrimosa as still as statues. 'Is *that* what you want?'

'Sorry . . . who is this we're supposed to be looking at?' said Granny. 'Oh . . . Igor's "old master"? The old Count Magpyr, I believe.'

The old Count nodded gracefully. 'Your servant, madam,' he said.

'I doubt it,' said Granny.

'Oh, no one minded *him*,' said Piotr, from among the Escrow citizens. 'He only ever came round every few years and anyway if you remembered about the garlic he wasn't a problem. He didn't expect us to *like* him.'

The old Count smiled at him.

'You look familiar. One of the Ravi family, aren't you?'

'Piotr, sir. Son of Hans.'

'Ah, yes. Very similar bone structure. Do remember me to your grandmother.'

'She passed away ten years ago, sir.'

'Oh, really? I am so sorry. Time goes so quickly when you're dead.' The old master sighed. 'A very fine figure in a nightdress, as I recall.'

'Oh, *he* was all right,' said someone else in the crowd. 'We got a nip every now and again but we got over it.'

'That's a familiar voice,' said the vampire. 'Are you a Veyzen?'

'Yessir.'

'Related to Arno Veyzen?'

'Great-granddaddy, sir.'

'Good man. Killed me stone dead seventy-five years ago. Stake right through the heart from twenty paces. You should be proud.'

The man in the crowd beamed with ancestral pride.

'We've still got the stake hung up over the fireplace, yer honour,' he said.

'Well done. Good man. I like to see the old ways kept up—'

Count Magpyr screamed.

'You can't possibly prefer *that*?! He's a *monster*!'

'But he never made an appointment!' shouted Agnes, even louder. 'I bet he never thought it was all just an *arrangement*!'

Count Magpyr was edging towards the door with his hostages.

'No,' he said, 'this is *not* how it's going to happen. If anyone really believes that I won't harm my charming hostages, perhaps you will try to stop me? Does *anyone* really believe that old woman?'

Nanny Ogg opened her mouth, caught Granny's eye, and shut it again. The crowd parted behind the Count as he dragged Magrat towards the door.

He walked into the figure of Mightily Oats.

'Have you ever thought of letting Om into your life?' said the priest. His voice trembled. His face glistened with sweat.

'Oh . . . you *again*?' said the Count. 'If I can resist her, little boy, *you* are not a problem!'

Oats held his axe before him as if it was made of some rare and delicate metal.

'Begone, foul fiend—' he began.

'Oh, dear me,' said the Count, thrusting the axe aside. 'And don't you learn anything, you stupid man? Little stupid man who has a little stupid faith in a little stupid god?'

'But it . . . lets me see things as they are,' Oats managed.

'Really? And you think *you* can stand in my way? An axe isn't even a holy symbol!'

'Oh.' Oats looked crestfallen. Agnes saw his shoulders sag as he lowered the blade.

Then he looked up, smiled brightly and said, 'Let's make it so.'

Agnes saw the blade leave a gold trail in the air as it swept around. There was a soft, almost silken sound.

The axe dropped on to the flagstones. In the sudden silence it clanged like a bell. Then Oats reached out and snatched the child from the vampire's unresisting hands. He held her out to Magrat, who took her in shocked silence.

The first sound after that was the rustle of Granny's dress as she stood up and walked over to the axe. She nudged it with her foot.

'If I've got a fault,' she said, contriving to suggest that this was only a theoretical possibility, 'it's not knowing when to turn and run. And I tends to bluff on a weak hand.'

Her voice echoed in the hall. No one else had even breathed out yet.

She nodded at the Count, who'd slowly raised his

hands to the red wound that ran all around his neck.

'It was a *sharp* axe,' she said. 'Who says there's no mercy in the world? Just don't nod, that's all. And someone'll take you down to a nice cold coffin and I daresay fifty years'll just fly past and maybe you'll wake with enough sense to be stupid.'

There was a murmur from the mob as they came back to life. Granny shook her head.

'They want you deader than that, I see,' she said, as the Count gazed ahead of him with frozen, desperate eyes and the blood welled and seeped between his fingers. 'An' there's ways. Oh, yes. We could burn you to ashes and scatter them in the sea—'

This met with a general sigh of approval.

'—or throw 'em up in the air in the middle of a gale—'

This got a smattering of applause.

'—or just pay some sailor to drop you over the edge.' This even got a few whistles. 'Of course, you'd come back alive again, I suppose, one day. But just floating in space for millions of years, oh, that sounds very boring to me.' She raised a hand to silence the crowd.

'No. Fifty years to think about things, that's about right. People need vampires,' she said. 'They helps 'em remember what stakes and garlic are for.'

She snapped her fingers at the crowd. 'Come on, two of you take him down to the vaults. Show some respect for the dead—'

'That's not enough!' said Piotr, stepping forward. 'Not after all he—'

'Then when he comes back you deal with him

yourself,' snapped Granny loudly. 'Teach your children! Don't trust the cannibal just 'cos he's usin' a knife and fork! And remember that vampires don't go where they're not invited!'

They backed away. Granny relaxed a little.

'This time round, it's up to me. My . . . choice.' She leaned closer to the Count's horrible grimace. 'You tried to take my mind away from me,' she said in a lower voice. 'And that's everything to me. Reflect on that. Try to *learn*.' She stood back. 'Take him away.'

She turned away, to the tall figure. 'So . . . you're the old master, are you?' she said.

'Alison Weatherwax?' said the old master. 'I have a good memory for necks.'

Granny froze for a second.

'What? No! Er . . . how do you know the name?'

'Why, she passed through here, what, fifty years ago. We met briefly, and then she cut off my head and stuck a stake in my heart.' The Count sighed happily. 'A very spirited woman. You're a relative, I presume? I lose track of generations, I'm afraid.'

'Granddaughter,' said Granny weakly.

'There's a phoenix outside the castle, Igor tells me . . .'

'It'll leave, I expect.'

The Count nodded. 'I've always rather liked them,' he said wistfully. 'There were so many of them when I was young. They made the nights . . . pretty. So pretty. Everything was so much simpler then . . .' His voice trailed off, and then came back louder. 'But now, apparently, we're in *modern times*.'

'That's what they say,' murmured Granny.

'Well, madam, I've never taken too much notice of them. Fifty years later they never seem so modern as all that.' He shook the younger vampires like dolls. 'I do apologize for my nephew's behaviour. Quite out of keeping for a vampire. Would you people from Escrow like to kill these two? It's the least I could do.'

'Ain't they your relatives?' said Nanny Ogg, as the crowd surged forward.

'Oh, yes. But we've never been much of a species for playing happy families.'

Vlad looked imploringly at Agnes, and reached out to her.

'You wouldn't let them kill me, would you? You wouldn't let them do this to me? We could have . . . we might . . . you *wouldn't*, would you?'

The crowd hesitated. This sounded like an important plea. A hundred pairs of eyes stared at Agnes.

She took his hand. *I suppose we could work on him*, said Perdita. But Agnes thought about Escrow, and the queues, and the children playing while they waited, and how evil might come animal sharp in the night, or greyly by day on a list . . .

'Vlad,' she said gently, looking deep into his eyes, 'I'd even hold their coats.'

'A fine sentiment but that ain't happenin',' said Granny, behind her. 'You take 'em away, Count. Teach 'em the old ways. Teach 'em stupidity.'

The Count nodded and grinned toothily.

'Certainly. I shall teach them that to live you have to rise again—'

'Hah! You don't *live*, Count. The phoenix lives. You just don't know you're dead. Now get along with you!'

There was another moment sliced out of time and then a flock of magpies rose up from where the three vampires had been, screaming and chattering, and disappeared in the darkness of the roof.

'There's hundreds of them!' said Agnes to Nanny.

'Well, vampires can turn into things,' said Nanny. 'Everyone knows that, who knows anything about vampires.'

'And what do three hundred magpies mean?'

'They mean it's time to put covers on all the furniture,' said Nanny. 'And that it's time for me to have a very big drink.'

The crowd began to break up, aware that the big show was over.

'Why didn't she just let us wipe them out?' hissed Piotr by Agnes's ear. 'Death's too good for them!'

'Yes,' said Agnes. 'I suppose that's why she didn't let them have it.'

Oats hadn't moved. He was still staring straight ahead of him, but his hands were shaking. Agnes led him gently to a bench and eased him down.

'I killed him, didn't I?' he whispered.

'Sort of,' said Agnes. 'It's a bit hard to tell with vampires.'

'There was just nothing else to do! Everything just went . . . the air just went gold, and there was just this one moment to do something—'

'I don't think anyone's complaining,' said Agnes.

You've got to admit he's quite attractive, whispered Perdita. *If only he'd do something about that boil . . .*

Magrat sat down on the other side of Oats, clutching the baby. She breathed deeply a few times.

'That was very brave of you,' she said.

'No, it wasn't,' said Oats hoarsely. 'I thought Mistress Weatherwax was going to do something . . .'

'She did,' said Magrat, shivering. 'Oh, she did.'

Granny Weatherwax sat down on the other end of the bench and pinched the bridge of her nose.

'I just want to go home now,' she said. 'I just want to go home and sleep for a week.' She yawned. 'I'm dyin' for a cuppa.'

'I thought you'd made one!' said Agnes. 'You had us slavering for it!'

'Where'd I get tea here? It was just some mud in water. But I know Nanny keeps a bag of it somewhere on her person.' She yawned again. 'Make the tea, Magrat.'

Agnes opened her mouth, but Magrat waved her into silence and then handed her the baby.

'Certainly, Granny,' she said, gently pushing Agnes back into her seat. 'I'll just find out where Igor keeps the kettle, shall I?'

Mightily Oats stepped out on to the battlements. The sun was well up and a breeze was blowing in over the forests of Uberwald. A few magpies chattered in the trees nearest the castle.

Granny was leaning with her elbows on the wall, staring out over the thinning mists.

'It looks like it's going to be a fine day,' said Oats happily. And he did feel happy, to his amazement. There was sharpness to the air, and the sense of the future brimming with possibilities. He remembered the moment when he'd swung the axe, when *both* of him had swung it together. Perhaps there was a way . . .

'There's a storm coming down from the Hub later,' said Granny.

'Well . . . at least that'll be good for the crops, then,' said Oats.

Something flickered overhead. In the new daylight the wings of the phoenix were hard to see, mere yellow shimmers in the air, with the tiny shape of the little hawk in the centre as it circled high over the castle.

'Why would anyone want to kill something like that?' said Oats.

'Oh, some people'll kill anything for the fun of it.'

'Is it a true bird or is it something that exists *within* a—'

'It's a thing that is,' said Granny sharply. 'Don't go spilling allegory all down your shirt.'

'Well, I feel . . . blessed to have seen it.'

'Really? I gen'rally feel the same about the sunrise,' said Granny. 'You would too, at my time of life.' She sighed, and then seemed to be speaking mainly to herself. 'She never went to the bad, then, whatever people said. And you'd have to be on your toes with that ol' vampire. She never went to the bad. You heard him say that, right? He said it. He didn't have to.'

'Er . . . yes.'

'She'd have been older'n me, too. Bloody good witch was Nana Alison. Sharp as a knife. Had her funny little ways, o' course, but who hasn't?'

'No one I know, certainly.'

'Right. You're right.' Granny straightened up. 'Good,' she said.

'Er . . .'

'Yes?'

Oats was looking down at the drawbridge and the road to the castle.

'There's a man in a nightshirt covered in mud and waving a sword down there,' he said, 'followed by a lot of Lancre people and some . . . little blue men . . .'

He looked down again. 'At least it looks like mud,' he added.

'That'll be the King,' said Granny. 'Big Aggie's given him some of her brose, by the sound of it. He'll save the day.'

'Er . . . hasn't the day *been* saved?'

'Oh, he's the King. It looks like it might be a nice day, so let him save it. You've got to give kings something to do. Anyway, after a drink from Big Aggie he won't know *what* day it is. We'd better get down there.'

'I feel I should thank you,' said Oats, when they reached the spiral staircase.

'For helping you across the mountains, you mean?'

'The world is . . . different.' Oats's gaze went out across the haze, and the forests, and the purple mountains. 'Everywhere I look I see something holy.'

For the first time since he'd met her he saw Granny Weatherwax smile properly. Normally her mouth went up at the corners just before something unpleasant was going to happen to someone who deserved it, but this time she appeared to be pleased with what she'd heard.

'That's a start, then,' she said.

The Magpyrs' coach had been righted and dragged up to the castle. Now it returned, with Jason Ogg at the reins. He was concentrating on avoiding the bumps. They made his bruises tender. Besides, the royal family was on board and he was feeling extremely loyal at the moment.

Jason Ogg was very big and very strong and, therefore, not a violent man, because he did not need to be. Sometimes he was summoned down to the pub to sort out the more serious fights, which he usually did by picking up both contestants and holding them apart until they stopped struggling. If that didn't work, he'd bang them together a few times, in as friendly a way as possible.

Aggressiveness did not normally impress him, but since in yesterday's battle at Lancre Castle he'd had to physically lift Verence off the ground in order to stop him slaughtering enemies, friends, furniture, walls and his own feet, he was certainly seeing his king in a new light. It had turned out to be an extremely short battle. The mercenaries had been only too keen to surrender, especially after Shawn's assault. The real fight had been to keep Verence away from them long enough to allow them to say so.

Jason *was* impressed.

King Verence, inside the coach, laid his head in his wife's lap and groaned as she wiped his brow with a cloth . . .

At a respectable distance the coach was followed by a cart containing the witches, although what it contained mostly was snore.

Granny Weatherwax had a primal snore. It had never been tamed. No one had ever had to sleep next to it, to curb its wilder excesses by means of a kick, a prod in the small of the back or a pillow used as a bludgeon. It had had years in a lonely bedroom to perfect the *knark*, the *graaah* and the *gnoc, gnoc, gnoc* unimpeded by the nudges, jabs and occasional attempts at murder that usually moderate the snore impulse over time.

She sprawled in the straw at the bottom of the cart, mouth open, and snored.

'You half expect to find the shafts sawed through, don't you?' said Nanny, who was leading the horse. 'Still, you can hear it doin' her good.'

'I'm a bit worried about Mister Oats, though,' said Agnes. 'He's just sitting there and grinning.'

Oats was sitting with his legs over the tail of the cart, staring happily at the sky.

'Did he hit his head?' said Nanny.

'I don't think so.'

'Let him be, then. At least he ain't settin' fire to anything . . . Oh, here's an old friend . . .'

Igor, tongue protruding from the corner of his mouth in the ferocity of his concentration, was putting the finishing touches to a new sign. It read 'Why not vysyt our Gifte Shoppe?' He stood up and nodded as the cart drew near.

'The old marthter came up with thome new ideath while he wath dead,' he said, feeling that some explanation was called for. 'Thith afternoon I've got to thtart building a funfair, whatever that ith.'

'That's basic'ly swings,' said Nanny.

Igor brightened up. 'Oh, I've plenty of rope and I've alwayth been a dab hand at nootheth,' he said.

'No, that's not—' Agnes began, but Nanny Ogg cut in quickly.

'I s'pose it all depends on who's going to have the fun,' she said. 'Well, be seeing you, Igor. Don't do anything I wouldn't do, if you ever find anything I wouldn't do.'

'We're very sorry about Scraps,' said Agnes. 'Perhaps we can find you a puppy or—'

'Thankth all the thame, but no. There'th only one Thcrapth.'

He waved to them until they were round the next bend.

As Agnes turned round again she saw the three magpies. They were perched on a branch over the road.

'"Three for a funeral—"' she began.

A stone whirred up. There was an indignant squawk and a shower of feathers.

'Two for mirth,' said Nanny, in a self-satisfied voice.

'Nanny, that was *cheating*.'

'Witches always cheat,' said Nanny Ogg. She glanced back at the sleeping figure behind them. 'Everyone knows that – who knows anything about witches.'

They went home to Lancre.

It had been raining again. Water had seeped into Oats's tent and also into the harmonium, which now emitted an occasional squashed-frog burp when it was played. The songbooks also smelled rather distressingly of cat.

He gave up on them and turned to the task of disassembling his camp bed, which had skinned two knuckles and crushed one finger when he put it up and still looked as though it was designed for a man shaped like a banana.

Oats was aware that he was trying to avoid thinking. On the whole, he was happy with this. There was something *pleasing* about simply getting on with simple tasks, and listening to his own breath. Perhaps there was a way . . .

From outside there was the faint sound of something wooden hitting something hollow and whispering on the evening air.

He peered through the tent flap.

People were filing stealthily into the field. The first few were carrying planks. Several were pushing barrels. He stood with his mouth open as the very rough benches were constructed and began to fill up.

A number of the men had bandages across their noses, he noticed.

Then he heard the rattle of wheels and saw the royal coach lurch through the gateway. This woke him up and he scurried back into the tent, pulling damp clothes out of his bag in a frantic search for a clean shirt. His hat had never been found and his coat was caked with mud, the leather of his shoes was cracked and the buckles had instantly tarnished in the acid marshes, but surely a clean shirt—

Someone tried to knock on the damp canvas and

then, after an interval of half a second, stepped into the tent.

'Are you decent?' said Nanny Ogg, looking him up and down. 'We're all out here waitin', you know. Lost sheep waitin' to be shorn, you might say,' she added, her manner suggesting very clearly that she was doing something that she personally disapproved of, but doing it just the same.

Oats turned around.

'Mrs Ogg, I know you don't like me very much—'

'Don't see why I should like you at all,' said Nanny. 'What with you tagging after Esme and her havin' to help you all that way across the mountains like that.'

The response was screaming up Oats's throat before he noticed the faint knowing look in Nanny's eyes, and he managed to turn it into a cough.

'Er . . . yes,' he said. 'Yes. Silly of me, wasn't it? Er . . . how many are out there, Mrs Ogg?'

'Oh, a hundred, maybe a hundred and fifty.'

Levers, thought Oats, and had a fleeting vision of the pictures in Nanny's parlour. She controls the levers of lots of people. But someone pulled her lever first, I'll bet.

'And what do they expect of me?'

'Says Evensong on the poster,' said Nanny simply. 'Even beer would be better.'

So he went out and saw the watching faces of a large part of Lancre's population lined up in the late-afternoon light. The King and Queen were in the front row. Verence nodded regally at Oats to signal that whatever it was that he intended ought to start around now.

It was clear from the body language of Nanny Ogg that any specifically Omnian prayers would not be tolerated, and Oats made do with a generic prayer of thanks to any god that might be listening and even to the ones that weren't.

Then he pulled out the stricken harmonium and tried a few chords until Nanny elbowed him aside, rolled up her sleeves and coaxed notes out of the damp bellows that Oats never even knew were in there.

The singing wasn't very enthusiastic, though, until Oats tossed aside the noisome songbook and taught them some of the songs he remembered from his grandmother, full of fire and thunder and death and justice and tunes you could actually whistle, with titles like 'Om Shall Trample The Ungodly' and 'Lift Me To The Skies' and 'Light The Good Light'. They went down well. Lancre people weren't too concerned about religion, but they knew what it ought to sound like.

While he led the singing, with the aid of a long stick and the words of the hymns scrawled on the side of his tent, he scanned his . . . well, he decided to call it his congregation. It was his first real one. There were plenty of women, and a lot of very well scrubbed men, but one face was patently not there. Its absence dominated the scene.

But, as he raised his eyes upwards in mid-song, he did notice an eagle far overhead, a mere speck gyrating across the darkening sky, possibly hunting for lost lambs.

And then it was over and people left, quietly, with

the look of those who'd done a job which had not been unpleasant but which was nevertheless over. The collection plate produced two pennies, some carrots, a large onion, a small loaf, a pound of mutton, a jug of milk and a pickled pig's trotter.

'We're not really a cash economy,' said King Verence, stepping forward. He had a bandage across his forehead.

'Oh, it'll make a good supper, sire,' said Oats, in the madly cheerful voice that people use when addressing royalty.

'Surely you'll dine with us?' said Magrat.

'I . . . er . . . was planning to leave at first light, sire. So I really ought to spend the evening packing and setting fire to the camp bed.'

'Leaving? But I thought you were staying here. I've taken . . . community soundings,' said the King, 'and I think I can say that popular opinion is with me on this.'

Oats looked at Magrat's face, which said plainly, Granny doesn't object.

'Well, I, er . . . I expect I shall pass through again, sire,' he said. 'But . . . to tell you the truth, I was thinking of heading on to Uberwald.'

'That's a hellish place, Mr Oats.'

'I've thought about it all day, sire, and I'm set on it.'

'Oh.' Verence looked nonplussed, but kings learn to swing back upright. 'I'm sure you know your own mind best.' He swayed slightly as Magrat's elbow grazed his ribs. 'Oh . . . yes . . . we heard you lost your, er, holy amulet and so this afternoon we, that is to say the Queen and Miss Nitt . . . got Shawn Ogg to make this in the mint . . .'

Oats unwrapped the black velvet scroll. Inside, on a golden chain, was a small golden double-headed axe.

He stared at it.

'Shawn isn't very good at turtles,' said Magrat, to fill the gap.

'I shall treasure it,' said Oats, at last.

'Of course, we appreciate it's not very holy,' said the King.

Oats waved a hand dismissively. 'Who knows, sire? Holiness is where you find it,' he said.

Behind the King, Jason and Darren Ogg were standing respectfully to attention. Both still had plasters stuck across their noses. They moved aside hurriedly to make way for the King, who didn't seem to notice.

Nanny Ogg struck a chord on the harmonium when the royal couple had departed with their retinue.

'If you drop in to our Jason's forge first thing when you're leavin' I'll see to it he fixes the bellows on this contraption,' she said diffidently, and Oats realized that in the context of Nanny Ogg this was as close as he was going to get to three rousing cheers and the grateful thanks of the population.

'I was so impressed that everyone turned up of their own free will,' he said. 'Spontaneously, as it were.'

'Don't push your luck, sonny boy,' said Nanny, getting up.

'Nice to have met you, Mrs Ogg.'

Nanny walked away a few steps, but Oggs never left anything unsaid.

'I can't say as I approve of you,' she said, stiffly. 'But should you ever come knockin' on an Ogg door in these parts you'll . . . get a hot meal. You're too skinny. I've seen more meat on a butcher's pencil.'

'Thank you.'

'Not necessarily puddin' as well, mark you.'

'Of course not.'

'Well, then . . .' Nanny Ogg shrugged. 'Best of luck in Uberwald, then.'

'Om will go with me, I'm sure,' said Oats. He was interested in how annoyed you could make Nanny by speaking calmly to her, and wondered if Granny Weatherwax had tried it.

'I hope he does,' said Nanny. 'I person'ly don't want him hanging around here.'

When she'd gone Oats lit a fire of the horrible bed and stuck the songbooks around it to dry out.

'Hello . . .'

The thing about a witch in darkness is that all you see is her face, bobbing towards you, surrounded by black. Then a little contrast reasserted itself, and an area of shadow detached from the rest and became Agnes.

'Oh, good evening,' said Oats. 'Thank you for coming. I've never heard anyone singing in harmony with themselves before.'

Agnes coughed nervously.

'Are you really going on into Uberwald?'

'There's no reason to stay here, is there?'

Agnes's left arm twitched a few times. She steadied it with her right hand.

'S'pose not,' she said, in a small voice. 'No! Shut up! This is *not* the time!'

'I beg your pardon?'

'I was, um, just talking to myself,' said Agnes wretchedly. 'Look, everyone *knows* you helped Granny. They just pretend they don't.'

'Yes. I know.'

'You don't mind?'

Oats shrugged. Agnes coughed.

'I thought perhaps you were going to stay on here for a while.'

'There'd be no point. I'm not needed here.'

'I shouldn't think vampires and so on would be very keen on singing hymns,' said Agnes quietly.

'Perhaps they can learn something else,' said Oats. 'I shall see what may be done.'

Agnes stood hesitantly for a few moments.

'I've got to give you this,' she said, suddenly handing over a small bag. Oats reached inside and took out a small jar.

Inside, a phoenix feather burned, lighting up the field with a clear, cool light.

'It's from—' Agnes began.

'I know who it's from,' said Oats. 'Is Mistress Weatherwax all right? I didn't see her here.'

'Er . . . she's been having a rest today.'

'Well, thank her from me, will you?'

'She said it's to take into dark places.'

Oats laughed.

'Er . . . yes. Er . . . I might come and see you off in the morning . . .' said Agnes, uncertainly.

'That would be nice of you.'

'So . . . until . . . you know . . .'

'Yes.'

Agnes seemed to be struggling with some inner resistance. Then she said, 'And, er . . . there's something I've been meaning to . . . I mean, perhaps you could . . .'

'Yes?'

Agnes's right hand dived urgently into her pocket and she pulled out a small package wrapped in greased paper.

'It's a poultice,' she blurted out. 'It's a very good recipe and the book says it always works and if you heat it up and leave it on it'll do wonders for your boil.'

Oats took it gently. 'It's just possible that's the nicest thing anyone's ever given me,' he said.

'Er . . . good. It's from . . . er . . . both of us. Goodbye.'

Oats watched her leave the circle of light, and then something drew his eye upwards again.

The circling eagle had risen above the shadow of the mountains and into the light of the setting sun. For a moment it flashed gold, and then dropped into the dark again.

From up here the eagle could see for miles across the mountains.

Over Uberwald, the threatened storm had broken. Lightning scribbled across the sky.

Some of it crackled around the highest tower of Don'tgonearthe Castle, and on the rainhat that Igor wore to stop his head rusting. It raised little balls of glowing light on the big telescopic iron spike as, taking care to stand on his portable rubber mat, he patiently wound it upwards.

At the foot of the apparatus, which was already humming with high tension, was a bundle wrapped in a blanket.

The spike locked itself in position. Igor sighed, and waited.

DOWN, BOY! DOWN, I SAY! WILL YOU STOP— LET GO! LET GO THIS MINUTE! ALL RIGHT, LOOK . . . FETCH? FETCH? THERE WE GO . . .

Death watched Scraps bound away.

He wasn't used to this. It wasn't that people weren't sometimes glad to see him, because the penultimate moments of life were often crowded and complex and a cool figure in black came as something of a relief. But he'd never encountered quite this amount of enthusiasm or, if it came to it, this amount of flying mucus. It was disconcerting. It made him feel he wasn't doing his job properly.

THERE'S A SATISFACTORY DOG. NOW . . . DROP. LET GO, PLEASE. DID YOU HEAR ME SAY LET GO? LET GO THIS MINUTE!

Scraps bounced away. This was far too much fun to end.

There was a soft chiming from within his robe. Death rubbed his hand on the cloth in an effort to get it dry and brought out a lifetimer, its sand all pooled in the bottom bulb. But the glass itself was misshapen, twisted, covered in welts of raised glass and, as Death watched, it filled up with crackling blue light.

Normally, Death was against this sort of thing but, he reasoned as he snapped his fingers, at the moment it looked as though it was the only way he'd get his scythe back.

The lightning hit.

There was a smell of singed wool.

Igor waited a while and then trudged round to the bundle, trailing molten rubber behind him. Kneeling down, he carefully unwrapped the blanket.

Scraps yawned. A large tongue licked Igor's hand.

As he smiled with relief there came, from far down below in the castle, the sound of the mighty organ playing 'Toccata for Young Women in Underwired Nightdresses'.

The eagle swooped on into the bowl of Lancre.

The long light glowed on the lake, and on the big V-shaped ripple, made up of many small V-shaped ripples, that arrowed through the water towards the unsuspecting island.

The voices echoed around the mountains.

'See you, otter!'

'Taggit, jins ma greely!'

'Wee free men!'

'Nac mac Feegle!'

The eagle passed overhead, dropping fast and steep now. It drifted silently over the shadowy woods, curved over the trees, and landed suddenly on a branch beside a cottage in a clearing.

Granny Weatherwax awoke.

Her body did not move, but her gaze darted this

way and that, sharply, and in the gloom her nose looked more hooked than normal. Then she settled back, and her shoulders lost the hunched, perching look.

After a while she stood up, stretched, and went to the doorway.

The night felt warmer. She could feel greenness in the ground, uncoiling. The year was past the edge, heading away from the dark . . . Of course, dark would come again, but that was in the nature of the world. Many things were beginning.

When at last she'd shut the door she lit the fire, took the box of candles out of the dresser and lit every single one and put them around the room, in saucers.

On the table the pool of water that had accumulated in the last two days rippled and rose gently in the middle. Then a drip soared upwards and plopped into the damp patch in the ceiling.

Granny wound up the clock, and started the pendulum. She left the room for a moment and came back with a square of cardboard attached to a loop of elderly string. She sat down in the rocking chair and reached down into the hearth for a stick of half-burned wood.

The clock ticked as she wrote. Another drop left the table and plunged towards the ceiling.

Then Granny Weatherwax hung the sign around her neck and lay back with a smile. The chair rocked for a while, a counterpoint to the dripping of the table and the ticking of the clock, and then slowed.

The sign read:

I ATE'NT DEAD

The light faded from can to can't.

After a few minutes an owl woke up in a nearby tree and sailed out over the forests.

THE END

INTERESTING TIMES

Terry Pratchett

'Funny, delightfully inventive and refuses to lie down in its genre'
Observer

'A foot in the neck is nine points of the law.'

THERE are many who say that the art of diplomacy is an intricate and complex dance between two informed partners, determined by an elaborate set of elegant and unwritten rules. There are others who maintain that it's merely a matter of who carries the biggest stick. Like when a large, heavily fortified and armoured empire makes a faintly menacing request of a much smaller, infinitely more cowardly neighbour. It would be churlish, if not extremely dangerous, not to comply – particularly if all they want is a wizard, and they don't specify whether competence is an issue…

'Imagine a collision between Jonathan Swift at his most scatological and J.R.R. Tolkien on speed… This is the joyous outcome'
Daily Telegraph

'Like Dickens, much of Pratchett's appeal lies in his humanism, both in a sentimental regard for his characters' good fortune, and in that his writing is generous-spirited and inclusive'
Guardian

9780552153218

MASKERADE

Terry Pratchett

'As funny as Wodehouse and as witty as Waugh'
Independent

'I thought: opera, how hard can it be? Songs. Pretty girls dancing. Nice scenery. Lots of people handing over cash. Got to be better than the cut-throat world of yoghurt, I thought. Now everywhere I go there's...'

DEATH, to be precise. And plenty of it. In unpleasant variations. This isn't real life. This isn't even cheesemongering. It's opera. Where the music matters and where an opera house is being terrorised by a man in evening dress with a white mask, lurking in the shadows, occasionally killing people, and most worryingly, sending little notes, writing maniacal laughter with five exclamation marks. Opera can do that to a man. In such circumstances, life has obviously reached that desperate point where the wrong thing to do **has** to be the right thing to do...

'Cracking dialogue, compelling illogic and unchained whimsy...Pratchett has a subject and a style that is very much his own'
Sunday Times

'Entertaining and gloriously funny'
Chicago Tribune

9780552153232

Feet of Clay

Terry Pratchett

'The work of a prolific humorist at his best'
Observer

'Sorry?' said Carrot. 'If it's just a thing, how can it commit murder? A sword is a thing' – he drew out his own sword; it made an almost silken sound – 'and of course you can't blame a sword if someone thrust it at you, sir.'

For members of the City Watch, life consists of troubling times, linked together by periods of torpid inactivity. Now is one such troubling time. People are being murdered, but there's no trace of anything alive having been at the crime scene. Is there ever a circumstance in which you can blame the weapon not the murderer? Such philosophical questions are not the usual domain of the city's police, but they're going to have to start learning fast…

'Like most true originals, Pratchett defies categorization… Deliciously and amiably dotty… Driven by Swiftian logic and equally intellectually inventive'
The Times

'Fantastical, inventive and finally serious… It's enjoyable as crime fiction, but the real attraction is the laughter waiting to be uncovered on every page'
Observer

'An explosion of imaginative lunacy'
Daily Express

9780552153256

Jingo

Terry Pratchett

'Generous, amusing and the ideal boarding point for those who have never visited Discworld'
Sunday Telegraph

'Neighbours...hah. People'd live for ages side by side, nodding at one another amicably on their way to work, and then some trivial thing would happen and someone would be having a garden fork removed from their ear.'

THROUGHOUT history, there's always been a perfectly good reason to start a war. Never more so if it is over a 'strategic' piece of old rock in the middle of nowhere. It is after all every citizen's right to bear arms to defend what they consider to be their own. Even if it isn't. And in such pressing circumstances, you really shouldn't let small details like the absence of an army or indeed the money to finance one get in the way of a righteous fight with all the attendant benefits of out-and-out nationalism...

'Pratchett's writing is a constant delight. No one mixes the fantastical and the mundane to better comic effect or offers sharper insights into the absurdities of human endeavour'
Daily Mail

'One of those very rare writers who appeals to everyone...He satisfies the need for fast-moving, breathtaking plots with entirely satisfying endings, and the equally primitive desire for an alternative world, full of thrills but benign, into which one can step for pleasure and enlivenment'
Daily Express

'Vintage Pratchett...Perennially funny...A sharp satire on the futility of war'
Metro

9780552154161

AG

The Last Continent

Terry Pratchett

'The perfect read'
Evening Standard

'Anything you do in the past changes the future. The tiniest little actions have huge consequences. You might tread on an ant now and it might entirely prevent someone from being born in the future.'

THERE'S nothing like the issue of evolution to get under the skin of academics. Especially when those same academics are by chance or bad judgement deposited at a critical evolutionary turning point when one wrong move could have catastrophic results for the future. Unfortunately in the hands of such an inept and cussed group of individuals, the sensitive issue of causality is sadly only likely to receive the same scant respect that they show to one another...

'Delightful...gleeful and downright mischevious. The pleasures on the page are so quirkily seductive. Puts one in mind of one of the greatest comic writers of them all, PG Wodehouse'
Sunday Telegraph

'A minor masterpiece. I laughed so much I fell from my armchair'
Time Out

'The humour sparkles as brightly as ever'
The Times

9780552154185